REVELS ENDING

BY VIC KERRY

Semmes felt eyes watching him. He turned to the door, still holding his gun and the obituary. A woman stood behind him. The shadows obscured her face.

"Why are you here?"

"I'm Detective Semmes of the Mobile Police."

"I know who you are. I asked why you are here."

"Official police business." He squinted trying to get a better look at the woman. "We have reason to believe this organization might be related to a missing person from Birmingham."

"Is that correct?" the woman asked.

Her voice and speech seemed artificial in some way. She flipped the light on. It blinded him, and he turned to the side to regain his vision. When he looked up, he almost lost his breath. The woman in the doorway was Marianne.

"Why are you here?" he asked.

"I have already asked that question to you," she said.

"I've been trying to find you, Marianne. Ashe is very worried. How did they mistake you for dead?"

"I am not dead," she said, "and I do not know this Marianne. My name is Ursula. Do you have a warrant, Detective Semmes?"

"Now that I've found you here, I don't need one."

Semmes eased toward the exit. He'd dealt with crazy people before. They could be unpredictable and stronger than normal. The last thing he needed was for her to attack him or cause any sort of ruckus. He needed to get back to his car and call for backup. "I do not know what you are talking about. I have always been here." "No, you haven't. Your name is Marianne Lenard. You were Ashley Shrove's fiancée, and about a week ago, you walked out of the morgue at University Hospital."

"My name is Ursula van Beckum, and we cannot allow you to leave."

DEDICATION

In memory of J.B. Spence. He was my best friend, first fan, and lover of Mardi Gras.

Laissez les bonnes temps rouler, mon ami.

Security Camera: Autopsy Room 2
University Hospital, 11:24 p.m.

Two technicians wheel a gurney into the room. A sheet-draped body rests on it. One of the technicians stands taller than the other. His curly hair springs out in all directions like he hasn't bothered to comb it before coming to work. The other technician is bald and muscle-bound.

They pull the gurney next to the autopsy table. The bald technician uncovers the cadaver's face. He shakes his head and points to it. The tall, curly-haired technician nods and tugs the sheet farther down to reveal the cadaver's B-cup sized breasts. He points to them and shakes his head. The bald technician says something, and the tall technician covers the cadaver's breasts back up but leaves her face visible.

They hoist her onto the table. Her head rests so that it is cocked up as if looking down her body. The technicians talk back and forth to each other. The bald one slaps the back of his hand against the tall one's chest. They laugh and wheel the empty gurney out.

The cadaver stares at the door. The eyes glare wide open as if in shock.

Security Camera: Autopsy Room 2, University Hospital, 12:03 a.m CST

A man wearing a complete surgical kit walks into the room. A canvas bag dangles from his shoulder. He pats the cadaver's shoulder as if sympathizing with her. Then he takes the bag and lays it on the cadaver's stomach. He opens the bag and takes out a series of electrode pads similar to those used with an EKG machine. Two are stuck to the cadaver's forehead. Two more are placed on her shoulders.

The man slides a boxy-looking machine from the bag. He takes a thumb drive from his pocket and jacks it into the back. A light on top of the mechanism flashes. He pushes a button. Static snows down the video image. When it clears away, the man packs the machine and electrodes back into the bag. He lifts it onto his shoulder and pats the cadaver again.

She sits up. The sheet bunches up around her waist. The man helps her to stand. He hands her the sheet. She winds it around her naked body like a sari. Once dressed, they walk out of the room, flicking the light off as they do. The room falls into blackness.

CHAPTER ONE

Ashley Shrove sat across a conference table from the chief medical examiner for University Hospital, the president of the hospital, the VP for nursing, and the director of media for the hospital. Detective Semmes of the Mobile Police Department sat to his right, and his quickly acquired lawyer, Scott Johnston, sat to his left. The room was stuffy. Ashe, as he liked to be called for obvious reasons, felt like all the hot air coming out of the hospital staff overpowered the ventilation system. They all sat looking at each other and not really saying anything.

"Please understand, nothing like this has ever happened at this hospital," the PR guy said. His glossy tag called him Ben Martin. "We've never lost a body from our morgue."

"On the phone, you didn't say that you lost Marianne's body. You said she got up and walked out with a doctor," Ashe said. "That's a whole different thing than losing a body, Mr. Martin."

"It's a matter of semantics," Martin said.

"It's a matter of a lawsuit," Johnston said. "There are several issues at stake here. One is wrongfully declaring someone dead. I would call that malpractice." He directed that to the medical examiner, whose tag named him Dr. Mott. "Then there's possible kidnapping. That will be for you to decide, Detective Semmes."

"I did not see Ms. Lenard when she was admitted to the morgue. I cannot be held responsible for the declaration of her death. Dr. Hemming did that workup," Dr. Mott said.

"Since you're the *chief* medical examiner, I assume that you are over every doctor that does postmortems. Am I right, Dr. Mott?" Johnston clicked his teeth together on the *T*s as if biting the end of the word.

Dr. Mott looked down. "Technically, that's correct."

"The woman was dead," Vera Wallace, VP for Nursing, said. "Dr. Hemming confirmed it. The EMTs on the scene confirmed it. Even Officer Semmes confirmed it."

"Detective Semmes if you please," Semmes said. "I did check Ms. Lenard's pulse myself. She didn't have one, and by the time I got to her, her skin had cooled."

"So what we have is a missing body," Martin said.

"If she was dead, and she walked out of the morgue, what we have is a zombie," Ashe said.

The hospital president, Dean Dennison, snickered, but tried to cover it up with a fake cough.

"I wasn't being funny, Mr. Dennison," Ashe said. "Either she was not dead, or she came back to life. If I know my horror movies like I think I do, a living corpse is a zombie."

"Or a vampire," Semmes said under his breath.

Ashe nodded his agreement.

"I think we should see the tape," Johnston said. "If you don't mind."

"I have it ready." Martin lifted a remote control and pointed it toward a large screen hanging on the wall.

The screen flickered and then showed the autopsy room. A time stamp at the bottom showed the time. Two technicians rolled Marianne in. They monkeyed around with her body. Johnston cleared his throat when the tall technician pulled down the sheet to reveal her breasts.

"That tech no longer works for us," Wallace said.

"Desecration of a corpse." Johnston made a check mark in the air. "Harassment if she is alive."

In the video, the technicians left the autopsy room. Martin fast-forwarded the video to save time. Blurry lines twisted across the screen, but nothing changed. No one came or went. Marianne lay on the table motionless and staring at the ceiling. Then a masked man entered. Ashe watched with a knot of anxiety in his stomach as Marianne stood, then wrapped her naked body in a sheet, and left with the stranger.

The mechanism used on Marianne looked familiar to Ashe. The colleague who introduced him to Johnston had a few of machines that looked like it. He should know because he'd built them.

"We've searched all the rest of our surveillance videos to see what happened to them, and have come up with nothing," Wallace said.

"We also cannot identify who the masked man was. He doesn't match any description of morgue personnel or any pathologist I know of in the hospital," Dr. Mott said.

"So she just walked out and disappeared?" Ashe asked.

"Apparently," Dennison said. "We're baffled too."

"And sued," Johnston said.

Ashe wished he hadn't involved a lawyer, but the news from Martin had been more than he could process. He'd met Johnston at a school party thrown for his friend, psychologist Erik Rogers. The lawyer seemed less sleazy in that situation, but Ashe thought perhaps he was being aggressive to make him feel better about the fact that his fiancée had either been stolen or resurrected. With Mardi Gras just around the corner and the focus on the most famous resurrection in history beginning, he didn't know which option he liked better.

"We're trying to keep this out of the media," Martin said. "For obvious reasons."

"I agree," Semmes said. "It'll be a lot harder to catch this freak if it hits Channel 3 news."

"I don't know about that," Johnston said.

"It's fine," Ashe said. "I don't need the interviews and attention." He looked at his lawyer. "Believe it or not, Marianne was a person before she died and came back or whatever. I loved her, and I'm hurting a lot."

"It was insensitive of me. I apologize; of course, we'll keep this under wraps," Johnston said. "Until enough time has passed."

"Do we have anything else to discuss?" Ashe asked.

All the hospital staff looked at each other. In succession, they shook their heads to the negative. Dennison stood followed by the rest of his staff.

"I suppose we're finished, Professor Shrove," he said. "If anything else comes up, we'll let you know."

Ashe, Johnston and Semmes stood as well. Johnston put his hand on Ashe's shoulder and turned him to the door.

"I'll be getting back with you," Semmes said to Dennison. "I'll probably want to see records and other things."

"We'll probably want to see a court order," Wallace said in a clipped tone.

"Vera," Dennison snapped back. "We will cooperate as far as the law allows."

"I thought you would." Semmes followed Ashe and Johnston to the door. "Don't worry, Miss Wallace. I wouldn't think of coming back without a court order for those records. I'll probably even have a fresh new subpoena just for you."

Ashe could tell by the tone of his voice that Semmes enjoyed saying that. The three men left the conference room and walked down the hall to the elevators. This part of the hospital smelled more like an office building than a house of medicine. There was no undertone of antiseptic cleaner. The sickly sweet medicinal smell most hospitals had was reserved for the floors that the high-ups didn't have to be on much, Ashe thought to himself.

The elevator doors slid open. Semmes, Johnston and Ashe stepped into the empty car. For some reason, all three men stood shoulder to shoulder as if the elevator were full. Semmes and Johnston flanked Ashe. He didn't mind. Strangely, he felt comforted.

"Could that video have been doctored?" Ashe asked.

"It might have been," Johnston said. "The only reason I could think of why they would was if they lost the body and were trying to cover it up with an elaborate and bizarre plot."

"Professor Shrove," Semmes said.

"Call me Ashe."

"Ashe, one of the first things I'm taking when I come back with that court order is the tape. I'm going to have our boys look for any anomalies in it. I'm thinking like your lawyer."

"You can call me Mr. Johnston."

Semmes cleared his throat. "Like Mr. Johnston said, they would only fake it if they lost the body or something like that, but you never can tell."

The elevator doors opened, and the men stepped out into the

lobby. Four people waited for the elevator and clambered on when Ashe and the others had barely stepped off. The men walked out of the lobby and into the foggy February morning without saying a word. Once they were out the door, Semmes dug into his pocket and brought out a pack of USA Gold cigarettes. Ashe thought that Mobile must not pay their cops very much for the detective to buy such cheap smokes. Semmes took one out and lit it. The smell of the cheap tobacco mingled with the briny smell of the sea fog. Ashe found the mixture less than pleasurable.

"Before I head over to Tech, am I still a suspect in a Marianne's death?"

Semmes blew smoke out of his nostrils. "As of right now, we don't know how she died. So, I'm putting the foul play investigation on hold." He took another drag. "Technically, we don't even know if she's dead. I don't mean any disrespect by that."

"I understand," Ashe said.

"But don't leave the country or anything," Semmes said.

"Don't worry about that. I've got a job and haven't earned tenure yet."

"Also, Mr. Semmes," Johnston said.

"You can call me Detective Semmes."

"Make sure that any questions you ask Ashe are when I'm present." Johnston gave the detective a Cheshire cat grin.

Semmes puffed on his cigarette and nodded his head. The winter fog started to chill Ashe. He'd been used to mild winters living in South Carolina, and expected the Gulf Coast to have no winter, but Mobile surprised him.

"I've got to get to work. One of my graduate classes is having a test, and I have to proctor it. If there is anything else, let me know."

"Working so soon after your fiancée's death?" Semmes asked. "Those Alabama Tech boys must be slave drivers."

"My personal choice," Ashe said. "Working keeps my mind off of things. If I stayed at home, I'm pretty sure I'd start drinking or crying into one of Marianne's blouses."

"I understand. I'll keep in touch," Semmes said.

Ashe walked across the circular drive. He stopped and turned back to Semmes.

"Detective?"

"Yes?"

"I recognized that device the man used on Marianne, or at least I think I do," Ashe said.

"Okay, how?"

"If it's what I think it is, I made it for Erik Rogers, who figured out how to record emotions. It looks like the recorder, but it shouldn't be able to raise the dead."

"Are you sure it's that device?" Semmes asked.

"Not completely, but I plan to ask Erik about it as soon as I get back to campus."

"I'll being following up on it myself, but let me know what he says."

"Be sure to let me know as well," Johnston said. "Remember, Detective, this is not incriminating evidence."

"I'll keep that in mind," Semmes said.

Ashe heard the dislike in the detective's voice. He felt it in his own stomach. Now, he wished he'd never bothered with the attorney.

Ashe opened his eyes when the light from the hallway spilled into his office. He'd lain down on the small couch he'd inherited from the office's previous owner. As his sleep-heavy eyes adjusted to the new light, he made out the outline of Cybil's head and shoulders jutting into the room.

"Did I wake you up?" she asked in her small girlish voice.

"Yeah, but I suppose I need to be getting up anyway." He looked at his watch. "I've got to give a test in twenty minutes."

Cybil pushed the door open and came completely into the room. She flipped the light switch on with her elbow. Ashe squinted as the lights came on. He saw that Cybil carried a bundle of papers under her arm.

"That's why I stopped by. I got the copies done. I was going to leave them with your assistant, but."

Ashe nodded. "I haven't not got one."

"Well, yeah. I could be your assistant."

He smiled and rubbed his chin. Sharp beard stubble scraped his palms. He hadn't shaved since his last shower which was some time before he'd been told by the Mobile police that Marianne had been found slumped over her computer in the stacks at the library.

"I don't think the department chair would like me making our work-study my personal secretary."

"I don't think he'd notice," Cybil said.

She walked to his desk and put the papers down. For some reason, Ashe noticed more about her than he ever had before. She wore her dark brown hair short in what he thought was called a pixie cut. Today, Cybil wore a strange kind of peasant blouse with a huge neck. It hung almost straight off her shoulder due to the lack of any breasts.

He'd noticed that before. Even in his best relationship, he would notice women's breasts. This work-study had boobs, but it was easy for her to hide them, even without trying.

"You look pretty rough." She put her hand on her hip. Her bright red fingernail polish stood out starkly against the deep black of her flowing skirt.

"I haven't had much sleep, or food, or a bath for that matter." He sniffed his armpit, not even trying to be polite in mixed company. "At least I don't smell."

Cybil sat beside him on the couch. She put her hand on his knee. "I heard about your fiancée. I'm so sorry. Do they know what killed her yet?"

Ashe shook his head. "No, and they won't."

"Oh, did she not believe in having autopsies?"

"No, someone stole her body from the morgue."

Cybil snorted but slapped her hand over her mouth. "I'm so sorry. I didn't mean to laugh, but that's crazy."

"I know. It gets worse." Ashe caught himself. Why was he telling his work-study this? "But I've got to get to my class and give this test."

He stood, and Cybil's hand finally fell off of his knee. She stood up too.

"I could give it for you."

"You haven't even graduated with a BS yet. I'm sure that my PhD students would not like an undergrad giving them their test." He noticed she looked a little offended. "Plus, this is advanced material. I know you're a good student, but there are things on this test they don't cover in undergrad classes. If one of my students had a question, I don't think you could answer it."

"I was just trying to help you out during this tough time," Cybil said. Some of the perkiness was gone from her voice.

"Thank you for that. Maybe you could help me get them graded and recorded. That's the hardest part anyway, especially running on as little sleep as I've had."

"When and where?"

"Here around 5 p.m. I've got to meet with Dr. Rogers after my test ends. It will probably take that long to get away from him."

Cybil rubbed her hands together. "All right, I'll see you then."

The work-study left. Ashe took his tests and headed to his class.

CHAPTER TWO

A she flipped a small device, similar to an MP3 player, over in his hands. He smelled the port where a USB cord could be attached and then where the electrodes were plugged into the device. Nothing of the usual acrid smell of burnt electrics was present.

"What did you say it was doing?" he asked.

"When I plug it into the computer, all the data comes up as gibberish," a middle-aged man with dishwater-blond hair said. Erik Rogers tapped on a computer keyboard. "I made this recording earlier this week with a student volunteer."

Ashe looked at the string of squares and dashes on the screen. He didn't really know what could have caused his device to malfunction.

"You're sure you haven't gotten it wet or anything?"

Rogers shook his head. "I keep that thing in an airtight, waterproof box when not in use. I wouldn't risk the safety of the machine that helped me discover the third law of psychology."

"What about the computer program? You programmed that. Have you checked it?"

"Several times. There are no changes in it."

"Virus."

"Mac-based."

"Power surge?"

"All my equipment is protected from that. Plus the other one doesn't seem messed up."

"You have the other one," Ashe asked, "and the component box, right?"

"Of course, and it works fine," Rogers said. "I've just gotten so many volunteers since the discovery that I need both to keep up with the subject pool size. I wish the prototype engram machine hadn't been stolen or whatever when we moved labs."

In all the hubbub surrounding Marianne's death, Ashe had forgotten about the missing prototype, but it couldn't have been the one that was used on Marianne's body. He'd rendered it inoperable after producing the two devices that Rogers now used.

"Let me take this and see what I can find out. I'll have this back to you in a couple of days. Will that be okay?"

"Take as long as you need. I'm not in a huge rush. Even if I was, I wouldn't push you after the whole thing with Marianne."

Ashe dropped the device into his shirt pocket. "You heard."

"Everybody on campus knows. The dean emailed us, but I know about the other thing too. Scott called me."

"So you and he are pretty good friends?"

"He's my lawyer too."

"I'm glad to see he doesn't have problems with confidentiality," Ashe said.

"Don't worry. He just told me because I asked out of concern. I feel like I have a vested interest in your well-being."

Ashe smiled. "Don't try any of your psychology stuff on me, Dr. Rogers."

"What psychology stuff?" Rogers twirled his finger at Ashe. "All kidding aside though, I think I have a friend you need to talk with. I asked him to drop by your office about a quarter until six this evening. He's a psychologist, a clinical one."

"I'll be there, but I don't think I need a shrink."

"He's notlike that. You'll like him, andhe's agreatpersonto-confidein. His confidentiality is a lot more secure than Scott's."

"That'll be all right then. I've got a set of tests to grade. One of the work-studies is going to help me out, so I should be able to talk to him."

Semmes starred at the computer screen until his eyes felt like they might fall out of his head. He blinked to bring the moisture back to them. The coffee he'd poured over an hour ago sat cold in its mug. He hadn't taken a sip of it. The cream coagulated on the top. He scrolled down the screen reading name after name of people from other cities and states. Every one was a supposed death where the body went missing. A brief description told of the details of the investigation.

Nearly all of them had been solved quickly. Some of the cases like the other two he found in Mobile and Baldwin Counties had been mistakenly labeled. The toe tags had somehow gotten switched with a person who had already been processed. The others varied from a necrophiliac embalmer in Portland, Oregon, to a case of wrongful death in Sault Ste. Marie, Michigan.

"This is hopeless, a wild goose chase," he said aloud to no one in particular.

"Try limiting your parameters," Cooper, his newly assigned partner from the sex crimes division, said from over his shoulder.

The detective looked up at the thirty-something woman in a Hillary Clinton pantsuit. "How long have you been there?"

"A few minutes," Cooper said. "I heard about this case. I thought our new partnership could get started on the right foot by me helping you out from the get go."

Semmes smiled. "You're a rookie. I don't think you'd be much help.

I've been on the force for eight years. That's not exactly a rookie status."

"I meant a rookie detective."

"I solved sex crimes for six of those years," Cooper said.

Semmes shrugged his shoulders and typed *unsolved corpse disappearances* into the search line and hit the enter button. A little hourglass turned over and over as the computer searched the databases all over the country, maybe the world. Semmes had no idea how thorough the database they used was. The small icon quit flipping, and a shorter list of names popped up on the screen.

"Told you so," Cooper said.

Semmes glanced over his shoulder at his not-so-rookie partner, and then looked at the dates on the list. Most were over thirty years old. He figured there was no connection to anything happening in his city. Then he stopped near the bottom. The date was the same as Marianne's death. He clicked on the hyperlink, and the whole report popped up on the screen.

Carol Heinz went missing from the morgue of St. Vincent's Hospital in Birmingham. He looked up at Cooper who read over his shoulder, a trait he detested.

"I think I found something," Semmes said. "I guess you might be of some help after all."

"Anything else that I can do for you?" Cooper asked.

"Yeah, get on the phone to the Birmingham PD and ask them to send down what they can about the Carol Heinz missing body investigation. Tell them that we've had something similar here."

"Can do."

Cooper walked away, and Semmes stopped feeling as if a vulture peered at him from a nearby perch. He stared at the words on the screen and tried to process things. The same section kept drawing his attention. Heinz died after being in ICU for three days. Her body was stored prior to organ harvesting. The body went missing under strange and classified circumstances.

"I bet she just got up and walked out." Semmes thought about Marianne coming up from the autopsy table and leaving the morgue with the mysterious man.

Cybil propped her feet up on an empty desk in the corner of Ashe's office. She leaned back in the office chair, twirling a pen between her fingers. The first page of a test flopped over the top of her other hand as she read over it. Ashe watched her but tried not to seem like he watched her. He could hear the faint sound of the music she listened to on her MP3 player. Why would a girl like her want to spend her evening helping a professor grade papers? Most work-studies kept to normal business hours and just made copies and coffee. Cybil looked over at him. She smiled. He returned the gesture.

"You want me to make some coffee?" she asked.

"You don't have to."

"What?" She pulled the earbuds free from her ears. The music from them became louder.

The song was familiar but played at a faster pace and seemed hard-edged. Ashe recognized it as an old Neil Diamond tune, "Sweet Caroline".

"I said you don't have to."

"I want some, but I'm not going to brew a whole big pot if you aren't going to have any."

"That's fine then. I'll drink some."

She took her feet off the desk and put the test down. She shoved a red pen behind her ear, pulling back a small amount of hair.

"Be back in a minute." She put one earbud back into her ear.

"You're going to make yourself go deaf listening to music that loudly," Ashe said.

She rolled her eyes at him. "Sure thing, Dad. Dr. Shrove, you act like you're old or something. I've seen the music you've got loaded on your computer. You don't listen to that kind of stuff softly."

Before he could protest like a proper professor should, she walked out. He supposed that he would bring up that fact of snooping on his computer when she came back with the coffee. The next answer on the test he graded was wrong. He marked it with his purple- ink pen. During his time in college, he hated professors who used different colored inks to grade papers, and now he did that very thing. Red got boring. Grading papers pushed the limits of tedium. His mind started to drift to Marianne.

He remembered the night she died. She'd been listening to a lecture she'd downloaded from Columbia University. Ashe had asked her to review the lecture by a professor there to help him plan an activity for his students. She'd gone to the library because he was working on his next project. Rogers needed a new device to capture his emotion engrams that could hold more data. Ashe had made schematics for a device with larger storage capacity while working on the original engram devices. He'd figured Rogers or some other researchers would want a bigger and better recorder and something more streamlined than the MP3- like device that had to be attached to a larger recording unit with USB external storage. Even thinking about it seemed clunky. Marianne understood. They both thought that getting involved with Rogers' research would skyrocket him alongside the psychologist. That rocket ride always excited

Marianne. Now, he'd be going to the moon alone.

A soft tap stirred him back to his purple-marked test paper. Ashe looked at the door expecting to see Cybil with the coffee. Instead a middle-aged man with salt and pepper hair stood framed in the door. He wore a black suit with a lavender shirt under it.

"Can I help you?" Ashe asked.

"You're Professor Shrove?" he asked.

"Yes."

"I'm Dr. Smalls, Erik Rogers' friend."

"Oh yes." Ashe stood up. "He told me you would drop by. Erik seems to think that I need a psychiatrist."

"Psychologist." Smalls entered the office. "Psychiatrists can write prescriptions."

"Should have said headshrinker."

"That I can do." Smalls smiled. His teeth were small and straight.

Cybil walked back in carrying Ashe's coffee mug and a Styrofoam cup. She stopped midway in the office and made a face that said that she wasn't expecting someone to be there.

"It's okay, Cybil," Ashe said. "This is Dr. Smalls. He works in the psychology department as a part-time teacher. He's come by to chat."

"Hi," Cybil said. "Would you like some coffee?"

"Thank you, that would be lovely."

She gave him her cup and sat Ashe's on his desk, then left the room. Ashe motioned for Smalls to sit down.

"I guess Erik told you that my girlfriend—fiancée died."

"He did, but he didn't think that was the part you needed to talk about."

"Her body was stolen from the morgue." Ashe drank his coffee.

"Erik said she walked out as if she weren't dead."

Ashe took another long drink of his coffee. "That's right. How does that make you feel?"

"Confused. I guess that's the best answer."

Smalls sipped his coffee. "I'd think that would be a mild reaction."

"Surprised. Terrified. Dead people don't just get up and walk around."

"Zombies do," Smalls said.

"I don't think that's funny."

"Neither do I. I'm being serious."

"And you *teach* psychology?"

Smalls laughed lightly. "Among other things. I also study paranormal activity that has potential religious overtones, like spontaneous resurrection."

Ashe almost spat out his coffee. "So you've come to investigate this, not help me out?"

"Both."

"The police are already trying to find out what's going on, and it wasn't spontaneous. Someone showed up and brought her back from the dead," Ashe said.

"A resurrectionist. Maybe a faith healer or a shaman." Smalls seemed to mumble this to himself.

"Dr. Smalls?"

"Sorry, my mind was wandering. I need to go. I have something else scheduled in a little while. Why don't you come by my office tomorrow around lunchtime? We'll talk more about your loss." Smalls stood. He took a business card from the inside pocket of his jacket and handed it to Ashe. "I'm going to want to know the name of the person down at the police station that's doing the investigation as well. If that's okay."

Ashe looked that the card. It had a crucifix on it. He thought about Dr. Van Helsing in the old *Dracula* movies. Then he noticed that Smalls' office was in St. Mary's-by-the-Bay on Conception Street downtown. "You're a priest?"

"Yes, butdon'tlet thatdiscourage you. Idosecularthery as well as pastoral counseling." He swallowed his last bit of coffee and tossed the cup into the trash can beside the door. "I'll see you tomorrow."

Smalls walked out of Ashe's office. He nodded at Cybil as she came back in with a fresh cup of coffee for herself. Ashe put the card in his top desk drawer. Cybil sat back down at the desk she had been at.

"You look rough. Maybe you need to go home and sleep."

"I can't," Ashe answered.

"Go home or sleep?"

"Both. I can't stand home right now, and every time I try to sleep I have nightmares."

"Let's go downtown then," she said. "We've got about an hour before the Buttercups have their parade. It'll take your mind off of things for a little while."

"I don't think I should," he said.

"It's not anything. I run into professors all the time at parades. During Mardi Gras, it doesn't matter. It's all about fun, beads and MoonPies."

"MoonPies?"

"Come on. You'll find out."

He knew that he needed to finish his papers, but they reminded him of Marianne. Home reminded him of her the most. Attending a Mardi Gras parade with a student seemed like something that could get him into hot water with the dean, but she was right, he needed to try and get his mind off of things.

"All right, but I'll drive," he said.

"Good, because I ride a Vespa."

Ashe shook his head as he stood up from his desk. "You are a strange lady, Cybil. It's wintertime, and you're riding a scooter."

"Come on; it's Mobile. It rarely gets that cold."

"True, but it does rain a lot."

"Who am I, the Wicked Witch of the West? I'm not going to melt."

"But you might catch a cold." He thought he sounded like his mother as the words came out.

"Okay Dad, I'll buy a Civic. Chill out, Dr. Shrove."

"I'll try."

He switched off his light as they walked out of his office. Cybil pulled the door closed behind her.

CHAPTER THREE

A she parked near the old train station on Water Street. All the other streets into downtown were closed off to regular traffic. Rivers of people flowed down the sidewalks on both sides of the street. When traffic lights stopped the flow of cars on Water Street, tributaries of revelers crossed toward downtown.

He and Cybil walked across the parking lot. Shards of broken glass glittered in the streetlight. The smell of the shipping canal hung heavy in the air. Ashe didn't go downtown much and when he did, it was mostly to Dauphin Street where the bars and bohemian shops and cafés were. The stench of fish and diesel fuel didn't waft that far up. The wind off the water added a bite to the February air. He pulled his trench coat around him and knotted the belt around his waist. Cybil buttoned up a black peacoat and tugged at a fuzzy-looking pink scarf around her neck.

"It's a little bit colder than I thought it would be tonight," she said as they stepped onto the sidewalk and headed toward the nearest crosswalk.

"I was thinking that myself." Ashe shoved his hands into his pockets. "You want to go back to school?"

"No. It's the first parade of the season, and maybe the weirdest."

"This is my first Mardi Gras parade, ever," Ashe said.

As they stopped to wait at the crosswalk, Cybil cut her eyes over at him. "Really? How long have you lived here?"

"This is my second year. Marianne and I talked about coming down last year, but it rained on Mardi Gras day, and we didn't feel like standing out in that."

The light changed, and the walk sign flashed white. He and Cybil started across the street with a handful of other people. Kids ran past them as their parents yelled for them to wait. On the other side of Water Street, Cybil took the lead and cut across the parking lot of a bank.

"Parades run every night for two weeks before the actual day," she said.

Ashe walked faster to catch up with her. They crossed a blocked-off street at an angle. "We didn't know that then. We had planned on going to a few parades this time, but."

Cybil stopped at the corner of Royal Street and St. Michael. "I'm sorry I brought it up. I didn't mean to get you feeling bad. We came down here to have a good time and to get your mind off of things."

"Everything is going to make me emotional right now," Ashe said. "My fiancée just died."

A burst of noise that sounded like an old air raid siren from World War II movies echoed down the street. Cybil grabbed him by the wrist and pulled him across St. Michael. They trotted. Ashe pulled his hand back. He didn't want to risk a student or worse a colleague seeing him being pulled along by a work-study. He reconsidered coming to the parade with her. If the chair of his department heard, he would be in trouble or least have a hard time explaining things. Ashe slowed down.

"Come on," Cybil said. "That siren means the parade has started. We've got to hurry to get in place. We're already not going to get on the barrier. We'll have to fight with all sorts of people for beads."

"Maybe I should go back to the car and wait. I'm going to be a wet blanket."

"Don't worry about it. You already are. Plus, I plan on drinking after this. You'll be sitting there a long time waiting." She smiled. "Maybe you can get a couple of drinks in you and help lighten your mood."

Ashe liked the idea of being able to down a few beers in a loud crowded bar where people might not know him, but certainly wouldn't sympathize with him. He nodded and started behind her. Cybil turned up the next street and cut through an alley. He followed her, until they came out on a busy street. All sorts of people milled around on the sidewalk. The air felt electric. People screamed and laughed. Cybil grabbed him by the wrist again and pulled him along. Finally they pushed through a group, elbowing them until they stood at a metal barricade.

"What are you doing?" a scruffy-looking man asked when Cybil pushed him to the side to get a place at the edge of the street.

"I'm here for the parade," she said with no fear in her voice. "You got a problem?"

"You need to get your girlfriend under control," the man said to Ashe.

"I'm not his girlfriend, you insensitive prick. She died yesterday, so why don't you step off before I shove my Doc Marten so far into your groin that you'll think you're eating oysters."

Cybil stuck her chest out at him like a rooster prancing before the hens in his barnyard.

The scruffy man backed down. He shook his head and slipped into the group of people behind him.

"That was a little bit—"

"Ballsy?"

"Scary. He could've broken you in half," Ashe said.

"And I could have made him taste his own foreskin for a month." She smiled and clambered onto the metal barrier as two police motorcycles passed.

Ashe looked up as the first float rolled down the street. A banner lit with LCD Christmas lights read The Buttercups: Ode to Joy. The float had a huge bust of Beethoven rotating on a platform. Revelers in powdered wigs and sequined harlequin masks wore candy-colored costumes that looked like tailed tuxedo jackets with matching knee britches and stockings. A shower of green, purple and gold bead necklaces rained down on the crowd. Ashe put his hand up to block the hard plastic beads from hitting him in the face. A few of the necklaces tangled in his fingers.

"Put them on," Cybil yelled at him while holding her hands out to the float.

She'd stripped off her coat and scarf. Several strings of

Mardi Gras beads hung around her neck. He pulled the two necklaces over his head. They hung loose on him. A small brass band walked between the floats. They played some jazz song that didn't sound like any song in particular.

"How's this?" he asked.

"You look better, but you've got to want those things. The first float will toss out things without any real reason. The later ones are a bit pickier. They usually have better stuff too." Cybil yelled as a masked man on horseback trotted by. He handed her a string of beads the size of silver dollars. Each looked like a multicolored mirror ball at a prom. "I got a fifth of Jack last year."

"Really. How did you get that?"

The next float came past. A cheap plastic toy hit Ashe in the head. He turned to the float and held his hands up again to block getting hit more than to catch something. A younglooking man with a bright red Venetian mask with a long beak-like nose taunted the crowd with a plush toy that looked like an alien giving the finger.

"Like this," Cybil said.

Ashe looked over to see her lifting her top up, revealing her small breasts. The cold air made her pinkish nipples stand erect. He looked away but not before the image of her fistsized milky breasts was seared into his memory. The big-nosed parade reveler tossed the alien to Cybil while giving her a big thumbs-up and flicking his tongue out.

"You have to be careful doing that though. The cops don't like it too much here in Mobile. You can usually get away with it at Bienville Square or on this stretch."

Ashe looked back at her while a high school band played a march as they passed. She shoved the stuffed toy into her pocket and readied herself to catch more beads. He turned back to the parade as well. Ethics training kept rolling over in his head as did the image of Marianne lying naked on the morgue table. The orderly jiggled her breasts in his memory instead of pointing at them like on the video. He saw in his mind's eye Cybil's boobs bouncing up and down as she tried to get that alien.

Beads flew at Ashe. He caught some but let others go. As

the parade progressed, he caught a few small silver-cellophane wrapped MoonPies that he shoved in his coat pockets. Some playful reveler on a float shaped like a piano with everyone dressed like Elton John on *The Muppet Show* tossed him a pair of thong panties. He shoved those quickly into his pocket before anyone saw them. Without being aware, he laughed at times. Toward the end he even looked over at Cybil without feeling guilty or embarrassed.

Red and white strobe lights flashed. A siren accompanied the lights. Cybil hopped off the metal barrier. She took him by the hand and pulled him back onto the sidewalk. A fire engine rolled past, and several men in coveralls with *City of Mobile* printed on the breast pocket came down the line of barriers. They lifted them up and slammed them back to the sidewalk. Ashe barely had his feet out of the gutter before the barrier slammed into the cement.

"You can get a hurt ankle if you're not fast enough," Cybil said. "Since you're a virgin and everything, I figured you wouldn't know about that."

Ashe knew she meant he was a virgin to the Mardi Gras experience, but he felt like a gawky awkward teen boy who had just gotten to second base and was hoping to round third. A large wad of shiny metallic colored beads rested on the small bumps of breast that he'd just seen her flash. Although he knew it was wrong and that thinking of stuff like that was not what he should be focused on right now, he wanted to see her breasts again.

"Thanks. The last thing I need is a broken ankle," he said, making eye contact with her as quickly as he could and hoping that it didn't seem like he was intentionally doing it. "I guess we head back to campus now?"

"If that's what you want to do," Cybil said.

"It's a school night." He felt like such a geek saying that. "I've skipped too many classes lately. The university isn't paying me not to teach."

She looped her arm under his and started walking. He followed her lead. They moved with the current of revelers making their way down Dauphin Street.

"Maybe they should," she said.

"Should what?"

"Pay you for not teaching. I've heard your lectures."

He looked down at his student worker. She smiled at him. He laughed.

"Maybe we could stop in for a drink." He paused in front of a bar called Grand Central.

"That's fine, but not here," she said. "There's a better place about a block away. It's less crowded and well, less that." She pointed to a few people going in who looked like stereotypical college students.

"Sounds good; lead the way."

Cybil pulled him down the street. All different sorts of people passed them as they moved slowly down the sidewalk. A few people dressed in evening wear with feather masks on laughed as they shoved past. Parents with small children weighed down in bead necklaces did the same. Ashe looked down at his feet as they walked. He didn't feel like making eye contact with anyone. Embarrassment burned at the edges of his psyche. If they ran into a colleague, he would be caught for sure, even though he hadn't done a single thing wrong.

His shoulder knocked hard into someone walking the opposite way. He looked up to apologize. A tall, slender black woman stood staring at him. Her eyes were amber and seemed distant but intent. They pierced into his. A feeling of déjà vu hit him as if he knew the woman from somewhere. He tried to think if she was on the faculty at Alabama Tech.

"I'm sorry," he said, letting Cybil's arm slip from his.

"No worries, friend," she said back with a flat tone. "I should have been watching where I was going."

"I didn't hurt you did I?" he asked.

"No, friend."

He felt Cybil's lips close to his ear. She whispered, "I think she must be some kind of religious nut."

"Have you been enjoying the parade and festivities?" the woman asked.

"Yes," Ashe said. "It was my first parade ever."

"Here comes the sermon," Cybil whispered again.

"I am the president of a new parading society, the Mystics of Mayhem. We will be parading on Mardi Gras night starting at 11:15 p.m., promptly. It would be appreciated if you came out to support us on our first year of revelry."

"Sounds fun," Cybil said. "How did a new society get that time so close to the end of the festival?"

"It is amazing what money will do." The woman laughed, but it sounded very artificial and forced to Ashe.

The president of the Mystics of Mayhem began to give him the creeps. Her stare never changed, and he hadn't noticed her blinking.

"We'll try to come, but I can't promise anything. It's still a while off," he said.

"I understand, but remember Mystics of Mayhem on Mardi Gras night promptly at 11:15 p.m. We have to be finished by 11:59."

"Why is that?" he asked.

"Because Lent starts at midnight," she said as if everyone should know that.

"Thank you," Cybil said and pulled Ashe down the street.

He looked back at the woman, who walked toward the bar Grand Central. Her steps looked stiff, but nothing else struck him as out of the ordinary.

"That was a strange lady," he said.

"Most of them are," Cybil said.

"Most of whom? Ladies?"

"No, presidents of parading societies. I've met a few while trying to get tickets to a ball. You'd be surprised what they expect people to do for those things."

"Like flash." Ashe didn't mean to say it, but the words just slipped out.

"I guess I should be embarrassed that my boss has seen my boobs, but I had to have that alien. They're my thing."

Cybil paused in the street and let her coat slip from her shoulder. She reached and pulled down the neck of her shirt to show the part of her back at her shoulders. A green alien head with big eyes stared up at Ashe. Its eyes seemed livelier than those of the woman they had just spoken with.

"That's…"

"Cool." She pulled her coat back up.

"Weird."

She slipped her arm back through his and pointed down the street. "The bar is just around the corner."

Traffic Camera: Corner of Dauphin and Conti Streets, Mobile, AL, 9:19 p.m. CST

Marianne walks across the middle of the intersection ignoring any traffic that is on the street. An SUV brakes violently before hitting her. The driver, a bulky man wearing a trucker hat, jumps out of his car. He walks up to Marianne and jabs his hands in the air at her, but she keeps walking slowly toward the other side of the road.

The driver reaches out and grabs her by the shoulder. She turns on him, grabbing his arm. He falls to his knees as she turns his forearm over. After letting him go, Marianne continues across the street. The driver kneels in the middle of the intersection. He screams at the sky and holds his arm, which dangles at his side. A woman climbs from the passenger side of the SUV. She helps the man up and back to the SUV. Then she looks down the street at Marianne. She takes a step in that direction, but then hurries to her SUV. The vehicle speeds through the intersection.

CHAPTER FOUR

A she waited at the bar for their drinks. Cybil had disappeared into the crowd to find a place to sit. Despite what she'd told him, this bar seemed more crowded than the one he'd wanted to go in. Everyone around him appeared to be of the same fashion persuasion as Cybil. He couldn't remember the last time he'd been in a place with so many people dressed in black and neon colors.

"Here you go." The bartender placed two longneck beers on the counter in front of him.

Ashe handed him his credit card. When he received his card back with his receipt, he waded into the people, looking for Cybil. The whole place smelled like clove cigarettes and the music that thrummed through it made his teeth vibrate. He found his companion after she waved to him from a table close to the far wall.

"Here you go." He handed her a beer. "You are old enough, aren't you?"

"Of course," she said and took a slug of the drink.

"So this is less crowded than the other place?" He hoped that it didn't sound mean but at the same time hoped it did.

"I guess I was wrong," she said. "Probably because they have live music tonight."

Ashe looked at the stage. A band's equipment was set up, but the music filling up the place was recorded.

"Who is it, Casper and the Ghosts?"

Cybil shook her head while taking another drink. "It's this local group called the Goth Sox. They play funky electronica punk semigoth stuff. They're between sets right now."

"Are they any good?" he asked.

"It's according to your taste in music, but if you're into Pat Boone, no they aren't."

He laughed. Pat Boone had never been to his taste. Back in the day he'd rocked out to Nirvana and Pearl Jam like most everyone else his age and a little bit older. An old photo or two might even have shown him in his flannel and ripped jeans phase, but he'd never understood the electronica rave music.

"I guess we'll have to see."

Finally he drank from his own beer. He hoped the alcohol would relax him just a bit. Tension still pulled at his insides. Cybil didn't seem to notice or if she did, she was hiding it well. His pants began to vibrate. For a moment, he thought he'd given way to his slight amorousness, but quickly realized he'd put his cell phone there when they came into the bar. He fished it out and answered it. The noise in the bar was too loud for him to hear.

"Hold on a second," he yelled into the phone. "I need to walk somewhere I can hear."

Ashe walked from their table to the door. He stepped outside into the cool, damp air. His ears rang slightly from the reverb of the speakers inside.

"Are you still there?" he asked.

"Yes, this is Detective Semmes. Sounds like a raging party."

"I came to the parade to try and get my mind off of things," Ashe said. "Then I ended up at a bar."

"Drinking doesn't make things better. It makes them worse most of the time."

"I promise I'm not trying to drink my blues away. It's just a beer, and a cheap one at that. I'm sure you didn't call to find out what I'm doing though."

"You're right. I like a man who gets straight to the point. I'm heading up to Birmingham tomorrow. I found out they've had a similar case at one of their hospitals."

"What do you mean similar?"

"They had a dead woman get up and walk out of the morgue at St. Vincent's Hospital. I thought you might want to ride up there with me."

"Why would I want to do that? I've missed quite a few days of classes. I don't think the university is going to let me just keep missing," Ashe said.

"For one thing, it might help me because you might notice similarities between Marianne and this woman. Another is that the police up there might not be very welcoming to me, but probably would think twice if I brought you," Semmes said.

"You want to take me along for sympathy," Ashe said. "I don't think so."

"Don't hang up. I really need you to go for the first part. If there is any similarity between the two women, it could give us an MO or something."

"What kind of similarities am I going to be able to see? I'm not a psychologist, Detective. Just because I built a machine for recording emotions, doesn't mean I understand them."

"That's not what I mean."

"So what do you mean?"

"I mean, physically."

"You mean carnally. You've got stills from the morgue video at University Hospital."

"Okay, you knew her *carnally*. I can't explain it, Ashe; I just need you there. You saw the video of Marianne. You have a doctorate, so you give it more credibility than just me. Even though I'm a detective, they might still think I'm crazy."

Harsh notes from a keyboard screeched from the bar's open door. Ashe cringed as the notes assailed his ears. The Goth Sox must have taken the stage.

"All right, when are you leaving?" he asked.

"Around 6 a.m. I've got your address so I'll pick you up at your house," Semmes said.

"I'll be ready."

Without another word, Ashe hung up and slipped his phone back into his pocket. He walked back into the bar. Green and red lights flashed from off the stage. A skinny woman with green and pink striped hair clutched a microphone in both hands. She sang something that sounded a lot like nothing to Ashe. He tried to block out the noise as he made his way back to Cybil. When he got there, a college-aged guy with eyeliner around his eyes sat beside her. She looked up at Ashe and smiled.

"Dr. Shrove, this is Stewart, a friend of mine."

Jealousy poked at Ashe as he stuck his hand out to shake with the guy. Stewart didn't reciprocate.

"I don't shake hands," he said. "Germs."

Ashe cut his eyes to Cybil. "I've got to go. The detective working on Marianne's case needs for me to ride up to Birmingham with him tomorrow. We're leaving early so I need to get in bed."

"The band just started," she said.

"Maybe Stewart could give you a ride back to campus," Ashe said.

"No, I came with you, and I'll leave with you. Besides, I left some stuff in your office, so I'll need you to let me in." Cybil snatched up the beer that had been his. She chugged it down. "No need wasting it."

She patted Stewart on the arm as she walked past him. Ashe and she left the bar.

Cybil let Ashe open his office door and turn the light on. She slipped past him, allowing her hip to brush against the front of his pants. Her backpack lay in one of the chairs he kept for visitors. She snatched it up and pulled it onto her back. The straps were tight and pulled her coat open. This drew her peasant blouse tight across her breasts. She turned to face Ashe, sticking her chest out as far as she could, which wasn't far.

"I got my stuff," she said.

He looked at her and then to his desk. "I think I left Detective Semmes' number in my desk."

He stepped past her. She smiled when she knew he couldn't see her. Ever since she'd flashed for the stuffed alien toy, he'd been avoiding looking at her anywhere except her eyes. She didn't mind it too much though. He had very pretty eyes. She could understand why Marianne had been with him even if he was a giant geek.

"I guess I'll be going," she said.

Ashe looked back at her and smiled. "Be careful. I'll see you in a day or two."

"Thanks for tonight. It was fun," she said.

He turned around and looked at her. "I should be thanking you for dragging me out to the parade and that bar. I'm sorry we had to leave so early."

"It's okay," she said, walking to him.

Cybil licked her lips. She thought about kissing him because there was no way he would kiss her first. Instead, she gave him a hug and put her mouth close to his ear.

"I'm sorry about everything. I'm around if you need anything," she whispered.

He let the embrace fall away and nodded his head. "Thanks again, Cybil. You've been really great to me these last few days. If you don't mind, tell my electrical engineering class to read ahead in the next unit, and I'll have a special make-up day for them. Also drop in on my graduate class, and tell them to download the lecture by Dr. Marcus O'Shea from Columbia University's website. It's the one about the emotional engram machine."

"Why not have them listen to one of your lectures on that, since you invented the thing?" she asked.

"He's the guy I asked for help. It was some of his theories that helped me make it," Ashe said. "I'll be back in a few days."

"Okay, sleep well, and have a good day tomorrow in the Ham." Cybil started out of the office.

"The Ham?"

She turned back and smiled. "It's slang for Birmingham. Goodnight."

He mumbled something as she left, but she didn't understand it. Deep inside her she wished that she could help him figure out what happened to his girlfriend. Maybe she would do some poking around while he was away for a few days.

A thin layer of fog settled over the campus when she left the building and headed to her Vespa. It would be thick by the next morning, she thought as she kicked the scooter into starting and headed toward her apartment.

Ashe sipped the police station coffee from a small Styrofoam cup. It tasted scorched and too bitter. Morning had come too soon for him. He slept poorly from the time he'd gotten home until his alarm sounded. As promised Semmes was at his house on the dot.

The four-hour drive north bogged down in Montgomery due to school and work traffic.

Although Semmes drove a marked Mobile PD cruiser, he refused to ride with the lights on even in the heaviest traffic.

After all that time riding, the lead detective on the case in Birmingham left them waiting in the main lobby of the police station. Semmes sat beside him on the hard wooden bench. He too sipped at a cup of coffee, but he seemed to enjoy it. His badge hung from the pocket of his sports coat.

"How much longer do you think we'll be sitting here?" Ashe asked.

"Probably just a few more minutes. They said this detective had a few people to interview this morning over at the hospital," Semmes said.

"We couldn't have just gone to that hospital?"

"According to the detective, the hospital isn't very excited about this and wants to keep it hush hush." Semmes took a slug of the coffee. "Plus I don't know how to get there. I don't get up here much."

The doors to the outside opened. A gust of cold wind blew inside. A bald man with dark brown skin that was almost the color of the coffee Ashe drank walked in. A young man with rumpled hair followed behind him. They both wore black peacoats. The bald man smiled and walked toward them.

"You must be Detective Semmes from Mobile." He extended his hand. "I'm Perry Monroe. We've been communicating back and forth about the Heinz case."

Semmes stood up and shook Monroe's hand. "Nice to meet you in person." He pointed to Ashe. "This is Dr. Ashe Shrove from Alabama Tech. He's the gentleman I was telling you about."

Ashe stood and put his hand out to Monroe. They shook. The bald detective introduced his partner as Joey Brewer. All four men crossed from the lobby into the interior of the police station. They ended up in a conference room on the third floor.

A large television covered the majority of a wall. A window

looking out on a downtown park made up another wall. They all sat grouped at one end of the conference table. Ashe and Semmes sat beside each other.

"So y'all had someone get up and walk out of a morgue down there in Mobile?" Brewer asked.

"It was more than just somebody," Semmes said.

"It was my fiancée who died mysteriously the same night," Ashe finished.

"I didn't realize that. I'm sorry," Brewer said.

"Rookie mistake," Monroe said. He turned his attention to Semmes. "You know how it is when you are first made a detective. We just can't seem to keep our mouths shut."

"We've got a long drive back home," Ashe said. "Can we get to it, please?"

Monroe nodded. He turned the on television and pressed play on the DVD player. The screen showed a cold storage room in a morgue. The camera was positioned so that it showed both walls that had drawers in them. A man in dark scrubs walked through the room and off screen. The time marker noted the time.

"This is a few minutes before the incident. We've interviewed that morgue tech. He said that nothing happened out of the ordinary," Monroe said.

"What was his name?" Semmes asked.

"Jackson. Steven Jackson," Brewer said. "He has a small record for misdemeanors like possession of drug paraphernalia, but according to his personnel records, he's been clean on every single drug test, even randoms."

"Someone is coming on the screen," Ashe said.

A man in a lab coat walked into the morgue. It was not the same man from Marianne's abduction in Mobile. This man was shorter and stockier. He walked to a drawer near floor level and slid it open. A black body bag lay in the drawer. He unzipped the bag. A woman's face stared up at the ceiling. Ashe couldn't tell anything about the detail of her face. The camera was positioned too far away from it. The only thing he could tell was that she was probably later middle-aged and a light-skinned black woman.

"That is Heinz in the drawer," Monroe said. "The doctor is unknown."

"No one saw him come in, or he wasn't required to sign in?" Semmes asked.

"There is a doctor on record entering the morgue at this time. The name on the sign-in was Smith. St. Vincent's Hospital has no doctor named Smith with privileges," Monroe said.

Ashe listened but kept his eyes on the screen. He saw no similarity between his fiancée and this woman. The doctor pulled out a device from his lab coat's deep pocket. The angle and distance of the camera made it difficult to see what it was, but he placed electrodes on the woman's forehead. After a few seconds, she sat up in the drawer. The doctor helped her down from the drawer. They walked out of the morgue. Monroe switched the television off.

"That's it," he said.

"Does that look familiar to you, Ashe?" Semmes asked.

"It's almost exactly what happened with Marianne, the device is even the same. The woman was much older than Marianne. I couldn't tell anything else about her from the camera," Ashe said.

"We have a photo of her," Brewer said.

He opened a manila folder lying on the table and took a picture from it. Brewer passed it to Semmes. Ashe looked at it as well. The face from the photo was pleasant and familiar. Ashe was sure he'd seen it before. He searched his memory.

"I saw that woman last night." He recalled the woman on Dauphin Street.

"That's impossible," Monroe said. "She's dead."

"Apparently not," Semmes said. "You saw her walk out of that morgue. Not many dead people can do that."

"Unless they aren't dead," Brewer said, "or are zombies."

"Rookies," Monroe said to Semmes. Then he turned to Brewer. "There are no such things as zombies or vampires."

"Don't be so quick to judge," Semmes said. "So far we have two women presumed dead, who have walked out of hospitals alive."

"Only after being visited by a mysterious doctor," Ashe

said. "I guess I should say doctors because that wasn't the same man who stole Marianne."

"I want to get back to what you just said," Monroe said. "You claim to have seen this woman last night. Where at?"

"Dauphin Street in downtown Mobile. It was after the parade last night," Ashe said.

"Except she had these weird amber-colored eyes instead of dark brown. It was the same woman though."

"She was alive?" Monroe asked.

"Very much so. She told me and the person I was with that she was the president of a society that would be parading on Mardi Gras night at almost midnight. She kept mentioning a very specific time that the parade would start and finish, 11:15 p.m. to 11:59 p.m."

"Did she try to eat your brains?" Brewer asked.

"What kind of a stupid question is that?" Ashe said. "I just told you she spoke to us. She didn't attack us or do anything unusual, except she walked a little stiffly."

"She is dead," Brewer said. "Rigor mortis made her shuffle just like a zombie."

"Rookie, we're going to have to have a talk after Detective Semmes and Dr. Shrove leave," Monroe said. He turned to Ashe. "Are you willing to sign an affidavit stating you saw her?"

Ashe looked at Semmes who nodded. "Of course. I've got no reason to lie about this."

"We'll get something drawn up and send it down to Semmes," Monroe said.

"I think we've gotten everything we're going to get from here," Semmes said. "We'll keep in touch."

The detective stood. Ashe did the same. They left the police station. The air outside still felt very chilled. As they walked down the sidewalk, Ashe put his hands in his pockets to keep them warm. The traffic moved steadily down the street.

"What was the name of that society Heinz said she was in?" Semmes asked. "I don't remember any society parading that late on Mardi Gras night."

"She said it was a new one called the Knights or Mystics of Mayhem," Ashe said. "This is the first time I've celebrated

Mardi Gras so I don't know all the names yet."

They crossed the street at an intersection and headed to the Mobile PD cruiser. Semmes pulled a cigarette out and lit it.

"I'll have to go check them out." He took a drag off it. "You about ready to head back south?"

"Yeah."

Ashe looked forward to nothing else. He needed some quiet time to process everything. Life seemed to be moving in a direction he didn't like, and he thought that he might need to be making some changes.

CHAPTER FIVE

Cybil carried a stack of papers down the hall toward Ashe's office. He'd left the keys in the mailroom with a note asking her to put any work from his classes on his desk. She jingled the keys trying to find the one that opened the door. His office smelled like Ashe. Although she'd been in his office many times when he wasn't there, the fact that it retained his scent had slipped her notice. She sat behind his desk and put the papers down, face up so that he would notice them.

Someone knocked on the door. Cybil sat up straight and fumbled to arrange the desk, trying to hide her surprise. She looked up. A uniformed police officer stood there. He held a large brown padded envelope.

"Can I help you?" she asked.

"Are you Ashley Shrove?" the police office asked.

"No, I'm his work-study, but I can probably help you."

"I'm supposed to leave this with him."

Cybil stood and walked to the door. "You can leave it with me. I'll make sure he gets it."

"I don't know."

"It's okay. I do stuff like this for him all the time. That's why they hire us, so we can do the dirty work."

"Are you sure it's not to give them something to look at?"

"I don't think they'd pay me for that. I'd probably have to pay them."

"You're pretty nice looking. You think you might go out with a cop sometime?"

Cybil looked at him. He was buffer than what she liked but had nice eyes. She didn't have much interest but figured

Marianne's computer was in that envelope. She wanted to try and find something out about her death. Ashe would be overly appreciative if she could find some clue that might help out.

"There's a bar downtown called Bayside. Do you know the place?" she asked.

"I've had to break up some fights there a time or two. It's a pretty rough place for someone your size," he said.

"It like it rough."

He grinned. She knew that look well. His mind instantly went to sex. All men's did, and she knew how to use that her advantage.

"Tomorrow night, 8 p.m. One of my favorite bands is playing there, but you've got to leave that with me." She touched the envelope.

"Sounds good." The police officer handed her the envelope. "I'll see you then."

"It's a date." The envelope was heavy. Now she was positive it had Marianne's laptop in it. "What's your name?"

"Zack McAllister."

"Cybil. I'll see you tomorrow."

He tapped the bill of his hat and walked away. Cybil returned to Ashe's desk. She put the envelope down and tore into it. A pink Dell notebook computer hid inside. A sticky note was stuck to the top. It thanked Ashe for letting them process the computer, but said they found nothing out of the ordinary.

"Let's see what I can find," she said aloud as she flipped the top up.

When the desktop pulled up, a picture of Marianne and Ashe smiled at Cybil. A few icons framed the photo, but it showed a happy couple. She felt sorry for Ashe. He seemed to love his fiancée. She even felt a little guilty that she was attracted to him. It would be a rebound for him if anything happened between them, but she figured that might not hurt him too much anyway.

The touch pad was more sensitive than the one she usually used on her own laptop. The arrow cursor soared across the screen. She reined it in and opened up the area for recent files opened. There were several Word documents there including one called guest list. Cybil figured it was a listing for Marianne and Ashe's planned wedding two years from then. He had told her at the beginning of last semester that he had planned a long engagement. Nothing seemed out of the ordinary.

Next Cybil opened the media player. She remembered being told that Marianne still had her earbuds in when they found her dead. The track listing showed a variety of interesting musical choices. Marianne seemed to be a big fan of chick music. Cybil recognized a few Liz Phair songs along with Joni Mitchell and Carole King. In the folder for lectures, she found several different ones including the one that Ashe told her to have his graduate students listen to. The last folder she checked was recently added. Several Elton John songs were there including "Goodbye Yellow Brick Road". She was getting ready to close this out when a song title caught her eye. "Pink-Striped Hair" was its name. She knew that song well. It was by the Goth Sox.

"Why would she have this?" Cybil said.

The music of the song started to play over the low-quality speakers of the laptop. She'd heard this song many times. The Goth Sox always opened and closed with it. It was their only *hit* song, meaning it was only one they had recorded in an actual studio. Something seemed off about the music. It echoed. Cybil stopped playing it.

"Dell speakers really suck," she said.

She shut the computer down and shoved it back into the torn-up envelope. Maybe she'd ask Ashe about why Marianne would have the Goth Sox on her computer since he'd never heard of them. Surely they knew each other's musical taste. She'd known all of her boyfriends' musical tastes. Sometimes that was the reason she'd broken up with them. The deal breaker list always included country, frat rock and party rap.

Her cell phone chirped. She dug it out of her pocket and answered it.

"Cybil, this is Ashe."

Her heart fluttered. He'd never called her on her cell before. "What's up?"

"We'll be back in about an hour. We're just coming to the delta. Is there anything I need to know about?"

"Not really, I gave out everything you asked for me to. Oh,

and the police brought back Marianne's laptop."

"Did they find anything?" he asked as his voice digitized some.

"No, but I do have a question." She heard more digitized talking. "Hello?"

Nothing answered back. She closed her phone and shoved it back into her pocket.

Ashe stood on the sidewalk outside of the D'Iberville Building on Alabama Tech's campus. The street lamps overhead made Semmes' cruiser look blue instead of white. The detective leaned out his window.

"You sure you don't want me to take you home?" he asked.

"I need to catch up on some work. Cybil—my student worker—was supposed to leave some stuff my classes have done. The college isn't going to keep paying me to do nothing," Ashe said.

"You've only missed a few days due to your fiancée's death," Semmes said. "How are you going to get home?"

Ashe shrugged his shoulders. "I'll catch a ride with someone." He looked up at the building; a few office lights were on. "My friend, Erik Rogers, is still here. He'll give me a lift."

"All right. If you need anything give me a call," Semmes said. "Oh, and until I get a chance to follow up on this new parading society, don't tell anyone about what we did up in Birmingham. I don't want things leaking to the public."

"No worries. Have a good night."

Ashe threw up his hand to Semmes and turned to walk into the building. He made his way to the third floor and into Rogers' office. The psychologist sat with his back to the door. He watched a program run on his computer. A single green line moved up and down at different beats. Ashe watched for a few moments then cleared his throat. Rogers turned around.

"Ashe, I haven't seen you all day. Where have you been hiding?" he asked while closing out the program.

"Here and there," Ashe said. "I came by to ask if I could get a ride back to my place when you leave."

"Sure. What's the matter with your car? Is it broken down?"

"I've been with Detective Semmes, the guy working on Marianne's case. He dropped me off here so that I could catch up on some work my student assistant was supposed to leave me."

"How did that turn out up in Birmingham?"

"I don't know what you're talking about," Ashe said.

"Cybil told me you had to go to Birmingham with that detective." Rogers scanned him up and down. "You'll tell your work-study where you're going but leave your best friend and confidante in the dark."

"I didn't realize that we were that close, but they had something similar to what happened with Marianne up there. This woman walked out of the morgue after a doctor used a device on her."

"Was it the same guy?"

"No, totally different guy." Ashe leaned against the doorframe. Although he'd been sitting most of the day he felt exhausted. "What is going on with your program?"

"Something strange," Rogers said. "I've been toying with the engrams I've recorded so far. I think I might be able to isolate different impulses for more emotions. All these emotions intertwine with each other. Just imagine if we can record people's feelings and find underlying negative and dangerous emotions like depression or dysphoria before symptoms appear."

"Sounds like another science award for Dr. Erik Rogers," Ashe said, glad that his friend changed the subject even if it was to brag.

"For both of us." Rogers held up the engram device Ashe had built. "Without this thing none of what I've been able to do would have been possible. We'll be the new Crick and Watson."

"I'm going to walk up the not double helix stairs to my office and get some work done. Come by and get me when you get ready to leave."

"I'll buzz you on your cell phone. That way I can save my knees."

Ashe left Rogers' office and climbed two more floors to his. Cybil had everything locked up, and the lights were out. He went in and lit up the room. Marianne's pink laptop lay on his desk. Although it was partially covered by a ripped envelope, he'd recognize it anywhere.

It had been a Christmas gift to her a few years ago.

He sat down at his desk. A note was stuck to the top of the computer. Cybil had written: *Accepted this from the police. I had to agree to a date so he would leave it. So you owe me. Sorry I opened the envelope, but I thought I might find something that would help figure out what happened with Marianne. Talk to you tomorrow.*

Ashe peeled the note off, balled it up and tossed it into the trash can. He felt a little bit angry that she had opened the envelope and probed into his fiancée's private matters, but she seemed like she wanted to help him deal with all the pain.

The temptation to snoop on the computer was strong, but Ashe found the papers from his undergraduate classes. He started grading. It was just the mind-numbing activity he needed. Marianne left his mind as did Cybil. Nothing of the Heinz woman in Birmingham lingered there until his phone buzzed an hour and a half later with a text message from Rogers. It was time to leave.

"Did my friend ever come by and talk to you?" Rogers asked.

"The priestly shrink? Yeah, he did." Ashe sipped his drink. He'd decided tonight he'd have a vodka and Coke, which he called a Russian libre.

"Did he help you any?"

"We only talked one time, so no."

A waitress brought them their food. Ashe didn't really want to eat out tonight. He and Semmes had stopped at a McDonald's somewhere between Birmingham and Montgomery for lunch. The idea of another greasy restaurant meal didn't appeal to him, but Rogers had suggested a seafood place. He decided that crab claws might not be that bad.

"So tell me more about what happened up in Birmingham." Rogers slurped down an oyster.

"I can't. Detective Semmes told me not to discuss that issue because he doesn't want anyone possibly involved to hear about it."

"Who am I going to tell?"

Ashe cracked opened a claw. "Your priest friend."

"Only in confession, which is protected information." Rogers chased another oyster with a swig of beer.

"I better not."

"You're going to tell Cybil, and she's just a work-study."

Ashe bit off a piece of crabmeat. As he chewed it, he watched Rogers. The psychologist's eyes seemed playful, but the words seemed loaded.

"There's nothing going on between us," Ashe said. "I mean my fiancée just died."

"She's cute."

"That doesn't matter." Suddenly the image of Cybil's small bare breasts filled up Ashe's mind. "She's younger than I am and a student."

"Please, like you would be the first professor to fool around with a student." Another oyster slid into his mouth. "You ought to talk to the literature professors sometime. It's like a soap opera mixed with an orgy in their department."

"I saw the woman who went missing in Birmingham last night at the Mardi Gras parade." Ashe tried to change the subject.

Rogers nearly choked on an oyster. "Seriously?"

"Yeah, she said that she was the president of some new parading society."

"Did she look like a zombie?"

"No, she looked like a normal person although she spoke and moved a little stiffly."

Rogers took a drink from his beer. "So who did you go to the parade with? Because I know you didn't venture down there by yourself."

Ashe bit off another piece of crabmeat. He tried to take as long as he could, chewing on it to avoid answering. It was apparent that Rogers wasn't going to let it go.

"Cybil."

"I knew it," the psychologist answered. "How was she? I bet she's a screamer. She looks like one."

"We watched a parade then went for a drink, which I didn't

get to have because Detective Semmes called me." Ashe took a long sip from his cocktail. "There is nothing going on between us."

"Is that Semmes guy trying to find this missing woman from Birmingham too?" Rogers asked.

"He's going to try and find out about this new parading society. I guess he figures there might be a connection between the disappearances and that society," Ashe said.

"That might be a pretty good bet." Rogers slurped down an oyster and then yawned.

"Let's finish up. I'm really tired all of a sudden."

"How many of those things have you sucked down?"

"I don't know, why?"

"I thought you were trying to lose weight and stay fit," Ashe said.

"I need the protein for the bodybuilding. Just like I need the sleep. Finish up already."

Ashe was happy to hear that. Nothing would feel better than to get to bed and try to sleep. He just hoped that Carol Heinz and Marianne wouldn't haunt his dreams.

Security Camera: Storage Facility, Michigan Avenue, Mobile, AL, 10:16 p.m. CST

Several people mill around the room. Only a small bulb dangling from the ceiling lights them. Most of the faces are lost in shadow. Carol Heinz stands in the middle of the people. She speaks to them, and although the others walk around, they seem to be listening.

Marianne walks out of the darker shadows carrying a costume. It looks like a mermaid outfit. The sequins on the tail fin sparkle and shimmer in the little bit of light in the room. All the others look at the costume and touch it. Carol points to the outfit and then to Marianne, who hands the costume to another person. With everyone standing around and staring, Marianne removes her clothes. She stands a long time naked in the midst of all the bodies. No one seems surprised, and not a single person ogles her. She takes the costume back and steps into it. Carol helps her fasten it in the back.

After Marianne twirls to show it off, Carol nods her approval. She speaks to the crowd again, pointing to Marianne the whole time. Then she claps her hands and the group disperses. Marianne turns around and lets her undo the back of the costume. She removes it and stands naked as she and Carol talk back and forth.

A brighter light floods the room as one of the doors opens and lets the bright street lamps from the back of the building shine inside. A man walks in, wearing a hooded sweatshirt with an Alabama Tech logo on it. The hood hides his face. He talks with the two women. Carol drops her head and walks off.

The man reaches out and caresses Marianne's breast. She does not recoil from him. He pulls her closer, and she moves toward him with stiff mechanical movements. She puts her arms around him, leaving enough room for him to fondle her breasts and then move to the area between her legs. After a few minutes, he leads her to the shadows while unfastening his pants.

CHAPTER SIX

Cybil knocked on the door as she entered Ashe's office. She did it more to warn him that she was coming than anything else. He looked up from some papers he worked on and smiled. She made her way into the office. Ever since opening up the laptop yesterday, she'd been worried what kind of reaction Ashe would have had to her doing so. Everything seemed fine.

"What do you need me to do today?" she asked. "Any papers that need copying?"

"No, I think I'm fine for today. Maybe you should check with some of the other professors. You don't work exclusively for me," he said.

She thought his words were clipped and curt. His eyes told her nothing of his emotional state except that he was tired. Dark purple bags hung under them and made him look much older than he was.

"I have. I went to everyone before I came here."

"I guess you can go to the lounge and attack homework or something like that," Ashe said.

"Can I do it in here? Your chairs are more comfortable."

"I don't know, Cybil. I think it would be better if you went someplace else."

"Are you mad at me? Is this about the laptop? I figured that you would want it back sooner than later."

"It's not about the laptop; although, I did find it a little bit strange that you agreed to go on a date with the police officer to get it."

She felt a bit embarrassed and flushed. "I really wanted to

get my hands on it to see if I could find anything that might explain why Marianne died."

"I'm not mad at you for that." He paused and took a long breath. She knew that he wrangled to find the right words. "I'm afraid that people think that we have an inappropriate relationship, something beyond student and professor."

They *were* more than professor and student, she thought to herself. She felt like they were friends. Who would care if they were friends?

"We are more than that, aren't we?" she asked.

"I don't know what kind of feelings you are harboring for me, but I am just your boss and professor."

"We're not friends?" She felt a little hurt.

He looked at her. His eyes brightened a little. "I guess we might lean that way, but that's not the impression I think others are getting."

"Do you mean people think we're getting it on or something like that?"

"Yeah."

"Who?"

"Other professors," Ashe said.

"Did they find out about me flashing at the parade? Because there was nothing sexual about that." She lied a little. Flashing had been in part to get the stuffed alien, but to also perhaps give him a free look, and maybe whet his appetite. It felt silly now. He'd just lost his fiancée.

"No, I think they just see you hanging out in here a lot," he said. "That's why I think you should deal with the other professors a bit more."

"All right," she said. "I'll be in the lounge if you need me for anything. I mean making copies or looking up research articles, not sex."

Ashe laughed even though he tried to hide it as a cough. He did smile though. Cybil knew that things weren't going to be as bad as they could be.

She walked back to the door and stopped. "I found something strange on Marianne's computer."

"What's that?"

"She had a song by the Goth Sox in her media player. Did she know the band?" She looked back at him.

"I don't think so. I'd never heard of them until the other night. I don't know, maybe one of her friends gave it to her."

"I tried to listen to it, but it sounded funny like it had an echo or something. I just thought you might like to know that."

"I'll check it out. Thank you." He smiled again, and it was warm and welcoming. She felt much better about their standing with each other, and she started into the hall. "When do you have to go on that date?"

She turned to look at him. "Tonight at a downtown bar."

"That's too bad. I kind of wanted to go to another parade. I don't really have friends who do that."

"We can still go. I'd like someone around just in case this guy gets fresh."

"Sounds good, but it's completely platonic," Ashe said.

"I'll write *I'm not doing Professor Ashley Shrove* on my forehead in permanent marker," she said.

"I'll see you this evening. We'll take my car again."

"Good because you'd look funny riding bitch on my Vespa."

Ashe opened Marianne's laptop. Cybil hadn't turned it off after she'd been searching it the night before. The screen woke from sleep mode. The happy picture of him and Marianne stared from desktop. If he kept the computer, he'd have to change that. Looking at the picture would depress him every time he worked on it. He opened up the media player software. The first song he saw on the play list was something called "Pink-Striped Hair" by the Goth Sox. He could only imagine what it would sound like after hearing a little of their music live.

"Knock, knock," Father Smalls said.

Ashe looked up and smiled at the priest. "I wasn't expecting to see you. What brings you by?"

"Erik told me that you went to Birmingham yesterday, and that you encountered something disturbing again."

Smalls walked in and sat in one of the visitor's chairs. He crossed his legs and folded his hands over one knee. Ashe double-clicked on the Goth Sox's song. It started to play from the speakers. The music was strained and harsh just like bad punk rock usually was.

"Apparently whatever happened to Marianne has spread to central Alabama," he said. "Excuse the music, but I need to listen to this."

Smalls curled his lip up as the music hit a very sour note. Ashe felt like doing the same thing. He could hear what Cybil had mentioned. The song did sound like it was echoing.

"What kind of music is that?" Smalls asked.

"A local band called the Goth Sox. Apparently Marianne had downloaded it."

"Did she like that kind of music?"

"No."

"What's the matter with it? It sounds like two versions are playing at the same time."

Ashe clicked on the stop button. The music quit playing. "That's exactly what it is. I was trying to figure it out. I think one version is playing faster than the other."

"Is that what punk musicians usually do when they record it, nowadays?" Smalls asked.

"It's a bit different from the Ramones or Blondie."

"I have no idea. This isn't my kind of music either, but I doubt it. I think something happened to the file."

Ashe opened the center drawer of his desk and rummaged around in it. His found a blue thumb drive. He pulled it from the drawer and shoved it into the laptop's USB port. Then he downloaded the Goth Sox song onto it.

"I thought maybe you might need to talk about things?" Smalls said.

"What kind of things?" Ashe transferred the thumb drive from the laptop to his computer.

A virus scan popped up automatically. He'd set up his computer to do that every time he inserted a USB device. Sometimes students turned in work from their personal drives. He didn't want to risk his computer crashing from some funky student-acquired virus.

"You've lost your fiancée recently. Then you go up to Birmingham to help them with a similar missing persons.

Erik said that you saw the missing woman down here at a parade."

"That's right. Remind me not to tell him any secrets. His mouth is way too big."

Ashe opened up the Goth Sox's song in a wave analysis program. He played the song. A green line started to pulsate on the screen as the music swelled up. On the good speakers attached to his desktop computer, the music didn't sound as bad. A few seconds into the song, another line began to pulsate on the screen. It kept close to the first.

"Erik was worried that you might be having a psychotic break. He's a clinical psychologist too, but doesn't specialize in actual therapy."

"You're right. He just electronically stores emotions. I think that he is off base. I actually saw that woman. My work-study student, Cybil, saw her too." Ashe thought that he probably needed to tell her about the woman as well.

"Erik mentioned Cybil too."

"Let me guess, he thinks that I've started a romantic relationship with her. We talked about that nonsense last night." He really wanted to say something stronger than nonsense, but wasn't going to curse in front of a priest.

"He said that you became very angry about him mentioning that," Smalls said.

"Because it's not true." Ashe stopped talking and put up his hand to stop the priest from saying anything.

The music changed. There were two competing versions of the song playing off sync, but something piggybacked with both. A third green line bounced up and down the screen.

The new sound was speech.

"What's wrong with that song?" Smalls asked.

"I don't know."

Ashe clicked through the menus on the screen. He dropped the two lines of the song out, leaving only the third echo. The words were garbled and not English.

Ratreuer eativ olam muc. Srom ibit teinev.

"Turn it off," Smalls said. "Hurry. *Benedicat nos Deus.*"

Ashe hit the pause button. "What's the matter?"

"That was an incantation in reverse Latin," Smalls said. "What band is that?"

"They're called the Goth Sox. I saw them play, and I doubt they know Latin. They sound like they would barely know English."

"Then someone who does know dark things has gotten to them."

"I still don't get your meaning."

"It is believed that Satan and his worshipers use reverse Latin in spells as a way to bring about his evil magic."

"Do all priests know this or just you?" Ashe felt like he'd drifted in some cheesy Hammer horror film.

"I don't think we all know this kind of thing, but I do. You remember I told you that I work adjunct for the school. I teach parapsychology. I'm an expert in psychoreligious phenomena."

"You mean like exorcisms or stigmata?" Ashe asked, having no real idea what he meant.

"I study incidents of levitation, glossolalia or speaking in tongues, exorcisms and other religious phenomena. I also have done studies in witchcraft and black magic. That sounded a lot like what I've encountered in that field of study."

Ashe felt sick to his stomach. "What would happen if some-one listened to that whole song?"

"They would probably get a headache from hearing the overlying music, but I don't know what the incantation would have done," Smalls said.

"Would it kill? Could it?"

Smalls shrugged. "Most psychoreligious phenomena have their power based in belief. If someone knew what they were listening to, maybe. If they didn't, I doubt that it would have done anything."

"What if it was real instead of some kind of mind trick?" Ashe asked.

"Then, it could have done great harm, but I don't think that Marianne was a victim of demonic evil. The only time I ever encountered supposed black magic phenomena I couldn't explain was in West Africa. I've only encountered hogwash in America."

"Is that the scientific term?"

"Of course."

Ashe smiled and picked up his phone and dialed the number for the lounge. When Cybil picked up, he asked her to come back to his office. If anyone would know something about that band it would be her. She seemed to have been a fan of them. Cybil walked in less than a minute later.

"What's up?" she asked.

"Have a seat." Ashe pointed to the chair beside Smalls.

She did, eyeing the priest the whole time.

"This is Father Smalls," Ashe said.

"Hello," she said. "I'm Cybil."

"You're his work-study student, correct?" Smalls said.

She pointed her thumb at the priest. "Is he the one who said we were having sex? I didn't think you guys were allowed to think about that kind of stuff."

Smalls appeared to blush. Ashe had to keep from laughing.

"No, he isn't," Ashe said. "He just dropped by to check on me. He's a psychologist and a friend of Dr. Rogers'."

"I'm so sorry," Cybil said. "I've never spoken to a preacher like that before. Please don't have God smite me or anything like that."

Smalls laughed. "I don't think I can do that anyway."

"Cybil, what do you know about that band from the other night?"

"The Goth Sox?"

"Yeah," Ashe said.

"They've been playing around Mobile for a few years. They play punk covers and few originals."

"Do they profess to be Satanist or talk about witchcraft or things like that?" Smalls asked.

"They're emo, but I don't think they do any of that." Cybil looked puzzled. "Why?"

"That song on Marianne's computer had a reverse Latin incantation on it. Father Smalls thinks it might be an attempt at a satanic spell," Ashe said.

"Come on." She looked at the priest. "You're serious?"

"Very much. I think whoever recorded it thought it was a

real spell. Do you know where the band members live or anything else about them?" Smalls asked.

"No. I'm not really friends with them. I've met the lead singer a time or two." She looked at Ashe. "That guy who was sitting with me at the bar the other night is her brother's boyfriend."

"Do you know where we can find them? Does your friend know?" Smalls asked.

"They're playing at the Bayside Bar tonight," she said. "That's where I'm meeting that cop."

"You feel like taking in a parade and maybe some live music?" Ashe asked the priest.

"*Laissez les bons temps rouler*," he replied.

Traffic Camera: Dauphin and St. Joseph Streets, Mobile, AL, 7:45 p.m. CST

A strand of beads cuts across the lens. It obscures some of the view, but a large parade float is still visible lumbering down the street. Revelers lean over barriers and stretch out to catch throws on both sides of the street. Ashe and Smalls stand behind Cybil, who waves her hands at the passing parade. A man dressed in a sequined tunic and mask riding a horse passes in front of her. She cheers and shoves something into her pocket.

Across the street, Carol Heinz stands against the barrier. She does not lift her arms up to catch beads or flying MoonPies. Several of those things bounce off her without her making a single movement. A man stands beside her. He too makes no movements to block or catch throws. The crowd around them pushes against them trying to get a better position for wrangling in the parade goodies. The man, who is broad and menacing in appearance, moves just enough to block anyone from getting in front of him and Heinz, but he does not take an actively aggressive stance. The crowd continues to push against them, but still neither gives room.

The lights of a fire truck flash. The last float crosses the intersection. On one side of the street Cybil climbs off the barrier. She, Ashe and Smalls step back into the crowd. On the other side, Heinz and the man turn, and the crowd swallows them.

Chapter Seven

A she, Smalls and Cybil stopped at the entrance to the Bayside Bar. She pulled her coat off and handed it to Ashe. Underneath she wore a low V-neck shirt that would have shown most of her small boobs if she didn't have so many beads around her neck.

"Aren't you cold?" Ashe asked.

"Listen. I agreed to meet this guy. He's not going to get anything else so I thought he at least deserved a good look," she said. "At least I'm dressed for a bar unlike our friend here."

Ashe looked at Smalls, who still wore his priestly vestments. The white tab of a collar was mostly covered with Mardi Gras beads, but it was still noticeable. He nodded his agreement.

"It would have been more appropriate if you had dressed down," Ashe said.

"What does it matter? I'm not here for a good time," Smalls said. "I'm here to investigate strange happenings."

"I'm going in," Cybil said. "Follow up in a few seconds so it doesn't seem like we're together."

"If you don't intend anything with this guy, what does it matter?" Ashe asked.

"That's not the reason. I just don't want to be seen going into a bar with a priest. It's like some kind of bad joke."

"That's only if a minister and rabbi came along," Smalls said. "I've heard a million of them."

Cybil shook her head and went inside the bar. Ashe counted off in his head until he reached two hundred and followed her in. This bar was different from the one they had gone to the night before. It stank of old beer and new whiskey. The smoke

that permeated the place wasn't the sweet spice of clove cigarettes, but the harsh funk of cheap cigars. The clientele looked a
bit different too. There were a few biker types, and some guys
that looked like they'd just gotten off of the barges that came
down the Tensaw River.

Ashe and Smalls started to get stares as soon as they walked
in. One older-looking man with a long braided beard slammed
his glass on the bar, tossed down a few bills and left.

"We don't serve your kind here," the bartender said.

"We're not gay," Ashe said.

"Ain't what I mean. We don't serve the clergy."

"I promise I'm not here for the booze," Smalls said.

"You certainly ain't come for the ambiance." The bartender
laughed.

"We're here to see the band. We need to talk to them about
something," Ashe said.

"That's fine but there's still a two drink minimum, for you
and the padre."

Smalls dug into his pocket and slammed a twenty-dollar
bill on the counter. "One shot of Wild Turkey and another of
your finest, cheapest vodka."

The bartender snatched up the money. He sat a shot glass
on the counter and poured the whiskey. Smalls snatched it up
and sank it. He banged the empty glass down on the counter-
top. The barkeep flipped it and filled it with poor vodka. Smalls
slammed this one too. He whistled against the burn.

"Satisfied?" he asked.

"Didn't even flinch," the bartender said. "Damned priests
are always the best drinkers." He looked at Ashe. "Don't worry
about the minimum, kid. My man right there gave me a good
enough laugh that I'll comp you." He handed Smalls his change.
"The band'll be out in a minute. By the way, they suck."

"We know," Smalls said. "That's why we like them."

Ashe and Smalls walked away from the bar toward the
small stage at the other end of the establishment. No one in the
place seemed interested in getting up close to the band. Most of
the patrons left the closest tables empty. Ashe and Smalls sat at
the table closest to the steps up to the stage. As soon as they had

settled in, Ashe looked around the room trying to find Cybil. He spotted her in the far corner at a tall round table, alone. She sipped from a glass, but across the room and in the dim light, he couldn't tell what she was drinking.

"Let's talk to these guys as soon as they step out to get onstage." Ashe turned back to Smalls.

"Sounds good to me. I don't like hanging out in places like this for too long."

"Are you afraid of sinners?" Ashe made sure the question sounded like a joke.

Smalls shook his head. "My business is dealing with sinners. I just don't like being in this much cigarette smoke. It makes me want to take it up again."

"You smoked?"

"Yeah, I've always been amazed at how many people think that because you wear a black suit with a white collar and read the Bible that you don't have vices. I am a human too," Smalls said.

Ashe pointed to a door at the edge of the stage. The band started in. Although the drum kit and amps were set up on stage, the bassist and guitar player carried their instruments in with them. They led the way in and up to the stage. Another man with a spiked dog collar around his neck and a hot pink do-rag on his head bounded onto the stage and took his place behind the drums. Then the singer walked in. Ashe recognized her from the other bar.

"Excuse me, miss." Ashe rose from the table and moved toward the singer.

"I'm sorry, I don't give autographs until after the show," she said.

"That's not what I want," Ashe said. "I just need to talk to you about a recording."

"Dude, you can talk to my manager about any recording. We don't make the deals ourselves," she said.

Smalls got up and came toward them. "He doesn't want to give you a record deal. We want to talk to you about an MP3 recording of a song called 'Pink-Striped Hair'. Who did the recording for you?"

The singer looked Smalls up and down. "This is the first time I've had a priest interested in our music."

"We don't care about your music," Ashe said. Frustration came out with every syllable. "We want to know about that particular recording."

"Hey, are these guys hassling, you, Hortense?"

Ashe looked up to the edge of the stage. The guitarist stood there holding his ax like he might club them with it.

"Just stay cool," Smalls said. "Who did the recording?"

"Why?" Hortense asked.

"We found something on one of the copies of it that my fiancée had downloaded," Ashe said. "The file was corrupted or something. It played two versions of the song a little out of sync and had a piggyback recording underneath."

"You mean like that Beatles song that had a message if played backwards?" The guitarist sounded a little excited.

"More like what people used to claim 'Stairway to Heaven' did if played backward," Smalls said.

"Dude, seriously?" Hortense asked. "It had a satanic thing on it."

"More serious than you can imagine," Smalls said. "There seems to be a reverse Latin incantation impregnated into the song."

"Did you guys do that on purpose?" Ashe asked.

"Seriously, dude?" the guitarist asked.

"I'm a good Catholic girl," Hortense said. "That freaks me out just a little bit."

The lead singer crossed herself, then kissed her hand and lifted it to the sky. Smalls did the same. Ashe figured it was something priests did for followers out of respect.

"So who recorded the track for you?" Ashe asked.

"He's here tonight," the guitarist said. He looked across the bar and pointed. "He's over there close to the door. Guy's name is Francisco San Roman. He said he was a scout for Warner Records."

Ashe looked to where the guitarist pointed. The man near the door was big. His broad shoulders framed his muscular body. The light hanging above his head set off the orange color of his hair, making his head appear to be on fire. Even across the room, Ashe could see the deep brown freckles on his skin.

"Does that guy look like a Francisco to you?" Ashe asked.

Smalls turned and looked at San Roman. "He looks like a Seamus O'Connell I once knew in Boston."

"Maybe it's a stage name," Hortense said.

"Strange stage name," Ashe said. "It doesn't really roll off the tongue."

"I guess we need to talk to him," Smalls said.

Ashe nodded. "Thank you for your help, and break a leg."

"If you find out anything about that spell or whatever, let us know." Hortense twisted the fabric at the bottom of her shirt around her finger. "I'm going to be freaked out until I get an explanation."

"We will," the priest said.

Ashe and Smalls walked toward the man identified by the band. Ashe glanced over at Cybil. She remained alone. She tipped her drink toward him and smiled. It was almost gone, and she looked bored. He waved at her when he caught her eye. He looked back to the way he was going after bumping into someone's chair. The last thing they needed was a fight in this kind of a dive. As soon as he and Smalls stepped up to the large man's table the band started playing a loud and too fast version of "Season of the Witch".

"Are you Francisco?" Smalls asked.

The red-haired man looked the priest up and down. "Who wants to know?" His words sounded mechanical.

"My name is Peter Smalls. The band told me that you work for Warner Records."

"Maybe I do, but we are not interested in recording Gregorian chants, Father."

Ashe stared at the man. His eyes were an amber color. The same shade as the woman he later found out was Carol Heinz. That made him more nervous than he had been.

"I don't want to record with your company," Smalls said. "I want to know about a recording you did for this band."

"Are you interested in buying them out from under my contract?" he asked.

"We didn't know you had a contract with them," Ashe said. "They didn't mention that."

"The whole band is not aware of this contract. I signed it with their manager only."

"That's interesting. Can you have a contract for them with just their manager's knowledge, Mr. San Roman?" Smalls asked.

"Yes," he answered. "How did you find out my name?"

"The band told us," Ashe said. "Strange you don't really look like a Francisco."

"You do not look like a man who would like a band like them," San Roman said.

"I don't. I'm trying to find out why my fiancée died," Ashe said.

"What is the priest here for?"

"I'm trying to figure out if there is something sinister involved in her death," Smalls said.

San Roman laughed. It sounded forced. "When it comes to death and rock 'n' roll, it is always sinister."

"An nescit mali?" Smalls asked.

San Roman smiled. "I do not speak Latin."

"Es usted consciente del mal?" Smalls asked.

"Good night, gentlemen. I just realized that I have an appointment." San Roman stood up and started to leave the bar.

His movements were stiff and looked artificial. Everything about him reminded Ashe of his encounter with the Heinz woman.

"Do you know Carol Heinz, Mr. San Roman?" Ashe asked.

San Roman turned and stared at Ashe. His eyes narrowed to slits, and it appeared that the amber-colored irises had changed to black. "I do not know who you are talking about, Dr. Shrove. Good night."

The large man turned again and left. Ashe and Smalls looked at each other.

"That was strange," Smalls said, "and in a joint like this that's saying something."

"He knew my name," Ashe said. "I didn't tell it to him."

Smalls thought for a moment. "Maybe I introduced you."

"No, you didn't. He just knew it."

"I'm not too surprised. He also knew I was speaking Latin to him, but didn't seem to know Spanish, although his name would suggest Hispanic origins."

"Well, guys, I got stood up," Cybil said as she walked up. "It looks like your date left in a hurry too."

"Yes," Smalls said. "I think we upset him."

"He was a scary-looking dude," she said. "I wouldn't have wanted to meet him alone."

"He reminded me a lot of the woman we met the other night at the parade," Ashe said. "He talked like her and moved stiffly. His eyes were even amber like hers."

"Maybe they were related," Cybil said.

"Maybe so," Smalls said. "I think we need to leave. I have something I need to research."

"Fine by me," Cybil said. "Without my cop date, I don't like my prospects."

"What do you need to research?" Ashe wanted to know what the priest thought.

"For some reason the name Francisco San Roman is familiar to me. I can't remember why, but something tells me it's important."

"That guy was named Francisco?" Cybil asked. "He didn't look like one."

"No he didn't," Smalls said. "That's why I think I need to get to this research as soon as possible."

Cybil sat in the passenger seat of Ashe's car. He'd brought her back to her apartment complex. She'd decided to leave her Vespa on campus. It was too cold to ride it back home in what she wore.

"Thanks for the ride." She fumbled for the door handle. "I've got no idea how I'm going to get to school tomorrow, but I'll figure it out."

"I'm sorry you were stood up," Ashe said.

"I'm not." She wasn't. "He was a meathead. I told you I just agreed to meet him to get the laptop. If he'd shown up, I'd have to fake interest in his cop talk. He'd try to get lucky. I'd slap him and would've ended up in jail for striking an officer."

"Before you go, I need to tell you something."

To her, his eyes looked worried. She hoped he wasn't going to fire her from being his assistant. The other professors would keep her on, but they were all too old to be fun.

"Okay."

"You remember the woman that told us about the new parading society the other night?"

"Of course, how could I forget her? She was so strange."

"I think she was the woman from Birmingham that I went to see the video of," he said.

"The dead woman who walked out of the morgue?" Cybil said.

"Yes."

"Come on. That's not a funny joke. Marianne did the same thing," she said.

"You act like I don't know that. I'm not joking. They showed me a family photograph of the woman. It looked exactly like the woman from the parade."

"That's creepy," Cybil said. "Is the detective doing anything about it?"

"I couldn't remember the exact name of the society she said she worked with, but I got as close as I could. I think he was going to investigate it."

She shivered not from being cold but from the gooseflesh that popped up from the thought that she'd made jokes about a dead woman. Speaking ill of the dead was bad karma. If the dead were walking around, she couldn't imagine what the results might be if she chose to speak ill of one of them. Her apartment was on the back side of the building. She didn't feel much like walking around to it alone.

"Walk me to my door, please."

"I didn't mean to scare you," Ashe said. "I just felt that you needed to know about it."

"I'm glad you did, and maybe I shouldn't be afraid, but this is like some kind of weird horror movie and right now I'm feeling a little bit like one of those bimbos that the monster gets."

She reached out and touched his hand as it gripped the steering wheel. It felt warm and comforting. Her fingers were so cold that she welcomed this. Ashe looked at her. She felt the understanding in that glance.

"All right, but no good night kiss," he said.

She removed her hand and smiled. "I promise."

They both got out of the car. The headlights flashed as Ashe locked the doors with his remote. They met on the sidewalk in front of the car. Cybil took Ashe's hand and led him down the sidewalk that disappeared into the shadows cast by the building. To her, their handclasp felt nice, but the kind of nice that occurred with children who were afraid of something and held to each other for strength and comfort. They walked up three short steps at the corner where two sidewalks intersected. The light from her stoop lamp spilled out onto the sidewalk. She let go of Ashe's hand so that she could dig her keys out of her pocket. When she looked up, the door to her apartment was open.

"Ashe," she said..

"I see it. Let me go in first."

He pushed past her and into her apartment. She followed close behind. Staying outside didn't appeal to her any more than going into her apartment first.

The lamp she always kept on shined its light from the floor where it had been knocked.

Stuffing poured from large slashes in the couch that sat near the door. All the pictures she had put on the walls lay on the floor torn and tattered. Cybil looked over the bar that separated the living room from the kitchen. All the contents of her refrigerator were poured on the floor. Streaks of mustard and ketchup clung to the walls. She walked toward her bedroom, but Ashe stopped her.

"We need to go back to my car, call the police, and wait on them there," he said.

"I want to see what they've done to my bedroom." Her voice quivered, making the volume of it low.

"We need to get out," Ashe said. His voice was firm.

Cybil looked at him, but he stared at the door to her bedroom. She looked at it now for the first time with clear vision. A long piece of paper was tacked to it. There was a message written there in dark, runny letters as if it were written in blood. She couldn't make out what was written there, but the language was different from anything she'd ever seen.

"You're right," she said. "The car is the best place to wait."

Without another word they turned and hurried back to Ashe's car.

CHAPTER EIGHT

Semmes decided to pursue his lead on the Mystics of Mayhem by himself. His new partner thought she had enough experience in the field to deal with a case as weird as this one was turning out to be, but she didn't. That was at least what he had told himself. The chief hadn't authorized his investigation of the society. Since Carol Heinz was from Birmingham and no real connection could be made between her and Marianne, Semmes was ordered that he couldn't harass anyone over her. Of course that only applied to work hours.

He sat in his own car looking at a building surrounded by a high chain-link fence with razor wire curled around the top. A sign hung on the fence warning that trespassers would be prosecuted. Semmes didn't worry too much about that. He was sure that no one at the department would try and put him away for investigating a lead to a case even if he wasn't authorized to do so. Other officers did worse than that almost daily. The radio he kept in his car screeched. The dispatcher announced an officer was needed in Birdville. He wasn't far from there, but he was off duty.

"Let one of the regular blues handle it," he said aloud, not taking his eye off the building.

Nothing about the place screamed that a Mardi Gras parading society was using it to make floats. It didn't look like any kind of office building either. Semmes assumed it had been used by some company that owned factories out at Brookley Field as a storehouse. Headlights flashed in his rearview mirror. He slid down in his seat to keep from being seen. A white-paneled van rolled down the street. It stopped just short of the gate. A large red-haired man got out and walked to the gate. He unlocked it and started to pull it open. Semmes got out of his car. He checked the clamshell holster in the back band of his jeans, pulling his coat over it.

"Excuse me," he said loud enough to be heard over the rumble of the van's engine.

The red-haired man looked at him, but kept pulling the gate open in silence. Semmes crossed the road. He pulled his badge out of his pocket and held it in front of him. It didn't seem to faze the man. Semmes looked into the van as he passed. The driver couldn't be made out. He wore a hooded sweatshirt, concealing his face.

"My name is Detective Semmes. I'm with the Mobile Police Department. I have a question about this facility."

"I do not own this establishment."

"Who does?"

The red-haired man looked at the van. Semmes looked back in enough time to see the van moving toward him. He stepped out of the way as the vehicle drove inside the fence. Once the van passed the gate, the red-haired man stepped to the other side and started closing the gate. Semmes tried to step over the line into the fenced area. The red-haired man pushed him backward with enough force to make him stumble.

"I apologize, but you cannot enter without permission."

"Can I talk to the driver of the van?"

"No."

"Who owns this property, and what is it used for?" Semmes asked as the gate clicked closed.

"The Mystics of Mayhem society owns this warehouse. We are constructing our floats for the Mardi Gras. I am afraid that is all I can tell you, Detective Semmes."

"What about your name?"

The man looked at Semmes. In the light cast down from the overhead security lights, his eyes looked amber. In all his time in police work, Semmes couldn't remember ever seeing a person with eyes that color.

"Francisco San Roman. I am a member of the society."

"Mr. San Roman, do you know a woman named Carol

Heinz? I think she might be in this society."

"I do not know a woman by that name."

"How about Marianne Lenard?"

The driver got out of the van. Semmes eyed him. By the build, the driver was obviously a man. He cleared his throat loud enough for Semmes to hear.

"So?" he prompted San Roman again.

"Do you possess a warrant officer?" San Roman asked.

"No."

"Then I have said everything I have to say to you."

"I'm just asking questions. I don't want to search the place, *yet*. If you cooperate then I may not even want to do that."

San Roman pivoted on one foot and turned his back to Semmes. The man then walked away with a stiff gait. Semmes felt like cursing at the guy, but figured anyone that strange wouldn't care. He shoved his badge into his pocket and crossed the street back to his car. As he started the engine, he noticed that the hooded man still stood outside the building. Semmes turned on his headlights and pulled from his parking place.

"I need a unit to head over to Rivera Apartments on South University Boulevard. There has been a break-in, possibly gang related. The renter, Cybil Fairchild, and her boss, Ashley Shrove, are waiting in the parking lot," the dispatcher said over the radio to no one in particular.

Semmes grabbed his transmitter. "This is Semmes, number 209. What's the apartment number?"

"401C."

"On my way," he said.

He didn't have a flasher to put on the roof of his car, but Semmes accelerated his Taurus up to 80 mph on the rough streets on the back side of Government Boulevard. He switched on his emergency flashers as he ran a red light that put him on Michigan Avenue. Keeping to the side streets would get him across town faster than hitting the main drags. The parade traffic would be gone, but folks would start leaving the downtown bars and heading back toward west Mobile.

After about ten minutes, he pulled his car onto Cottage Hill Road. His tires squealed and probably smoked. He didn't pay attention. Few cars drove westbound. He ran the light at the intersection with University Boulevard, turning right. The blue flashing lights from two cruisers lit up the night as the entry-way for the apartment complex came into view. He drove onto the service road and then through the gates. A parking space was available beside a Mobile County cruiser. He parked and hopped out of his car. A sheriff's deputy hurried to him waving his arms for him to stay back. Semmes dug his badge out and flashed it to him.

"Detective Semmes, Mobile PD." He brushed past. "I've been investigating the disappearance of Dr. Shrove's fiancée."

"Semmes," Ashe said from ahead of him.

He saw the professor step away from the other police car. Ashe didn't look too well. All the different lights from the cars and the street lamps caught in the hollows of his face, mak-ing him look much older than he was and very tired. Semmes shoved his badge back into his pocket.

"What's going on?" Semmes asked.

"Someone broke into Cybil's apartment. I brought her home from the parades. She was afraid to walk to her apartment alone so I escorted her, and we found it ransacked."

"Why was she scared to go by herself? Do you think she knew about the break-in?" Semmes asked.

"I told her about Carol Heinz."

Anger steeped inside of Semmes like boiling tea. He sucked air through his teeth, making a whistling sound. "I thought we agreed no one would know about that."

"We did, but she was with me when I met that woman. I figured she had a right to know, just in case there is something bad going on."

"You might be right, but still, if too many people know, it could compromise the investigation. You know that every-one wants to keep this stuff hush-hush until we know more." Semmes said. "Who's working on this from the PD?"

Ashe pointed to an officer standing by a police car with Cybil. He recognized the officer although he'd never worked with him. The officer worked well but always seemed to end up on night duty. He walked toward the officer.

"How is everything?" he asked and looked at the officer's name badge. "Brewster."

"Detective Semmes, what brings you to a breaking and entering?" the officer asked. "I figured you'd be after a murder case."

"I have reason to believe that this might be related to a case I'm working on. Do you think you could walk me through the scene?" he asked.

"Of course. Just let me finish this interview," Brewster said.

"She can come with us; he can too." Semmes pointed to Ashe. "They are both well versed in my investigation."

"Do you think this is related to Marianne?" Cybil asked.

"Possibly," Semmes said.

Ashe walked to them. "I know it is."

"Why is that?" Semmes asked.

"I'll show you when we get to the apartment," Ashe said.

Semmes let Brewster lead the way. He brought up the rear with Cybil and Ashe between the two. When they entered the apartment, Semmes started to make mental pictures of what was around. He noted all the pictures on the floor in tatters. Everything that would be worth money was still there, but smashed. A smell hung in the air. It reminded him of rotten eggs.

"What's that smell?" he asked.

"We haven't figured it out yet," Brewster said.

"Do you guys have any idea?" he asked Ashe and Cybil.

"No, it smells like rotten eggs," Cybil said, "but I haven't bought eggs in ages."

Semmes made a mental note of the smell with a big red mark beside it to keep it fresh in his memory. He walked around the room. It seemed that the burglars left nothing untouched if not destroyed. The door leading to the bedroom was open. He poked his head inside. The same amount of devastation was there. Someone had slashed the mattress and pulled out the stuffing. The fluffy material lay all around the room. Pages from textbooks lay crumpled up on the floor. Even Cybil's underwear was torn up and strewn across the room.

"Thorough, weren't they?" Brewster asked.

"Yeah," Semmes said. "Ashe, is this what you're basing your assumption on? There's a lot of damage, but I don't know how it would relate to Marianne's disappearance."

"That tells me it's related." Ashe pointed to the note in blood still pinned to the door.

Semmes recoiled from it like a rookie on his first encounter with a decomposing body. He didn't know how he'd missed it. If it had been the perp, he'd probably have had a bullet in his head. Voodoo stuff freaked him out a bit. Even if the note wasn't part of that weird religion, it still seemed dangerous. The letters looked normal, but the language perplexed him.

"What is it?" he asked Ashe.

"I believe it's a note in reverse Latin," he said.

"Reverse Latin? What does that have to do with anything?" Semmes asked.

"Cybil found an MP3 on Marianne's computer that had some auditory anomalies on it. I broke it down with some of my equipment and found a message in reverse Latin under the song. A friend of mine who is a parapsychologist and a priest was there. He said that oftentimes reverse Latin phrases are used as incantations in satanic rites," Ashe said.

"Oh great," Cybil said. "Now I've got Satanists after me."

"Come on," Brewster said. "There's no such thing as satanic cults. Oral Roberts and Pat Robertson made that up to scare kids from listening to heavy metal music."

"I'm just telling you what Father Smalls said," Ashe related. "He didn't seem to believe in that kind of Satanist either."

"It doesn't matter if they are in cahoots with the Devil or not. If these guys think they are doing something to please him, they're likely to do anything," Semmes said. "But I don't think there's enough to put everything together."

Semmes was disappointed about that. Marianne could have downloaded the song from some pirate site and the whole reverse Latin stuff could just be a coincidence.

"Are we good?" Brewster asked. "I'd like to get back to taking Ms. Fairchild's statement."

"Yeah, I think I've gotten everything," Semmes said. He took Ashe aside. "I don't really see a link right now. I mean it would be nice if a cult was doing this, but I don't think that's the case."

"Would it be okay if I took a picture of the note with my camera so that I can show it to Father Smalls?" Ashe asked. "I think he might have some insight into it."

"Do it while Brewster is distracted. Otherwise, you might get arrested for tampering with evidence." He looked at his watch. "I've got to get going. I'll keep you up to date from my end."

Ashe took his cell phone out of his pocket and aimed it at the note. The machine flashed as he took the picture. "I'll do the same."

Voice Mail: Office of Ashley Shrove, PhD, 11:45 p.m. CST

Dr. Shrove, listen to me. You don't know me, and there is no reason to try and trace this call because you won't be able to. Let it suffice to say that I am a friend who is looking out for your personal safety.

Quit trying to figure out what happened to your fiancée. You're going to stir up more trouble than you could ever imagine, not only for yourself, but everyone else you're around as well. You can already see how it's affected the life of Ms. Fairchild, and she has very little to do with anything.

There are forces at play here you cannot realize. None of the people you are working with can either. Just let Marianne go. It's not worth it. I promise that worse things will come if you continue to poke your nose into this.

Dr. Shrove, move on. Resign from Alabama Tech and find another school a long way away. It might be the only thing to save you and everyone around you.

Goodbye.

CHAPTER NINE

A she put his arm around Cybil and pulled her to him. She
snuggled in. He was warm and strong enough to offer some
relief from the horrible feeling nagging at her. The intruder left
little for her to use. All of her clothes were destroyed, as were
her books and personal mementoes. When the police told her
she couldn't stay there, it didn't faze her. Anyplace would be
better than there, even the Salvation Army shelter.

"What now?" he asked.

"I guess I need you to take me to a motel or something. It's
too late to call any friends for a place to crash."

"You can stay the night with me. I've got a spare room. If
that's not good enough, I have a horrible lumpy couch."

"Thank you."

It didn't matter where he put her at in his house; she knew
she wouldn't be sleeping tonight. Ashe walked her to the passenger side of his car and opened the door for her. She sat down.
He crossed behind the car and climbed into the driver side.
They left her apartment complex.

As they passed through the almost empty streets of Mobile,
Cybil thought about everything. She didn't understand why
someone would have broken into her apartment or treated her
stuff so horribly.

"They didn't leave me a single thing to wear," she said, as if
she been speaking her thoughts. "Did you see my panties? He
tore the crotch out of every pair."

Ashe looked over at her as he turned the car into his driveway. "I thought that was just the kind you wore."

He smiled, and she knew he was trying to cheer her up, but

nothing was going to help. "Sorry to disappoint, but I'm not that kinky."

"You can wear a pair of Marianne's. She'd just bought some before she died. I found them still in their packaging," he said, getting out of his car.

She did the same. His house looked accommodating from the outside. The driveway ended by a small fence. When they walked through the gate, she saw a small patio and an even smaller yard. A door led them into the kitchen. There was nothing extraordinary about it.

"The bathroom is through there." Ashe pointed through a dark hallway toward a door. "The towels and washcloths are on the rack over the toilet. Soap and shampoo are in the shower. I'll find you something to wear and leave it outside the door."

Cybil looked into the darkness. Although the hallway was very short, the idea of walking down it alone frightened her. As Ashe started to walk the other way, she grabbed his arm.

"Please go check it for me," she said.

He walked through the doorway into the hall and flipped on the light. The shadows disappeared. He started down the hall. She walked right behind him. They entered the bathroom him first and her on his heels. There was nothing there that wasn't supposed to be. He pushed back the shower curtain to let her see inside.

"You going to be okay?" he asked.

"I think so. Thank you."

Ashe walked out. Cybil turned on the water and put her hand under the stream. It was warm. She wanted it scalding and adjusted the water until steam rose. She took off her top and tossed it to the floor. Without much thought, she disrobed completely and stepped into the shower. The water felt wonderful. It boiled the chill from her bones. The shower was something that she needed. The ball of emotion inside her let loose, and she cried. Her tears mixed with water running down her face. After a few minutes, she stopped the water and stepped out of the shower. True to his word, Ashe had left a pile of clothes on the floor on the other side of the door. Cybil snatched them up and pulled them into the bathroom.

A wrapped pack of panties lay on top of a pair of green flannel pants. He'd left her a T-shirt from his undergraduate college. It hung long on her body, hiding the fact that she didn't have on a bra. She knew that her breasts were small enough that it didn't matter. A wicker basket sat in the corner by the toilet. Cybil wadded up her towel and tossed it into the basket.

She opened the door and stepped into the hall. The entire house glowed with the light from every fixture and lamp in the place. There wasn't a dark corner anywhere. Ashe stood in the kitchen drinking milk from a fluted glass.

"Fancy for milk, isn't it?" Cybil asked.

"I always drink milk out of these glasses. It's a habit I guess," Ashe said. "You want anything?"

"I'm tired. I think I'll just go to bed."

"You have a choice. The guest room is through the living room. The couch is in the living room across from the television. I've got both ready for you."

"I'm going to take the bedroom if that's okay with you. I don't think sleeping on a couch is going to do it for me. Tonight I need the comfort of a warm mattress."

"I understand that. Do you want me to walk you in there?"

"I've got it." Cybil walked past him and into the living room. She saw the door to the bedroom. "Good night, Dr. Shrove."

"It's okay to call me Ashe," he said from the kitchen.

She nodded even though he couldn't see her. "Good night, Ashe."

Cybil slipped into the bedroom. After giving it a once-over glance to make sure nothing hid in the corners, she turned off the lights and crawled under the turned-down sheets. Her limbs felt leaden. The softness of the mattress helped to lighten them. Even though she didn't think it would, sleep overtook her.

Once Cybil settled into the guest bedroom, Ashe decided that he needed a shower too. The day had been long. Much longer than what he had wished for. The filth of it seemed to weigh him down. Nothing would be better than to wash it down the drain.

He carried his pajamas into the bathroom and laid them on

the tank of the toilet. The humidity from Cybil's shower still hung in the air. Ashe turned on the water. As it cascaded down from the showerhead, he put his hand in the stream. Judging by the steam that fogged the mirrors, Cybil had used a lot of hot water. He hoped it would hold out for him to get finished.

The warmth washed over him as soon as he stepped into the shower. He stuck his head under the water and let it roll down his body. With his eyes closed he reached for his bar of soap. It wasn't there. Cracking his eyelids just enough to see, he found it on the shelf below where he usually kept it. It had been a long time since he'd shared a shower with someone who didn't know his routine. He lathered his hands with the soap and rubbed his body over with sudsy hands. The lather rinsed off almost as soon as he applied it. Another rubbing of the soap between his hands and he washed his face. Keeping his eyes squeezed tight, he rinsed. Once his face was free from the soap, he reached around for the shampoo. He grabbed it and started to shake it to the top of the bottle.

Cybil screamed from the guest room. It was ear piercing even muffled by two closed doors, several walls and the sound of the shower. Ashe dropped the shampoo bottle. It thudded on the bottom of the tub. With a fluid movement, he tore open the shower curtain and leapt out. He grabbed a towel off the rack over the toilet as he rushed out the door. By the time he made it to the guest room, it was wrapped around his waist. Water footprints tracked his path through the house.

It had taken only a matter of seconds for him to make it through his house to the guest room. The sound of Cybil's scream still echoed in his head although she hadn't made another sound. He pushed the door hard, and it opened with little effort. Ashe almost fell inside.

The bedside lamp lit the room. Cybil sat up in the bed. The sheets bunched up at her waist. Ashe made a quick scan of the room. There was nothing out of place.

"What's the matter?" The water on his skin and the rush of adrenaline made goose bumps rise.

"I'm so sorry," she said. "I had a nightmare. I just closed my eyes, and horrible things started to go through my head."

"You scared me," he said. "After everything tonight, I thought someone had broken in here too."

"This is going to seem silly, but could you give me a hug or something?" she asked. "I feel so helpless."

Ashe walked to the edge of the bed. He bent to embrace Cybil.

"I'm kind of wet and naked."

"I don't care." Her voice was full of emotion.

He bent over farther. She wrapped her arms around his neck. He wrapped his around her and squeezed. The water from his skin soaked through the fabric of her sleep shirt. He tried to pull away, but she kept a tight squeeze on him.

"I need to go shut off the shower and dry off," he said.

Cybil let go, but before he straightened to a standing position, she kissed him. Her tongue probed his mouth, even as he tried to break the kiss off. Her hands reached down. He felt her fingers brushing down his bare torso, until they touched the top of the towel. Then he felt the cool air surround him as his towel fell away. She quit kissing him, long enough to pull her top off. Ashe stepped away, grabbing his towel to wrap back around him.

"I need to go back and turn the shower off," he said.

Cybil reached out one hand. "Please."

He took it, and she pulled him to the bed. Deep inside him every emotion he'd ever experienced tumbled over each other. He knew that what he was doing was wrong, but everything in him kept urging him onward. *Did grief make you do such things? How about trauma?* He didn't know.

They kissed again. It was passionate, full of rubbing hands and deep gasps for air. Ashe started to take the lead, although he continued to feel pangs of guilt inside himself. He moved from kissing Cybil on the mouth to her chin, then her neck. As she ran a fingernail down his flank, he took her nipple into his mouth. Ever since she'd flashed at the parade, he'd kept thinking about her breasts, and what it would be like to caress and suck on them. It was what he imagined and far more.

Cybil pushed up on his chest, and Ashe rolled onto his back. She came out from under the sheets and straddled him just above his pelvis. She'd wriggled out of the flannel sleep pants and panties while still under the covers. Now her bare buttocks brushed against his stiffened manhood. She leaned over him and kissed him on the mouth, then followed a similar pattern of love pecks to those that he had made that ended by her flicking her tongue around his nipple.

The guilt that Ashe wrestled with in his psyche was pinned to the mat. Ashe grabbed Cybil just above her hips. He lifted her, at the same time sliding himself up the bed. When he placed her down again, his stiffness slid inside her.

He lifted himself up as she pushed down. She lifted as he let himself down. All the time they kissed and groped and sucked on each other. Her body, which had been tense when he'd entered the room, softened. Ashe noticed that his own stress melted away as they continued to writhe with each other. They rolled over as a unit and continued to give and take from each other until the tense excitement shuddered through Cybil's body. The same rushed through Ashe shortly after.

They lay beside each other. Ashe had his arm under Cybil's head. She rested one of her hands on his hipbone. For the first time in many days, he felt nothing bad. All the anxiety and fear was expelled from his body for the moment, an almost orgasmic feeling.

Sunlight peeked through the curtains of the dining room. Ashe stared at the floor while sitting at the table. He'd been in there since Cybil fell asleep. His nerves had driven him into the refrigerator for a beer, but he'd decided to just drink coffee. He'd had two pots over the last four hours. Beer would have done a better job of calming him, but if he wasn't going to sleep, he needed the caffeine to keep him up and moving.

After the initial absence of bad feelings, ghosts started moving around his house. He felt a lot like Scrooge on Christmas Eve. Different spirits of the past and present and future harassed him as he sat naked underneath his bathrobe, sipping his Maxwell House.

The present visited first. That ghost appeared not long after he and Cybil had finished having sex. The guilt that came over him made him want to run away. He realized the mistake he was in the middle of the whole time it was going on. This ghost drove him out of bed and into the kitchen.

The future spirit slipped in while he drank the first cup of coffee. This one visited like a hallucination playing out before him. His department head sat across the conference table. All the other faculty in the electrical engineering department lined the table between them. Even though their faces were little more than blurs, he could read every one of them. Having a sexual relationship with a student was frowned upon, so much so it would probably cost him his job.

"Dr. Shrove, you are on leave for the rest of this semester," he heard the chair say. "You will not be brought back for the next."

Then the whole thing flashed to an academic board meeting for Cybil. This one was not as nice. They kicked her out of school and rescinded all her credits. The ghost of the future ravaged all and left only scorched, salted earth across its path.

As the sun started to rise, the last ghost visited. Ashe heard Marianne's voice loud in his ear although it was a whisper. She accused him of many things. Infidelity was the worst. She called him a letch, and Cybil a whore.

He had a conversation with Marianne in his head.

How could you sleep with someone so soon after my death? she asked.

"I didn't plan it. It just happened," he said.

Things don't just happen, Ashley. You wanted it.

Now Marianne had become his conscience. He *had* wanted it, but still, he would have never acted on those impulses if not compelled by extraordinary circumstances.

"No, I know better than that," he said. "I'm not some pervert who tries to sleep with all my students. She's not even my student."

That makes it worse, Marianne said. *She's your work-study. You can't even give her a grade or a raise. You've ruined her life too.*

"You're not being fair. Stress causes people to do a lot of strange things, things they wouldn't normally do."

That's like going to a prostitute or sleeping with a stripper, not taking advantage of a student. Marianne's voice was so real. *You're so screwed, Ashley Shrove. I'm glad I'm dead.*

"You're not dead," he said. "I saw you walk out of that morgue. Who are *you* out fooling around with?"

Marianne's voice went silent, but the ghost of the past lingered on. He felt it around him, circling like a predator waiting to pounce. She was thinking of something cutting to say. He expected it to sting.

"Go on, give it to me. I can take it. I'm a big boy."

"Who are you talking to?" Cybil said from behind him.

The sound of her voice instead of Marianne's shook him out of the daydream he was having. He turned and looked at her. She stood dressed only in the T-shirt that hung well down her thighs.

"No one... Myself... Ghosts."

"Ghosts?"

"Not literally," Ashe said. "I've been arguing with myself most of the night. I've had memories and shadows of the past come to me. That's what I was calling ghosts."

Cybil touched him on the shoulder. "Have you been arguing with yourself about what happened last night?"

"Amongst other things."

"What happened, happened. If it helps any, we were both in a very high stress situation. It doesn't have to change anything. We both went a little crazy."

"I've been telling myself that, but I don't believe it. Everyone is going to find out. Then I'll be discharged, and you'll be kicked out of school."

"Hold your horses," Cybil said. "They can't kick me out of school for having sex."

"With a professor?"

"With anyone. That is a major violation of personal rights. I don't know what your contract says, but if they had to fire every teacher who made it with a student, then the whole English department would be completely full of nuns."

"You're kind of nonchalant about all this."

The idea of just being a lay to her offended Ashe for some reason. Even with all the angst about dealing with the repercussions of the happening, he thought there was more there or maybe, he wished it.

"What do you want me to do, go all doe-eyed and lovey dovey?" She took his coffee mug and drank from it. "It was fun, and I think that we have some kind of chemistry, and I don't regret a thing, but I know you just lost your fiancée. I know that I'm a student and younger than you. I'll understand if this is just a one-time stress-related thing. *Que sera, sera.*"

"You're not that much younger." Ashe didn't like being made to feel old either.

"I know that." Cybil rolled her eyes and handed him back the coffee mug. "I'm going to take a shower before we head to school. I've got class at nine."

"I've got one then too," he said. "I probably need another shower."

"You can join me if you want to," she said.

Ashe turned and looked at her. Her face didn't give away anything. Once was a mistake, but he wanted to again. She felt so good last night, the kind of good that you want more of.

"I better not, just don't take too long," he said.

"Whatever."

She walked into the kitchen, pulling the shirt over her head as she did so. Her skin looked alabaster in the dimmer kitchen light. The lines of her body as she walked nude to the bathroom made a different ghost disappear. After all, Ashe was a man, who in the old days wouldn't have passed up tail for very much of anything, mostly because he didn't get a shot at it very often.

"Maybe I'll take you up on that offer after all."

He finished off the swig of coffee and followed her. She stopped in the bathroom doorway. When he was close enough, she turned, showing him all her nudity, and tugged the knot loose in his robe's belt. He let it fall open and then slide down his shoulders. She pressed herself against him. His skin began to tighten and flush as he felt the softness of her skin again.

The last bit of his conscience to bother him at that moment evaporated, as Cybil pulled him into her.

CHAPTER TEN

As soon as Ashe walked into his office, he hit the button for his voice mail. A metallic voice announced seven new messages. He thought that wasn't too bad for missing a whole day at the office. The first was a student calling in sick to class. She was in his largest class, and Ashe couldn't remember what she looked like. He'd address what she'd missed with her tomorrow when her class met again. As the next message started playing, Rogers stuck his head into the office.

"Dean Allred is looking for you," he said.

"What for?" Ashe asked.

"Said it was important."

"Why didn't he call me?" Ashe asked.

"He said he left you a voice mail."

Ashe looked at his phone. He hung up and headed out of his office. The dean's office was on the top floor of the building. The future ghost from that morning started to haunt him again as he rode the elevator up three floors. His mind played out the scene. He'd be ushered into the dean's office and sat down. Then Dean Allred would start the reprimand with positives before pinning him to the wall with the accusation that he had slept with Cybil. The dean would even know it was twice, with one time being in the shower. Ashe didn't try to reason in his daydream how the dean would know that, he just knew he would.

The elevator door opened. He stepped out into the wood-paneled hallway. The dean's office was at the end of the hall to the right. As he walked toward it, his shoes clicked on the wooden floors. Dean Allred always kept the door to his outer office open, so Ashe walked in. The secretary looked at him.

"Dr. Shrove, I see you got the message," she said. "I'll let the dean know you're here."

"Can you tell me what this is about?" he asked even though he knew the answer.

She put her phone to her ear. "I think it's better if he talks with you." She told the dean that he was there. "He said to come in."

Ashe put one hand in his pocket and went into the office. Dean Allred sat behind his oversized mahogany desk. A large window was behind him. From that height, it overlooked the bay. Two large potted palms flanked the window. The dean looked like a Lilliputian, surrounded by such huge office fixtures.

"Have a seat, Dr. Shrove."

Ashe sat down in one of the overstuffed visitor chairs. He sank into the supple leather. The dean's face showed no sign of what he was going to talk about. Ashe assumed that if he encountered a hard stony look then he was in trouble. Dean Allred's face was smiling. It was a real, mellow smile.

"I know that you have been having a hard time, Ashe. That's why I decided that I needed to tell you this instead of the department chair."

The shoe was about to fall. Ashe looked over his head almost absentmindedly to make sure that a sword wasn't dangling there. Only a gaudy light fixture hung above his head.

"I can explain. She stayed with me because her apartment got trashed by burglars and she was very afraid. We shouldn't have done it. I know it was unethical, but things happen."

Dean Allred looked confused. "What are you talking about?"

"Cybil Fairchild and I? Aren't you going to fire me because we had relations last night?"

The dean laughed. "That's not what I was going to talk to you about at all. How would I have even known about that?"

Ashe shrugged. A weight lifted off him even as an embarrassed flush ran up his body. He'd just told his personal business to a coworker, and not just any coworker, but the dean.

"Sorry about that. Things have been tough lately."

"I understand," Dean Allred said, "and don't worry. We've

all fooled around with a student at some point. Have you ever been to the English department?"

"That's what I've heard. I guess I need to check it out."

"Maybe you should, but I am afraid that I've called you here on some important business that doesn't concern Ms. Fairchild." The dean's expression changed. He looked grave. "Three of your graduate students were found dead last night in their dorm."

"What?" All the joviality and relief left Ashe again. The emotional rollercoaster was getting a little bit out of control. "Which ones?"

"Samuels, Bertram and Haggardy. They were all found in the same room."

"What happened?"

"It's still under investigation, but that building is heated with natural gas. The current theory is carbon monoxide poisoning. Another student in your class who lives there too said they had gotten together to listen to a lecture and compare notes."

"Samuels, Bertram and Haggardy were my best students. I was Haggardy's thesis chair, and on Samuels' committee."

"That's why I've decided to give you a bit of break. I don't think it would be appropriate for you to continue this semester as an instructor with all that's happened."

"No, Dean Allred, I can still teach. I have other students to help with research. I'll go crazy if I'm not working." Words gushed from Ashe like water from a hose.

"I'm not suspending you, Ashe. I'm giving you a sabbatical if you will. An adjunct instructor will take your classes. You can come to the office every day or not, and work on any research you want. I just want you to move on your own time at your own pace. I can't afford to lose such an important professor," Dean Allred said.

"So why don't you want me to teach? You don't think I've had anything to do with the deaths, do you?"

"Of course not. It's a series of unfortunate coincidences. I do think, though, that you might burn out with so much going on, and you are a valuable member of our team. Your work with Dr. Rogers has really put Alabama Tech on the map. Since the engram recorder came out, admission applications for our college have tripled. We're getting applicants both undergraduate and graduate that would normally try for MIT or Cal Tech." The dean took off his glasses and wiped his face with a handkerchief. "You're going to keep the college of engineering bankrolled for the next ten years."

Ashe felt better. At least his job wasn't in danger. He shook his head. "This is unbelievable."

"I understand. Why don't you go home and rest? You look like you didn't sleep much last night." Dean Allred chuckled. "I guess you were up to other things."

"I'm very embarrassed about that outburst, sir. Can we forget it?" Ashe felt flush again.

"Water under the bridge. Go home, get some sleep. Take that student, Ms. Fairchild, home with you if you need to, but just take care of yourself."

Ashe walked into his office. Rogers sat behind his desk with his feet propped up on an open drawer. The psychologist smiled like a cat that had just eaten the canary.

"What is it?" Ashe asked.

"I hear that you had a little adventure last night," he said. "I believe a fair young lady was involved as well."

"Cybil's apartment was broken into. Whoever did it completely tore the place apart. They destroyed everything including her underwear and pictures that hung on her wall. Sick stuff. I think they even took a dump somewhere and hid it. The whole place smelled like rotten eggs."

"So where did she stay?" Rogers asked.

"With me, because it was late and she didn't want to bother anyone else. She, Father Smalls and I had gone to a parade and then to a bar."

"A threesome with a priest, this girl is freaky," Rogers said. "I like it."

Ashe rubbed the bridge of his nose and started gathering up some papers. "Father Smalls and I needed to talk to a band that she knows. That's all."

"Sure it is." Rogers took his feet off of the drawer. "Are you going home?"

"The dean has put me on sabbatical. I'm not allowed to teach classes until further notice. He's as good as told me to just do as little as I want to." He shoved the files into a canvas satchel.

"Wish I had him as a dean."

"Maybe your dean will force you on a mental health vacation if three of your graduate students end up dead less than a week after your fiancée died." Ashe slung the bag over his shoulder. He scooped his keys up from his desk and shooed Rogers up and toward the door.

"I'm sorry. Do they know what happened?" Rogers asked, walking out the door.

"They think carbon monoxide poisoning, but they're not sure yet. I don't want to talk about it or think about anything. I'm going home to try to sleep."

Ashe turned his office lights off and pulled the door closed. He remembered that Cybil had left a backpack in his office the day before. It probably had her Vespa key in it. He didn't want to lock that away from her and risk her not making it home.

"If you see Cybil, tell her I left my office open, and that I went home. Tell her I have my cell if she needs me."

"Now that you're not teaching classes, she probably won't. I might take her on as a work-study." A look of lustful deviance came into Rogers' eyes.

"She's not in your department's budget."

The door of the elevator opened without Ashe punching the call button. Two students he recognized as aerospace undergrads got off. He stepped on and held the door for Rogers.

"I've got to see Dr. Mendev," Rogers said. "You still had voice mails on your phone. Aren't you going to check them?"

"When you find Cybil, because I know you're going to look for her, tell her to check them for me and write down any important ones."

Ashe punched the ground floor button and let the doors close. He blinked his heavy eyelids and looked forward to going home and sleep.

Security Camera: Autopsy Room, Providence Hospital, Dictation Recording, 10:12 a.m. CST

A young man's body lies on the table. A folded sheet covers only his pelvic area. His large gut hangs off both sides of his body, making him appear like a beached whale. A technician in a lab coat wheels a cart into the room. All sorts of instruments used in pathology are on it. A doctor with her hair in a ponytail with the top covered with a surgical hat follows. She pulls on her latex gloves. A clear plastic shield covers her face. She stops beside the tray. The man hands her a scalpel.

The technician walks to a table and flips a switch to a machine sitting on it. He comes back to the side of the doctor. She makes an incision at the base of his chest, near where the man's belly bulges upward.

The doctor speaks into a microphone pinned to her scrubs, recording into a dictation machine. "This is Dr. Sydney O'Hara conducting an autopsy on Jason Samuels, a twentytwo- year-old Caucasian male. Death is unknown but believed to be carbon monoxide poisoning. Samuels, however, would have been considered morbidly obese while alive. I am beginning the incision near the base of the sternum."

A crashing noise comes from the next room. Both Dr. O'Hara and the technician look up and toward the noise. Glass shatters from the same direction. The doctor nods her head toward the noise. The technician hurries that way. She slices through Samuels' belly fat until she reaches his navel.

Another crash echoes through the autopsy room. Dr. O'Hara puts her scalpel back on the tray and starts around the autopsy table in the direction of the noise.

"What's going on?" she asks.

Before she makes it all the way around, a naked man runs from the side of the room where the noise originated. She tries to dodge him, but he hits her with his shoulder lowered like a defensive back. Both hit the floor with a loud thud. A man dressed out in full operating room garb comes in after the naked man. He takes the scalpel from the tray and bends down over Dr. O'Hara.

"What are you doing?" she yells. "Let me go. Please don't kill me. I'll do whatever you want me to."

"We want you to die," the naked man says.

Before she can scream, the man dressed like a surgeon kneels and slits her throat. He stands and tosses the bloody scalpel across the room. He looks Samuels' body over. The naked man runs his finger down the long incision in the corpse's body.

"Can we still use him?" the naked man asks, his voice sounding distant in the recording.

"No, the incision is too deep. His guts would spill out. I wish I would have gotten here earlier. I was only able to get you. This puts me behind. The boss isn't going to be happy," the man dressed like a doctor says.

"No, he will not be."

The clothed man snatches the sheet off of Samuels' body. He drapes it over the nude man. As they walk to door, three tones beep over the loudspeaker .

"Code black in the morgue, code black in the morgue, code black in the morgue," a voice repeats over the speaker.

"We've been seen. We need to hurry," the man in full surgery garb says, barely audible due to his distance from the dictation microphone.

Both men run out the door. A uniformed security guard rushes into the room from the way the others had come. He kneels over Dr. O'Hara's body and then vomits.

CHAPTER ELEVEN

Cybil punched the code into Ashe's office phone to retrieve his voice mails. She dug through the center drawer in the desk until she came up with a pen and pad. The first message was from a student who had a question about an assignment. She copied down his name and contact info.

Someone knocked on the door. She looked up to see Father Smalls and waved him in.

"Where is Ashe?" he asked.

"He was sent home for the day," she said as she skipped past the automated message from some journal trying to sell copy.

"Not for anything bad I hope."

"He didn't do anything wrong, but three of his graduate students died last night in the dorms. The dean decided that he needed a vacation or at least that's what Dr. Rogers said."

"I heard about the students' deaths. I didn't realize they were his students. Things aren't going very well for him, are they?"

"Understatement of the year." She paused the playback. "Can I help you with anything?"

He shook his head. "I came by to talk to him about that man we met last night. I found out something interesting."

"Really, have you talked to Ashe today?" she asked.

"No, if I had, I wouldn't have come by. Why?"

She took a deep breath. Talking about the break-in made her very uncomfortable. Some of her classmates had asked. Retelling the tale scared her almost as much as when it happened.

"Someone trashed my apartment last night. They left a note in blood or something that looked like blood. Ashe—Dr.

Shrove—took a picture of it on his phone. He wanted you to look at it."

"Blood? What did it look like?"

"Dr. Shrove said it looked like reverse Latin, but he wasn't sure."

"Maybe I should go and see him. I think you might want to come as well," Smalls said.

"I need to finish copying his voice mails, but I can just ride my scooter over there," she said.

"Nonsense. Finish his messages, and you can ride with me. It's too cold to ride a scooter across town, plus I don't know where he lives," Smalls said.

Cybil hit the play button on the voice mail. "I don't want to leave my scooter on campus again."

"I drive a truck. We can put it in the back."

"Okay. Just a few more."

She took up her pen as the next message played. The first part passed without her paying much attention. The person hadn't left a name. She was about to delete it for being some nut who had read about Ashe in the newspaper.

"Quit trying to figure out what happened to your fiancée. You're going to stir up more trouble than you could ever imagine, not only for yourself, but everyone else you're around as well," the caller said. Cybil paused and gave it more attention. "You can already see how it's affected the life of Ms. Fairchild, and she has very little to do with anything."

As the rest of the message played, her stomach sank. She looked at the priest. His jovial face turned granite hard. Lines of concern drew down from his mouth. As the message ended with the advice to leave the university, Smalls reached across the desk and silenced the voice mails.

"Grab your stuff. We need to go," he said.

Cybil didn't hesitate. She wanted to be far away from that office at that very moment.

Ashe sat up and stretched his arms out. Everything looked fuzzy. He blinked hard and got the sleep out of his eyes. The doorbell rang again.

"Hold on," he yelled at the door, which was just feet from the couch.

He walked to the door and opened it. Smalls and Cybil stood on the stoop. The wind blew in his face. The air raised goose bumps on his bare arms. He'd fallen asleep in his undershirt and khakis, which were unfastened. Cybil grinned and pointed that out using her eyes. He moved from the doorway to allow them in and to zip up. Smalls closed the door behind him.

"What brings you two here?" Ashe asked.

"A couple of things," Smalls said. "I've got a feeling we probably need to be sitting when we discuss them."

"Sounds like I'm going to need a beer for this." Ashe walked toward the kitchen. "You two want one?"

Smalls shook his head no, but Cybil agreed. Ashe went into the kitchen, grabbed two bottles from the refrigerator and came back. He handed a bottle to Cybil as he sat by her on the couch. Smalls perched on the end of the recliner. Ashe twisted the top off the bottle and took a slug of it.

"All right, I'm ready," Ashe said.

"I heard about your students. I'm very sorry," Smalls said. "It seems that things just get worse and worse for you. Cybil also told me about the break-in at her apartment. She said that you took a picture of a message left in what looked like blood."

"It's on my phone," he said. "I can get it."

Ashe reached over the back of the couch. His phone lay on the table there. He probed around blindly until he found it. A few flicks of his thumb brought up the picture. He handed it to Smalls.

The priest squinted and then put the phone close to his face. "It's too small. I can't make it out. Can you upload the picture onto a computer so it can be larger?"

"Sure." Ashe stood up and took his phone back from Smalls.

He left his guests sitting in the living room and went into his bedroom. His computer lit up when he moved the mouse. He plugged his phone into a cord that stuck out from a USB jack. A window popped up with all the pictures on the phone.

Ashe clicked on the one of the writing. It opened up in a separate box. He printed it off and brought it back to the priest.

Smalls took the paper and stared at it. He didn't say anything, but his lips moved pronouncing each syllable silently. After he was done, he shook his head.

"We're dealing with a sick individual here," he said.

"What did it say?" Cybil asked.

"It warns Ashe to back off trying to find out what happened to Marianne," Smalls said.

"Just like the voice mail," Cybil said.

Ashe looked from Smalls to Cybil. "What voice mail?"

"That was another thing that we needed to discuss," Smalls said.

"I was checking your voice mail like you asked me to. Father Smalls came in while I was doing so, that's how he knows about this. So, the last message I listened to was from a man that said you should quit trying to figure out what happened to Marianne. Then he said that other bad things would happen."

She stopped talking. Ashe could tell that she was upset. He took her hand. This didn't seem to help, because she remained silent. It didn't make him feel any better either.

"The message said that others around you would get hurt if you didn't, and then it mentioned the break-in at the apartment," Smalls said.

"What did the guy sound like?" Ashe asked. "Did he sound familiar?"

"He almost sounded like one of those reader programs on a computer," Cybil said. "The voice was very artificial, almost mechanical."

"They probably used one of those programs," Smalls said. "It would help to keep his identity a secret."

"Or her identity," Ashe said. "If it was a program, it could have been either gender."

"True," Smalls said. "This is beginning to become a mystery best suited for Sherlock Holmes. I have one more piece to add to this puzzle."

"What's that?" Ashe asked.

"It's about our friend from the bar, Francisco San Roman. I did a search of that name because it sounded so familiar to me. Then I found it."

"Where? Who is he?" Ashe asked.

"Francisco de San Roman was the first Protestant burned as a heretic in Spain," Smalls said. "Years ago I wrote a paper on witchcraft in the time of the Inquisition. Heretics were often accused of having extrasensory powers. His name came up then. That's why I remembered him."

"What does that mean?" Cybil asked. "Lots of people could have that name."

"True, but being inquisitive by nature I decided to run another search for missing persons. I looked for people that resembled the supposed Francisco San Roman," Smalls continued. "This is who I found."

The priest reached into his pocket and pulled out a folded piece of paper. He handed it to Ashe who unfolded it. The man from the bar stared back at him. The picture looked like one somebody would see in an advertisement for an insurance company, but it was definitely the man from the Bayside Bar.

"Who is he?" he asked.

"Harold Conner, a State Farm agent from Natchez, Mississippi. He went missing about three weeks ago after spending a weekend in Biloxi at the casinos," Smalls said.

"What does this all mean?" Cybil said.

"In light of all the new information, the note, the voice mail, I think that Mr. San Roman or Conner is some kind of sociopath who is after Ashe," Smalls said.

"Why me?"

"I don't know that. I study psychic phenomena, but I'm not psychic myself. He probably has seen things about you in the news related to Erik's research with emotion. People will become obsessed with the strangest of celebrities."

Ashe stared into the eyes of the insurance agent. Nothing seemed different, until he looked closely at the eyes. Conner's stared back in a deep green, but the man in the bar had amber eyes like those of woman at the parade. He was about to question Smalls about that, but remembered that a person could get contacts in any color, even amber. He folded the paper up and handed it back to the priest.

"What do we do now?" Cybil asked. "He's apparently after us."

"We can go to the police," Ashe said, "but I don't think it will help anything. All we have is a suspicion."

"You're right," Smalls said. "We need more evidence before we can move on this."

The doorbell rang. Ashe handed his beer to Cybil so that he could answer the door. He hated when people kept their drinks in their hands when they greeted people.

"Who's there?" He felt cautious just in case San Roman/ Conner knew where he lived.

"It's Detective Semmes."

Ashe opened the door. The detective stood on the stoop with another police officer. Both held their badges out for clear viewing.

"What's going on?" Ashe asked.

"Ashley Shrove, you're under arrest for defilement of a dead body." Semmes pulled handcuffs out of his pocket. He turned Ashe around and put his hands in them. "You have the right to remain silent, and I suggest that you do so."

As Semmes quoted him the Miranda rights, Ashe felt like he was in some kind of bad movie. He saw Smalls and Cybil get up and rush to the door.

"What are you doing?" she asked. "He hasn't done anything."

"Please don't interfere," the other officer said.

Ashe shook his head at Cybil, and Smalls pulled her back into the house. When Semmes finished the rights, he said that he was sorry.

"Stay here," Ashe said to Cybil. "Stay with her please, Father Smalls."

Both nodded as Semmes led him down his front steps and to the police car. All around, Ashe could feel his neighbors staring out their windows at him. He'd never felt quite as embarrassed and angry as he did then.

Semmes watched Ashe through the two-way mirror. He didn't

think the professor had stolen the body. Marianne's corpse hadn't really been stolen at all. She'd gotten up and walked out. The deaths of the students and a doctor—along with one of the corpses going missing—meant something had to be done. He, unfortunately, was the only logical suspect, especially after mentioning that the machine the perp used looked like the device he had invented to measure those brain waves or whatever they were.

Ashe sat at a wooden table in a straight-backed wooden chair. He looked down at the tabletop. Semmes knew that he was aware of the mirror. He didn't know if the professor knew *he* was watching him. Almost as soon as they'd gotten to the station, Ashe had demanded that his lawyer be present. That would usually annoy him, but this wasn't any old perp.

The door behind Semmes opened. Cooper stepped inside.

"The perp's lawyer's here," she said.

"The perp has a name, rookie. It's Ashe."

"A perp's a perp, and I'm not a rookie."

"Not in this case. You've got a lot to learn about homicide. Not everyone we pick up is guilty." He stared at Cooper. Tomorrow he was going to the chief and getting this woman reassigned. He'd tried when they assigned her to him, but this definitely spoke to her inability to work the kind of cases homicide had to deal with. "Let Ashe's lawyer in. I'll be there in a minute. Just watch. We won't need good cop, bad cop on this one."

Semmes walked out. He went to the coffee pot and poured out three cups of joe, and hoped that everyone liked them black. It would be a juggling act just getting those cups to the room. Holding two Styrofoam cups in one hand, and his own in the other, Semmes made his way toward the interrogation room. Cooper passed him carrying a brown envelope.

"Rookie, stick that under my arm. I need it," he said.

She followed his instructions without complaint. Semmes walked to the interrogation room door and opened it with the hand holding the single cup of coffee. As he walked in, Ashe's lawyer got to his feet ready to protest.

"Hold your horses," Semmes said. He held out the hand

with the two cups of coffee. "Take one, and give Ashe the other."

"Dr. Shrove, if you will," Johnston said.

"Scott, it's okay," Ashe said. "He can call me by my first name."

Johnston took the cups of coffee. "Whatever you say."

"Please note that we are being recorded," Semmes said. "I don't figure you've ever been in a situation like this so I want to let you know from the start."

"Ashe may not have been in this kind of situation, but I have," Johnston said. "I promise that he will not say anything that will incriminate him."

"Mr. Johnston," Semmes said. "I'm trying to be as nice and pleasant as I can. I would appreciate a little bit less of an adversarial tone."

"Acting buddy-buddy isn't going to butter us up, Detective," he said.

The urge to punch the lawyer was strong. Ashe was innocent of what they'd booked him on, and Semmes knew it. All the effort he was trying to take to let them know that's what he thought wasn't working. It was time to go a bit rogue.

"Rookie, turn off the recorders." He looked at the mirror.

"What?" Cooper said over a speaker.

"You heard me. I said turn it off. I'll take responsibility for whatever happens."

"They're off," she said.

Semmes looked at Johnston. "Get out."

"What? This is violation of my client's constitutional right to representation."

"I'm not going to question him. I have something to say that I don't need you or anyone else to hear. It's going to benefit him, but I know how you lawyers are. You'll screw me over the first chance you get. So, I don't have any recording devices going, which includes you; so either get out or get punched out."

Johnston's face turned red. His throat started to swell up like a bullfrog about to croak. Ashe reached out and touched his lawyer on the arm.

"I trust him," he said. "Give us one minute."

"Forty-five seconds," Semmes said.

"Thirty," Johnston added, getting up from the table. He walked across the room and through the door. "Starting now."

The door closed. Semmes opened the manila envelope and pulled a small stack of black and white photographs from it. He slid them over to Ashe.

"Those are stills from a security camera in Providence Hospital's morgue," Semmes said.

"That's my student, Jason Samuels," Ashe said.

He flipped to the next photo, which showed two men entering the morgue, and then to the third, which was the murder of Dr. O'Hara. The last was of the room after the murderers left.

"Did you recognize anyone else?" Semmes said.

"The guy with the killer was Eddy Bertram, another one of my students, but he's supposed to be dead," Ashe said.

"Exactly." The door opened, and Johnston came back in. "I think that someone is trying to get you."

"What do you mean?" Johnston said.

Semmes ignored him and looked back at the mirror. "Turn the recorders back on."

Johnston took the pictures from Ashe. He flipped through them. "Are these the evidence against him?"

"Not necessarily," Semmes said.

"He's not in these pictures. You don't have him on camera when Marianne went missing. I saw that film myself at University Hospital. You've got nothing," Johnston said. "We're going to take you to the cleaners on this one, Semmes."

"I think I'm being framed or set up or something," Ashe said.

"By whom?" Semmes asked.

"Don't answer that," Johnston said.

"I don't know anyone who would do something like this. I don't know anyone who could pull something like this off," Ashe said.

"I told you to stay quiet."

"Do you know anyone who might?" Semmes asked.

"As your lawyer, I'm telling you to keep your mouth shut," Johnston said.

"No. I don't know anyone who could raise the dead."

"All right, that's it," Johnston said. "This interview is over. I want to speak to a judge right now and get this thrown out. This is a gross miscarriage of justice."

"Do you think that there is a connection between this and the break-in at Ms. Fairchild's apartment?" Semmes asked.

"Ashe told me about that. He was with her the whole night, and she will verify this,"

Johnston said. "You're pulling at straws, Semmes."

Ashe gave Semmes a look that told him he was getting it. He willed his supposed suspect to hear his thoughts about how he was only trying to protect him.

"Where were you last night between 9 p.m. and 1 a.m.?" Semmes asked.

"I'll answer," Ashe told Johnston. The lawyer shook his head in defeat. "I was with Cybil Fairchild and Father Peter Smalls until about 11 or so. Then I took Ms. Fairchild home where we discovered the break-in. You showed up at about midnight. Then I took her to my place. We were there the rest of the night."

"Where were you at about 10 a.m. this morning?" Semmes asked.

Johnston threw his hands up in frustration. "Answer! Answer! I don't care. It's your money we're wasting."

"I was in Dean Allred's office being put on forced sabbatical because of all the stuff going on in my life," Ashe said.

Semmes looked at the mirror. "We got nothing, rook." He turned to Johnston. "He's got a rock-solid alibi. He can go."

"I should hope so. Expect a lawsuit, Semmes," Johnston said.

"No, you shouldn't," Ashe said. "I won't be pressing charges."

"What do you mean?" Johnston looked like a deflating balloon.

"I'm getting out. This was more of an inconvenience than anything else. I'm on sabbatical so it's not like I had anything better to do," Ashe said.

"My partner will make sure you get your stuff back and all the appropriate papers are signed," Semmes said.

He got up from the table and opened the door. Johnston and Ashe walked out. Semmes went back to the table and returned the pictures to their envelope. Something was going on, and he didn't know if it was really about Ashe or not, but it was something strange. He decided that the warehouse out near Birdville needed another visit.

CHAPTER TWELVE

A she walked into his house to find Cybil asleep on the couch. She had an afghan pulled over her, but despite her small stature, it still didn't cover her all the way. He smiled when he saw her. The levity in his mood changed as he closed the door behind him and darkness fell across her. What if she was the next target? He wished that he hadn't gotten her involved in things, but he didn't know how he could have stopped it. Everything that started happening to him started without him knowing it.

Smalls stepped out of his bedroom. "Don't worry, I've been here the whole time," he whispered. "I've just been doing some research on your computer. I hope that's okay."

"I guess it's too late if it hadn't been," Ashe said. "What's up?"

"Come in here so we don't wake her."

Ashe walked into his bedroom with Smalls. He sat on the edge of his bed and let the priest use his office chair. A mosaic of pixels shifted on the screen. Marianne had put that screen saver on the computer. Ashe had never cared for it but hadn't removed it yet. He supposed he might just leave it as a tribute to her.

Smalls moved the mouse. A sinister-looking picture appeared on the screen. It was a painting of impish-looking monsters poking people with a variety of different sharp instruments. Other characters that looked like priests stood around the periphery. A flaming brazier took up the center on the painting. A man crucified upside down dangled above the flames.

"What kind of stuff have you been looking at?" Ashe asked.

"Satanic stuff, mostly. I've been trying to contact a colleague of mine who specializes in all things evil."

"Is he a parapsychologist too?"

"No, he's just a normal priest, but the Vatican uses him to investigate things like possession and events believed to be perpetrated by real Satanists, not just a bunch of yahoos thinking that they're worshipping the Devil."

"Is that his website?" Ashe asked.

"These are some of the images he has there. This painting was made by someone who accused the Inquisition of being started by the Devil. Note the priests standing around not stopping the demons. Of course there is also Christ being crucified upside down over the flames of Hell."

"So what have you found out?" Ashe asked.

"We might have a real case on our hands." Smalls twisted around in the chair and looked at him. "I've not encountered a real religious happening in many years."

"What was the last thing you encountered?"

"Technically, it's the only real phenomenon that I've encountered. It was a case of stigmata in a Guatemalan girl living in south Texas."

"Never anything like this?"

"A few cases of supposed Satanism back in the early 1990s. It was just a bunch of headbangers riding the coattails of the Devil-worshiping craze from the '80s. They killed a few pets. One of them was trampled trying to rape a horse."

"Rape a horse?"

"He read in some fake spell book that having sex with a horse would raise Satan. It had something to do with the Jersey Devil. The problem was he was too stoned to notice that he was having relations with a stallion."

"No resurrections though?"

"None." Smalls looked at him. Ashe felt like the priest was reading his mind. "What do you know, and why are you back so soon?"

"Semmes had to arrest me, but he knew I couldn't have taken part in some of the grave robbing or whatever you want to call it. He had to let me go because you and Cybil were my alibi for last night."

"They thought you killed your students?" Smalls asked.

"Possibly. They also tried to accuse me of murdering a doctor in the Providence Hospital morgue, and stealing the body of Eddy Bertram, one of my dead students. Dean Allred was my alibi in that situation."

"Are you saying it happened again? Another corpse walked out of the morgue here in Mobile? Was the stranger with it?"

"It looked like it. The stranger also killed the pathologist."

Ashe looked at the priest. Smalls' face drooped as worry started to play across it. He shook his head and rubbed his chin.

"This is bad, Ashe. I think something very bad is happening."

"Like what?" Cybil stepped into the bedroom.

"I don't know," Smalls said, "but it's more than just some stalker breaking into your apartment and possible necrophilia."

"How long have you been listening?" Ashe asked.

"Since you got home." She walked over and sat beside him. They clasped hands. "Are we in serious danger?"

"Probably," Ashe said. "Semmes actually brought me in to warn me without giving away any sensitive police information."

"Does he think it's Satanists?" Cybil asked.

"He doesn't know what to think, except that we might be in danger." Ashe looked at Smalls. "You're probably not safe either."

"That will be between me and the Lord I suppose," he said. "I am going to leave now. There are a few things I need to research in-depth."

Smalls didn't wait for them to say another word. He stood and walked out of the bedroom. The front door opened and closed. Cybil squeezed Ashe's hand tighter. He felt her trembling. It wasn't fair for her to have been dragged into things.

"Maybe you should leave town for a little while until we figure out what's going on," he said.

"Where would I go?"

"To your parents' house," Ashe suggested.

"That'll be the day. All they'd talk about is how I'm too old to still be in college. They've been on about that for years now."

"You're just what, like twenty-two?" Ashe asked.

"You've drank with me and screwed me twice, and you don't know how old I am," she said.

Ashe couldn't tell if she was angry or joking. He didn't know what to say so he banked on silence. She raised an eyebrow.

"I just figured you were that age because you're a senior in college," he said.

"Twenty-seven. I'm a senior because I quit when I was nineteen and twenty-one. Then I changed majors at twenty-two and twenty-three."

Ashe let out a sigh. "I feel relieved. I started to feel like that dirty old man in *Lolita*."

"Humbert Humbert," she replied. "One of those majors was literature, and you're not a dirty old man. But you are a douche bag."

"So I guess you're staying in town," he said.

"I guess I'm staying here," she said. "If someone is out to get us, I don't want to drag any of my friends into it."

"That makes sense." Ashe was happy. Cybil made the place feel less like quicksand. "I'm sorry you got dragged into it."

"I don't know how I did. All we did was go to a parade. How did you get in the whole mess?"

"I don't know."

Ashe started to rack his brain again. He figured that somewhere locked up in there he might find the missing puzzle piece to answer that question. Nothing came up. They kept holding hands. He rubbed her thumb with his. She put her head on his shoulder.

"I'm a little bit hungry," she said.

He looked at his watch. It was well past eight p.m. He hadn't eaten all day, but didn't seem any the worse for it. "I don't have a lot in the kitchen. I haven't been shopping in a while."

"I'm sure I can find something to fix, and after that maybe we can take another shower."

Ashe looked at her. She wasn't joking although she smiled. "Really?"

"Sex is my coping mechanism. It really helps relieve stress. Right now I'm under a lot of it."

"We'll see."

Ashe felt guilty because his feelings for Marianne were still so raw. The guilt also stemmed from the fact that he didn't know if he was expressing his feelings for Marianne with Cybil or if he was having real feelings for her. He'd always felt a little bit attracted to her. It didn't matter. He would do it anyway. She'd gotten dragged into the whole mess, and fooling around was the least he could do to make this situation a little more tolerable.

CHAPTER THIRTEEN

Semmes parked in front of the warehouse he'd been at the night before. The gate was still closed tight, and now a padlocked chain secured the gate closed. He watched the place for an hour before making his move. After no one came in or out of the place, he got out of his car. His 9mm rubbed the small of his back as it sat in its clamshell holster. He opened the trunk of his car and took out a pair of bolt cutters.

The street was well lit by street lamps. Their hum was the only noise except for the faint sound of work going on inside the place. Semmes put the padlock's arm into the jaws of the bolt cutters. With a little effort and a good twist, the metal snapped in two. He took the lock out of the links of the chain. The gate slid open with ease. The chain dragged through the fence's links, filling the air with its metallic sound. Semmes kept looking at the warehouse and then down the street both ways. His eyes never stopped moving until he'd opened the gate enough to slip inside. He propped his bolt cutters against the fence and pulled his pistol from the holster.

Semmes walked straight across the parking lot to the door of the warehouse. The knob twisted, and he opened it enough to peek inside. The door led into an office area. All the lights in the room were off, but enough spilled in from the adjacent room that he could see the clutter around. He stepped inside, closing the door carefully behind him. Noise came from the other room. Hammering and grunting kept step with each other. An occasional buzz of an electric saw drowned out the rest. Semmes slipped across the room to a desk that stood against the far wall. It was covered with papers, but the light at that end of the room was much dimmer. He shuffled a few of the top sheets. They were pink carbon copy receipts from hardware stores. He could only make out the stationery logo. The inventory lists were handwritten, and the scarce light made the lettering difficult to read. He riffled through more papers. Some he could read better than others. There was a computer printout from a Mardi Gras supply store. Another was for costumes. Nothing seemed incriminating, or worth breaking in for.

Semmes opened the middle draw of the desk. The light was enough for him to see several printouts from the *Mobile Press-Register*. He took one and leaned into better light. The headline read: *Psychology Professor at Alabama Tech has Scientific Law Named for Him*. A picture was beside the article. He didn't recognize the man in the picture, but the caption identified him as Erik Rogers. Ashe had told him that he worked with a professor named Rogers.

He put that article back into the drawer and pulled out the next. It was a much larger write-up. The printout was folded in the middle. *Two Alabama Tech Professors Record First Emotion*. This time the large photo was of Rogers and Ashe. They both held small devices in their hands. Something about this bit of newspaper felt important to Semmes. He folded it up and stuck it into his pocket. The next bit of paper he brought out was Marianne's obituary.

The noise in the adjacent room stopped. Semmes felt eyes watching him. He turned to the door, still holding his gun and the obituary. A woman stood behind him. The shadows obscured her face.

"Why are you here?"

"I'm Detective Semmes of the Mobile Police."

"I know who you are. I asked why you are here."

"Official police business." He squinted trying to get a better look at the woman. "We have reason to believe this organization might be related to a missing person from Birmingham."

"Is that correct?" the woman asked. Her voice and speech seemed artificial in some way.

She flipped the light on. It blinded him, and he turned to the side to regain his vision. When he looked up, he almost lost his breath. The woman in the doorway was Marianne.

"Why are you here?" he asked.

"I have already asked that question to you," she said.

"I've been trying to find you, Marianne. Ashe is very worried. How did they mistake you for dead?"

"I am not dead," she said, "and I do not know this Marianne. My name is Ursula. Do you have a warrant, Detective Semmes?"

"Now that I've found you here, I don't need one."

Semmes eased toward the exit. He'd dealt with crazy people before. They could be unpredictable and stronger than normal. The last thing he needed was for her to attack him or cause any sort of ruckus. He needed to get back to his car and call for backup.

"I do not know what you are talking about. I have always been here."

"No, you haven't. You're name is Marianne Lenard. You were Ashley Shrove's fiancée, and about a week ago, you walked out of the morgue at University Hospital."

Marianne or whatever she called herself looked at him with amber eyes. Nothing seemed to look back. It was almost like having a staring contest with a doll. Crazy people would look at someone like that sometimes. Semmes remembered reading something about a psychological disorder where people forgot their identities and made up new ones.

He wondered if this had happened to Marianne.

"My name is Ursula van Beckum, and we cannot allow you to leave."

"Try and stop me."

The door at Semmes' back pushed inward. It knocked him off balance. He stumbled forward, looking behind him. Eddy Bertram, the dead college student who walked out of Providence Hospital's morgue, came through the door. Gaining his footing, he stood and put his back to the wall so that Bertram was to one side and Marianne to the other. Now another woman joined the group. It was Carol Heinz. None of them looked normal. They all stared at him with amber, doll eyes.

"I don't know what's going on, but if any one of you tries to do anything I'll shoot," Semmes said.

In all his years on the force, this was the first time he knew he'd have to shoot his way out of the situation. His mouth was dry, and his throat started to clamp shut. They laughed, and Bertram advanced on him. Not thinking twice, and running on almost total adrenaline, Semmes aimed his 9mm and squeezed the trigger. Bertram jerked back as the bullet went into his chest, but he kept coming toward Semmes. Blood poured down the student's body. It spurted out with force. Some of it hit Semmes in the face.

He shot again and again. More wounds opened up in Bertram, but it didn't stop him. Semmes dropped his pistol as the student grabbed him around the neck with both hands. Fingers pressed deep into his throat. His windpipe started to crush inward. The pain was like nothing he'd felt before.

Black spots began to dance around in Semmes' vision. Thoughts came quick and jumbled to his mind. He guessed he was having that life-before-your-eyes flashback. That was the last thought he formed before he felt his spine crushing into his windpipe, and then snapping.

CHAPTER FOURTEEN

Cybil tiptoed into the kitchen, carrying two plastic bags in each hand. Fitful sleep roused her early. She decided to fix breakfast for Ashe as a surprise, but knew there was nothing in the house. She sneaked out, borrowing his car, and drove to the local grocery store just a block away.

She turned the small television in the kitchen on as she started the meal. Bacon crackled in the pan. A bit of the hot grease popped up on her. She rubbed her hand and added eggs to the pan and scrambled them. The weather came on. She looked at it to see the extended forecast while mixing the Bisquick batter to make pancakes. The weather report was nothing too different for that time of the year. There would be heavy fog several mornings with temperatures in the sixties for highs.

Commotion came from the living room. Cybil poured the batter onto a griddle pan, flipped the bacon and moved the eggs around to keep them from burning. Ashe walked into the room. His hair stood on end.

"What smells so good?" he asked, stretching and scratching.

"Breakfast."

"What's wrong with some Cap'n Crunch and OJ?"

"Nothing, but I woke up way too early and wanted to do something special."

Ashe walked to the coffee maker. He took the carafe from the warmer and poured the old coffee into the sink. "It smells like bacon."

"It is bacon, eggs and pancakes," Cybil said. "OJ if you want to drink it or apple juice, milk, or if you're making it, coffee."

"I am making it." He emptied out the filter tray and put

a fresh one in it. Two scoops of coffee went into the filter. He poured the water into the reservoir and replaced the carafe.

"Hope you like plain old Maxwell House."

"I drink tea at breakfast, Lady Grey," Cybil said.

"I don't have that," he said. "I don't know if I've heard of it."

"She was Earl Grey's wife, and you didn't have any. I went to the store and got the other things you didn't have like bacon, eggs, Bisquick."

"Apple juice," Ashe added.

Cybil started taking up the bacon and eggs. She plated them and flipped the pancakes. The television came back from a car commercial. Ashe poured himself some of the coffee that hadn't finished brewing yet. A drop hit the warmer. The smell of burnt coffee overpowered that of breakfast.

"Can't you wait a few minutes before drinking that stuff?" she asked. "You've got the place stinking like scalded coffee."

"Sorry. I need my jolt first thing in the morning. I have to get my hair on my head."

She took the pancakes off the griddle. "Looks like it did that itself."

He laughed sarcastically. With his hair standing out everywhere, Cybil thought he looked cute, like a little boy. His face bore some stubble as well. She liked the way he looked in the morning. Making breakfast for him might be something fun to do in the future as well. He pointed his coffee mug at the TV.

"What's on?" he asked.

"Local news. I wanted to catch the weather for the rest of week. You might get a vacation, but I've got to go to class and work."

He pointed again. "That's Detective Semmes."

She looked at the screen. A picture of Semmes levitated in a box above the newscaster's shoulder. It was a younger photo and looked like something that the police department might have in his personnel file. His name was written underneath the box. She turned up the volume.

"The body of Mobile Police Detective Alexander Semmes was found at the entrance to the Outlaw Convention Center's parking deck this morning. A guard walking the perimeter stumbled upon the body wrapped in a tarp at about five a.m. There is no official cause of death, but the police suspect foul play," the newscaster said.

"That can't be right," Ashe said.

Cybil heard the strain in his voice. He must have been working hard to keep from sounding overwhelmed. She looked at him. His mouth stayed gaped open. Cybil put some eggs, bacon and a couple of pancakes on a plate. She handed it to Ashe.

"Let's eat," she said.

"How can I do that? He's dead."

"You've got to eat," she said. "I know it's tough, but I've got a feeling that this isn't the last we'll be dealing with this."

All they needed was for Ashe to get arrested again. Semmes helped him out last time, or so Ashe had said. Cybil didn't like nor dislike the police officer. He'd helped out at her apartment break-in, but seemed obsessive and intense.

"That voice message is coming true," Ashe said.

Cybil had thought about that no sooner than the newscaster had announced the death. She started to worry about herself. If someone could get to Semmes, who was a hard-boiled egg, how easily could they get to her? She thought about her parents' place in Florence up in Lauderdale County. Breaking her vow to never return would make her mother the winner, but being so stubborn that it might get her killed accomplished nothing as well.

"Maybe I *should* think about visiting my folks for a while. You could go with me," she said.

"I'm not sure Daddy and Mommy would like me too much, and anyway if this person is trying to get to me, he might follow me there and do things to your family. I won't risk it."

"We have to do something. I feel like a sitting duck." She tried hard not to yell or carry on.

"I do too, but I don't know why they picked me of all people to come after."

"Let's eat and try to come up with something."

Ashe sat at the computer in his office at the university. He didn't spend his time working on critiques of student theses. Instead, he stared at pictures of grisly murders. Someone out there wanted to kill him for some unknown reason.

Someone knocked on the door. He looked up to see Rogers standing there. The psychologist's usual demeanor was jovial. Today he looked stoic at best, deeply saddened at worst.

"You look like you lost your best friend," Ashe said.

"No, but I've got more bad news for you," he said.

"Am I being arrested again for something? Because I have a watertight alibi for where I was last night during that time."

"Janie Hack is dead."

"The one who's been working with you on emotion research?" Ashe asked.

"The same one. She died of unknown causes," Rogers said. "It's a shame because I was training her up to be my shadow when I left the university."

"Detective Semmes is dead too. They found him out near the bay," Ashe said.

"That's the cop who was helping you try and find out what happened to Marianne?"

"Right. Now he's dead, and I've been getting threatening voice messages about how everyone around me is in danger," Ashe said.

"Things are getting tougher. I'm going to call Peter to come over and talk with you some more," he said.

"I've talked to Father Smalls enough. I don't know if he can help me; maybe he can help you. I mean your protégée just died."

"Nonsense. I don't want you committing suicide and the amount of stress you've been under makes you a prime candidate for that. I know how to handle this kind of thing."

Ashe shook his head. "I've got someone out there trying to kill me. I don't think I need to help him along."

"Maybe you should talk to Peter about this paranoia," Rogers said.

"It's not paranoid if it's true." Ashe turned a yellow legal pad around for Rogers to look.

He'd written out the names of all the people who he knew had died of mysterious reasons recently. He even included Carol

Heinz from Birmingham and Harold Conner from Natchez. He circled the names of the people directly connected to him in red, and the ones only vaguely so in green. The stolen engram recorder was listed in blue on the bottom corner of the page. Rogers looked down at it.

"A little late for a Christmas list, isn't it?" Rogers asked.

"The ones circled in red are the mysterious deaths I have a closer connection with. The green circles are people who I have no connection with but that I've interacted with. All of them are dead or presumed dead." He looked at Rogers. "Strange how I'm a central figure, don't you think."

Rogers took a blue pen from his pocket. He circled several of the names. Then he took a pencil off of Ashe's desk and circled a few more names.

"Same dead people," Rogers said. "I've circled the ones directly connected to me in blue and the ones vaguely connected with pencil." He wrote Janie Hack's name down and circled it with blue ink. "I'm just as much a target according to your logic."

"You haven't run into two supposedly dead people at Mardi Gras parades either," Ashe said.

"Have you?"

He pointed at Conner's name and then Heinz's. "I met him at a bar. Smalls was with me. Cybil and I met her downtown."

"Harold Conner is dead?"

"Probably. He's a missing person from Mississippi."

"Cybil knows what that woman looked like. You've shown her a picture of the woman on the video walking out of the Birmingham morgue?"

"No, I haven't."

"How do you know that you're not mistaken? Eyewitness testimony is very unreliable, although people don't seem to think so, and a missing person isn't necessarily dead."

"You think I've made it all up?"

"No, of course not, people have died. Supposedly dead people have walked out of the morgues, but I don't think you've met Carol Heinz or Harold Conner at Mardi Gras. Think about it, Ashe. What I've said is rational."

Ashe thought for a minute. Anger stirred in his belly. The woman from downtown was Carol Heinz. He could remember everything about her face when he'd seen it in Birmingham. Smalls had been with him when they met Conner, but that man called himself San Roman. Could the priest be wrong? Was he just making things up in his mind? Rogers waited with his cool, poker-face eyes.

"Maybe you're right. It just seems like a lot of people around me have died lately," he said. "I guess I want to make them fit together."

"That is what humans do. We strive for a gestalt view of things. If you don't believe me ask Peter, he'll tell you the same thing. Half of what his research is on deals with people dreaming up phenomena."

Rogers stood up. He pulled the small emotion-recording device from one pocket and the cranial electrode pads from another. Ashe still felt angry but now it wasn't for having his own irrationality pointed out to him. He was angry because he'd been so irrational. Scientists were supposed to have better grips on reality than that.

"Mind if I get a recording off of you?" Rogers asked. "I haven't gotten a sample of nonclinically- induced confusion and self-doubt."

"Always the scientist." Ashe lifted his bangs up off of his forehead. "Go ahead."

Rogers leaned across the desk. He pressed three of the pads to Ashe's head. One toward the right temple, another in the middle of his forehead, and a third at his left temple. He felt a little tingle as Rogers turned the machine on. The tingling stopped. Rogers took off the pads, pulling a little bit of hair with the one positioned at the left temple. Ashe rubbed where the hair was torn from.

"Think that'll do it?" he asked.

Rogers shrugged. "I'll look at the pattern compared to induced guilt, but I have nothing on self-doubt at all. I'm anxious to run this and see what I get."

"Not a very large sample size," Ashe said.

"When dealing with something like self-doubt, a case study might be in order."

"I'm not going to be your personal guinea pig, Dr. Rogers. I don't like wallowing in self-pity."

Rogers smiled. "I hope that's not what you've recorded on this thing. I have more of that than I know what to do with. I recorded the entire Auburn University football team the day after they lost homecoming to UAB. Self-pity off the charts."

"I might get that joke if I followed football," Ashe said.

"You ought to. It's a great game, and your alma mater has had a pretty good team the last few seasons. Mine hasn't."

"Remind me again of where you went to school?" Ashe asked.

"Duke University. I'm a Blue Devil through and through."

"Oh yeah." Ashe had known Roger's alma mater all along. "I guess you need to switch to basketball. I hear they're pretty good at that."

"Ha, ha." Rogers pocketed his machine. "I'll let you know what I find."

Ashe turned back to his computer search. One of the pictures from Jack the Ripper's murders looked back at him. The prostitute's neck had been sliced open. According to what he read, the attack was so violent that her head was almost cut off. The face of the victim changed to that of Marianne. He saw her body in that photo. Then it morphed to Cybil.

He typed a new address into the web browser. A search engine pulled up. He searched for the lecture he'd assigned his graduate students before he had gone to Birmingham. Two sites pulled up first. He clicked the link that took him directly to that professor's website. When he tried to download the MP3, he received an error message about the file being temporarily unavailable. Clicking back, he went to the other hit. It brought up a friendshare site, but the MP3 loaded from there with no problem.

The file began to play. Ashe leaned back in his seat and closed his eyes. The professor's voice droned out of the computer speakers. He couldn't believe how boring this was. From all the talk he'd heard about this guy, he'd expected a lot better. No wonder his students had complained in previous classes about this lecture. Marianne had volunteered to listen to it this

semester because she knew that he was a bit overwhelmed with
a new introductory class he was building for the next semester.

The recording hiccupped. Ashe opened his eyes and looked
at his computer. The line that pulsed up and down with the
voice moved with the rhythm of the speech. Another hiccup
and the recording stalled. He clicked on the play button, but
nothing happened.

Then the cursor changed from a pointing finger to a twirling hourglass. Ashe moved it along, trying to get the computer
to do something else. The screen went blank.

"Great," he said. "Just what I need."

He banged on the side of the monitor with his hand. As if
this were the magic touch, the screen flashed back on and the
line of the media player started to move again. Instead of the lecture, harsh electronic chords came through the speakers. Then
a manic drumbeat followed by the thumping of bass. Lastly, a
bad guitar riff started. Ashe dragged the cursor over the media
player. A white box popped up. Inside were the words *Goth
Sox: Pink-Striped Hair* scrolling across in black letters. Now he
noticed that another version of the song was playing beneath
the first. He hit the stop button, and the music ceased.

Ashe switched back to the lecture and tried to get it play
again. As soon as he hit the play button, the Goth Sox song
started playing back at the same point he cut it off at. He hit the
stop button again, and pushed away from his computer desk.
He snatched up his telephone and hit the speed dial for Rogers'
office. When the psychology professor answered, Ashe asked
him to go ahead and call Smalls. Apparently, he needed the
priest after all.

Security Camera: Beauregard Hall, ATU, 3:23 p.m. CST

A few students stand near a metal railing that has several
bicycles attached to it. They smoke. The wisps of smoke disappear quickly in the gray nothingness of the grass. A tall, broad-
shouldered man approaches them. They do not seem to give
him a second thought.

He taps one on the shoulder. When that student ignores

him, he twists the student around. Hands fly up as if the student is surrendering. The cigarette falls to the ground. A thin twist of smoke escapes from it during the plummet. Now the student gestures toward the building with his whole hand. The broad-shouldered man points to the building with a single finger. The student nods.

The large man asks a question. The student answers and for extra emphasis holds up all the fingers on one hand as if talking to a little kid. The man pats the student on the shoulder, turns and stiffly walks up the sidewalk toward the entrance to Beauregard Hall.

The student snatches a cigarette from the lips of one of his compatriots. He takes a drag off it, and then puffs, blowing smoke like an old steam locomotive.

Chapter Fifteen

Cybil hurried down the fifth floor hallway. Her backpack was slung over her shoulders, and her arms were burdened with several reams of paper. One of her other bosses had sent her to the campus bookstore to pick up several printouts of the manuscript he was working on. The bookstore usually boxed up those kinds of things, but not this time. Her luck had doomed her to rushing around with loose papers stacked in the right order. The copy people hadn't even stapled the stupid things together.

She turned the corner that led to the south hallway. Her shoes, slick from walking over a mopped floor near the elevator, nearly slid out from under her. This hall always made her a little bit nervous without having the extra burden of a few manuscripts. The baseboards and moldings in this hall were scrolled with strange-looking creatures that resembled goat men. Supposedly when the school had been a military academy well before the Civil War, this floor was devoted to the humanities and especially ancient languages and history. She'd been told the goat men were satyrs from Greek mythology, little gods of mirth. They made her feel creepy not jovial.

Dr. Milton's office came up on the left. Cybil kept her balance and skidded to a halt just inside his door. The old professor looked up at her and pointed for her to put the stacks of paper on his desk. She did so without being told twice. The muscles in her forearms jumped and quivered now that they were free from the burden.

"Anything else?" she asked.

"No, thank you. I hope these aren't stapled," Milton said.

"No sir they're not, and every page should still be in the right order."

"Good, good. You can go."

Cybil wasted no time. Dr. Milton's office smelled like old man, and it bothered her just a little bit. She wondered what Ashe was up to and if he might want to grab a coffee or something. For some reason, the professors ran her ragged today. She started down the hallway toward the side staircase. The route took her past Rogers' office, which she would have rather avoided, but the spiral side staircase was closer than walking to the other side of the building for the other set of stairs or elevators. As she passed his office, she saw that the door stood slightly ajar. Even though an encounter with the psychology professor was the last thing she wanted, Cybil stopped by the door. Rogers never left his door closed when he was in his office, but he never left it ajar if he was gone.

She stopped and listened. No sounds came out of the office, but then there was clatter, a huff, and some under the breath cursing. She almost pushed the door open to make sure there were no burglars, but then she thought about her own apartment and what might have happened to her if she'd made it home earlier. Instead she listened closer. Rogers spoke, and someone answered. She didn't recognize the voice, which wasn't a big shock because there were lots of students at the college. However, this voice sounded too deep and old to be a traditional student.

"How stupid do you have to be coming here?" Rogers asked.

"I had no choice in the matter; I received orders to fetch you. Things require your attention," the other voice said, sounding clipped and forced.

"I'm busy," Rogers said. "Tell him that I have other important business to attend to, and that he'll have to wait."

"Why should I?" a third voice said.

The third man spoke in a raspy voice that demanded respect. Something about the accent set Cybil's teeth on edge and made her stomach flop. It didn't sound artificial like the other, but sinister.

"It's your business I'm trying to get organized," Rogers said.

"My business is your business as well," the foreigner said.

"What is it?" Rogers asked.

"We need more emotional recordings. We lost one the other night when John Balby died," the man with the forced speech said.

"I've given you about half of my collection of emotional recordings. I have to keep some for legitimate research," Rogers said.

Cybil eased around so that she could see through the crack between the door and the wall. Through the small opening, she saw Rogers at his desk. The other two men couldn't be seen. Rogers dug around in his desk and brought out what looked like a thumb drive. He handed it over. An olive-colored hand took it from him.

"Ashe is suspicious about the *missing* engram prototype device," Rogers said.

"Might I remind you, Dr. Rogers, that none of this would be possible without my assistance," the foreigner said.

"I know that."

"I would think that your cooperation would be more forthcoming. Great things await you yet," the foreigner said. "What emotions are on this?"

"I just recorded and processed that today. It's genuine self-doubt."

The foreigner laughed. The sound resonated through the walls. Cybil felt it in her chest cavity. She stepped away from the door hoping that the feeling would subside.

"I love that emotion. It is so powerful," the foreigner said. "Take this back with you, and do what needs to be done."

Cybil heard a grunting noise, and the door started to open more. She turned her back and started down the hall at a pace that didn't seem like she was trying to run away, but didn't seem like she'd just started walking. The temptation to look over her shoulder to see who came out of the office was strong, but she avoided it and made her way to the stairwell. As she opened the door to the stairs, she took a look behind her. A broad-shouldered man followed her down the hall. He looked familiar, but not in an obvious way.

Cybil slipped inside the stairwell and started up a flight of stairs heading to Ashe's office. She stopped on the next landing and peered down as the door from the fifth floor opened. The man walked in. He started down the steps, almost hopping on each step as if he couldn't bend his knees properly. She ducked back from over the rail as he stopped and looked up. His heavy hops down the stairs echoed up to her. Cybil waited until she heard the door on the ground floor slam closed. It echoed up to her. She opened the door and stepped into the sixth floor hall.

Her heart beat fast in her chest as if the man had chased her. She didn't really know why she was so excited. The only thing too bothersome was the foreign man, and it was just his voice. She walked down the hall toward Ashe's office attempting to calm herself so that she didn't burst in ranting.

Ashe and Smalls walked out of his office. They talked with each other as they came toward her. Ashe almost knocked into her before he looked up.

"What's the matter with you?" Ashe asked. "You look like you've seen a ghost."

"I just overheard Dr. Rogers and two men talking," she said.

"That was scary?" Smalls asked.

"I've heard how he talks around other guys," Ashe said. "It can be scary."

"I think that he's involved with the Mafia or something," Cybil said.

She really wasn't sure that's what she actually thought. The broad-shouldered man moved like the woman from the parade, but the two men talked like gangsters in old movies.

"The Mafia?" Smalls said. "What makes you think that?"

"These two guys were hassling him for more recordings of emotions. One of them said they needed a new one because someone died. The other guy, who had an accent of some kind, said that if it hadn't been for him, Dr. Rogers would have never been able to figure out how to record emotions at all." Cybil tried hard not to rant, but she felt like she'd failed at that.

"I'm not sure the Mafia is interested in emotional engrams," Smalls said, "nor do I think that they could help Erik discover them."

"I know what I heard."

"I'm not saying that you misheard anything. I'm not sure it was the Mafia is all," Smalls said. "It must have been disturbing though to get you this worked up."

"Maybe we should stop by and visit him on our way out," Ashe said.

"Where are you going?" Cybil asked. She didn't want to be alone; plus, she'd ridden to school with Ashe.

"We were going to head downtown to that bar we went to the other night," Ashe said.

"The Bayside Bar?" she asked.

"No, the one that you and Ashe went to after meeting the woman from the parading society," Smalls said.

"Why?"

"We need to find the Goth Sox," Ashe said. "Somehow and for some reason, that song you found on Marianne's computer has been attached to the only downloadable copy of that lecture I assign students. It pops up automatically with all the issues that the copy on Marianne's computer has."

"You don't think that the band is out to get you, do you?" Cybil asked.

Smalls shrugged his shoulders. "All I know is that the song has an incantation on it. When I did some research into that incantation, I found that it is very old."

"Didn't you say it was in Latin?" she asked. "I'd think that would make it pretty old."

"It's older than that," Smalls said. "Much, much older. It's the Latin translation of an ancient Hebrew translation of a Sumerian incantation."

"Let's get down to Erik's office before he leaves for the day. We can talk about all this incantation stuff later," Ashe said. "I want to settle your nerves, Cybil." He smiled at her. She felt genuineness in his sentiment. "Maybe when we get to that bar and find the band, I can get mine settled."

Cybil joined them as they walked to the stairwell. Without saying much they walked down to the next floor and to Rogers' office. Ashe knocked on his door. No one answered.

"How long ago did you come past here?" Smalls asked.

"Not long. I came right upstairs as soon as the big guy came out," Cybil said.

Ashe twisted the doorknob. The door opened. He stepped inside. Cybil moved so that she could see in. Smalls stood behind her. The lights were off, and the room empty. A strong odor filled her nose. It smelled almost like rotten eggs.

"Smells like someone farted in here," Ashe said. "After eating Indian food."

"More like rotten eggs." Cybil put her hand over her nose and mouth. The smell was bad, but she could taste it too.

"You're both wrong. That's sulfur," Smalls said.

Ashe pushed past her and back into the hall. She didn't waste time getting back out either. Smalls pulled the door closed. The smell made her eyes water. She worried that it might make her eyeliner run because she'd bought the cheapest stuff at the grocery store that morning.

"Are you sure that was sulfur?" Ashe asked.

Smalls nodded. "That is one of those smells that once you've smelled it you always recognize it."

"Sort of like pot." Cybil took her hand away from her face. She noticed that Smalls and Ashe gave her a strange look. "Like you've never done it."

"I haven't," Ashe said. "In case you haven't noticed I'm a bit of nerd."

"It's exactly like that," Smalls said. "I have smoked and been around it many times. Sulfur is another one of those smells."

"Why would Dr. Rogers have sulfur in his office? Is that part of recording emotions?" Cybil asked.

"It's all electrical," Ashe said. "There aren't any chemicals used at all."

Smalls rubbed his chin. "Didn't you say that you smelled something like rotten eggs at your apartment after it was broken into?"

Cybil nodded. "Yeah. I thought someone had taken a foul dump or something, because I didn't have any eggs."

"That's interesting," Smalls said.

"Why?" Ashe asked.

"I'm not positive just yet, but it's something to think on,"

Smalls said. "I think Erik's gone for the day. Let's get to that bar."

Cybil thought that the priest was a strange duck, but she'd been raised to think that all priests were a bit off. She took Ashe by the hand as they walked to the elevator. Being close to him comforted her some, even though she thought he might be thinking that she was a bit of strange duck right then as well. Why did she say Mafia? Now they'd think she was crazy.

Security Camera: Storage Facility, near Michigan Avenue, Mobile, AL, 5:07 p.m. CST

A group of people work on a large float. The face on the front is grotesque, snarling like a gargoyle on a cathedral. Several men of varying sizes carry boards to the float. Others lift them onto it. None of them move smoothly. They all look like robots in a factory assembling the thing.

A man in a dark hooded sweatshirt comes in. He points to the workers and then somewhere to the side. All the workers stop what they are doing and go where they are directed. The hooded man touches the face of the float. He inspects the under-side and taps the structure with his finger. He looks around. No one is there except him. He beckons in the direction he came from. A woman walks toward him. Her movements are stiff. When she gets to him, she looks up at the ceiling. It is Marianne Lenard.

The hooded man unbuttons her blouse and pushes it off her body. She is naked underneath. He cups one of her breasts and pushes it up. At the same time he stoops and puts the nipple into his mouth. She moves her head around as if enjoying it.

He comes up and unfastens her pants. She pushes them down. The hooded man fondles both of her breasts. She stays stiff with her arms beside her. He appears to say something. She moves and undoes his pants. They fall to the floor. She begins to stimulate him. The hooded man pulls her face to his. They kiss.

With a sudden movement the hooded man turns Marianne around and puts her hands against the float. He pulls her hips out toward him. She moves closer to him and they start to gyrate. The movements become so swift that the hood falls free from his head revealing light-colored hair. He doesn't replace the hood but keeps pumping away.

Just above them, a swarthy man appears. He looks down and smiles.

CHAPTER SIXTEEN

The hipster bar looked different from the night he and Cybil had come to it. Even though Ashe, Smalls and Cybil showed up around the traditional happy hour, only a few people milled around in the place. All the lights were on as well. It almost looked cheery, for a bar, Ashe thought. The bartender with a towel tossed over her shoulder came over to them when they sat down in a row at the counter.

"So what can I get for you three? Today's special is piña coladas," she said. "I know what you're thinking: it's a little early in the year for those. I told the manager that, but he really likes them so we've got them on happy hour special."

"I'll have one," Cybil said.

"All right, and you gentlemen?"

"I think I'd just like a Pepsi," Ashe said, "and a few answers."

The bartender stopped and gave him the eye. He recognized the look. She didn't trust him.

"Are you cops?" she asked.

"No," Smalls said. He unwrapped the scarf he wore from around his neck. It revealed the white tab in his collar. "We're just some folks who are curious about a band that plays here."

"As long as you aren't cops," she said.

"I come in here all the time. Surely you've seen me," Cybil said.

"Doesn't mean you're not some kind of narc."

"He's a priest, and I'm an engineering professor. We might be total nerds, but we're not narcs," Ashe said. "What do you know about the Goth Sox?"

"Give me a second and let me think." The bartender walked

to the soda machine and dispensed some Pepsi into a glass. She brought it to Ashe. "They suck."

"We knew that already," Smalls said. "Can you tell us the next time they're playing here or if you know where they rehearse?"

"Are you going to drink something or just hassle me?" the bartender asked.

"Whiskey, straight," Smalls said.

She walked to the area covered with whiskey bottles. "I've got no idea on either question."

"Got any idea who might?" Ashe asked.

She looked him up and down as she handed Smalls his whiskey and started working on Cybil's piña colada. "The boss might, but he's not here right now. Before you ask, I don't know when he'll be back."

Ashe drank his warm soda. It had been a waste of time coming back to this place. He hated bars like this. Dives always made him uncomfortable. Cybil got her piña colada. It was white and frothy in a fluted glass. A swizzle straw stuck up from the froth. She sipped from it.

"Maybe we should move to a table to finish our drinks," Smalls said.

"Fine with me."

They moved from the bar after Ashe put the drinks on his credit card. He signed a tip to the bartender. She would have gotten more had she given up more information. They sat at a table near the door. Ashe figured they shouldn't get too involved in the ambiance of the place.

"This is a burnt run," he said.

"Not really," Smalls said.

"How is that?" he asked.

"I got a free whiskey."

Ashe shook his head and took another sip of warm Pepsi. "I got an overpriced warm soda from a surly daylight bartender. I don't guess you get to say that every day."

"Fancy running into you guys here."

Ashe looked up to see Rogers standing at their table. His hair was mussed, and he looked like he'd been sweating. The gray T-shirt he wore had dark places under his arms and at his chest.

"Why are you here?" Smalls asked. "This is certainly not your kind of bar."

"I called in for my messages. They told me you had stopped by to see me. When I called to find you, Ashe, they told me you were coming here with Peter. I decided to come on down and see what you needed." He sat in the available chair and waved toward the bartender.

She looked at him and waved back. Rogers let out a laugh and gave her the finger.

"Who told you?" Ashe asked.

"My assistant." Rogers reached over and took Cybil's drink from her and took a swig from the glass. "Piña colada."

"Since when do you have an assistant?" Ashe asked.

"Since I became famous." Rogers pondered Cybil's drink again. "A bit early in the year for a piña colada, isn't it?"

Cybil reached and took her drink back. She looked at it and pushed it back to him. "It was on special. Why don't you finish it?"

He smiled. "I can handle that. I'm thirsty." Another swallow went down his gullet. "Been at the gym. I have to start getting in shape for summer."

Ashe picked his credit card out of his pocket and gave it to Cybil. "Go get yourself something else." He looked at Rogers guzzling the drink. "Get me something too."

Cybil got up and walked to the bar. Rogers watched her walk past. He wiped the white froth moustache on his arm and smiled at Ashe.

"I bet that's fun to hit. How do you get them, Ashe? I mean Marianne and now that bit of freak," Rogers said.

"You know that he's a priest, right?" Ashe asked.

"He doesn't care. He knows a hot piece when he sees one," Rogers said.

Smalls took a drink from his whiskey. "You just have to deal with some things, like it or not."

"I don't know what you're talking about anyway," Ashe said. "I'm still dealing with what happened to Marianne as well. You're supposed to be a psychologist and sensitive to that kind of thing."

"I'm not that kind of psychologist, and I know you've been getting it on with her. You told Dean Allred about it. You might as well have put in the newsletter."

"So what did you come down for, Erik?" Smalls asked.

"To see what you guys wanted. I figured it must be important if you had both come by. I'm not in trouble am I?"

"Are you?" Smalls asked.

"Not that I know of."

"How is the research going with the engrams?" Ashe asked.

"I'd like for it to be going a little faster and smoother, but I'm in no way in trouble. I'll have some more publishable stuff soon."

"Did you get what you wanted when you took my recording?" Ashe asked.

"Oh, yeah that was a great data set. The amplitude of that was amazing. I've yet to see engrams like those. I need to record more naturalistic emotional outbursts. Lab-induced just isn't the same. It's like canned peaches versus the fresh ones."

Ashe knew that he was talking about Cybil and Marianne again. He didn't know why he dealt so much with the scientist. It probably had to do with the fame they were connected by. If Rogers hadn't come up with the theory and idea of how to record emotional engrams, then he would have never built the recorder. Equally, if Ashe hadn't been such an electrical engineering genius then Rogers would have never been able to find the evidence he needed to make his law. Ashe saw nothing narcissistic about looking at things that way.

"Erik, there was a strange smell in your office when we came by," Smalls said. "It kind of smelled like rotten eggs."

"I'm a bit embarrassed about that," Rogers said. "I've been on this new regimen trying to bulk up muscle so that I can be buff."

Cybil handed Ashe a beer. She sat down with one as well. Rogers looked at her.

"Don't stop because of me," she said.

"I don't really want to talk about it around a lady," he said.

"Come on, Erik; it's not like everyone on campus doesn't know how you are," Smalls said. "My students do."

"Mine too," Ashe said.

"So I want to get all buff because I've picked up so much exposure with this engram thing and women are just throwing themselves at me. I've been using this supplemental drink. It's horrible and gives me wicked gas. That's what it was."

"That was some rank gas," Cybil said. "I assume we're talking about that smell in your office."

"That's why it's embarrassing. If I wasn't getting such good results, I would quit using it, but look."

Rogers pulled the sleeve of his shirt to his shoulder. He flexed his arm. The bicep muscle looked large and defined. Ashe remembered that when he started working with Rogers the psychologist was flabby and didn't have much muscle tone at all.

"Where did you get that stuff?" Ashe asked. "If it'll make your arm look like that I might need some."

Rogers took another drink from the piña colada. "I can't tell you. It's not exactly legal in the US."

Ashe was not surprised, and it explained the smell even better. He'd probably picked up something that was heavily laced with sulfur. Rogers might even be using a product similar to methamphetamine, which sometimes had a heavy sulfur base.

"Was that all you guys wanted to know?" he asked.

"Pretty much," Smalls said. "I guess we were just concerned because you've been losing so much weight. I guess we misinterpreted your weight loss attempt to get sex as stress related."

"Sex is a great stress reliever," Rogers said.

"True," Smalls said.

Ashe looked up at the priest. He noticed that the others had as well.

"I'm a clinical psychologist as well as a priest. I know about stress relievers even if I don't use them."

"I'm going to get out of here. I need to get some work done," Rogers said. "You know it's weird that you guys hang out here because I met this chick the other day that plays here a lot."

"She's in a band?" Cybil asked. "I probably know her. I come here a lot."

"I don't remember her name, but she played in some band called the Bobby Socks or Red Sox or something like that."

"The Goth Sox." Ashe felt a flush inside him.

"Yeah that's it. Let me tell you something. Amazing. She had this piercing." Rogers stopped and looked at Cybil. "I'll stop there."

"Do you know where we can find her or the band?" Ashe asked.

"Why? You interested in strange piercings?" Rogers asked.

"We need to ask them some questions. They may be connected with Marianne's death or disappearance," Ashe said.

"I've got no idea. I had a one-nighter with her and threw her number away. It was good but not getting attached good. Sorry." Rogers took one more drink to empty the glass. "I'll catch you later."

He hurried out of the bar. Smalls finished off his whiskey and stood up.

"I think I'm going to hitch a ride back with him," Smalls said. "I need do some work on campus as well."

Ashe nodded. The priest ran after Rogers. Cybil reached over and took him by the hand. Her fingers were cold, probably from holding her beer. He looked into her eyes. She looked innocent. He wished that he hadn't gotten involved with her. She was in as much danger as he was now.

"He's a charming guy that Dr. Rogers," she said.

"He's a pig."

"I know that. I've known that since the first week I started working in the building."

"How?"

"He tried to get me to blow him in the copy room the first time we ran into each other."

"He was probably just joking. He razzes everyone. I don't think he's ever heard of sexual harassment."

Cybil drank from her bottle. "Maybe he was, but he pulled it out and pointed it at me."

Ashe took a big swig from his beer. Marianne hated Rogers. She always said that he came onto her as many times as he could. He even seemed to remember that his junk slipped out of his running shorts one time when they encountered each other in the library stacks.

"He wouldn't try anything now. As long as we're friends, he'll respect that." Ashe doubted his own words as soon as they came out.

CHAPTER SEVENTEEN

Since they were downtown, Cybil and Ashe decided to take in the parade. By the time they'd left the bar after two more bottles of beer, the crowds on Dauphin Street kept them from getting to the barricade.

"It's crowded tonight," Ashe said.

"There's a good parading society tonight. People love their floats and their throws." Cybil stood on her tiptoes to try and see the street. She looked at her watch. There were still a few minutes before the parade would start to roll. "I know a better place to stand so we can get closer to the street."

She took Ashe by the hand and pushed back through the crowd. They walked across a few side streets and down an alley by the most popular gay bar in Mobile. The balcony of the old Victorian house was empty, and the music coming from inside was subdued. Cybil stopped as they passed.

"Sometimes Hortense comes by here to hang," Cybil said. "We may find her there after the parade."

Ashe looked at the building. He pointed at the rainbow pride flag flying from the side of the porch. "You want to come back here?"

"You're not a homophobe are you?" she asked.

"No, but this isn't my kind of a place," Ashe said.

"You want to find somebody from the band, right?"

"Yeah."

"She'll probably be there. Don't worry; I'll hold your hand the whole time so that no one mistakes you for one of *them*." Cybil giggled.

She must have had more of a beer buzz than she thought

because the giggle turned into a big belly laugh. Ashe pulled on her hand to start back walking. She did, but laughed all the way to Government Street.

At the corner of Joachim and Government, she led him back toward the bay. Very few people stood on this stretch of the parade route. A few children hung off the barriers into the street.

"I told you that this street would be better." Cybil let go of Ashe's hand, running to an empty spot at a barrier.

He kept up behind her. Once she was on the barrier, he leaned in to her. She felt his hot breath on her neck. It smelled of beer, but not like he'd had an all-nighter, milder than that.

It was manly and a little sexy. That confirmed her buzz was stronger than she had thought.

"You're not going to flash with all these kids around, are you?" he whispered.

"Not a chance. Even though there are fewer people around here, the cops are a lot stricter; plus, this guy doesn't want to see it."

Cybil pointed to a man in an electric wheelchair. He wore an Auburn ball cap and held a large cardboard box in his lap.

"Leave me out of this," he said. "I'm just here for the medallion necklaces. They changed them this year, and I need the new one."

"I guess your prudishness is safe," she said to Ashe.

Across the street behind Government Plaza cheers rose up, muffled by the distance. She gave him a peck on the lips, slipping her tongue in just enough to be a tease. He tried to kiss her back, but she kept away from him. "Always leave them wanting more" was her motto. As the spotlight mounted behind an Alabama National Guard Humvee that led every parade flashed in the air like a signal to some superhero of Mardi Gras, a man leapt over the barrier on the opposite side of the street. He ran to the middle and started waving his hands.

"The end is near," he yelled. "I have seen the dead walk. They come for us. They want us, the living, to become like them. The Devil walks the earth seeking who he may devour like a roaring lion."

"Shut up!" someone in the crowd yelled.

"Nut job," the man in the wheelchair said.

Cybil looked at Ashe. He held onto the barrier and leaned into the street. People started throwing things at the bum. She felt sorry for him as McDonald's cup slammed into his back. One hit him on the head and burst. Vanilla milkshake ran down his face.

"Come over here," Ashe said. "Get out of the street."

"Don't invite him over," the wheelchair guy said.

"I thought you said to keep you out of our doings," Cybil said.

"Whatever."

"The time is near," the bum yelled, coming closer to them. "The dead walk with Satan."

More people hurled things at the man. Cybil started to yell for them to stop. Music swelled down the street. The cadence of a marching band drumline rumbled toward them. Police sirens whined. She looked as two police motorcycles rode down the street. The engines revved when they got to the old man.

"Sir, you need to get back behind the barriers, or we'll arrest you," one of the motorcycle cops said.

"It's all over by Ash Wednesday," the bum said. "Satan and the dead will have us as part of their kingdom."

"Okay," the other police officer said.

Each of the motorcycle cops took the man by one arm. They started to ride their bikes down the street at just enough speed to keep them upright, with the old man trotting between them. He ranted the whole time. Cybil wanted to yell for them to leave him alone, or that he was her grandfather and demented, but she didn't. Ashe seemed ready to jump the barrier himself. She grabbed him by the shoulder to keep him from it.

"They'll haul you to jail too," she said. "He's just a crazy old man."

"Did you hear what he was saying?" Ashe asked. "He said he saw the dead walk."

"Just a crazy old man," she said again. "Come on; let's go back to that bar and wait. We'll get you a drink to calm you down."

As the first float rolled down Government Street, Cybil took Ashe by the hand and led him back to the gay bar. His hand felt clammy and trembled a little bit. She couldn't imagine what was going on in his mind. The bum was crazy. No one ranted and raved about that kind of stuff in the open, but Ashe claimed that he had watched at least two dead women walk out of the morgue. He'd supposedly seen photos of another corpse doing the same thing. They stopped at the door of the bar. The bouncer held the door open. He wore a Venetian carnival mask with a long nose that looked a little like a penis. Cybil peeped inside. It seemed that the few patrons milling around all wore some kind of mask.

"Is there a theme tonight?" she asked the bouncer.

"Honey, there's a theme every night, and that theme is fabulous," he answered back. "You'll be fine." He eyed Ashe. "I don't know about him though."

"Come on," Cybil said. "Geek is chic."

"He must be Mr. GQ then," the bouncer said. "Come on in. Two drink minimum no cover."

Cybil and Ashe went inside. The bass coming from the speakers rattled through her chest. She attempted to read Ashe's face again, but came up short. He kept a serious unreadable look.

"You're not crazy," she said.

"I know that, but I'm not sure that guy was either." Ashe held up two fingers to the bartender. "He may have seen the dead walk. I've seen it several times."

The bartender brought over two beers. They looked cheap to Cybil. She never drank much of the stuff so she wasn't certain. Ashe moved deeper into the bar. She followed. They sat down at a round table in a back corner. The lighting was bad, leaving him mostly in shadows so that she couldn't watch or study his eyes.

"I think the stress is just getting to you—to us both," Cybil said.

"Maybe." Ashe took a drink from the bottle. "All I know is that I'm sitting in a gay bar waiting for someone who may or may not show up."

"Cybil?" A patron wearing a feathered masked stopped by the table. "What are you doing here?"

"I'm just here having a beer with my boyfriend waiting on somebody," Cybil said. She had no idea who the guy was but tried hard not to show it.

"I'm doing the same thing," he said. "Who are waiting for?"

Cybil drummed her fingers on the table. "I'm not sure who I'm talking with."

The patron pulled his mask off. He was dark skinned with deep green eyes rimmed with eyeliner. His lips were shiny and his cheeks sparkled. Cybil recognized him. It was

Dean, Stewart's boyfriend and Hortense's brother.

"We're waiting on your sister. Is she going to be here tonight?" Cybil asked.

"Be here? She is here up on the second floor. What you need her for?"

"I need to ask her some questions about her band." Ashe perked up.

Dean looked him up and down. Cybil knew it was for nothing else but to get an idea if

Ashe was a narc or not. "Are you a narc?"

"No."

"A record producer? Because you don't look like one."

"I'm not that either. I'm just an electrical engineering professor with a few questions," Ashe said.

"She doesn't know anything about that, but like I said, second floor." He started away. "Maybe I'll see you there in a few."

"You want to head up before the crowd comes in after the parade?" Cybil asked.

Ashe nodded. They got up and started toward the stairs. He took her by the hand. She felt a little bit of a flush come over her. No one in the place was going to hit on him, but having him act like a teenage boy afraid that it might happen was cute. The stairs to the second floor were wooden with barefoot prints on them in different colors of paint. Mardi Gras beads hung from the banisters. At the landing, a boa greeted patrons with a feathery brush across the face or forehead depending on the height of the person. Ashe let her hand go when he got to this part. He swiped at the feathers. Cybil laughed.

"Afraid much?" she asked.

"I just don't like the way the feathers feel when they brush over you. It tickles."

She goosed him in the ribs. "Don't like being tickled?"

Ashe jerked away from her. Some of his beer splashed out of the bottle and onto her top. She started to wipe it off with her hand.

"That's what you get." He reached up and started brushing his hand across the wet spot over her breasts.

She slapped at his hand and turned her back to him. "That's what you don't get."

"I think I'm being stalked," Hortense said from behind them.

Cybil quit trying to wipe the beer from her shirt. She turned around and saw the woman sitting at a round table near the wall. Only Hortense and a few men sat around the table. No one else was on the second level.

"Don't flatter yourself," Cybil said.

Hortense always got under her skin. Usually she just called her Tense Whore, but tonight she planned on being on her best behavior for Ashe's sake. A tip of the hand with her beer bottle in it was how Cybil formally greeted her.

"I've been looking around town for you," Ashe said.

Hortense looked at her friends. "What did I tell you? I'm almost famous."

"Which is a synonym for obscure," Cybil shot back even though she tried to keep from it.

"Why have you been looking for me, and where's your priest friend? Was he afraid to come into a gay bar?" Hortense asked.

"He had other things to do," Ashe said. "I need to know more about that song your band recorded."

"What song would that be?" Hortense asked.

"It's not like you've had that many songs recorded," Cybil said. "Answer the question. We're trying to figure out something very important."

"Maybe I don't want to help," Hortense answered.

"The song that had the incantation on it," Ashe said.

To Cybil his voice sounded cold and flat. He was all about business now. She needed to keep her own emotions under control, or she could risk getting nothing out of Hortense.

"That one." Hortense's voice became soft. She crossed herself, kissing her fingers at the end. "How can I help?"

Cybil thought that she changed her tune quickly. She thought about commenting on it, but let it pass. Hortense looked scared. Her bravado and narcissism faded away into that visage. That change made her uncomfortable too. Although she'd been in on all the discoveries that Ashe and Smalls had come up with, somehow Hortense becoming frightened sent a chill into her. She shivered.

"The man that recorded the song, Francisco San Roman. Is that his real name?" Ashe asked.

"As far as I know. He doesn't look Hispanic, but I don't know why he would lie."

"Could it be a stage name, like yours, *Amanda*?" Cybil asked.

"Maybe. I don't know. All I know is what he told me. That's not much," Hortense said.

"Do you know where San Roman lives?" Ashe asked.

"No idea. I don't even know if he lives in Mobile."

"How about your manager?" Cybil asked. "Would he know?"

"Sure, but he's out of town."

"Where did he go? Was it sudden?" Ashe asked.

"No, he's from Huntsville originally. He had an appointment of some kind up there. He'll be gone the rest of the week. Thus, why I'm sitting here with my boyfriends," she said.

The men around her laughed. Cybil thought that the bravado might be coming back. She didn't like that idea; it meant that the flow of information was about to run out.

"Did you know that your song has been attached to a recording of a lecture from Columbia University almost like a virus?" Ashe asked.

"No, but at least, people are hearing it," Hortense said.

"It's the version with the incantation on it," Ashe said.

Hortense's demeanor changed again.

"Maybe you'll finally be totally famous," Cybil said. She paused to set up the next jab.

"For killing people."

Ashe looked at her. His eyes threatened. Cybil shrank down some. All in all, she was still a little freaked out and that look made her even more so. Ashe wasn't dealing with things as well as she'd thought he would.

"I don't know what to tell you," Hortense said. "If that's the case, I can't stop it. I just sing the songs. I don't know anything about the computer stuff."

Before either Cybil or Ashe could ask another question, Hortense's cell phone tweeted and buzzed on the table. She snatched it up and looked at the screen. A large grin crossed her lips.

"I'm going to have to cut you two off," she said. Then she looked at her companions. "Booty call. I thought this guy would never get back with me."

One of her companions held his hands up with a length of about a foot between them. She giggled and nodded. The man looked at her, puckered his lips and then waved her away.

"I think we should talk a little bit longer," Ashe said.

"I'm not missing this," Hortense said. "I'll be here for the rest of week. You can find me then."

Hortense hurried away. Cybil took a long drink off her beer. She looked at Ashe over the rise of the bottle. All that showed was his eyes that stared out with a dumb amazement. When she lowered her bottle, she saw his mouth was slightly agape.

"Don't look so shocked," Cybil said. "They don't call her Tense Whore for nothing."

"You know you're wrong," the measurement man said, "but so right too."

"Maybe we should follow her," Ashe said. "She might know more, or might even be in danger herself."

"Good luck catching up to her with the parade letting up. You might as well wait until tomorrow," the measurement man said.

"Do you know who"—Cybil held her hands about a foot apart—"is?"

"Somebody she met on a one night stand or something like that. She said nobody ever worked her like him. She's been talking about it for weeks and weeks. Made me jealous."

Ashe looked at Cybil. He looked defeated. "I guess we can head out."

"Let's finish these beers, and we will."

CHAPTER EIGHTEEN

A she stood on the street across from the high-rise court-house. The wind blew from the bay, cold and damp. A low fog roiled along the sidewalk blanketing everything in deep gray mist. All the revelers along the stretch of street stood stiff like cardboard cutouts. Nothing moved, except the wind, the fog and him. The noise of the parade carried on, however. Plastic horns blew; people shouted and laughed. The atmosphere felt electric just like the other parades he had been to.

Cybil stood beside him, her pale skinny torso bare. Nothing moved. Not a single hair fluttered in the harsh wind that was heard but not felt. Ashe looked down the street toward the bay. The glittering and flashing lights of a parade moved along a street several blocks down. From that distance, he could see no other movement. The roiling fog helped little. It bubbled and curled into the air higher in that direction.

He looked up the street back toward the bulk of town. People lined the barriers. The noise of the crowd was there, but there was still no movement. Everyone's face, except for Cybil's, was blank. The skin of their faces pulled out where a nose should have been, but it was just a flesh-colored lump. The same was true of the chin.

"What's going on?" he asked.

His voice crashed down the street like an echo from a deep canyon. The crowd noise dissipated into his own voice. The fog appeared to separate to allow his words to pass by just to close up over the empty space.

A section of brass horns sounded. The trumpets played a familiar tune like something he heard at church when he was a child. Ashe looked back toward the bay. The parade turned the corner onto his street about two blocks down. A group of men playing horns led the way. They slipped through the fog but didn't really move. Their limbs remained still as if they were mannequins being pulled along on roller skates. The first float loomed out of the fog. The gray mist built up around the hull of the ship-shaped float. Only two people were on the float, a man dressed like a jester and another dressed like the Devil. They ran around the whole float. For a moment, the jester chased the Devil; then they would change, and the

Devil would pursue the jester.

"Folly seeks damnation," Marianne's voice said from the fog. "Then damnation chases folly."

"Where are you Marianne? Let me help. Where are you?"

"Folly leads to damnation." Her voice faded into the fog.

As the float passed directly in front of him, Ashe saw that the ship was named *Loathing*. At a closer view, folly and the Devil moved around with motionless limbs. They must have been running on a track, he told himself.

The fog swelled up and engulfed the *Loathing*. The next float came out of the fog. A gaping lion's mouth held a few revelers. Their masks had long noses. They tossed nothing out. As the tawny float passed by, Ashe looked up. Only one person rode atop the float. It was the bum who had been arrested at the parade.

"The Devil walks like a roaring lion seeking who he might devour," he yelled and tossed out a book.

Ashe caught the throw. As the lion-shaped float slipped into the fog, he opened it. On the inside of the book, the incantation written on Cybil's apartment wall glowed in a chartreuse green. He closed it and tossed it to the ground. The fog that swirled at his feet parted as the book hit the pavement. The mist gathered around it but never covered it. The words glowed through the cover.

The odor of sulfur like what he'd smelled in Rogers' office filled the air. The next float slithered out of the fog. A Chinese dragon's head spewed sparks from its mouth and yellow smoke billowed from its nostrils. Music came from this float. He'd heard it before. It warbled and seemed to have a dual beat. Then the words started. As one line ended, another echoed right after it. It was the song by the Goth Sox. Hortense stood on the float. She moved to the music and sang. Both vocals came from her mouth. Then the incantation started. It wasn't in Hortense's voice.

A man dressed in a shiny tunic wearing a long-nosed Venetian mask rose from behind Hortense. His mouth moved to the words of the incantation. Ashe tried to plug his ears, but it didn't help. The words continued to echo through his mind. When the masked reveler finished, he drew a knife from behind him. It was long and gem-studded. He pulled back Hortense's head, and slid the blade across her throat. Blood spurted into the night air. Some of it splattered on Ashe's face. It ran into his mouth. The ferric taste of the hot blood turned his stomach. As he vomited, he screamed, and jerked awake.

Ashe reached up and swiped away something warm that ran down his face. Through the dim light cast into his bedroom from the streetlight outside, he saw it was sweat. His heart pounded so loudly he thought it might wake Cybil. She slept on her stomach, the covers bunched at her waist. The bare skin of her back looked even paler in the wan light. He watched her until he saw her back rise with breath. His own came so quickly that he felt light-headed.

He tossed the bedclothes off him and planted his feet on the floor. The hardwood felt cold on the soles of his feet, but he welcomed it. Sweat poured down his body. He grabbed his robe as he stood up. Nothing could be hotter than a terrycloth robe, but he preferred it to putting on actual clothes. There was enough light in the room for him to navigate out into the much darker living room. He closed the bedroom door behind him. Cybil needed to sleep. She had places to go tomorrow. Well before they had made love and fallen asleep, he'd decided to spend the next few days at home. She could borrow his car to get back and forth. If he needed anything, he could walk the two blocks to the grocery store or just wait until she got in. A few days alone might help clear his head a bit.

The walk across the dark living room proved less than

eventful. He made it to the kitchen. Opening the refrigerator, he let his robe fall open. The cool air felt good on his night-mare-sweat dampened body. The silver label of a beer bottle winked at him in the light radiating from the fridge. Although he wanted a drink, he let the bottle stay where it was. Too much alcohol probably brought the nightmare on in the first place. He grabbed a bottle of water and closed the door. The cool air snuffed out as soon as the seal hissed.

Marianne's voice continued to speak to him from the dream. Her part had been only a small one but besides the horrible death it was the most disturbing. He took a sip of the water as he walked into the living room. The crispness of it helped to cool him. He knotted his robe as he continued into the small guest bedroom, which had been Marianne's. Ashe hadn't gone into it without having a clear objective like making up the bed for Cybil the other night. Even then, he didn't like to look at its door. As he reached out for the doorknob, his hand began to shake. He steadied his nerves and went inside.

It was very dark. Ashe flipped the light switch. The room lit. The small bed was turned longways to the back wall. A chest of drawers sat against the wall next to the window. A small vanity with a round mirror was opposite that. The whole place smelled liked Marianne. Other places in the house did as well, but nothing as strong as this. Ashe wondered how he could have started a relationship with Cybil so quickly. Just the thought of Marianne's voice mixed with her aroma ripped at his guts. He closed the door behind him and sat on the bed. A balled pair of socks rolled down the mattress and rested against his leg. It was time to box her stuff up.

Ashe grabbed the socks and squeezed them. He hated the idea of tossing Marianne's belongings out, but she was dead. *Was she?* He had seen her walk out of University Hospital's morgue. If she were really alive, why hadn't she tried to contact him? A lot of uncertainty rattled around in his head. He stood and walked to the closet. Inside he found several plastic boxes stacked inside of each other. Their tops were in the top one. He dragged them out and started to separate them.

The early morning hours weren't the best time to start a

project like this, but sleep wasn't going to come either. Although he was tired, he knew that he would be able to catch up on sleep while Cybil was at class.

Ashe pulled out the top drawer in the chest. It was full of bras and panties. He didn't think much about them and tipped them over into the first plastic box. The undergarments toppled in with a few landing on the carpet. He picked those up and crammed them in with the rest. Replacing the top drawer, he moved to the next. Socks rested in the second drawer. He did the same with those as he did the contents of the first drawer. In the next drawer he found T-shirts rolled into cylinders. Ashe remembered that always drove him crazy about Marianne. She rolled his T-shirts like that as well. He never understood why she thought that way saved space. This drawer looked like it was full of stacked multicolored firewood.

His eyes burned as he emptied the drawer into the plastic box. As he put the lid over the clothes that had covered her most intimate parts, tears slid down his face. He didn't sob nor sniffle. Hot tears just came to him. The last drawer was full of papers and envelopes of pictures. Ashe wanted to flip through them to see what was there, but nothing looked important. He grabbed a second box and dumped the contents into it. Everything fell in without a problem. He put the drawer back.

A small wooden box sat on the chest of drawers. Marianne kept what she called her blue jean jewelry in it. This meant junk jewelry. He snatched it off the piece of furniture. The urge to toss it into the box was strong, but he knew that all the plastic earrings and bead necklaces would spill everywhere. Someday he might want to go through and take out things he remembered the best or just give them to people who knew Marianne. He placed the jewelry box into the plastic one. As he did so, a clothbound book caught his attention. A rose was etched into the cover. He traced it with his finger, and then lifted the journal out of the box.

Ashe couldn't remember seeing it. Marianne read all the time, but mostly from trade paperbacks or the kind she got at the grocery store. This book was beautiful. He opened it up. The first page was a yellow color and lined with brown college rule lines. Marianne's distinct cursive sprawled across the page. The date in the corner of the page went back two years. He'd found her journal. She'd never told him that she kept a diary, and she must have wanted to keep it a secret because she'd kept it hidden.

Marianne haunted him tonight more than any other night since she'd died. Perhaps he had started to mourn her like he thought he should. Cybil slept in the master bedroom. They had a relationship now, but his emotional investment seemed minimal. It didn't seem like that when they had made love and then gone to sleep, but he had a good buzz going as well. Had he cared about her at all except through lust? Ashe didn't know. He took the diary and returned to the bed. The springs sank in again as he sat. He pushed backward until the wall pressed against his back. The ink used in the diary look faded. She must have used a cheap pen, but he could read it without much strain. Maybe taking the journey through her private thoughts would exorcise her from him for a while. He started to read.

Cybil felt hot, not just hot, but burning. The heat around her felt like the hottest day she had ever spent on a beach. She looked at her usually alabaster skin. It reddened before her eyes. The skin tightened around her arms and began to crack like chapped lips. She opened her eyes against the scorching heat. Everything was white. Sky and land could not be distinguished.

"I can cool you off." Rogers appeared out of nothing.

"How?" she asked.

"I have my ways."

Her skin ached from the heat. Any relief was welcome even coming from him. "So?"

Rogers looked at her. His eyes penetrated to the depths of her soul. She had never seen anything like this stare. Nothing existed of his irises. The entire area was black. Flames seemed to sprout up from those eyes.

"You have to do just what I say," he said.

She nodded. If he took much longer, she was sure she'd burst into flames or wither up.

"Take off your clothes."

"No."

"Then burn to death. I offer you the only way out, so take it."

The burning sensation overwhelmed her. It was as if the temperature had been turned up. She pulled at her shirt. It crumbled into ash in her hands. The rest of her clothes did the same. Her tender parts felt the heat for the first time now.

It was not the same. A feeling of ecstasy came over her. The brutal heat she had felt turned to erotic warmth. It vibrated through her, bringing her to the point of orgasm. As her eyes began to roll back in her head, she glimpsed Rogers. He gyrated, but not in a sexual way. It looked as if he vibrated. The air filled with voices. They chanted words that she did not know, but thought she had heard somewhere before.

The orgasm overtook her. It expelled its energy and coherent thought returned. Opening her eyes, she looked at Rogers. The psychology professor no longer stood in front of her. His figure had changed. Now an unknown man stared at her. His eyes were amber in color. His visage was as stern as if carved from granite. The chanting grew louder. She knew what it was, now that the overpowering feeling of ecstasy had passed. The voices recited the incantation that was on the song that downloaded onto Ashe and Marianne's computer.

Cybil threw her hands over her ears. She screamed to stop, but the words made it only as far as her lips before evaporating into the air.

"Open your eyes," a voice said over the chanting.

She did. The man who had replaced Rogers held a knife in front of him. The blade looked old and rusty. What little bit of the handle she could make out, look knurled. It appeared to be some kind of ceremonial weapon.

Before her eyes, Hortense appeared from thin air. She was naked and looked drugged. Her eyelids lay heavy over her eyes, and her mouth sagged. The man brandished the knife and gave it a histrionic flourish before jerking it across Hortense's throat.

Finally, a scream escaped from Cybil. It expelled outward with as much force as thunder through the sky. At the same time, blood spewed from the gash in Hortense's neck. The chanting turned to uproarious laughter. Hot blood splattered on her face. Cybil wiped her fingers across her lips. They came back dripping with thick blood. As the metallic taste swelled in her mouth, she awoke.

Sweat poured down her face. It pooled on her lower lip. She licked it away, preferring its salty taste to that of the blood in the nightmare. In the not so dark bedroom, she reached out for Ashe, but felt nothing but the sheets beside her.

Her mind began to race. Was the dream over?

She fumbled for the lamp switch. Its light chased away the shadows in the room. The red numbers on the clock told the time as a quarter until five. It was earlier than she would have liked to wake up, but there was no way sleep was coming back after that. For a long time, she sat up in bed letting her heartbeat slow down. It pounded so hard it hurt. The sweat beaded up on her back and breasts started to evaporate and cool her off. The room had a chill to it. Being awake after a bad nightmare always seemed to put a cold streak into Cybil. She wanted to find Ashe even if he was just in the bathroom. He calmed her nerves better than anything.

Cybil climbed out of bed. She grabbed her crumpled clothes from the floor. The drinks she and Ashe had downtown translated into a flurry of tossed clothes discarded in the throes of passion. She pulled her panties on and buttoned her blouse without putting on her bra. The moisture on her skin absorbed into the fabric. She left the room and entered the dark living room. Ashe was not there. She turned around scanning the whole room. A slip of light seeped from the space under the door to the spare bedroom.

Ashe told her it was Marianne's. When he said that, he used air quotes. He meant that Marianne kept most of her stuff in there. She hadn't seen any of his fiancée's stuff when she'd slept in there. For the sake of decency, Cybil had decided to not poke around looking for anything. The idea of decency concerning Marianne almost seemed laughable. She'd jumped Ashe's bones almost immediately. Her body might as well have been warm. According to everything Cybil had heard Marianne might still be alive.

The nightmare still toyed with her mind. The images and feelings of the heat and the blood running down her face stayed with her despite all her ruminations about Marianne. She needed Ashe for comfort, which seemed strange. Never had she needed a man or anyone to help her deal with emotions.

"Ashe, are you in there?" she whispered into the crack between the spare bedroom's door and the wall.

No one answered. Cybil put her hand on the doorknob. It moved free from the lock. She cracked the door and peeked inside. Ashe sat in the middle of the small bed. He leaned against the back wall, reading from a small clothbound book. She eased her head inside.

"Ashe?" she said, a little louder than a whisper.

He looked up at her. His expression was stoic, nothing readable in it.

"Is it okay if I come in?"

Ashe waved her inside. She eased in, closing the door behind her as if someone might barge in. He returned to his reading. She made her way across the room dodging the boxes on the floor and sat down on the bed. He barely acknowledged her presence. His coolness bothered her. She thought that maybe she was still dreaming. Looking at all the boxes, she realized that he had been awake for a while. Several of the boxes were full of the flotsam of life.

"How long have you been awake?" she asked.

"I don't know, a bit."

"What are you reading?" she asked.

"I found Marianne's diary that she's been keeping since we started our relationship."

"Oh."

Cybil felt guilt tug at her. It was bad enough that she had violated Ashe and Marianne's intimacy by moving in on him so soon after the death, but now she intruded on an even more personal level.

"Would you believe that Erik harassed her nearly every time he saw her?" Ashe asked.

"No. What kind of harassment are you talking about?"

"Sexual. According to this, he propositioned her all the time."

Ashe dog-eared the page he was on and closed the book.

Cybil felt uncomfortable. Rogers did almost the same thing to her. She wasn't sure if Ashe knew that or not, but at that time, there was no reason to tell him.

"How does that make you feel?" she asked.

"I don't know. Erik isn't really a friend. We wouldn't have much to do with each other if we hadn't worked on the emotional engram device. I think I'm more upset that she never told me."

"There are some things that people don't feel comfortable doing at times." She thought maybe she needed to tell him about Rogers' advances toward her.

"Why are you up? I figured you would still be sleeping it off."

"I wasn't drunk," Cybil said, "but I had a nightmare."

"So did I."

"Both of us on the same night. That's kind of strange, isn't it?" she asked.

"Not really. We've been under stress, and that usually causes them. Plus the beers probably didn't help."

Cybil knew that stress caused nightmares. She'd taken introductory psychology. Her transcript would show that for a while, she majored in psychology. When Rogers came on the faculty, she switched to math. He'd started making advances toward her almost as soon as he began teaching. Back then, he was pudgy and unattractive, but no less a letch.

"I dreamt about that crazy man from the parade and Marianne," Ashe said. "I decided to get up and start putting her to rest. Maybe I won't have any more dreams like that."

He pointed to the boxes on the floor as if punctuating his sentence. She figured he'd found the diary while rummaging through the boxes.

"I think I dreamed about Hell," she said. "I'm not sure. It was hot and there was this man who appeared with Hortense. He cut her throat."

Ashe looked at her. His face became ashen. "You dreamt about Hortense having her throat slit?"

"Yes, it was horrible. The blood splattered everywhere. It even hit my face."

"I dreamt that too. The blood hit me as well."

Cybil knew that stress brought on nightmares, and that they had both been under a lot of it, but shared dreams weren't covered by the stress theory. Dual dreams that specific didn't bode well. She put her arm under his and laid her head on his shoulder. The sun couldn't come up soon enough. Only a light that powerful could ward off the uneasiness that settled deep inside of her.

Security Camera: Parking Lot, Water Street, Mobile, AL, 1:00 a.m. CST

Only two cars are parked in the large lot near the bayside railroad tracks. Light from the overhead lamps casts a circular glow over everything. Two people stand by the white car. One is the man in the dark hooded sweatshirt. The other person snuggles close to him. They kiss. The second person steps back.

She tries to push the man's hood off his head. He stops her, turns her toward the white car, and bends her over the trunk. Without much flare, her jerks her pants down and does the same to his. They begin having sex.

She puts her hands flat on the trunk lid. They slide up and down the metal as they get deeper into their activity. Headlights flash on them as a car passes on the street. It does not faze them; they continue. She tosses her head back in ecstasy.

As their sexual activity becomes more passionate, a hulking man ambles up from the street. They do not seem to notice him.

The hooded man grasps the woman by the hair and pulls on it, making her back arch downward. Their efforts become harder. Both jar with the force of their actions. He lets her hair loose and grabs her hips as he gives hard thrusts. After a few moments of this, he pulls away.

The hulking man steps up behind her as the hooded man pulls his pants up. He motions toward the woman who remains draped over the trunk of the car, her bare bottom half reared up. The hulking man pulls her to a standing position. She turns and looks at him. She tries to escape, but he pulls a buck knife from a holster on his belt. The blade slides along her neck.

She bucks and convulses in his arms. The hulking man

pushes her back onto the car. He and the hooded man walk away. The woman slides down the trunk and crumples to the pavement. Blood streaks across the white trunk.

CHAPTER NINETEEN

Smalls laid an old tattered book on the table. His study was lit by a small lamp. He'd been up before sunrise. A nightmare woke him that early. He'd dreamed that Hell burst through the ground, opening the graves of the recently dead. Many of those corpses rose. Marianne walked the streets of Mobile, along with the woman from Birmingham. Francisco San Roman or the man who claimed to be San Roman led the resurrected through the streets. It ended with the sacrifice of the Goth Sox lead singer. Her throat was slit like a ceremonial goat. The blood from the wound splattered on him. He awoke after wiping it from his face, the stain on his palm forming a satanic pentagram.

He had spent enough time researching paranormal phenomena to recognize a psychic dream, although he'd never had one himself. During research, however, he had recorded the dreams of some very reliable sources. The book in front of him was an old copy of an ancient treatise on psychic dreaming. He put on his glasses and began to read.

The book had no index for easy reference, and the text was entirely in Latin. If the Church found out he had a copy of it, he could be excommunicated. A papal decree had made it blasphemous centuries before. The inquisitors used it to proclaim witches during the dark times of the Great Inquisitions. For the first time, Smalls definitely thought that everything going on around him concerning Ashe and the disappearance of bodies from the morgues was supernatural in nature, even bordering on satanic.

He scanned the text. The best thing about the book was it had headings for different sections. After a search of these, he found the one listed as *Hell Raised*.

The book detailed imagery in dreams related to prophecies of demonic invasion of the Earth. Smalls had seen many supposed psychoreligious phenomena including possession, but things described within the text were foreign to even him.

Dreams of the dead rising from the grave bodes ill not only for the dreamer but the world. Evil is at work. Oft times when Devils cannot enter people in a waking state, they haunt the dreams.

Smalls picked up his pen and jotted this on a piece of paper. Something in the back of his mind wanted to surface. He knew somewhere he'd seen information related to demons not being able to completely possess the living. At the time, he found it a strange theory and little else, but the memory wouldn't come. A nice walk in the crisp early morning air might help jar his memory.

The wind off the bay gave the air an extra chill that Smalls hadn't expected. His light jacket still hung on the coat hook near his front door. The Alabama Tech hooded sweatshirt he wore wasn't quite enough to cut that damp cold, but he'd gone too far to justify going back for it.

Nothing much moved downtown. Cars belonging to people who either lived in the low-rent apartments on the streets around the downtown or were too drunk to drive home after the parades lined the streets. Half strands of broken beads lay in the gutter as Smalls passed down Dauphin Street in front of random bars. He always felt that the lively nightlife area looked so different in the morning light. The old feel of the area was strong much like the Vieux Carré in New Orleans in the middle of the morning. All the good timers were gone, and the natural flow of an old French town could be seen.

He turned up St. Joseph Street and walked north. The financial firms along this stretch of street were still empty. Morning business would not begin until much later. As he walked past the intersection of St. Louis, he spied Water Street several blocks away. Traffic moved along that thoroughfare between the interstate heading north and I-10 heading across the bay.

Wind swept down between the tall buildings. The nip in it chilled Smalls deeply. He pulled the hood over his head and tugged the strings to tighten it around his face. Nothing made him feel worse than cold ears. His mind started to turn things over and over as he passed by the power company, which had been the site of an old slave auction before the Civil War. A plaque memorialized the historical significance of the location. The place always gave him the creeps. He thought about all the terrified souls that had been bought and sold at that very location. Some of them would have just been off the boats from Africa, jerked from everything they had known to be put on the block. The negative psychic energy felt overwhelming. He was surprised no one had ever reported some kind of paranormal phenomenon at that location.

St. Anthony Street intersected St. Joseph just past the old slave auction. Smalls decided that the morning air had done its job. He turned down the street heading toward the bay. A walk south on Water Street would bring him back to Dauphin and his circle would be complete. He remembered where he had read about demon possession that had plagued his memory. The only problem now would be finding it down in the basement of the church with all the other books he'd put into storage.

He'd been walking much faster than he usually did, and he could feel the effects. His leg muscles burned a little. Smalls stopped when he reached Water Street. Across the street in a large parking lot on the bay, numerous police cars idled with lights flashing. Yellow tape cordoned off the entrance to the lot, and uniformed and plainclothes officers milled around. He thought of poor Detective Semmes who ended up dead and abandoned at the conference center. Butterflies flurried in his stomach. He began to worry about Ashe and Cybil and even Rogers. With all the craziness surrounding his friends, something very bad and very strange could have happened to one of them.

Smalls made sure that nothing sped down the street. He crossed the first two lanes then the next and entered the parking lot. A uniformed officer trotted over to him with his hand held up.

"Excuse me this is a restricted area," the officer said.

"I understand, but I live nearby and thought I might be able to help with the investigation," Smalls said. "I'm a priest at St. Mary's-by-the-Bay."

"It doesn't matter if you're Moses," the officer said. "This is a secure murder investigation area. You need to go back to your church, Father."

Smalls could see beyond the police cars. A few cops poked around a white sedan. Long streaks of blood covered the rear section of the car. A lump underneath a plastic tarp lay at the back of the car. He couldn't tell anything about it.

"I am worried about my friends," Smalls said. "I knew Detective Semmes who was murder a few days ago. I was assisting him in an investigation into the missing bodies from the morgue."

The officer looked him up and down. Then he turned toward some of the plainclothes officers behind him. "Chief, I need you over here."

Smalls recognized the man who walked over to him as the police chief. The county sheriff came with him. They both looked the priest over. Neither of them gave away any thoughts through their expressions.

"Who are you?" the chief asked.

"I'm Father Smalls from St. Mary's-by-the-Bay. I was help-ing Detective Semmes on his investigation into the missing the bodies from the morgue. I was taking a walk this morning and saw the commotion."

"And just decided to wander on over?" the sheriff asked.

"I was concerned for some friends of mine. There have been some very strange things occurring around here. I was afraid that one of them may have fallen victim to the goings on."

"Do you live over at St. Mary's?" the chief asked.

"In an apartment near it," Smalls said.

"So you know a lot of the folks that live and work around downtown?" the chief asked.

"I suppose, even if it's just seeing them in passing."

The chief of police and sheriff looked at each other and nod-ded. The sheriff put his hand on Smalls' shoulder and pointed toward the body.

"We found the victim earlier this morning. She had no ID

on her. Maybe you'll recognize her," the sheriff said.

"I'd be happy to try."

Smalls and the two high-ranking police officials walked past the police cars to the body under the tarp. A few of the forensic techs swiped samples of the blood from the car. A photographer snapped pictures. The chief pointed to one of the techs and made a gesture to uncover the body.

When the cover was lifted, Smalls recognized the face immediately despite the ashen complexion and gory gash in the throat. Hortense stared up at him with dead, fish scale eyes. He crossed himself.

"Do you recognize her?" the chief said.

"Yes."

"Who is she?" the sheriff continued.

"All I know her by is Hortense. I've got no idea what her last name is, but I do know that she was lead singer in a local band called the Goth Sox."

"I've heard them," the tech said. "They suck. She looks a little bit different though."

"Maybe it's because she's dead," the chief said.

"I think that we should be more respectful," Smalls said. He never liked people making comments about the recently deceased. He found it distasteful. A worse feeling than distaste came over him though. She had died just like in his dream, a slit throat over an altar, even if it was a car. "Do you know how she died?"

"By the looks of it, heart attack," the sheriff said with a large dose of sarcasm. "Her throat was cut."

"I know that, but do you know who did it or how? Was she raped or kidnapped?"

"According to our brief investigation, it looks like she may have had some kind of intercourse. Her pants are down around her ankles," the chief said. "We also have video surveillance showing her murderer and his accomplice."

The sheriff pointed to a security camera mounted just overhead. Smalls looked up at it. A hard wind blew and ruffled his hood. If he hadn't tied it on so tightly, it would have blown off.

"It also showed that she had sex with the accomplice who

allowed her to be murdered," the sheriff said.

"So you've got faces. That is great. Maybe everything can get worked out," Smalls said.

"I think we've pretty much got it wrapped up," the chief said. He pulled a small snubnosed pistol from a clamshell holster and pointed it at Smalls. "You're under arrest for the murder of this girl."

"What do you mean?" Smalls said. "I'm a priest."

"That surveillance camera shows a man wearing a shirt, just like yours, with the hood up, just like you've got on, having sex with her before she got it. He's even got your build, and you know the victim," the chief said.

"If the glove fits," the sheriff said.

"It doesn't fit. I'm a priest and a professor at Alabama Tech. That's why I have a sweatshirt from there," Smalls said.

"Okay, so where were you last night about one a.m.?" the chief asked.

Smalls looked down at the ground. He was dreaming about Hortense's bloody death, but they weren't going to hear about that until he had a lawyer. "At home asleep."

"You live with any other priests?" the sheriff asked.

"I live alone."

"No alibi and you match the video evidence," the chief said. "You have the right to remain silent."

The chief continued the Miranda rights as a uniformed police officer put handcuffs on Smalls. He breathed in deeply and tried not to sigh. Now he knew something beyond the normal was at work, something that dealt death and despair to anyone who interfered.

Cybil pushed a cart piled with reams of paper out of the engineering department's copy room. For some reason, the adjunct professor who had taken over Ashe's class decided that the textbook being used didn't cut it. He had her copy every page out of another textbook for the entire class. This was the third trip she'd made with the overloaded cart. As she walked down the hall, a group of undergraduates stood around the announcement bulletin board. They were talking louder than usual, especially when classes were still being held on that hall. She stopped.

"Guys, what's all the noise about?" she asked. "You need to hold it down, classes are still being conducted."

"Hortense from the Goth Sox is dead," one of them said and pointed to a photocopied poster for one of the band's shows. Someone had written "cancelled" across it in what looked like blood.

Cybil tore the poster off the bulletin board despite the jeers of the other students. A wave of heat seemed to wash over her. Everything started to feel distant. The voices of the students took on a tinny quality as if her head were in a bucket.

She laid the poster on the cart and walked toward Ashe's office. He had given her the key to the door so she could bring him some items that he needed. She opened the door and went inside. The room was dark. She walked to one of his guest chairs and collapsed into it, not bothering to turn the lights on. The world seemed a little off kilter. The room began to slowly turn over. The feeling of vertigo overwhelmed her. Her stomach tossed like the waves on the bay during a storm. At the same time, her chest tightened, and her heart beat so hard it felt like it might explode. Her lungs couldn't get enough air. Everything piled up on her. She knew that she'd pass out or die.

Images zipped through her mind. Hortense at the bar leaving to meet the mystery man. The gory death of the singer from her dream imposed upon that. All the while she sang "Pink-Striped Hair" over and over. As the blood from Hortense's dream murder splattered out, the contents of Cybel's stomach would stay down no longer. Cybil jumped up and made it to the trash can before vomiting.

Not much came out except bile. She'd been too tired to eat lunch and hadn't fooled with breakfast either. Another wave of nausea came over her, and she puked again. She lifted her head and wiped her mouth on her sleeve when the door opened and the light flickered on. Rogers stood in the doorway.

"Are you okay?" he asked.

"I'm having a bit of a thing with my nerves." The urge to vomit hit her again, and she spewed into the trash can.

Rogers brushed what little hair hung in her face away. His touch was soft and almost caring. She sat up and wiped her mouth again. Everything seemed to come back under control.

"What's the matter?" Rogers asked.

"Have you ever had a dream come true?" she asked.

"You mean like having a law named after me?"

All the panic left her as she considered what a narcissist Rogers was. "No, like an actual dream like you have when you sleep."

"You mean a psychic dream?"

"I guess if that's what you psychologists call them."

"I've never had one, but I've done research about them. There is evidence that some people are capable of dreaming of future events. Why? Have you had one?"

"That girl we were looking for at the bar yesterday evening was murdered. I dreamed about it last night."

"A psychic nightmare," Rogers said. "Those are very rare. Let me help you up."

She gave him her hand. He pivoted and pulled her up, but too much, sending her off balance. She began to fall over, and he caught her under the arms. His hands just happened to be in position near her breasts. As he helped to steady her, his thumbs brushed over her nipples. He acted nonchalant about it, but Cybil felt he had done it on purpose.

"I don't appreciate that," she said.

"What, helping you up?"

"No, copping a feel. What would Ashe say if he knew?"

"Knew what, that you almost fell and I caught you?"

Cybil shoved him into the door. "And made sure to put your thumbs on my nipples. Were you trying to see if I had on a bra?"

"What do you think Ash will do? You're a rebounder. He's screwing you because he's emotionally confused right now. If you want meaningless sex, just let me know. I'll bang the hell out of you with no strings attached."

Cybil glowered at him. He meant what he said. At the same time his words infuriated her, she thought that maybe she was just a rebound for Ashe. She shoved the professor back into the door.

"I hope that gangster you were talking with yesterday kills you," she said and started out the door.

Rogers caught her by the arm. The pressure from his grasp felt like pliers squeezing down. "What do you mean?"

She tried to jerk her arm away from him, but couldn't. He tugged her to him and pressed her close. His stare pierced, and his breath felt hot.

"I heard you talking about the emotion engrams and giving them to some shady people. Are they sponsoring your research?"

"Be careful." He squeezed her arm harder. "You might be getting into something that you don't want to. Those men are dangerous and will do anything to keep their business lucrative and secretive." He dropped his other hand down and squeezed her crotch. "Anything."

Cybil broke free from Rogers once he'd had his say. She felt dirty, and his look was no longer lustful but hateful. Everything inside her wanted to scream out. She needed relief from the dream and the murder, from the feelings of betrayal from Ashe, who hadn't done anything except what Rogers had implied, and of course from the violation he had committed. The college would do nothing to him. They almost encouraged professors to fool around with students.

"I'll tell Ashe about this," she said.

"That's fine. He knows how I am."

Cybil spat on Rogers and ran down the hall to the stairwell. She needed to get out and get back to Ashe's before she went crazy and did something even rasher.

CHAPTER TWENTY

A she sat on the uncomfortable wooden bench in the lobby of the Mobile city jail. Just a few days ago, he was sitting in the interrogation room after being arrested for grave robbing. Now Smalls, a friend he had made quickly, sat behind bars booked on murder charges. The whole place made him uneasy. The idea that the police thought that Smalls had killed Hortense didn't help. The fact that she had died just like his and Cybil's dreams may have bothered him the most. He hadn't heard from Cybil today, and only left her a note about where he was going. She had his car, so he'd braved traveling across town on her Vespa.

He decided to try and call her. Her phone played a song as he waited for her to answer. He didn't recognize it.

"Hello," a deep voice said.

"I'm trying to get a hold of Cybil Fairchild," Ashe said.

"Well you got me," the voice said.

"I'm sorry. I must have dialed the wrong number."

"No, you got the right number, but you got me instead of Cybil."

The voice seemed sinister. It rumbled through the cell connection like a strange thunder. Ashe's stomach clenched down.

"So where is she?"

"I've got no idea. She left school in such a hurry that she forgot her phone in your office, Dr. Shrove."

"So are you one of her friends?"

"Not really."

"A classmate."

"No."

"Then who are you?"

"Someone who has to tell you that you've gone too far. Now you are in real danger. Quit while you still can."

"Quit what?" Ashe asked. "What are you talking about? Who are you?"

"Others will suffer if you don't listen to me."

The line went dead. Ashe looked at his phone. The other person had hung up. This was the second time he'd heard this warning. Someone knew an awful lot about his life, and apparently had access to his office and maybe even his house. He needed to leave and find Cybil. They had to get out of Mobile before both ended up in the morgue, in jail, or worse, but he had to stay long enough to get Smalls out. They all needed to get out of town.

The door to the outside opened. Ashe looked up. He had every time the door opened. Scott Johnston walked in carrying his briefcase. Rogers was with him.

"So where do they have him?" Johnston asked Ashe.

"Somewhere back there," Ashe said. "I've got no idea. They haven't been very helpful. All they really told me is that his bail has been set at $200,000."

"Chump change," Rogers said.

Ashe didn't find it funny. He stared at his colleague. The thought of Rogers harassing

Marianne almost every day made him want to punch him where he stood, but that was not a good idea in the middle of the jail. Johnston walked up to the desk; he stooped to look through the small hole in the glass at the officer behind the desk.

"I'm Scott Johnston, legal representative for a prisoner you have in there. Father Peter Smalls."

"All right, who are these yahoos?" The officer pointed to Ashe and Rogers.

"My assistant counsel. This is a murder arrest. I don't usually do these by myself," Johnston said.

"Have a seat. Someone will be with you shortly," the officer said.

"Remember that I am an attorney, and making me sit here too long doesn't benefit anyone," Johnston said.

The officer glared up at the lawyer. Ashe could see the

disdain in the cop's eyes, but he picked up a phone and mumbled something into it. Johnston sat down beside him; Rogers sat on the other side of Johnston.

"Why did you do that?" Ashe asked.

"What? Pretend that you are legal counsel?" Johnston said. "Dr. Rogers knows Father

Smalls very well, and you called me to represent him. Also, you were just in here the other day. I don't want them picking you up for killing that detective."

"I don't think there's a chance of that. As I understand it, there's video of three men dumping his body," Rogers said. "I've seen the grainy stills from it on the news. None of them looked like Ashe."

"There's video of the murder they've got Father Smalls in here for too, but they still arrested a priest for sexual assault and murder," Johnston said, "and people call us sharks and cutthroats."

The heavy metal door that led to the interior of the jail swung open. Detective Cooper came out. She looked them over.

"Are you three the attorneys for Father Smalls?" she asked.

"We are," Johnston said. "Can we come back to see him now?"

"I have him in one our interview rooms, so yes you may. By the way, I know you're lying."

Johnston nodded. He stood and motioned for Ashe and Rogers to follow him. As soon as he stepped through the doorway, the smell of the place made Ashe shiver. He'd spent only a few hours in there but that time was enough to scare the living daylights out of him. His whole life had been spent avoiding trouble to keep out of juvie and then jail. Now he voluntarily walked into what he started to think of as the belly of the beast. They walked down the corridor until they came to one of the interrogation rooms. Cooper opened the door and let them inside.

Smalls sat at the end of a short wooden table with his hand-cuffed hands resting on it. He wore an orange jumpsuit. His eyes drooped and looked haggard. Johnston scanned the room, but Ashe and Rogers sat down.

"I assume there is no recording device," Johnston said.

"You would be correct," she said.

"No one is behind that mirror on the far wall?" he asked.

"Not a soul."

"Your name is?"

"Cooper. I'll be leading the investigation into the murder of Amanda 'Hortense' Moore."

"So you're a detective?" Rogers asked.

Johnston looked around at him. "I'll handle the questions, if you don't mind."

Rogers puckered his lips and nodded.

"Are you a homicide detective?" Johnston asked.

Cooper shook her head. "I investigate sex crimes. I was training with Detective Semmes for homicide. Since he's been murdered, I'm dealing with this." She looked at Ashe and then to Smalls. "If you need anything or when you're ready to leave hit the red button by the door and talk to whoever answers."

"Thank you, but this isn't my first time doing this sort of thing," Johnston said.

She looked at Ashe again. "I know it's not."

Cooper left the room, pulling the door shut behind her. Johnston set his briefcase on the table and plopped into a chair. He opened the case and took out a yellow legal pad.

"I didn't do it," Smalls said. "I had nothing to do with that girl's death."

Johnston looked at him and wrote something down on the pad. "Of course not."

"So how did you end up in here?" Rogers asked.

Smalls told them his story. Ashe only heard bits and pieces of it. Most of his concentration focused on the threat he'd received. He didn't even know if the mystery man had found Cybil's cell phone or kidnapped her. As far as he knew, she might be dead, murdered by whoever had killed Semmes and probably Hortense.

"They arrested you because you were wearing a hooded sweatshirt," Johnston said, "and the man on the video had on a similar one."

"According to the officers, we were of similar height and build as well," Smalls said.

"This isn't going to stick," Johnston said. "That's all circumstantial evidence. They cannot hold you on such a high bond for that. The fact that you're a priest and have been for a very long time should cancel all that out."

Smalls turned his eyes down to the table. He twiddled his thumbs. "It's not going to though."

"Why not?" Johnston asked.

Ashe turned more attention to the conversation now. The idea that being a priest wouldn't be taken into consideration intrigued him.

"I became a priest because of a problem I had. I felt it might be the best cure for it," Smalls said.

"What kind of problem?" Johnston asked. "Do you mean homosexuality? Because if you're gay, that will help."

"It's not that," Rogers said.

"How do you know what it is?" Ashe asked.

"Erik and I didn't meet as professionals. We first met at a meeting for an organization we're a part of," Smalls said.

"You're an alcoholic," Johnston said. "Problematic, but not a big deal."

"We're addicts," Rogers said, "but not alcoholics."

"Then what are you addicted to? I don't have all evening," Johnston said.

"Sex." The word came out of Smalls' mouth as a matter of fact. "Nothing illegal, I've never raped anyone, but I was a user for a very long time. It was causing me great problems including almost failing out of my doctoral program and losing loads of money. I decided to cure it with celibacy, and the best place for that was the church."

Johnston blew out a long breath. "That might be a wrench in the gears. A sex addict priest isn't going to get much sympathy. You can thank those in your profession who've ended up as child molesters for that."

"So now you see my dilemma."

Ashe looked at Smalls. Nothing had physically changed about the man but now he saw him in a different light. He also started to remember things from the night that Hortense died. She had to leave to meet a mystery man who hadn't contacted her in a while. Smalls was elsewhere at that time, having left with Rogers.

"I dreamed about her death," Smalls said. "Even the detail of her throat being slit."

"So did I," Ashe said. His distrust of the priest at that moment disappeared. "So did Cybil."

"She told me about that before she left campus today," Rogers said.

"You saw her leave campus?" Ashe asked. "Was she alone?"

"Yeah, but in a hurry. She was freaking out because some students told her about this girl's death. Why are you so concerned about her?"

Ashe glanced around the table. "I called her cell and some man answered. He said she'd forgotten her phone, and he'd found it. Then he told me to get out of town or I might end up in trouble."

"Do you have a recording of this?" Johnston said. "It might be important."

"It was just a conversation," Ashe said.

"Strange because you got a message like that earlier, didn't you?" Rogers asked.

"I did."

"Mr. Johnston," Smalls said. "Something very strange is going on around me and everyone in this room. It may be beyond our understanding. I need to get out of here so that I can figure it out before it is too late."

"Strange things?" Johnston asked. "I'd call that an understatement, but I don't think it's going to happen. You've got a couple of things against you. There's enough to keep you in here until we can have some kind of hearing before the judge."

A knock came on the door and it opened. The female detective poked her head inside. "Time's up."

Johnston stood up. "I'm going to see what I can do."

Rogers also stood. "Hang in there."

Johnston and Rogers walked out. Ashe looked at the detective.

"Can I have just one minute with my client alone?" he asked.

"Thirty seconds, and you can drop the character, Dr. Shrove." She closed the door.

"What's the likelihood that the three of us would have such a similar dream?" he asked.

"Very rare, so much so I would think it would have statistical significance."

"What does this mean?"

"I went for my walk this morning because I was trying to piece something together. I read about psychic dreams concerning the resurrection of the dead. It reminded me of another piece of research I read years ago. The book is in the basement of the church. I store my old books there. It was called *Possessions in Modern Day*. See if you can get it to me."

Ashe turned the title over in his head a few times. "Will I have any problems at the church?"

"Hopefully not, but I'll try to call them tomorrow."

The door opened, and the detective walked in. "Time's up."

Ashe nodded and stood to leave. "Anything else?"

Smalls looked at him and licked his lips. "Sometimes sulfur is called brimstone."

The detective looked at Ashe with an expression that told him she didn't get what the priest was talking about. If he had to tell her the truth, he didn't either. Stress must have been getting to Smalls for him to make such a random statement.

Cybil sat on the couch with her elbows on her knees and her head in her hands. She'd found Ashe's note on the door but didn't understand what it meant. All he said was *gone to jail*. Had he been arrested again? She had called the jail, but was told nothing because of privacy issues. Her Vespa was gone as well. She had no idea what that meant.

The high-pitched rumbling of a vehicle echoed outside. It sounded like her scooter. She jumped to her feet and tossed open the front door. Ashe parked her Vespa behind his car. He wore her skullcap helmet, which looked funny, but she was overjoyed to see him.

"Where have you been?" she asked.

"I left a note. Didn't you get it?"

"All it said was 'gone to jail'. I had no idea what it meant.

He walked up the sidewalk while removing the helmet.

"They arrested Father Smalls for Hortense's murder. They have a man on video that matched his description."

"What does that mean?"

He took her by the arm and led her back into the house. It felt warm and welcoming because she'd stepped out in just her T-shirt.

"He says that he didn't do it, but there are some circumstances that make him a very likely suspect."

"Like what?"

"He's a sex addict. That's how he and Erik met, at a sexual addictions meeting."

The fact that the priest was a sex freak surprised her, but Rogers not so much. She went back to the couch and sat down. He joined her.

"I tried to call your cell, but."

"I left it at school because I was in such a hurry to get away."

"It's been found, and I don't think the person who has it will give it back."

She looked at him. His voice sounded worried. "Why?"

"He threatened us again. Said we needed to get out of town before it was too late. I hope this doesn't upset you more. Erik told me how bothered you were by Hortense's death."

"I ran out because he fondled me," she said.

"What?"

"Your colleague might as well have threatened my life today," she said. "I didn't want to tell you but I need to. He told me to be careful and mind my business then he groped me."

"He threatened you? I wonder if he was the one on the phone."

"I don't know but he said that he was being pressured by some heavies who didn't like being listened in on. He said that they were protecting their interest in his research."

Ashe put his arm around her and pulled her closer to him. It felt good and comforting. She wanted to cry, but wouldn't. Only vulnerable women in bad movies did that.

"I'll talk to him about this tomorrow after I go to St. Mary's-by-the-Bay."

"What do you have to go there for?" she asked.

"Smalls needs a book that's stored in the basement. He said it's important to figuring out what's going on, but I don't know."

"Why? I still trust him even if he's a pervert," she said.

"I think he's going crazy. He told me something completely insane when I left him at the jail."

"What was it?"

"Sometimes sulfur is called brimstone."

She looked at Ashe to see if he was joking, but he wasn't. "That is weird, but I'm sure he had a reason."

"I think he's going for an insanity plea," Ashe said. "I really think he might have killed Hortense. I've been thinking, and we really don't know very much about him. He hid being a sex addict from us. What else might be hiding?"

Now everything seemed topsy-turvy. If the man who seemed to know so much about how to handle this kind of situation might be causing the problems, Cybil didn't know what to think.

"I think I want to lock the doors," she said.

"I'll get the back door if you'll get the front," Ashe said. "Don't forget to throw the dead bolt."

The air in the vestibule of St. Mary's-by-the-Bay smelled stale. Ashe hadn't been to many Catholic churches in his life. If he was honest with himself, he hadn't been in many churches period. Cybil had come with him. She said that she didn't want to go back to school after her encounter with Rogers. He tried to convince her to file a grievance with the dean of students, but she said that it wouldn't get anything accomplished. Ashe knew she was right.

"I am sorry I wasn't ready for you," a priest said, coming out of a door near the bathrooms. "Father Smalls called me this morning to let me know that you would be coming by to look through his books, but I just lost track of the time." He motioned for Ashe and Cybil to follow him. They stopped in front of a small ornate door beside a statue of some saint. "We get a lot of confessions around this time of year. Almost as many as on Easter, but nothing close to the amount we get between Christmas and a few days after New Year's."

"That's interesting," Ashe said as if he cared. The priest seemed very excited about hearing people's problems. "How hard do think it will be to find this book?"

The priest unlocked the door and pulled it opened. A small flight of stairs descended into the darkness. The air that came out smelled staler than the vestibule.

"I've got no idea. He put a bunch of boxes down there a few years ago. The man has a huge library."

"We'll find you when we get finished." Ashe reached inside and flipped a light switch.

A single bulb in a fixture attached to the wall lit up. The light didn't chase many of the shadows away. The stairs down were made of stone. Ashe felt a little bit like a character in an Edgar Allan Poe story walking into an ancient crypt. The cool air was heavy with the stale smell that so many basements had. Cybil stayed close behind him. He could feel her brush against his back. By the time he stepped into the low-ceilinged basement the feeble stairwell light was gone. He felt along the wall for another light switch. It was an old-fashioned button type, which he'd only seen in movies. He pressed one of the buttons and several bare bulbs hanging from naked fixtures flickered on.

Ashe walked a little deeper into the basement, keeping his head bent to avoid hitting it. Cybil still stayed close behind him. She whistled.

"That guy wasn't lying, there are a lot of boxes down here," she said.

Ashe was trying to not focus on the number of plastic boxes stacked down there. The wall of multicolored containers looked like a giant Lego-block wall. They went almost to the ceiling, and he couldn't tell how far back. The idea of finding this book in there seemed like the old needle in the haystack saying. He sighed and took down a box. Cybil did the same. They began rummaging through the books looking for the text.

By the time they got to the last two boxes, Ashe's back hurt. Every time he lifted a new heavy container of books, it felt like he was ripping pieces of his back muscles away. Cybil sat Indian-style on the floor. He handed her one box, and opened the last one. His box was full of psychology journals. The white covers with black writing looked like what they had found in a majority of the containers. He dug down into the box, but only felt the slick glossy binding of the journals.

"Nothing but journals," he said.

Cybil held up a glossy magazine-like book that could be a mirror image of the ones he looked at in his box. "Same here."

"This has been a total waste of time." He flung a journal back into its box. "A wild goose chase."

Cybil put the lid back on the box she had been searching. "I thought someone had to put you up to a wild goose chase."

"I'm not sure that he didn't."

"Did you find what you were looking for?" the priest said from the stairs.

Ashe looked at him. "No. We found mostly old psychology journals."

"Like I said earlier, he has a lot of books. Perhaps he just forgot where he placed this one, but I'm glad that you've finished all the same. Someone needs to see you," the priest said.

"Who?" Ashe asked.

"Archbishop Harrington," the priest said. Ashe gave him a look that he hoped said he had no idea who the bishop was. The priest smiled larger. "He's the head of the Archdiocese of Mobile."

"Why?" Ashe asked.

"I am afraid I'm just the messenger and not privy to such information." The priest leaned forward and lowered his voice. "I will tell you that if he has come here personally it must be very important."

Ashe looked over at Cybil and motioned for her to start upstairs. She quit what she was doing and walked to the stairs. He gave the room one last look to make positive that there were no more boxes that hadn't been scavenged through. Once he was convinced that all of them had been searched he went to the steps after the priest.

During the walk back to the vestibule, he pondered why Smalls would have sent him to look for a book that wasn't there. This led to the question of why the Archbishop of Mobile would want to talk to him. Cybil waited on him when he stepped out into the well-lit foyer area of the church. The priest bounced on his heels like a kid in a hurry to get somewhere.

"Come on this way, His Excellency is a very busy man," the priest said.

"He can wait as long as he needs to," Cybil said. "He called for us, not the other way round."

The priest stopped bouncing and stared right at Cybil. "He actually just asked to see Dr. Shrove. You can wander around out here or if you will stay quiet, you can sit in the back of the sanctuary or do anything else you feel necessary." He looked at her. "Are you Catholic? If so, our confessional is open."

"I'm not," she said, "and if I were, I have nothing to confess."

"Just telling you," the priest said. "I didn't mean anything by it."

"Sure you didn't," she said.

"Take me to the archbishop," Ashe said. "Before this comes to blows."

"Of course, come this way. I have him in the reverend monsignor's office."

Ashe followed the fidgety priest across the vestibule and into a side hall. At the end, a large wooden door with an elaborate stained glass window that depicted a gruesome scene of the crucifixion rested in the wall. The priest knocked and slipped inside. Ashe stared at the glass visage of Christ. Ruby-colored drops of glass speckled his forehead where the intertwined crown of thorns represented by gold glass rested. More red glass gushed from the wound just under the man's ribs. He'd never seen such a gory depiction of the scene, especially not in stained glass. It almost looked like it might come to life.

The priest's shadow moved on the other side of the window. It darkened the vibrant colors of the glass. Ashe remembered a story from his childhood that he'd heard on one of the occasions he had gone to church. As he remembered, when Christ hung on the cross an eclipse occurred, plunging the world into darkness. The priest's shadow seemed to be doing this to the stained glass scene. The door opened, and Ashe was happy. He couldn't stare at the dying man much longer.

"You can come in," the priest said.

Ashe stepped inside. The smell of rich old wood filled his nostrils. A large window with a red rose in the middle of it was in the back wall. Each of the sidewalls was lined with books. A man with a beak of a nose sat behind a large desk. His hair was plastered to his head, and his jowls hung loose. The priest smiled at Ashe and held his hand out to the other man.

"Dr. Ashley Shrove, this is His Excellency Archbishop Harrington."

"Nice to meet you," Ashe said, stiff and uncomfortable. "Am I supposed to bow or something?"

Harrington laughed. His jowls shook back and forth. "No, you can just shake my hand."

Ashe stepped closer to the desk and extended his hand. "I'm sorry about that. I've never met an archbishop, and I'm not Catholic."

Harrington took his hand and pumped it. "Nobody's perfect." He motioned to the priest. "You can leave us."

Ashe sat in one of the visitor's chairs. He sank into the overly plush cushion. Harrington said nothing until the door to the office closed. He smiled at Ashe. It didn't look like a sincere one. The silence between them seemed to last a very long time.

"So what is it that you needed me for?" Ashe asked.

"Right to the point. I like that." Harrington reared back in his chair. "I understand that you are a friend of Father Smalls."

"I guess you could say that. I've only known him around a week or so. I don't usually consider that a strong and lasting friendship."

"How did you meet him?"

"My coworker, Dr. Erik Rogers, introduced us after the death of my fiancée. Because Father Smalls is a psychologist, Erik thought he might be someone good for me to talk to," Ashe said. "We really haven't talked about Marianne's death though."

"Dr. Rogers? I know him well. He and Father Smalls have been friends for a while. I can't say that I care too much for him," Harrington said. "I guess that's a horrible thing for an archbishop to say."

"Trust me, not many people like him," Ashe said. "I still

don't understand why you needed to see me."

"What have you and Father Smalls been doing if not talking about the death of your fiancée?"

"Research."

Harrington leaned onto the desk, propping himself on his elbows. "What kind of research? And remember that I am man of God."

"I'm not supposed to tell. The police might take issue with it, and I don't think the confessional privilege counts in this situation."

"You've been investigating the bodies that have walked out of the morgues," Harrington said. "Your fiancée was one of them."

Ashe huffed. "If you knew that then why all this show?"

"You know that Father Smalls is in jail suspected of murder and sexual assault."

"Yes, I've met with him there. That's why I've been in your basement for the last two hours looking for a book that isn't there."

"Do you know why he became a priest?"

"He said he joined to help his sexual addiction," Ashe said.

"That is correct, and up until now, there has never been an issue concerning Father Smalls and sex, but there have been many occasions when he has come dangerously close to heresy."

"Heresy?" Ashe had to keep from laughing. "I didn't know that still existed."

Harrington pulled out a drawer and reached inside. He took out a large old book. When it hit the desktop, the noise thundered through the wood. Even across the desk from the tome, Ashe could smell how old it was. The archbishop opened to about midway through the volume.

"This book is restricted. A papal decree made it forbidden to any Catholic, especially clergy."

"What's so bad about it?" Ashe asked. "It just looks like an old book to me."

"The problem is that Father Smalls had this book. Because he does a lot of research into psychoreligious phenomena, the archdiocese could overlook the fact that he owned it. I assume it is a good guide to finding out what is real and what isn't, but he didn't let us know about it."

"Do you give up the right of privacy when you join the church?" Ashe asked.

"Somewhat. I found this when I accompanied the police in a search of his apartment." Harrington seemed to notice the look of concern that Ashe felt cross his face. "Don't worry, they had all the legal paperwork and a justifiable cause. I had justifiable reason because of the PR nightmare this whole thing could start if it got out. So far, the Mobile police have done a good job keeping it covered up."

"Just like Marianne and the others walking out of the morgue."

"Exactly. You may be aware that the murder of the doctor happened at the hospital that is under my jurisdiction."

Ashe shook his head. His patience was wearing out quickly. He needed to find that book or find out why he couldn't. The day was getting away from him, and there were other things that needed to be handled before he and Cybil sequestered themselves in the house. After Smalls' arrest and Hortense's murder, they decided to stay inside as much as possible.

"I don't understand why you need me."

"I have the book that you are looking for," Harrington said. "I also want to suggest that you get out of town. For some reason, you have been singled out for all this to happen to you. It's not going to get better, just worse."

"What about Father Smalls? He needs that book to figure out what's going on."

"I'm going to get the book to him, along with this one." Harrington jabbed his finger into heretical text. "He'll be out soon, but you need to be far away."

"Who's after me?" Ashe asked.

"I'm afraid it might be more like what's after you. In a short and sweet way, the Devil." Harrington crossed himself. "He's getting closer and closer with every new person that dies."

Ashe looked at the archbishop. There was no sign of levity in his face. He was serious.

"I don't believe in the Devil," Ashe said.

"That's what he wants. When people believe in him, they avoid him at all cost, but when people do not, he can walk around like a roaring lion seeking whom he may devour."

The crazy man from the parade said something very similar. Not only that, much of the imagery of his most recent dream seemed satanic. Cybil even said her nightmare was about Hell.

"Where did you hear that phrase?" Ashe asked.

"The Bible. St. Peter tells the recipients of his divine letter that the Devil goes around like this. In this case, he is making a lot of noise that we're not going to be able to keep quiet much longer, Dr. Shrove."

"What can I do to stay safe?"

"Leave town."

"I've seen enough horror movies to know that Satan can go anywhere. So leaving town isn't going to cut it," Ashe said. He didn't much like the idea of running away when people he cared about might still be in harm's way.

"I don't literally think that the Devil is after you, but I do think there are people who believe they are doing his bidding who are. They aren't everywhere," Harrington said. "I suppose you could stay at home and not go out unless it is absolutely necessary."

"Cybil and I had already planned that."

"Then I will let you go. I would suggest prayer to you, Dr. Shrove, even if you don't believe in the Devil." Harrington stood up.

The holy man must have been slumping in his seat because once he was fully standing, he towered over Ashe. The archbishop held his hand out to be shook again. Ashe stood and did so.

"I will send Father Smalls to stay with you as soon as he gets out. Expect him later this evening."

"How is that?"

"The woman found murdered had sex shortly before her death. Evidence shows that the partner wore a latex condom."

"And?"

"Father Smalls has a very bad allergy to latex. It blisters his skin as if he was burned. No blistering anywhere on his body.

He couldn't have been the man in the video."

"That's a relief," Ashe said, but he wasn't sure if it really was.

"Be careful, Dr. Shrove, and remember that the Church is looking out for your interest."

Ashe nodded to the archbishop and left the office. Something didn't seem quite right. Everything felt a little too convenient. He decided to keep it to himself until he had more time to ponder on things. After all he was a scientist who made a living solving complex problems; this wouldn't prove too strenuous.

Smalls sat in the cramped visitation area of the jail. It smelled like sweat and other things he hadn't thought about in a very long time. The fact that he was the fifth person to sit in the place in the last hour and a half didn't help things. He watched other prisoners go in and then some woman go in after. The smell pulled at him. Old habits and longings came back to him despite how long he had kept them under wraps. He hoped they'd bring in his guest soon.

The door opened, and one of the guards let Archbishop Harrington into the room. The archbishop wore street clothes, which made Smalls happy. The last thing he needed was for other prisoners to see a church official coming to see him. They already accused him of being a child molester, even though he and the guards had assured them that he was in on suspicion of murder. Harrington sat in the wooden chair across from him.

"It stinks in here," the archbishop said.

"It's the smell of visitation in jail," Smalls said. "Lifelong churchmen, like you, wouldn't recognize it."

"I know what it is," Harrington said. "I might have spent the majority of my life in the church, but I wasn't born a priest."

Smalls laughed. He wandered what Harrington wanted. The judge should have already let him out. The evidence for his release was stronger than that for his continued incarceration.

"Are you getting me out?" he asked.

"Not at this moment. I am assured that you will be out before much longer. Definitely before tomorrow. I have come to give you a new assignment."

"Moving me out of your archdiocese?"

"On the contrary, I need you here more than ever." Harrington gave a sinister smile. Smalls never liked to see him do that. It ran chills deep inside him. "When you get out, I want you to stay with Dr. Shrove."

"Why him?"

"He came by St. Mary's today looking for one of your books," Harrington said.

"I told him to. I need it."

"We've removed all your books that could cause you trouble."

"So why do you want me to stay with Ashe then?"

"Because he needs the kind of protection I feel only you can offer. Of everyone in this archdiocese, I have the greatest confidence in *your* abilities to serve the church to the fullest."

Smalls nodded his head. He knew that he was the only expert in psychoreligious phenomena for three hundred miles or more, but still something seemed off.

"I need my books if I'm going to figure this all out."

"Heretical books aren't going to help you. All they can do is make things worse. I won't let that happen." Harrington stood up. "If you're good on the outside, I might see if you can't look at those books for a few hours." He pushed the door open and walked from the room.

"If you behave."

The door swung closed, and Smalls sat alone in the foul-smelling room again. The essence of it overwhelmed him. He needed to get laid; it was the only thing that might clear his mind.

Security Camera: Storage Facility, Michigan Avenue, Mobile, AL, 3:43 p.m. CST

The swarthy man stands in front of a large float. The face sculpted onto the float snarls in a frozen look of either pain or ecstasy. The eyes screw up to the ceiling and the tongue protrudes. The swarthy man smiles and holds his arms out. The man wearing an Alabama Tech hooded sweatshirt walks to him. They embrace.

The swarthy man points at the float and flourishes his hand around the room as if showing off other things. Although the hood is over the other man's head, his nodding in agreement can be seen. The two men walk around the large room. The swarthy one points out different things along the way. Several props and costumes for a parade line the periphery. Every now and then the hooded man touches them or nods.

The two men then step back to the main float. The swarthy one perches on a stool and begins to talk animatedly, using his hands to punctuate different things. The hooded man listens. After the conversation ends, the swarthy one snaps his fingers and waves to someone on the periphery. Marianne walks to them in a stiff and almost artificial movement. She pulls her clothes off, and the hooded man takes advantage of this while the swarthy man watches and smiles.

Chapter Twenty-One

A she tried to watch television, but the only show he could find bored him. All he could think about was his conversation with Archbishop Harrington. Why was he so insistent that he and Cybil allow Father Smalls to stay with them? Why the special attention on him? Harrington raised more questions than he answered.

"When is Father Smalls supposed to get here?" Cybil walked in from the kitchen carrying a cup of tea.

"I don't know. All the archbishop said was that he would be getting out today and would come here to stay with us."

She sat down beside him on the couch. The cinnamon smell of her tea wafted to him. The aroma seemed to make him feel at ease just a bit. He never kept that kind of tea in his house, but once he had been warned that if he couldn't leave town to stay inside as much as possible they went to get some essential groceries.

"How do you feel about all of this?" she asked.

Ashe turned off the television and gave her his full attention. "I'm not comfortable with this at all. I don't even know why I'm listening to him."

"He's an archbishop."

"I'm not Catholic. I have no reason to listen to this guy, as far as I know he's the one out to get us."

"You trust Father Smalls though?"

He looked at her. "Do I? I did, but now I just don't know. Is there anyone I can trust?"

"Me."

"Huh."

"I haven't done anything."

"You discovered the file on Marianne's computer and heard the first warning call."

Ashe looked at her. He didn't really know why he was saying these things. She wasn't doing anything to him. He was pretty sure of that. "You're the one who supposedly heard Erik talking with those strange men."

She looked down and then back up at him. Her eyes flamed with anger. "How dare you? I'm just as scared as you are. I had a dream about Hortense dying the same as you. In case you haven't noticed, I'm stuck here as much as you are, and they ransacked my apartment."

"Brimstone."

"What?" she asked.

"Before I left him the other night, Smalls told me that sometimes sulfur was called brimstone. I think he was trying to tell me something instead of just being crazy like I'd thought."

"I remember you mentioning that. Do you think he meant something like the fire and brimstone in Hell?"

"I don't know, but we smelled sulfur in your apartment and in Erik's office. The archbishop talked about the Devil. Maybe there is something like that going on."

"I don't know."

"But Father Smalls could have caused that smell. I remember being able to buy stink pellets as a kid. It smelled just like rotten eggs," Ashe said. He chuckled. "I bought some one time and burst one outside the door of my English class in the eleventh grade. The whole room stank most of the period. My teacher was furious. She kept pacing back and forth holding a lacy handkerchief under her nose." He held his hand up to show miniscule height. "She was like that tall, but a pure bulldog. It was great. I think she almost vomited everywhere."

"Why didn't she just open the window?"

"It was the wintertime and too cold."

Ashe took a moment to enjoy the paranoia-free thinking before turning back to his and Cybil's situation. She appeared to enjoy the moment of levity as well. He wondered how many people had ever been faced with a predicament like his. So many people around him had ended up dead, including his fiancée who came back to life and disappeared into the city. He wished that he could do that, just evaporate into the winter fog.

A loud rap on the door focused Ashe back to reality. Cybil jumped up off the sofa, spilling a little of her sweet-smelling tea. She looked at him, and he back at her. For a moment, he didn't know what to do. The wood on the door cracked again as someone knocked on it. Cybil moved to answer it, but Ashe took her by the arm and shook his head. He would answer the door. If something horrible was on the other side of it, he didn't want to risk it getting to her first. His throat dried out as he stepped to the door. The handle felt cold in his hand, almost too cold. He was afraid for just a slip of a moment that his hand might stick to the metal.

"Who is it?" The words barely came out louder than a whisper over his parched lips.

"Father Smalls. Please let me in."

Ashe took a deep breath and let it out slowly through his nose. He flipped the lock with his thumb and opened the door. Father Smalls stood on the doorstep. He held a green suitcase in one hand. A leather duffle bag hung from his shoulder. He looked tired but no worse for wear. Ashe stepped aside without a word to let the priest inside. He closed the door behind Smalls and locked it.

"We've been expecting you," Cybil said. "I was getting worried."

Smalls set both of the bags on the floor. "Why is that?"

"You seemed like you were running late, although I had no idea when you would get here."

"I stopped by my apartment to get some clothes and take a shower. I found it rather turned over." He looked at Ashe who still stood behind him. "I guess the police had to search the place."

"That's what Archbishop Harrington said," Ashe said. "The way he made it sound he searched it too."

"Yes, I am afraid he found a couple of my books. That is unfortunate."

"Why?" Cybil asked.

"Because I wasn't supposed to have such texts. I tried my hardest to keep them hidden and secret, but when you're in jail accused of murder, you can't go back and clean your office up to hide any contraband." He looked at her mug. "Is that coffee or tea?"

"Cinnamon tea," she said. "Would you like a cup? I'm sure the water in the kettle is still hot enough."

"That would be nice." Smalls looked at Ashe. "Where can I put my things?"

Ashe looked at the bags. He didn't want to stick the priest in Marianne's room since he wasn't sure that Smalls was innocent in her death and resurrection. The thought of him and Cybil sleeping in there didn't sit well with him either.

"In the spare bedroom. Ignore the boxes all over the floor. I've been clearing out some of Marianne's stuff. She kept it all in there."

Smalls looked toward the other room and back to Ashe. The priest's eyes seemed piercing. He didn't know if they always seemed so soul-searching or if it was a recent attribute that came along with his paranoid distrust.

"If you aren't comfortable with me being in there, I can sleep on the couch or on the floor. I've been a priest long enough to get used to some less than desirable sleeping arrangements. I was a cad long before that, which meant I ended up sleeping in a lot of unusual and uncomfortable places."

"I'm not comfortable with any of this," Ashe said. "It's not just you sleeping in there. Imagine getting told that the Devil is after you."

Cybil walked back in with a mug. She handed it to Smalls. He took a long sip out of it after blowing the steam away.

"So he told you my theory," Smalls said. "I wish he had let me do it."

"Needless to say, I find this all very dubious."

"Obviously." Smalls drank more of the tea. "Thank you, Cybil. It's very good. Just what I needed."

"Archbishop Harrington told me those books were heretical," Ashe said.

Smalls nodded. "He's right. That's the reason I tried to keep them hidden. They contain valuable information for people like me."

"What do you mean?" Cybil asked.

"I investigate things like possession and other psychoreligious phenomena. Sometimes books that aren't sanctioned by the Church or are even right out forbidden have the best information." He looked at Ashe again. "One of those was the text I asked you to get for me."

"We couldn't find it," Ashe said.

"He must have gotten to it." Smalls shook his head. "I was afraid of that."

"Who got it? Archbishop Harrington?" Ashe asked. "He said he did."

"Too bad," the priest answered. "It was the puzzle piece that I needed. Harrington has forbidden me to look at any of my confiscated books."

"What was so important about it?" Cybil asked. "Maybe you can look it up on Google."

"I doubt it would make a website. It was an obscure theory from very early on in the church put forth by a church philosopher when the age of miracles was ending."

Ashe felt his cell phone buzz in his pocket. He took it out. Erik had sent him a text message. He needed help with the engram recorder. Ashe put the phone back into his pocket.

"I need to go to school," he said.

"Why?" Cybil asked.

"Erik's broken one of his engram recorders again. I've got to fix it."

"Let it wait," Smalls said. "It's not safe for you to leave the house."

"I have to. I'm the only one who can fix the thing. I have as much riding on these engram experiments as Rogers. If these machines keeps accurately recording emotion engrams, I could be a multimillionaire."

"I still think it is not a good idea," Smalls said.

"What would make it safer? Do I need a crucifix or holy water? What about a wooden stake?" Ashe said. "I can't completely quit working. I'll go crazy."

"I'll go with you," Cybil said.

"No." Ashe didn't want to leave her with Smalls, but Erik had made advances toward her and she didn't need to be put into that position again. "Stay here. It won't take me long to fix the thing. He broke one the other day. It was a simple issue."

Ashe grabbed his coat off the hook near the door and left the house. The outside air was cool and refreshing. He hadn't realized how warm the house was until just then. As he walked to his car, he told himself that Cybil would be fine with Smalls. The priest wouldn't do anything. Despite all the inconsistencies with the man, Ashe still trusted him more than not, at that point, but he thought any little thing could tip the scales.

The building seemed abandoned when Ashe walked in. No one walked up and down the steps. Students didn't mill around the front, smoking cigarettes. Not a single bicycle was chained to the metal post under the live oak tree. His footsteps echoed down the hall as he walked to his office. The whole place felt like no one had been there all day. He went into his office. Everything inside was just like he'd left it the last time he'd come to campus. This shouldn't have surprised him but it did. Deep inside of him, he felt like he'd been off campus for months.

Ashe went to a filing cabinet at the back of the room. He fumbled with his keys, looking for the tiny one that unlocked this particular cabinet. There were so many of the small keys on his ring; he needed to organize them better. After a few tries, the correct one slipped into the lock and allowed the top drawer to slide open. Ashe reached in and brought out a small plastic toolbox. All the small tools he needed to work on the engram recorder were inside. Some of them he made special for that project. Keeping these safe was one of the most important things to him, almost as important as keeping himself alive. He thought that he should carry them home to ensure their safety.

"About time you got here." Rogers walked into the office.

"I got here as quickly as I could. Doesn't look like anything's that pressing anyway. Where is everyone?"

"I don't guess you get memos that often since your forced vacation. The school has cancelled class for a few days to help the student body deal with the recent student deaths."

"I guess that's nice of them. It would be stressful to have to go to school with that going on." Ashe opened his toolbox and looked inside. Everything seemed to be in its place. "What have you done to the recorder this time?"

"I'm not sure. It does not want to download the data into the computer. When I put it into the USB port, it tells me that it cannot read the device."

Ashe closed the top of the toolbox. "That might be a software issue instead of a hardware one. Have you consulted the programmer?"

"It's not that. I have the software on several computers. None of them will recognize the thing. It's down in my office. Come on and I'll show you."

He and Rogers headed downstairs to the psychologist's office. A fan blew the air in the room around. Papers on Roger's desk fluttered. It looked like the psychologist had been working all night for several days. Beside the untidy stacks of papers on his desk, empty potato chips bags littered the floor and empty soda bottles sat here and there. Looking at him a bit closer, Ashe thought Rogers appeared tired, although he didn't show typical signs like dark bags under his eyes.

"Been burning the midnight oil?" Ashe asked, setting his toolbox down on a Zapp's Crawtators bag.

"I'm working on a deadline, a very important deadline."

"Working on a grant?" Ashe asked.

The door to Rogers' lab opened. A man with black hair swooped into a pompadour walked inside the office. A scar ran from the bridge of his nose to the corner of his mouth. He smiled and revealed small white teeth.

"I wouldn't call it that," he said with a strong accent.

Ashe looked from the man to Rogers and back to the man. He felt butterflies in his stomach again. Cybil talked about a man with an accent threatening Rogers. He only half believed that Rogers might have been conferencing with a strange fellow. Even when she said that Rogers had told her that people needed her to mind her business, he thought it was just Rogers being a douche bag. The man walking toward him with the less than friendly smile didn't look like any professor Ashe had ever met.

"You have no reason to be afraid of me, Dr. Shrove. I won't hurt you." He held out his hand to Ashe.

"I'm not afraid," Ashe said, taking the man's hand. It felt very soft like it belonged to a person who had always kept it in a glove full of lotion. "You just startled me; that's all."

"My name is Mikal Czernobog. I am a business associate of Dr. Rogers'."

"I don't know if I'd call us that," Rogers said.

The increasingly unnerving smile turned to the psychologist. "I don't know. We have a deal. I did some chores for you and now you have to do some chores for me."

"Listen, just give me the engram recorder, and I'll get it fixed," Ashe said. "I don't want to have any more involvement in your agreement than that."

"Dr. Shrove, I was hoping that I could convince you to lend me your services as well. It seems that our dear friend Dr. Rogers is very clumsy with your device. He seems to break it frequently. I need better and quicker results. You show much technical genius. How quickly could you make five more of those devices?"

"The full contraption? About three years," Ashe said. Although Czernobog made him very uncomfortable, he couldn't keep the sarcasm out of his voice. "The engram recorder isn't something that I'm set up to mass produce. It is a delicate instrument."

"But if I could provide a facility and ability to mass produce it, how long?" Czernobog asked.

"That's not possible," Ashe said. "It's far too sensitive for that kind of work. Each one has to be handmade."

"I can provide the hands," the other man said. "How long?"

"Can you provide the expertise in engineering as well?"

"You do not understand, Dr. Shrove. I have unlimited resources at my disposal."

"Almost unlimited," Rogers said.

Czernobog cut his eyes toward the psychologist. The smile disappeared, replaced by a look that Ashe couldn't describe if he had to. The air in the room almost became electric. Ashe took the chance to snatch the engram recorder that lay on the desk. He dug into his toolbox and got the tool he needed to fix it. As the other two stared at each other like gunfighters in some Old West movie, Ashe finessed the mechanism. It looked like the other one had. Rogers or this guy had been using the recorder to broadcast emotions out. He closed the mechanism back into its plastic shell and replaced it on the desk.

"I'm done," he said. "I suggest that you use the recorder for what it is designed to do, which is record and download onto a specific program, not playback on something else."

Czernobog turned back to Ashe. "Is there nothing I can do to convince you to work with me? I really need more of those recorders as quickly as possible."

"I'm sorry," Ashe said, "but I've got enough trouble right now without dealing with the KGB."

"KGB, indeed," the Russian said and laughed. "I have nothing to do with that organization, but I am sure you will come to see things my way, Dr. Shrove." He reached into the breast pocket of his coat and brought out a black business card with silver lettering. "Take this and call me. You can ask any price."

Ashe looked at Rogers, but the other professor made no eye contact. He took the card and stuffed it into his toolbox. Without saying another word, he left. As Ashe walked down the hallway, he heard Czernobog.

"Do that again, ever, and you will experience wrath like you cannot imagine."

He tucked the toolbox under his arm and wasted little time getting to the stairwell and out of the building.

CHAPTER TWENTY-TWO

Noodles bobbed up and down in the boiling water. Cybil flipped the ground beef over in the pan as it sizzled. Every time she turned the meat, it broke into smaller and smaller pieces. Father Smalls read in the spare bedroom. He'd gone in there almost as soon as Ashe had left to go back to the college. Cybil had been a little bit worried that if the priest was some kind of killer he might come after her during that time, but he hadn't done anything since then. She popped her head in to see if he wanted anything for supper. He had said it didn't matter much, that anything was better than the food in jail. She decided to make spaghetti, one of the only things she knew that she made well enough to serve to other people.

Some of the grease from the meat popped on her arm. She hated when that happened and let the meat simmer in its own fat. The jar of marinara sauce sat on the counter beside the stove. She grabbed it and tried to open it. Her hands slipped around the slick metal lid. She tried again using the tail of her shirt to cover her hand but had the same result.

"Father Smalls," she yelled as she took the jar and headed toward the spare bedroom. "I need your help opening this jar. My hands are too slick."

Cybil rounded the corner from the dining room into the living room. As she did, the jar slipped from her hand and hit the floor. It bounced on the carpet and rolled under the couch. A scream caught in her throat. Three large men stood in the living room. The front door hung open, and the cool February air came in. The largest of the men moved toward her. His movements were stiff like something automated instead of alive. The scream finally escaped.

The door to the spare bedroom flew open. Father Smalls rushed out. He stopped short almost toppling over his own feet as the smallest of the three men turned on him.

"What's going on?" Smalls asked.

Cybil couldn't answer. She turned and ran back into the kitchen. It sounded like Smalls threw something. Then she heard a meaty thump, and somehow knew he'd either been killed or knocked unconscious. She ripped open the silverware drawer looking for a knife as the largest man lumbered into the kitchen.

"You are to come with me, Cybil Fairchild," he said with a voice as artificial as his walk was.

"I don't think so."

She pulled a paring knife from the drawer and swiped at the man. He knocked her hand away, and the knife clattered to the floor. His hand closed around her wrist. Cybil reached out and grabbed the frying pan of sizzling meat. She flung it at the man. The half-cooked ground beef flew through the air. It splattered on the man's face and slid down. Although his skin blistered, it didn't seem to faze him.

Terror locked down everything inside of Cybil. Never had she been this scared before. It all seemed unreal. She fumbled with all her effort to grab the pan of boiling noodles. The man jerked hard on her arm. Her hand fell on the hot eye that the frying pan had been cooking on. She squealed as her skin burned.

"We have to go. No more of this."

As she drew her stinging hand to her stomach, he pulled a cloth sack from his pocket. He tugged it down over Cybil's head. Everything went dark, and she smelled a tangy smell like alcohol mixed with some kind of strange fruit. Her head swam. Vertigo overwhelmed her and then nothing.

Something wasn't right. Ashe knew it deep down inside of himself. It wasn't just nerves from the meeting in Rogers' office. There was something seriously out of whack. The traffic on Azalea Road moved along faster than it usually did for that time of the day. He usually avoided using that street except late at night or early in the morning, but it was the shortest route back home. Ashe wanted to get there without the usual twisting and turning through Mobile's side streets. As he got closer to his neighborhood, a plume of dark black smoke billowed up over the pines and green leaves of the live oaks. It looked like a storm cloud descending from the blue sky. The next block, a stretch that included a gas station Ashe frequented because they had cheap coffee, brought him closer to the smoke.

The feeling of dread and anxiety overpowered him. He ran the red light at the intersection where he turned onto his street. The smoke was definitely from his block. The tires squealed as he turned onto Boleyn Court. The street was clogged with fire trucks and police cars. The red and blue lights flickered and strobed on the neighborhood houses. Ashe stopped his car so hard that he hit the steering wheel. He didn't turn it off as he jumped out and ran toward his house or what was left of it. The smoke billowed up from the little square of property that he'd bought when he started at Alabama Tech. Flames lapped the sky at the rear, which would have been somewhere around the kitchen. The firefighters sprayed water over the front of the house. He stopped when a police officer stepped in his path.

"I'm sorry, sir, but you can't go any farther," the officer said.

"This is my house," he said. "I live here."

"Detective," the cop yelled. "Here's the owner."

Cooper, wearing a long raincoat, hurried over from a group of police officers. She pushed past the cop that had stopped Ashe and stuck her hand out to him.

"We meet again," she said.

He took her hand and shook. It seemed strange to shake hands at an event like this, but he didn't know what else to do.

"Yes. This is my house."

"I understand. When I heard this fire come over the radio, I hurried over. I'd like to ask you some questions."

"I would like to ask a few too." He pushed past her and closer to the house. "Like where are Cybil and Father Smalls?"

Cooper followed him. She put her hand on his shoulder with force to slow him down. "There wasn't anyone inside, as far as the firefighters could tell. A neighbor called the fire in not long after it apparently started, but it burned really fast."

"My friends, Cybil Fairchild and Father Smalls, were there when I left." He looked toward his small garage that he didn't use, but that Cybil's Vespa had been parked in front of. The scooter was not there. "Her Vespa's gone. Maybe they left to go somewhere."

"Actually, they moved the scooter away from the house in case the fire jumped to the garage. They didn't want it exploding and causing more problems. The same neighbor that called in the fire told the first officers on the scene that something like a moving van came up before the fire."

"I wasn't expecting anything to be delivered." Ashe stopped. "Father Smalls said that Archbishop Harrington was supposed to bring by some books he had confiscated."

"Do you mean the head of Mobile archdiocese?" Cooper asked.

"I guess. Is there more than one archbishop in Mobile?" Ashe asked. "I have no idea. I'm not Catholic."

"I think we might need to go sit in my car and talk," Cooper said.

"Why? My house is burning down, and you want to talk." Ashe almost started to cry.

"Please, I think this might be just part of the worries you need to have right now."

He looked at the detective. Her eyes were serious but concerned. Something weighed on her mind. He nodded and followed her to a white Ford Escort. She motioned for him to get in on the passenger side. Ashe walked around and sat in the car. Cooper slid under the steering wheel. She turned the car over and fastened her seat belt.

"Where are we going?" Ashe asked.

"Away from here," she said. "I think you're in a lot of danger."

Ashe wanted to roll his eyes. Everyone kept telling him that, but not until he saw everything he owned and still loved eaten by fire had that idea hit home.

"Really?"

The car maneuvered past a few police cars and was free to accelerate the rest of the way down Boleyn Court until it made a U-bend and turned into Seymour Place. Cooper kept her eyes on the street. Ashe kept his on her.

"Am I under arrest?" he asked.

"No, but I need to keep you close to me for your own protection."

"Sounds like protective custody to me," he said.

"You watch too many cop shows. The description of the van your neighbor gave matched the one on the surveillance video at the Outlaw Center."

"What are talking about?"

"It was the same van that Semmes' killers used to dump his body. Now you're telling me that the only thing that you expected to be delivered was from the head of the Archdiocese of Mobile."

"Do you think that whoever came in that van, took Cybil and Father Smalls?"

"I think they took Cybil, but I think your priest friend was in on it." Cooper turned onto Azalea Road. "Remember I am investigating the murder of Amanda 'Hortense' Moore. I was never convinced that Smalls didn't kill her. By the way, clever how you got that lawyer to say that you were his associate."

"That was his idea, not mine."

Ashe felt guilty. He hadn't trusted Smalls enough to leave Cybil alone with him, but he had. Now, she was gone and might end up like Hortense and Marianne. Smalls was some kind of sociopath to use his position as a priest to do such things.

"I'm going to take you up to a safe house in Saraland. We use it to keep suspects protected. You have to do a few things for me though. Don't answer your cell phone unless you get a text from me telling you to."

"They can't trace a cell phone to a location," Ashe said. He knew it was possible but didn't figure that Smalls had that kind of technology or savvy. "What about my job and clothes? What about Cybil? Are you going to try and find her?"

"We'll use whatever leads we can. Right now the only thing we have to go on is a dead end that Semmes was looking at."

Ashe wrung his hands. "What is that?"

"A parading society called the Mystics of Mayhem.

Apparently, he thought they had something to do with your fiancée's disappearance from the morgue. He found the location where they were building parade floats, but never found any kind of evidence. We'll get a warrant and search the place."

"How long will that take?" he asked.

"Not long, when we have a possible kidnapping with all these strange murders and other strange things going on."

He hoped that would be the case. As soon as they found Cybil, he planned to get her and get out of the area. His cousin lived in Memphis. That wouldn't be too far to get in a quick amount of time, until he could figure something else out. He settled back into the seat and looked out the window as the detective drove onto the interstate. The afternoon light started to fade more and more. The sky across the bay began to turn an indigo color. He hoped they'd get to Cybil before nightfall. Bad things happened at night. He'd known that since he was a kid and listened to campfire stories and ghost tales. Now it seemed he was involved in his own horror movie.

Everything was dark, but Smalls was awake and aware. He and his kidnappers had been driving a long time. They had stopped at one point not long after he regained consciousness and unloaded Cybil. Then they moved on. After the stop and go traffic of the city, the vehicle drove a long while without much stopping or slowing down.

Smalls assumed he was being driven into the countryside. He didn't think that the kidnappers had taken the interstate because the road noise hadn't sounded like that. This made him happy because he wasn't being dropped off in the delta north of the city to be left to the mercy of the alligators, who would still be moving about even in the winter.

The vehicle began to slow. It stopped. He heard the door slide open, and a hard breeze gusted into the van bringing cool air. A pair of strong hands grasped him under the arms. He felt the helpless sense of being heaved up and out. The sack over his head jerked off as he flew a few feet and crashed onto hard-packed sand. Smalls looked up in time to see the door to a white van being pulled closed. The van turned and sped away tossing sand into the air. Bits of the stuff landed on him. A few grains entered his eyes. He tried to reach around and wipe them, but his hands were secured behind his back by what felt like duct tape. Smalls blinked hard and tears welled up, making everything a blur.

As he waited for his vision to clear, Smalls sat up and took in the things around him using his other senses. The wind felt not only cold but damp. The smell borne on it was musky with brine. The scent smelled stronger than the breezes that blew in off the bay on his walks around downtown. The air even tasted salty. Not that far away he heard the ocean washing up on the shore. The bay didn't have waves like that and the delta or a bayou wouldn't have waves at all. Finally the sand exited his eye, and the tears started to clear out. Although the sun had almost slipped down the horizon, he could see enough to know where he was at.

"They dumped me on Dauphin Island," he said.

Smalls struggled to his feet, which was harder than he'd expected. Once standing, he turned around, taking in the vista. To the west, the sand, and small dunes extended out. The south had a dune with wild sea oats sticking up and blowing in the wind. The gulf was on the other side. To the east, there was more sand and the tire tracks from the van. He couldn't see the paved street that ran the length of the island until the point where the city and county had restricted people because of past hurricane damage. The kidnappers had gone past the barrier and dumped him well on the sandy side of the island. The roofs of a few vacation houses that were rebuilt after Katrina were just visible in the dying light. The island was a good forty-five minutes away from the city. His kidnappers hadn't wanted him getting back in quickly, even though they wanted him alive for some reason.

"It's not getting any lighter," he said, and trudged toward the south and the small dunes separating the sandy land from the strand.

Smalls wasn't afraid of getting lost. He knew if he kept walking in the direction of the houses he'd make it back to the street, but walking through the soft, loose sand with his hands behind his back was difficult. His balance kept tipping to one side or the other. He topped the small dune and slipped down the other side. The surf from the Gulf of Mexico washed cold around his knees as he stood back up. He turned toward the east and headed down the sliver of packed sand that marked the beach. The hard sand was much easier to walk on, and he hoped to get to a house or store before too long. He needed to get back to the city and find Ashe. Things were moving faster than he thought they would.

Security Camera: Storage Facility, Michigan Avenue, Mobile, AL, 7:24 p.m. CST

Cybil sits alone in a wooden chair. The whole space has been emptied out. Only a few remnants of float preparation lay around the room. She moves her arms, but they are tethered to the chair with rope. Hindered by the restraints, she stretches her neck to look as far behind her as she can.

A door at the back of the long room opens. Two men walk in behind her. One is the man in the hooded sweatshirt. The hood is pulled over far enough to conceal his face. The other is the swarthy man. They say nothing to each other.

Cybil yells for help and tries to crane her neck to see them. The chair nearly tips over with her. She rights it while saying something. The men continue walking toward her. Once they get to the chair they separate and walk on both sides. She looks at the swarthy man first and then at the one in the sweatshirt. Her expression changes from strained worry to disbelief.

"It's you," she says, expressive enough to be read on her lips.

The swarthy man laughs and slaps the one in the sweatshirt on the shoulder. He slips his hand into the pocket of his black suit coat, bringing up an ornamental-looking knife. Cybil's eyes dart up and down from the man's face to the knife.

The swarthy man shakes his head and waves his free hand as if telling her not to worry. He uses the knife to slice through one of the tethering ropes, and then the other. Cybil moves her arms free of the restraints. She tries to get up, but the swarthy man pushes her back into the chair. As he walks around behind her, he slips the knife back into his pocket. The man in the hood reaches out and caresses Cybil's cheek. As he strokes it, his other hand slides down her neck and plunges into the neckline of her shirt. He fondles her breasts. She tries to move away, but the swarthy man, ever smiling with small teeth, pushes down on her shoulders. The hooded man removes his hand and begins to rub his crotch. He tugs at the zipper and starts to pull himself out of his jeans.

The smile disappears from the swarthy man's lips. He waggles his finger at the hooded man. He speaks, and his words are heard.

"You will not rape her. If you must express your lustfulness use your usual one."

The swarthy man claps his hands. From out of sight, Marianne walks up. She is completely naked. Cybil looks at Marianne. Her eyes widen. She looks as if she might run away, but the swarthy man continues to hold her down by the shoulders. The hooded man walks to Marianne. He pushes her to the ground and then drops his pants. They have sex in front of the swarthy man and Cybil. She closes her eyes and tries to plug her ears with her fingers, but the swarthy man will not allow her to.

"You must hear this," he says "It will explain much."

CHAPTER TWENTY-THREE

The safe house ended up being a room in an old Howard Johnson motel that had lost the franchise. The only way Ashe knew that the room used to be part of a HoJo was the fact that the towels still had the company's name on them. The only chair was an orange vinyl seat that had seen its best days sometime in the late 1970s. It sat beside a small round table with drink rings and cigarette burns on the top. He sat at it watching The Weather Channel. The bed looked too frightening to sleep on. The orange spread that matched the chair had large holes in it and a few mystery stains.

The few belongings he had were spread out over the room. His billfold and car keys lay on the nightstand. His cell phone sat in the center of the round table. He kept his shoes on his feet for fear of what might be living in the shag carpeting. Everything swirled around his mind. Smalls and Cybil were gone, either dead or missing. Had the priest killed Cybil and fled or had he kidnapped her? Either way, Ashe was sure the priest had something to do with it all. The police abandoned him in the roach motel with instructions to sit still and do nothing.

Ashe walked to the window. He pulled the curtain back and looked out at the parking lot. The evening grew darker, and the street lamps glowed orange light out on the parking lot. He knew he was facing south back toward the city of Mobile. Somewhere people plotted against him. Theoretically, the reanimated corpse of his fiancée wandered the streets. This was the first time he had thought of Marianne as a *reanimated* corpse. It made her sound like a zombie, but that's what she would be. Perhaps she would be wandering around in the crowd of revelers at the parade that would be rolling through downtown in a few hours. Was she trying to tell people about that new parading society along with the dead woman from Birmingham?

His cell phone rang and vibrated. It moved across the disgusting table with each electric shudder. Ashe grabbed it and looked at the number on the small screen. It was Marianne's. He pressed the green answer button.

"Hello."

"Dr. Shrove," a flat, emotionless voice said. It was not that of Marianne.

"You've got him."

"My name is Anne Askew. I believe we have met before one night in downtown Mobile."

"I thought your name was Carol Heinz," Ashe said.

"I do not know the woman, but I do know Cybil Fairchild. Do you know her, Dr. Shrove?"

"Where is she? Let me speak to her."

"You are in no position to make demands. We have something that you want, and you have something that my master wants. He believes that everyone can come to an agreement."

Ashe stared at the table. The coffee rings began to dance as he thought about what was being told to him. Why had the police left him alone? Weren't they supposed to stay and protect him? His phone might be bugged. He thought about that for a moment, but didn't know how. The military used satellites to listen in on suspected terrorists' cell phone conversations, but he doubted that the Mobile police had those kinds of resources.

"Are you still there, Dr. Shrove?" Askew asked.

"I'm here." Ashe thought for what seemed like a millennium but he knew it could only be a few seconds. "What do I need to do, and how do I know that Cybil is safe?"

"I will text you a picture of her and a message. Follow those instructions. Goodbye, Dr. Shrove."

The phone went dead. Ashe set it back on the table. He wanted to grab it up and call the police, but what was the use? They couldn't do anything. If they could, his house wouldn't be in ashes, and Cybil wouldn't be a captive. The cell phone vibrated as the message came in. Ashe picked it up. The screen showed a fuzzy pixelated image of Cybil. She was bound to a chair, but looked unharmed as best he could tell through the distortion. The picture disappeared as a text message popped up on the screen. The vibrations of the phone tickled his hands, and he almost dropped it.

We will be for you shortly. Watch for a white van in the parking lot of your motel. It will arrive within ten minutes. Do not forget your billfold on the table.

The message burned a scar into Ashe's mind. How could they know that his billfold was on the table? He looked around the room. Cameras had to be placed somewhere to keep an eye on him. He wondered if that was why the police had not remained. They had been in on it the whole time. How else would this Anne Askew know where he was and be so close that it would only take ten minutes? The van would have had to be en route during their conversation if it was coming from Mobile. In the evening rush hour traffic, it would have had to be on the way not long after he was dropped at the motel if it was coming from somewhere south of Airport Boulevard.

Ashe put his phone in his pocket and gathered up his stuff, making sure to get his billfold. Then he stared out the window and waited for the white van to pull up. The people he dealt with weren't fooling around, and he didn't want to leave them waiting. More than his safety was on the line if he upset them.

Smalls made it to the public beach as the last of the sun's beams disappeared. The wind coming in off the gulf felt damper and colder. He tried to keep far up the beach from the water, but there were places where he had to let the surf splash at his ankles in order to keep on the hard-packed sand. No one milled around on the fishing pier or on any of the viewing areas. Smalls made his way up the soft sand. His feet felt like cold blocks of cement. Winters on the Gulf Coast weren't terrible, but the water was colder than he would have liked.

When he made it over the dune that separated the beach from the street, he found the parking lot empty. None of the businesses that had once made a steady profit opposite the beach had built back after Katrina. Smalls walked across the parking lot and then made his way down the bicycle path that ran the length of the island. He'd been there enough to know that a few service stations and tourist-trap shops were a mile or so east.

After a few minutes of walking with no one driving down Bienville Avenue, Smalls came to the major intersection on the island. To the north, the road ran over the tall bridge to the mainland and on to Mobile. A BP station sat on the corner. The large green starburst glowed in the dark. The interior lights showed a few people milling around inside the store. Smalls scurried across all the lanes of the road and into the store. The air as he entered felt like a strong trade wind blowing in from the Caribbean in the summertime. He welcomed it. His wet feet gave him a chill all over. The cashier looked at him through the bulletproof glass she had to stay behind during evening hours. Smalls never understood why places like that required the protection only at night. Service stations were just as likely to get knocked over during the daytime, but this wasn't his concern.

"I need to use your phone," he said into the metal grated hole in the glass.

The cashier looked at him. "I can't let you in here. Rules."

"It is very important. It's life and death as a matter of fact."

She shrugged. "Life or death doesn't matter to the BP corporation. Don't you remember that oil spill?"

"If you don't let me use a phone, people might die, and not from the extended effects of oil exposure, but from something so horrible, I cannot describe it."

"Drama," the cashier said. "Rules are rules. No entrance."

"Is there a pay phone around somewhere?"

The cashier looked him up and down. "You look like a priest, but you sound Amish. You do know this is the twenty-first century right? It's called a cell phone. Get one."

"I had one until I was assaulted, kidnapped and dropped off on the west end of this island. Needless to say, my legs and feet didn't get wet from me walking from my car to in here nor did I tie my hands up. I need to call the police. That's why I need the phone." Smalls held nothing back. "Don't let this little white tab of a thing fool you, I can be quite a bastard when I need to be."

"I didn't know." The cashier grabbed the phone. "I'll call 911 and stick the receiver out the door."

"I need you to call another number first," he said and gave her Ashe's cell number. He'd been able to remember it well for some reason. "And could you cut my hands free?"

She cut the tape loose and dialed the number and held the phone out. It rang several times, and then the voice mail picked up. It wasn't Ashe's voice but the prerecorded message that the phone company provided on some phones that didn't say a person's name, just their number. Smalls left a quick message about being alive and on Dauphin Island. He decided to not mention that he had no idea what happened to Cybil. The cashier took it back and dialed 911. The dispatcher said that she would contact the Dauphin Island police and that they should have someone to him shortly. Smalls handed the phone back to the cashier.

Smalls wished he'd gotten ahold of Ashe. He almost had it all worked out, but something wouldn't click into his mind. He had hoped that Ashe had figured something out. Maybe he had, and when they got with each other everything would fall into place just like a puzzle after the aha moment. For now, Smalls decided to roam around the small gas station and wait for the police to arrive and hopefully take him back into the city.

Security Camera: Storage Facility, Michigan Avenue, Mobile, AL, 7:25 p.m. CST

Ashe stares at a large float. It depicts an ancient ship like something the Greeks would have used. A giant painted eye stares from the side. He stands alone free of any kind of bindings. The float towers over and around him.

He turns and looks behind him. The swarthy man comes into view. Ashe has a look of recognition on his face. The swarthy man smiles and flourishes his hand toward the float.

Ashe looks back at it. He nods his head as he listens to the swarthy man. Several other people enter the room. They range in sizes from short and fat to tall and skinny. Each moves with stiff, almost robotic movements. They close in around Ashe and the other man.

Ashe stiffens and clenches his fists as the others encircle him. The swarthy man puts his hand on Ashe's shoulder. The engineer relaxes the tension in his muscles but keeps his fist tight and ready for a fight. The swarthy man flourishes his hand again. The stiff moving crowd parts, and a slender woman walks through the gap. She pushes Cybil in front of her. Tape covers her mouth and binds her hands behind her back. Ashe's hand falls out of a fist. He reaches out for her, but the swarthy man pushes his arms back down.

The dark man shakes his head in disagreement. Another hand flourish sends the tall woman and Cybil receding into the circling crowd. Ashe reaches out to her again, but it does nothing. He looks back to the swarthy man who pats him on the shoulder as if he is trying to console him. Then he takes the engineer by the arm and leads him away from the float. The crowd separates and allows them to walk away.

CHAPTER TWENTY-FOUR

"Why did you kidnap Cybil?" Ashe asked as soon as he was led into an office space in the large warehouse facility.

Mikal Czernobog rubbed his chin and smiled. "It was the only way I could get you to cooperate."

"So you *are* part of the Russian Mafia. What do you want with technology for measuring engrams? Spy stuff?" Ashe asked.

"Dr. Shrove, I am not some James Bond villain who is going to reveal my plans to you, nor am I part of the Russian Mafia."

"Then what is this?"

Ashe did not like what was going on. The people in the large area of the warehouse had moved like the woman who looked like Carol Heinz and the music producer from the bar. They all had a strange vibe to them. Czernobog gave off the strangest. He seemed more than just a strange man.

"What do you want more than anything in world, Dr. Shrove?"

"For Cybil to be safe." Ashe didn't hesitate to say that although several things floated around in his mind. He thought about asking for Marianne to be returned to him, but that seemed very stupid.

Czernobog smiled at him. His small teeth had a pearly sheen to them. "There is nothing else. You don't wish to be rich or famous? You have no desire to have some grand scientific discovery to your credit?"

Those things sounded wonderful, but all Ashe really wanted right then was for Cybil to be released and for him to be safe.

Not having to be paranoid that everyone was out to get him would be better than anything else he could imagine.

"All I want is for Cybil to be let go and be safe," Ashe repeated.

Czernobog laughed. It sounded hollow and cavernous. Ashe had never heard a laugh quite like it. The noise echoed from the Russian's mouth. It reverberated around the room like thunder and vibrated through Ashe's body like the bass at a rock concert.

"A regular Jesus Christ, aren't you," he said once his laughing stopped. "I offer you anything in this world you could want or desire, and you put others first. I will grant you this wish if you do something for me."

"What is it?"

"Make a few devices for me. One needs to broadcast audio information. The second needs to be able to record and store emotional engrams without the use of electrodes and en masse. The third is a mechanism that can place those stored engrams back into the minds of people, without electrodes."

Ashe looked at Czernobog. "The first one is easy. It's called a stereo. They've been around in America for a long time. Maybe in Soviet Russia, you didn't have them."

"I am not Russian."

"In the Ukraine then."

Czernobog's eyes burned into Ashe. He felt like the man was trying to kill him with a glare. "I need the device to broadcast a sound that is heard while delivering a hidden layer. It is easy to do with MP3 and headphones, but doesn't work through stereo speakers."

"You're the one who has been layering those songs." Ashe felt a horrible idea crash into his brain. "You killed Marianne."

"I resurrected her as well."

He clapped his hands. It sounded like the popping of a bull-whip. The door to the office opened, and Marianne walked in. Her movements were stiff and artificial like the people

Ashe had seen since being brought to the warehouse. Despite that, the woman was her.

"Marianne," he said. "How?"

She looked at Czernobog. "Who is Marianne?"

"You are," Ashe said.

"I am Ursula van Beckum," she said.

"You are Marianne and were my fiancée," Ashe said.

"My name is Ursula van Beckum, and I am no man's betrothed." She looked at Czernobog again. "Master, I do not understand."

"You are Ursula van Beckum, but your body once belonged to a woman named

Marianne. She was this man's betrothed before you took ownership of her corporeal vessel."

Ashe felt a streak of pain run between his temples. He squeezed his eyes closed and opened them again. Marianne still stood in the room, and Czernobog still sat across from him.

"This doesn't make any sense. Who are you? What is all of this? Is Archbishop Harrington trying to raise the dead or something?" Ashe asked.

The other man laughed his deep otherworldly laugh. "The archbishop has nothing to do with this. Dr. Shrove, I am who you might call the Devil."

At that moment, Ashe realized that he was surrounded by madmen. The woman in the room couldn't be Marianne. She had died. Even though he saw someone that looked like her leave the morgue, it could have been this Ursula dressed to look like her. As he stared at the woman, he thought she looked less and less like his fiancée and more like a mirage of Marianne.

"Where are your horns?" Ashe asked.

Czernobog lifted his hand into the air and squeezed it into a fist. When he opened it, flames shot up. A tongue of fire flickered for each finger with the main trunk of the hand being a large blue flame. Even as far away as Ashe was he could feel the heat of the fire. The light was more intense than any he'd ever seen, but the fire produced no smoke or smell. Czernobog wiggled his fingers. The fire moved just like flesh and bone.

The man who claimed to be the Devil drummed his flaming hand on the desk. As he did so, the fire extinguished. Long thick talons clicked on the table. The fingers attached to the claws were covered with hard red scales. Czernobog ran the claws through his hair. When he brought his hand across it from back to front, the hand changed into a tentacle like that of an octopus. He reached out with it, and it grew longer and longer until it wrapped around Ashe's neck.

The tiny suckers pricked the skin on his neck. The slimy thing began to flex. The air entering Ashe's body began to get less and less until it was cut off. Ashe looked at Czernobog and tried to speak. Nothing came out.

"What was that? I cannot hear you," he said.

As Ashe tried to speak again, the tentacle was gone, and Czernobog sat with his fingers laced together. The words came out.

"Please stop," Ashe blurted out with too much vigor.

He felt a little embarrassed by this. Had he realized that the tentacle would disappear he would have tried to control the volume of his voice to seem calm and under control.

"All you had to do was ask." The other man rubbed his forehead with both hands. Goat horns appeared where he had rubbed. "Horns, just for good measure."

Ashe looked deeply into the other man's eyes. Somewhere in there he saw the flicker of a fire. He felt like it was not a normal fire but something greater and stronger than anything he would have ever encountered in his normal everyday life. Czernobog smiled. His small teeth now looked cannibalistic. Ashe was sure that he would be devoured like so many sticks of beef jerky. The Devil folded his hands and laced his fingers together again.

"And so," he said.

"Prove to me that Cybil is safe and has not been turned into one of these." Ashe pointed to the shell of Marianne with the name of a heretic.

"I will do this."

A giant blue flame erupted from the floor less than two feet from Ashe. It put off no heat or smoke. The light from it was not harsh but almost pleasant. Inside it, he could see Cybil seated at a card table eating takeout. A man wearing a hooded sweatshirt stood just at the edge of the visible area that the flame showed.

"You've shown me some amazing tricks," Ashe said. "How

do I know this isn't one of them?"

The Devil chuckled. "I do love humans. They never take anything on face value. Speak to her. She will hear and see you."

"Cybil."

As soon as he said this, she looked directly at him. Her eyes showed both joy and terror at the same time.

"Ashe, where are you?" she asked.

"I'm with Mr. Czernobog. Are you safe?"

"So far, but I think it's only because that man wants you to do something. If it wasn't for that, I'm sure I wouldn't be."

The man in the hooded sweatshirt turned to face Ashe. He pulled the hood away from his face. Rogers beamed. His smile looked almost as ravenous as Czernobog's.

"She's probably right," Rogers said.

Before Ashe could say anything else, the flame disappeared. He looked back at the Devil with an appeal on his lips.

"That was enough. I believe you get the point," Czernobog said.

"So you offered Erik a psychological law named for him in exchange for his soul?" Ashe asked.

"No. He found the engrams on his own. I offered him something far more personal for the exclusive use of what he found, and the ability to record them."

"I figured that out," Ashe said.

"Did you now? How did you come up with the idea?"

"Brainstorming."

"Liar." Czernobog slammed his hand on the desk. The whole room shook. "You dreamed it up, literally. One night you dream about the schematic and all the programming needed.

I could give you a detailed account of that dream. Do I need to?"

Ashe looked at the floor. Somehow Czernobog knew exactly how it had happened. He'd tried hard to keep that aspect of his discovery a secret mainly to keep the media and other scientists from downplaying his idea.

"You're right."

"Of course I am, I gave you that dream. I put all the pieces together for you because you'd never figure it out yourself.

Mortals are easily distracted by the noise of life."

"I didn't sell my soul to you," Ashe said.

"Not yet, but there is always time."

"It will take more than promising me a law for me to do that."

Czernobog smiled and flourished his hand at Marianne/ Ursula. She disappeared in a puff of smoke. In her place, another blue flame flared up. Ashe watched as Rogers pulled Marianne's pants down. They began to have sex on the table that Cybil had just been eating at.

"Why are you showing me this?" Ashe said, almost crying.

"To show you what your *friend* sold his soul for." Czernobog appeared to enjoy the horror that Ashe felt. "You can blame him for Marianne's death and yourself for her resurrection."

"I didn't bring her back," Ashe said.

"Your invention did and mostly so that Erik Rogers, PhD, could do that to her corpse." The flame disappeared, and the Devil leaned across the desk and stared into Ashe's eyes. "If you don't want him to do this to Cybil's very alive body, I suggest that we get down to the brass tacks."

"So I have to build these machines, and you'll let her go," Ashe said.

"Yes, and you will have your freedom as well, barring me owning your soul."

"Why can't you do this yourself? You are the Devil," Ashe asked.

"I am not an engineer. I can only unleash people's hidden ability. They reap the benefits." He smiled. "I can, however, kill people at will."

Ashe thought the threat proved that the Devil felt vulnerable. Times when he'd dealt with people with limited abilities, they'd always seemed to try to intimidate people. Apparently, the Devil *could* only do so much. "How quickly do you need these things done?"

"We have a very short deadline to work with, by Mardi Gras."

"That's only a few days from now. There's no way I can get it done," Ashe said.

"You will be given all the help you need." The Devil broke his horns off. One turned into an old fashioned quill; the other to a scroll of parchment. "All you have to do is sign this."

Ashe looked at the quill and at the contract. Czernobog smiled at him, but the thought of Cybil safe, away from them was the most important thing he could think of.

"This is all so that you can bring Hell to earth?"

"That is an indelicate way of saying it, but you get the gist," the Devil said.

Ashe shook his head. "I'll build these things, but if I do, you don't need my name on a contract to get my soul. I'll be damned forever."

Czernobog raised an eyebrow. "How do I know that you will keep your word?"

Ashe returned the look. "I suppose we'll have to trust each other."

The Devil laughed. "It has been many a century since I entered into a verbal agreement. I look forward to this."

Chapter Twenty-Five

By the time the van from St. Joan of Arc Church got to the island, Smalls' pant legs were dry, and the salt from the gulf's water clung to the skin beneath. He raked his fingers over his ankles as the interning priest from the parish drove down the wide lanes of Rangeline Road north toward the city. The trail from his nails formed white lines down his leg. The priest who drove had said nothing since picking him up from the island. Archbishop Harrington hadn't sounded very happy when Smalls told him that he'd been dumped on Dauphin Island, but he also didn't ask any questions. The archbishop simply said that he would send a van for him.

"Where are we going?" Smalls felt he needed to know. If he was going to see Harrington, he needed to get his story in line to make sure he detailed everything.

"Archbishop Harrington wants to see you," the priest said. His voice was flat but had tinges of French to it.

Looking at him, Smalls thought he was probably French Canadian. "Are we going to St. Mary's-by-the-Bay?"

"He wants to see you at St. Joan of Arc."

"Why?"

"Ours is not to reason why. Ours is but to do and die."

The words rattled around in the older priest's head for a moment. Then they sank like lead to his feet, pulling his guts down with them. Paranoid thoughts began to turn over and over. He only got a blurry half-dazed look at the van that stranded him on the island. Although this priest was not one of the large men who assaulted him and Cybil at Ashe's house, he could just as easily be part of the whole thing. Smalls licked his lips. The van had just gone through a series of red lights at Tillman's Corner near the Walmart. They were turning to head down Government Street. Enough traffic lights stretched down this street that bailing out would be easy and might not cause much injury. He slid to the end of the bench seat close to the sliding door.

"What do you mean?" Smalls slipped his hand under the door handle.

"I always say that when I don't know why I'm supposed to do something. It is from a poem by Tennyson," the priest answered.

"I'm familiar with the poem. It just seemed like a strange response to an easy question," Smalls said. "You have to understand that I've had a stressful day, so talking about dying doesn't sit well with me. By chance you wouldn't happen to know what happened to my friends, would you?"

"I don't know anything, Father Smalls, except that I was supposed to pick you up from a gas station. They didn't even tell me why you were there."

"Kidnapped."

"You should have called the police."

"I did. They took my story down but wouldn't bring me back. Probably because I just got out of jail."

The priest turned around to look at him, disregarding the traffic down the busy street. "What?"

"I was falsely accused of murder and rape," Smalls said. "Please watch the road."

The younger priest turned back to driving. "They did know you were a priest, right?"

"Yes, but I looked like the suspect they had caught on one of the street cameras downtown. When it comes to the law, it doesn't matter what profession you are."

"Is that why someone kidnapped you?"

"I don't know. I just know someone wants me and my friends out of the way. So maybe now you can see how your quote from Tennyson was bothersome."

"I'm sorry."

The younger priest said nothing else. They drove down

Government Street past the old motels that would have been nice during Mobile's heyday, but had grown old and sketchy as the years passed. The neighborhood St. Joan of Arc Church was in was much the same as those no-tell motels: it had known better years. The van stopped, and the young priest looked back at Smalls.

"I'm supposed to let you out here," he said.

Smalls looked out the window toward the church. Light from the open church door haloed Archbishop Harrington. He opened the van door and climbed out. The driver gave just enough time for the door to close then pulled away. The archbishop stepped down the stairs from the door to the sidewalk. Smalls walked toward him.

"It's good to see you, Father Smalls."

"It's good to be here, I suppose."

The two priests met in the middle of the sidewalk. Smalls tried to enter the building, but the other took him by the arm and led him into the yard of the church.

"I don't really want to talk inside," Harrington said. "Out here I'm sure that we will not be heard."

"Has the church been compromised?"

"You know that we must always leave the doors open to those who wish to enter. I just feel safer here."

They stopped under an old live oak tree. Tendrils of Spanish moss hung from the limbs and blew in the breeze. The sky through the limbs looked brown under the lights of the city. The air smelled like a mixture of diesel exhaust and brackish water. It was an unsettling perfume.

"What's happening?" Smalls asked.

"I'm not sure, but it seems that the powers of evil have descended on this city, and for some reason have chosen to come after you and your friends."

"Why us?"

"I thought maybe you would know. You have looked these people in the eye if they kidnapped you. Didn't they talk on the way to the island?"

"They knocked me out. The last thing I remember there was a huge man in Ashe's living room. He looked unreal like a living corpse, not a zombie like in movies, but his eyes weren't right."

"I believe it may be demons possessing people," Harrington said. "That book you had Dr. Shrove looking for has been stolen with a few other volumes of your heretical texts."

"How could they steal them from the basement of St. Mary's? Surely demons cannot cross over into a church."

Harrington leaned against the tree. His hair blew in the breeze and blended in with the swaying moss. He rubbed his face. Smalls heard the scratching sound of a stubble beard. In the low light around the church, he'd only been able to make out the grosser details of the archbishop's face.

"One of the books you sent Dr. Shrove for talked about possession. It postulated that demons cannot possess humans since the death of the last disciples who were given the miracle of casting out demons."

Smalls nodded his agreement. He'd wanted that book more than any other. "I needed that one the most. I almost have my finger on something, but needed to reread it."

"It said that demons cannot possess people because they cannot handle humans' past memories. Once they enter, they stay only until they are so overwhelmed by memories that they must flee or perish." The archbishop looked at Smalls. The priest tried to hide any emotion from his face but knew he must look amazed that the other had read the text. "I wanted to see why the book was considered blasphemous."

"I remembered that, but if you remember when I talked to you the first time about Ashe we discussed that his fiancée supposedly rose from the dead and walked out of University Hospital's morgue. Maybe the demons have possessed the dead," Smalls said.

"Only Christ is the king of dead," Archbishop Harrington said. "Satan cannot rule over a dead body, and that book postulates it is because demons must have emotions to exist."

"Dead people don't have emotions," Smalls said as if he'd suddenly been given this as an epiphany.

"I do not know what is going to happen, but I'm not sure we can resist it. Ash Wednesday is upon us, and I fear that something bad is going to happen before it gets here. The Devil is the strongest during this period of temptation."

"What happened to Ashe and Cybil?"

"Dr. Shrove's house burned to the ground. There was no sign of Cybil or him there, so I don't know."

Smalls crossed himself then rubbed the edges of his forehead. His eyes burned with tears for his friends. Both men stood a long time in silence. The cool February air whipped around them with every breeze.

"What now?" Smalls asked.

"I want you to stay here at the church. The monsignor has made provisions for you in one of the classrooms." The archbishop reached into his pocket and brought out a cell phone. He handed it to Smalls. "I assumed that yours has been lost or destroyed."

"That would be correct."

"I made arrangements for this one to have your old number, just in case Cybil or Dr. Shrove try to contact you. Be safe, Father Smalls."

Archbishop Harrington patted Smalls on the shoulder and walked off. Smalls stood under the tree a little bit longer. The wind chilled his skin, but the thought of Ashe and Cybil being at whereabouts unknown chilled him to the bone.

Traffic Camera: Intersection of St. Ann and Government Streets, Mobile, AL, 9:34 p.m. CST

A black Lincoln Continental idles behind a white van with the windows covered over from the inside by canvas material. The van's right turn signal blinks, but the vehicle remains stopped. The Lincoln flashes its lights at the van. Three large men lumber from the back of the van. One steps in front of the car. Another hurries to the rear passenger side. The Lincoln lurches and tries to shift to the left to get around the van. The third man runs to driver's door and tries to open it. When he fails, he rams his elbow into the window, shattering it. A black-clad arm fights against the third man as he paws inside the car. The third man grabs hold of the driver's arm and pulls him through the window. The driver falls to the road as the

Continental rolls slowly into the rear of the van.

The third man stomps his foot down on the head of the driver until a pool of dark blood forms around the head. As this happens, the second man pulls the rear door open. He drags Archbishop Harrington from the vehicle. The first man helps the second to secure the archbishop. They carry him back to the van. The third man finishes crushing the driver's head into the pavement then joins the other men. The van turns right onto Government Street. The Lincoln rolls through the intersection leaving the dead driver bleeding on Ann Street.

CHAPTER TWENTY-SIX

Ashe's eyes burned, and his back ached. He'd been hunched over a worktable for he didn't know how long, but it felt like years. Czernobog had stuck him in a room fitted out better than any university electronics or engineering lab he'd ever seen. Several of the undead heretics milled around the room as well. The Devil assigned them to shadow what he did so that they would be able to make more of the recorders in the amount of time needed. Cybil stayed trapped somewhere in the warehouse. The thought of her slowed Ashe down as he worked. He wanted her to be safe, and Czernobog promised it would be so if he kept working. Ashe couldn't help but wonder how much he could trust the Devil.

"Dr. Shrove." The sound of the voice so heavily accented twisted into Ashe's spine.

He turned to see Czernobog standing behind him. A small smile was on the Devil's face. He looked almost pleasant and welcoming.

"Yes."

"I think that you can stop for the evening. I don't want you to get exhausted and make an inferior product. My whole plan relies on these things working as effectively as possible."

Ashe rubbed his eyes and stood up. The muscles in his back and neck thanked him for letting them stretch. He reached over his head, bouncing on his tiptoes. "Thank you. I felt like I might snap."

"I may be the Devil, but when I have a deal I try to take care of my investment." The smile remained the same while he spoke. "I have made arrangements for you to have a small place to sleep here at the warehouse."

"Is it with Cybil?" Ashe asked.

"I am afraid not. I cannot allow you two to stay with each other. You might come up with a scheme for escape."

"Can I at least see her before you cloister me away?"

Czernobog laughed. It fell flat in the room, a joyless sound. "You make it sound like you are monk, Dr. Shrove. You also make it sound like I am forcing you to do this."

"Aren't you?"

"No. You agreed to do this, and you can walk away at any time you want. Just remember that we have a verbal agreement and breaking it would result in me keeping to my promise."

Ashe's mouth ran dry like a drainage ditch in August. The other man's eyes did not have an ounce of dishonesty in them when he spoke those words. He realized that he could trust the Devil, that he might be the only thing in the whole universe he could trust to keep his word one way or the other.

"So can I at least see her?"

"I am afraid she has already been moved to my other facility. I promise that she is safe though and that Dr. Rogers is far, far away from her." The creepy smile still crossed his lips. "I have him on another mission tonight."

Czernobog put his hand on Ashe's arm and started moving him toward the door. The undead *engineers* still worked at their engram machines. They moved slowly and with stiff motions. He wondered if they were nimble enough to make the precise connections and manipulations to work on such sensitive instruments. Ashe allowed himself to be pushed through the door of the lab and back into the cavernous work area of the warehouse where a float was being constructed. Czernobog followed him, closing the door behind him.

They walked past the float as other undead heretics attached decoration to it. The float looked like nothing Ashe had seen at the parades he'd been to. The colors were dark. The whole of the body of the float appeared to be black velvet and a bloodred moon hung over all.

"It's the final float," Czernobog said. "That's when your invention gets to come into its own. It will be glorious."

The Devil sounded like a madman at the moment. Ashe

found it a little funny. He choked back a laugh. Czernobog stared at him. His eyes flashed with hellfire.

"I need something from my office at the university," Ashe said.

"I don't think so."

"If you want these things to work right, then you'll reconsider."

"Tell me what it is; I am sure my people can find it with no problem."

"I don't think so. It's on my computer and saved behind lots of security."

"I am the Devil, and you think a series of passwords can confound me."

"Actually, yes I do."

Czernobog's visage changed. The lines in his face became deep and dark as if coal dust had settled in them. The whiskers of his beard ruffled. "Who do you think you are? How dare you say such to me?"

Ashe saw that the other man's teeth had sharpened to points, and his tongue appeared forked. "You know I'm right. You told me that you were no engineer. If you could manage technology, you wouldn't need any of this."

The Devil wrapped his fingers around Ashe's neck and squeezed. He felt the power in the Devil's grasp. His windpipe clamped off, and no air seeped into his lungs. The other man stared at him.

"What makes you think I cannot?" Czernobog asked and let his grip go.

Ashe reached up and touched his own throat. He rubbed it where the crushing grip hand been the tightest. It took a few moments for the air to fill his lungs up enough for him to speak. His mind already had his answer back to the Devil.

"Because you let me go."

Czernobog quivered. "I will take you there myself. Any trickery and I let Rogers have her and make you watch. After Rogers rapes her, you can watch every male I have under my control do the same thing until she dies. I am Satan, Prince of Darkness. I will not be mocked."

Every inch of the large room smelled of sulfur, and yellow smoke floated in the air. At that moment, Czernobog looked more like a demon than a man. Ashe understood that the Devil meant what he said, but he needed access to his computer because if he didn't get the algorithms he needed, the engram machines wouldn't work. The Devil would kill them all anyway.

"I have no tricks in mind. Without my algorithms, this won't work. They are far too complicated for me to memorize."

Smalls lay on his very uncomfortable cot. A poster with a cartoon Noah looked down at him. A mobile of the days of Creation twirled above his head. Light from the street shone straight in his face, but the small size of the classroom that had been set up as his bedroom made moving his cot to a different position just about impossible. His new cell phone lay on his chest. The priest willed it to buzz or beep and let him know what had become of Ashe and Cybil. Then it did.

The small mechanism's vibration tickled down deep into his chest. He snatched it up and looked at the LED screen. The deep green letters scrawled there said he had an email.

Smalls pressed the okay button, and the message popped up. He scanned it quickly, looking for the sender. It was from Ashe. He quickly read it.

Smalls,

Cybil and I have been kidnapped. I don't have time to detail what has happened. Send me back some religious incantation that wards off demons. Do it now. I won't have another chance to check my email.

Smalls jumped up from his cot, but drew a blank on anything to reply with. Any other time, he would have seven or eight such incantations on the tip of tongue. He wondered why Ashe needed something like that and what was happening. If the message was truthful and his friend might not have another opportunity to check his email, he didn't want to waste it with a question instead of the information that was requested.

Like a bolt of lightning, one of the incantations came to him.

Smalls flipped out the keyboard on his phone and started spelling out the words. It was a rough translation of a Buddhist mantra, but it was all he had right then. After a quick check to make sure autocorrect hadn't fixed anything, he finished the email with *where are you*. Green letters scrawled across the screen that said the email had been sent. Smalls stood staring at the little cell phone screen like a kid watching some great toy commercial during Saturday morning cartoons. It seemed as if an eternity passed. The screen remained dim, and so did Smalls' hope of a response. He tucked the phone into his pocket and sat back down on his cot.

In times of great doubt and distress there were few things better for a priest to do than pray. So he did. As soon as he crossed himself after uttering amen softly to himself, the phone vibrated. He slipped his hand into his pocket and brought the phone out.

I don't know, but I think it's the warehouse where the Mystics of Mayhem are building their floats. I think that Detective Semmes knew about it.

Smalls read the email and knew what he had to do whether he wanted to or not. He would have to contact the Mobile police and find out what they knew about Semmes' investigation. It probably meant they would think he was crazy. He got up and put his shoes on because he figured there was no better time than the present to get things started.

Ashe sat in the back seat of a Jeep Cherokee. The windows were darkly tinted. Next to him, Czernobog drummed his fingers together. One of the undead heretics drove them back down Michigan Avenue toward the warehouse. It felt strange that with all he had experienced in the last few hours the proximity of the warehouse to the university was what bothered him the most. He thought the feeling might be what it's like to realize you were being stalked after the person was caught.

"How much of a problem do you think it will be to get those devices up and running before Mardi Gras night with those algorithms?" Czernobog asked.

"Not much. The algorithms are the linchpin in the whole

recording engram formula. I'll just have to make a few adjustments so that the matrix holds up when you reverse them en masse."

"And you can do that, easily?"

"With all the equipment set up back at the warehouse, very easily."

The Devil smiled his confident smile. He drummed his fingers together harder. Ashe could see the cogs turning in the demon's mind. Something big was in the works. He wished that he could jump out of the car and make a run for it, but knew that wasn't going to happen. Czernobog assured him that the doors would only open from the outside and that the windows were locked.

Cogs turned in Ashe's mind as well. Smalls had given him an incantation that should ward off demons. He would have a little trick up his sleeve for the Devil, and now that he was positive that Czernobog couldn't read minds, he wasn't afraid of doing it. Ashe almost wanted to drum his fingers together like the Devil, but instead he watched the very dim lights of the city pass by as they rode on toward the warehouse.

Security Camera: Morgue Room 1, Singing River Hospital, Pascagoula, MS, 12:59 a.m. CST

A doctor and his assistant stand over the body of a small African-American woman. A slender microphone headset rests on the doctor's head. He speaks into the microphone.

"Beginning autopsy of Debra Henry, identified only by the driver's license in her purse. Person, who wished to remain anonymous, brought patient into this hospital's emergency department, DOA. Claimed he found her in a parking lot off of Highway 98. Cause of death unknown and thus the reason for the autopsy. Dr. Simon K. Folds is dictating and performing the autopsy at 12:59 a.m."

The doctor reaches for a large sawlike instrument on the tray table beside him. The assistant removes the white sheet covering the corpse's torso. The sound of a metal door slamming open is picked up by the microphone. The doctor and his assistant look toward the far wall. Two large men lumber into the room. Erik Rogers follows them.

"What are you doing here?" the doctor asks. "No unauthorized persons are allowed in this room."

One of the large men advances on the doctor. He knocks the autopsy instrument to the floor and snaps the doctor's neck in one move. The assistant looks from the doctor crumpled on the floor to the men and runs away.

"Don't worry about him." Rogers' voice is faint and sounds like it is spoken from one end of a cavern. "Stand guard outside and make sure no one else comes in."

Both men lumber out the way they came. Rogers walks to the woman. He takes a small box from his pocket. Electrode pads dangle from wires attached to the device. He places the pads on the woman's head in selected areas. After Rogers presses a button on the mechanism twice, the woman sits up on the table and removes the pads from her head. She stands, and Rogers motions for her to leave the room. He winds the wires around the small device and shoves it back into his pocket. Kneeling down beside the dead doctor, he removes the microphone headset and straightens.

"Testing: one, two, three." His voice is loud and breathy sounding from the proximity to the dictation microphone. "Just to let whoever finds this tape know." He points to the camera then waves. "I killed this woman about half an hour before I brought her into the ER, and now, she's walking out a new woman. Try and catch me."

Rogers cackles and drops the microphone. Feedback squeals out when it hits the hard floor. He smiles at the camera and blows a kiss toward it before walking out of the autopsy room.

CHAPTER TWENTY-SEVEN

Smalls hadn't slept. All he could do was pace around the classroom that had been made his temporary quarters. After he rushed to the police station downtown, the sergeant on duty told him that no one was there at that time of night that could help him, but he could check back in the daylight. The problem was it took daylight forever to get there, and worse, it was a Saturday morning. The detective he needed to speak to wouldn't be there, but as soon at his watch told him it was 8 a.m., he lit out for the police station again.

It took him about half an hour to walk from St. Joan of Arc Church to the police station. Cold rain drizzled on his way there, which made him walk faster. When he stepped into the police station, the officer who had told him to come back in the morning was still on duty.

"Father," he said. "I'm glad you came back."

"I told you that I would. It's imperative that I speak to Detective Cooper."

"It's imperative I speak to you." Cooper came from behind a cubicle partition. "I called the number we had for you, and St. Mary's-by-the-Bay."

"What is it? Have you found Ashe or Cybil?"

"I don't really want to talk about this in the open. Come to my office."

Smalls followed Cooper into the bowels of the police station. Her office was unkempt with Styrofoam coffee cups sitting all over her desk. Papers of different sizes and colors spilled from piles. She sat behind her desk. The area in front of her was the only area devoid of clutter. Smalls sat across from her.

"I'm glad to see that you are well," Cooper said.

"That's surprising since the last time we saw each other I was sure you wanted me nailed to the wall by my scrotum."

"I did, but that was before I found out you were innocent."

"I'm glad to know that the police are impartial, but what about Ashe and Cybil?"

Cooper flipped open a tan manila folder that lay on a precarious pile of forms. She took out three pieces of paper and handed them to him. "I was hoping you could tell me. Those are pictures from a motel room up in Saraland. I left Dr. Shrove there yesterday evening with express instructions to stay put and only answer calls from me. When he didn't answer his phone, I sent a patrol to check on him. That's what they found."

Smalls examined the pictures. They showed a motel room badly in need of updating. All the colors and fabrics looked like they had stepped out of a 1970s porno. The bed was made. One bedside lamp glowed from under the orange shade. It appeared no one had been in the room.

"I don't see anything wrong. Am I overlooking something?" he asked.

"Yeah, Dr. Shrove. That room doesn't look like anyone has been in it, although I dropped him off there myself."

"He contacted me late last night and said that he'd been kidnapped. Probably by the same people that broke into his house and left me on Dauphin Island. He said that he was sure they had him in the warehouse that Detective Semmes checked out on Michigan Avenue that belonged to that parading society."

Cooper shook her head. "I doubt that. After Semmes' body was found, we sent some officers to that place. It was completely empty. Some Russian guy said he owned the place and was waiting for a supply of Eastern European goods to come in. He said he was opening an import business."

"Are you sure they went to the right place? I'm sure that Ashe wasn't lying."

"What else did he say?"

"He wanted me to email him an incantation against demons."

Cooper's eyes widened, and it appeared she tried to hold back a laugh. "Demons?"

"You've taken over Semmes' case about Ashe's girl-friend walking out of the morgue over at University Hospital. Archbishop Harrington, he's over the Archdioceses of Mobile, and I had been working under an assumption that her disap-pearance might be demonic in nature. One of the things I study is psychoreligious phenomena. I'm an expert in it."

The detective reared back in her chair and rubbed her face. Before saying anything else, she took a few more pages from the manila folder and handed them to Smalls. He looked at the top one. A grainy black and white image showed a black car behind a white van. Three large men stood around the car. One appeared to be stomping the head of the car's driver with his foot. He flipped to the next picture. Another of the men man-handled what looked like Harrington. The third picture was of the white van pulling away. Smalls set those photos on top of the ones from the motel room.

"What does that mean?" he asked.

"Archbishop Harrington has apparently been kidnapped. Those men indeed killed his driver, a Father Thomas, by smash-ing his head into the pavement. It happened late last night at the intersection of Ann and Government."

"I had no idea."

"We're keeping it a secret, along with this." She took some more pictures and handed them over.

These were of a morgue. The time and date were stamped on the corner. He thumbed through the pages. They acted almost like an old-fashioned flipbook as he watched the corpse on the table sit up and walk out. He also recognized two of the people in the photo. One was the assailant from Ashe's house. The other was Erik Rogers.

"That's Dr. Erik Rogers," he said. "He's a colleague of mine at Tech. One of the big men attacked Cybil and me at Ashe's house yesterday."

"That Dr. Rogers' body type and style of clothing match the man on the surveillance video of the Amanda Moore murder. The van that was used to kidnap Archbishop Harrington was the same one that dumped Semmes' body," Cooper said.

"Rogers was also working with Ashe on recording emotion

engrams." Smalls' words tapered off as he became lost in deep contemplation.

The tumblers began to click into place and the door that led to the memories Smalls had been trying to find opened. Somehow Rogers had figured out that demons couldn't possess the dead because they didn't have emotions. He used Ashe's device to put emotions into the corpses and allow the demons to possess them. When Cybil heard the two men in Rogers' office, they wanted his engram recordings. Those were the ones that he used for *research*. The people bringing back the dead were using his engrams gathered for studies to allow the possession of dead bodies.

"We've got to find Rogers," he said.

"I've already tried. He's not at home or at Alabama Tech. Any idea where he might be?"

"Have you tried that warehouse again?"

"Why would I? It's a dead lead, Father Smalls. You might be an expert on the paranormal, but police work is my forte." Cooper took the pictures and stuck them back into the folder.

"This may be both. I think it's worth a shot."

"I guess it's better than any lead I have right now. Let me get an officer to go with us out there, just in case."

Smalls nodded and then crossed himself. The detective gave him a skeptical look.

"Just in case," he said.

The ride to the large warehouse on Michigan Avenue not far from St. Joan of Arc Church took only a few minutes. Cooper made Smalls ride in the back of the unmarked car. The uniformed officer drove, and she rode shotgun. A high fence surrounded the whole compound, so they had to park across the street.

"I'll do all the talking," Cooper said as they crossed the street.

"Do you know all the questions to ask?" Smalls asked.

"I'm a detective. Asking questions is my job."

They stopped at the fence. A talk box hung from a thigh-high metal pole near the gate. Cooper pressed the button under the speaker.

A rigid-sounding voice came over the box. "Can I help you?"

"I am Detective Cooper with the Mobile Police Department. I need to ask the owner of this warehouse a few questions. Do you think I could come in?"

The speaker went silent. Cooper looked at her watch. Smalls decided to do the same thing. It seemed to him like they were getting a cool reception. The traffic on the street seemed brisk. Several different kinds of personal vehicles drove past. A few of those blasted varieties of loud music that could be heard clearly even though the windows were up. Two tractor-trailers rumbled past. Foul-smelling diesel exhaust wafted around them. Smalls coughed. The caustic odor always nauseated him. The back of his tongue felt heavy as if he might vomit right there. He bent over enough to hopefully alleviate the symptoms.

"Are you okay?" the officer asked.

"Diesel fumes just get to me a little bit. I think I'm going to be okay."

"Buck up," Cooper said. "I thought you'd be made of stronger stuff."

Smalls straightened back up. "Even the hardest stuff cracks under enough pressure. Don't you think we've been standing here for a little too long?"

"I was just about to do something about that."

Cooper reached to press the button again, when the speaker crackled and popped.

"Can I help you?"

The heavy accent in the voice sounded Eastern European or Russian to Smalls. The wave of nausea subsided. He felt they had found the right place. Cybil had told them she'd overheard Rogers talking with a man who sounded Russian. Although Mobile was a major port city, he hadn't run into many Russians in his time living there.

"This is the police," Smalls blurted out before Cooper could say anything. "We have questions, and we want answers. No is not going to suffice as one though."

The detective pushed him so hard that he almost tripped over his feet. She mouthed for him to shut up, but he had no intention right now.

"Do you have a warrant?"

"We don't need one," Smalls answered. "You're not accused of anything, we just need some answers about a missing persons report in the area. If you want us to, we'll be happy to get one and haul you downtown."

"That will not be necessary. You may come in."

The speaker crackled, but the fence popped as the electric pulley engaged. The gate slid open, shuddering as it did so. Cooper stepped through the gate first, followed by the uniformed officer. Smalls brought up the rear. The detective kept staring back at him as they walked across the small paved area between the gate and the door. He was sure if she could have she'd have put a bullet between his eyes with her service revolver. They stopped at the door, which was locked.

"What happened to letting me do the talking?"

"Heat of the moment," Smalls said. "Besides that guy sounded Russian."

"What does that have to do with anything?"

"Cybil said that she overheard Erik—Dr. Rogers—talking to a Russian and sounding like they were engaged in some bad business."

"That still doesn't justify why you talked. You're not even a cop."

Smalls decided to tip his hand on this one before Cooper exploded. "I think Erik is involved in demonic activity. Those photos you have of him from Mississippi should tell you he's into something serious. Besides murder, he did resurrect the dead."

Cooper snorted in derision. "So you think this Russian guy is a Devil worshiper? Didn't we decide all that stuff was an urban legend?"

"I don't think he's a Satanist." Smalls licked his lips and took a deep breath. He hadn't uttered his suspicion aloud yet for fear that Cooper would think he was out of his mind, but she needed to know just in case. "I think he *is* Satan."

The uniformed officer burst out with a loud laugh. Smalls watched Cooper's mouth drop lower than he imagined a human mouth could do. Her eyes said that she wanted to laugh and curse at him at the same time, but before anything else could be said the door rattled and swung open. A short, swarthy man stood framed in the door. His dark eyes looked as if there was no difference between his pupil and iris, as if there was a huge hole in the sclera. He smiled to show small teeth, precisely lined up in his mouth.

"What questions can I answer for you?" he asked.

Cooper looked at him. Her mouth slowly closed. Smalls could tell that she was a bit surprised by him, almost as much as he was. She swallowed.

"May we come inside? It's a bit cool, and we've been standing out here for a while," she said.

"No. I am afraid that I cannot allow you inside, although I am happy to answer your questions." He looked at Smalls. "I thought you were all police officers."

"We are." Cooper pointed to Smalls. "He's a priest, but he is assisting us in finding this missing person."

"Oh really?"

"Yes. Can I get your name for the record?" she asked.

"I am Mikal Czernobog. C-Z-E-R-N-O-B-O-G."

"Archbishop Harrington, the head of the Archdiocese of Mobile, was kidnapped not far from here last night. His driver was killed. I was wondering if you have seen anything unusual."

Czernobog smiled. "I am looking at something unusual right now. How often do American police officers carry a priest around with them?"

"Not often, but have you seen the archbishop?" Smalls stepped toward Czernobog.

"I do not know. I have never seen the man to know what he looks like."

"Do you know Dr. Erik Rogers or Dr. Ashley Shrove?" Smalls pressed.

"No."

"What about Cybil Fairchild, Marianne Lenard, or Amanda 'Hortense' Moore?"

"Father Smalls, please," Cooper said.

Czernobog licked across his teeth and narrowed his eyes. "No, and I believe that we are done with the line of questioning. If you want more, I suggest getting a warrant. I may not know much of your laws, but I know about that."

"We understand." Cooper grabbed Smalls around the arm and pulled him away from the warehouse.

The uniformed officer tipped his hat to Czernobog and followed. The Russian remained in the doorway watching them. When they were through the gate, it began to close. Smalls jerked himself free from Cooper and grabbed hold of the chain link.

"What about Francisco de San Roman? Ever heard of him?"

Czernobog looked at him as he began to back into the gloom on the other side of the open door. "I have. He was burned as a heretic a long time ago. I don't think you need worry about him being kidnapped."

"I know. Thanks."

Smalls watched the Russian close himself back into the warehouse. He stepped away from the fence and back to the car. Cooper drummed her fingers on the top of the car. She looked livid.

"What was that about?" she asked. "I ought to arrest you for hindering an investigation."

"I haven't hindered anything. I just proved that he knows everything."

"How do you figure that?"

"Why else would he become so angry when I mentioned such random names? Also, he knew who Francisco de San Roman was."

"What does that prove?" Cooper asked.

"Do you know who he was?" She shook her head. "Neither did I until a met a man claiming to be him. It turns out that like Czernobog said, he was burned at the stake over 500 years ago."

"So Satan and a dead heretic are doing all this?" Cooper asked, sliding into the car.

Smalls crawled into the back seat. "That's what the archbishop thought, and told me the night he was kidnapped. I believe it too, especially since there is supposed to be a demon named Czernobog."

Cooper looked at the uniformed officer. "Not a word about this to anyone."

CHAPTER TWENTY-EIGHT

"What are you doing?"
Ashe raised up on his elbows and opened his eyes. Rogers leaned against the doorjamb. He held a tray with a steaming bowl of something on it.

"Napping. I have a headache."

"This will make you feel better, a big bowl of tomato soup, with little oyster crackers," Rogers said.

His tone was playful as if everything going on was some great big game. Ashe sat up and swung his legs off the cot. A sharp pain streaked across his temples. The time he'd spent bent over the engram mechanisms in not so good light had taken its toll on his eyes. With eyestrain came a headache, it was always the way.

"I think Advil and a day off would be better."

Rogers walked over and handed Ashe the tray. "You should ask Czernobog about that.

I'm sure he'd give you a break."

Ashe swallowed a spoonful of soup with a soggy cracker. "I'd rather not. The less amount of time I have to spend with him the better."

"You don't know what he can give you. Anything you want, and pow, it's yours." Rogers snapped his fingers. "Look at me."

"I've seen you. I don't want to be you. The Devil has nothing to offer me."

"You are a horrible liar, Ashe."

"Dr. Shrove. Only my friends call me Ashe."

"I am your friend. I wanted you included in this bottle rocket ride. We can have anything we want. Don't you understand? We can be the kings of the world."

"Kings of a world of zombies." Ashe handed the tray back to Rogers and stood up. "You sold your soul for a good body and sex with my fiancée."

"And every other woman or man I want. Don't forget about the fame as well."

"But for what, Erik? What does it really accomplish?"

"Everyone knows who I am and always will."

"Don't you understand that there isn't going to be anyone left to care? I'm making those things so that everyone around the parade on Tuesday turns into a possessed corpse, just like Marianne, who you've been raping."

"Why are you helping if this is so bad?"

"Because I want Cybil to be safe, and he promised that he would let her go, if I helped him." Ashe knew he had selfish motives.

"You don't think he'll go back on his offer? He is the Devil."

"If he does, then I'll go back on mine."

"Whatever. I'm feeling horny; I think I'll go get me a piece of zombie Marianne."

Rogers grabbed his crotch and squeezed then walked out, closing the door behind him. Ashe kicked his cot across the room. It hit the far wall, and one of the legs broke off. He snatched the broken leg from the floor and started smashing things around the room. A small electrical meter flew from a table and slammed against the wall. Pieces of plastic and metal clattered to the floor. An empty glass with milk residue on the sides met the floor and the fate of a thousand pieces. The box with several completed engram recorders sat near the edge of a table. The heretic zombies had left them there for him to troubleshoot.

He swept the box from the table, and the recorders scattered across the floor. Ashe raised his foot to stomp the first one. The tiny blue device that looked like an innocent thumb drive had a picture of Czernobog on it. His mind had produced that image. He eased his foot back down. If those devices didn't work then Ashe would have reneged on his word and Cybil would be as good as a blow-up doll for Roger's use. It didn't matter too much; eventually they'd all be possessed corpses anyway. There was the better plan of using the email from Smalls. He bent down and scooped the little plastic sticks up and put them back in their box. The devil left him a computer to work on. It wasn't connected to the Internet, but Ashe had his thumb drive with engram algorithms on it. He popped it into the hard drive tower and pulled up the formulas. The string of letters and numbers blurred together. His head hurt, and his eyes wouldn't stay focused for long at a time, but he had work to do for his own soul's sake.

Smalls stood in the hall outside of Rogers' office along with Cooper. He was surprised that she had let him come along after her almost losing it when he took over the interrogation of the Russian. She knew that he had insight into Rogers that others might not and that had won out over her anger.

"Open this thing," she said.

"I don't have a key," Smalls said.

"I didn't say unlock it. I said open it."

He decided to take out a little frustration. A hard kick with all the effort he could put into it broke the door away from the jamb. It swung open. Cooper stopped it before it could recoil closed. They stepped inside. The place looked like a bomb had gone off. Smalls knew

Rogers well and had never seen him so disorganized. Papers lay everywhere. The trash can was overturned. Empty Diet Coke bottles made a zigzag from the plastic bin. A brown dust covered most of his desk and chair. The whole place smelled faintly of chocolate. Cooper eyed the dust on the desk.

"What is that stuff?" she asked.

Smalls looked on the floor around the desk and under it. He saw a plastic tub and brought up to be viewed. "Just like I thought, protein powder. Chocolate flavored. Erik drinks the stuff like mother's milk."

"A bodybuilder?"

"Only recently. After he discovered how to record emotions, he went on this weight loss kick and dropped mega pounds and beefed up a little. I guess he thought fame would be better if he were in shape," Smalls said.

"Is he always this messy? He makes me look like *Good Housekeeping* magazine."

"Never. He likes to keep everything in order so he can find it easily. I think someone has come in here looking for something." Cooper flipped on the light. The room filled with harsh fluorescent light. She tapped on a filing cabinet. "Look at this."

Smalls walked over. It looked like the lock on the filing cabinet had been melted away. There was a circle on the side of the cabinet where the lock would have been and a long line of melted metal ran from it like a steel teardrop. Black soot surrounded the hole. He ran his finger around the edge of the hole. It was smooth as if finished by a master metal worker.

"What could have done that?" he asked.

"A blow torch. People use them all the time to get into safes." He took her finger and put it into the hole. "It's smooth, too smooth."

She opened the top drawer. A fireproof box sat in the otherwise empty drawer. The lid was open after the lock mechanism had been burned off just like the one on the filing cabinet.

"What about that?" Smalls ran his finger around that burned area as well.

"I don't know. Why wouldn't they just take the box and open it elsewhere?"

"Because he didn't have to," Smalls said, lifting the box out of the drawer. A slight smell of sulfur wafted up to him as he did so. "The Devil has great power."

"Not that again."

"Smell." He shoved the box under her nose. "Just like rotten eggs, right? It's not though. That's the smell of brimstone. I believe that we are dealing with satanic powers and plots beyond anything we can hope to handle. If we arrest Rogers, it will get worse."

Cooper looked worried. "At least he may be able to answer some questions."

"I don't believe that will happen." The tone of the voice fell flat.

Cooper jumped, and Smalls turned around. He already knew what he would find standing in the doorway. Sure enough, the man who claimed to be the manager for the Goth Sox filled up the only way out of the room. His face remained steely calm and stone firm. The eyes had as much personality as the flat verbalizations.

"Who are you?" Cooper asked.

"Francisco San Roman."

"A heretic burned at the stake many centuries ago, am I right?" Smalls asked.

"Heretic is a harsh word. Only those who burn others for their beliefs and practices would use such a word."

"He looks good to be a long dead heretic," Cooper said. "Only looks about 45 or so."

"That's because the body isn't that old. The soul is that of Francisco de San Roman," Smalls said. "Why are you here?"

"My master wants to know the same of you. You do not have the right to be in this place."

"Where is Dr. Rogers?" Cooper asked. "He's wanted for questioning about a murder in Pascagoula."

San Roman cocked his head to one side and seemed to be studying the two of them. To Smalls it appeared that the man had to process who she might be talking about. The large man remained silent for a little too long. It made him seem unreal or at least out of sync with the current reality.

"I do not know of whom you speak."

"Don't give me that crap. You know exactly who I'm talking about. Now that I've gotten a good look at you, I'm pretty sure you assisted him in the murder of Amanda Moore in the old dock parking lot a few nights ago."

"I do not know what you are talking about."

This time San Roman answered too quickly to be truthful. Cooper eyed him just like Smalls expected a seasoned detective to do when dealing with a liar.

"Where's the man who owns this office?" Smalls asked.

"I will not tell you. My master gave me one duty and that is to eliminate you both."

"The power and light of God and our Lord Jesus Christ compels you to answer me." Smalls fished his rosary and crucifix from his pocket. He pushed it out in front of him.

San Roman laughed a deep hollow laugh. It sounded like a corpse laughing. All the joy associated with such an action, even when villainous, was not present in the noise coming from him.

"Although we know of God and the power He has, your petty attempt at evoking that power does nothing to stop me."

He advanced into the room. Smalls and Cooper retreated a little deeper into the office. The priest fought with himself on the inside. He should not fear something like San Roman. The power of God was with him. As the looming heretic-possessed corpse kept lumbering into the room, Smalls searched through all his knowledge of paranormal religious activities. The email he had sent to Ashe popped to the front of his mind. The Buddhist incantation to make evil spirits and good spirits live in harmony might do the trick.

"I can destroy you," Smalls said. A look of derision came on San Roman's face. It surprised the priest. He thought that the reanimated corpse couldn't have an affective response. "I will if you do not cooperate."

"I hope that it is better than your last try, priest."

San Roman grabbed Smalls by the front of his shirt and pulled him closer. The hair on the back of Smalls' neck stood on end. The feel of the other man's grasp was as unearthly as his countenance. Now the heretic's other hand reached for his neck.

"Where is Ashe Shrove?" Smalls twisted his head from the hand.

"I do not know of who you speak."

Smalls began to chant the Buddhist exorcism prayer. He did so in the English translation. A slight tremble from San Roman's hand ruffled his shirt. The heretic retracted his other hand, and his grip on Smalls slipped. The priest pushed himself away from the heretic. Something was happening. He continued to chant the mantra over and over.

The large man backed up, stumbling over his feet and slamming against the doorjamb. The whites of his eyes became visible as they rolled back into his head. It looked like San Roman was having a seizure. Smalls pressed on with the mantra. The room began to change. Objects elongated as if being pulled toward the door by a strong magnet. The overhead lights blew. One of the fluorescent tubes shattered. Bits of powdery glass showered down on Smalls. He closed his eyes and continued.

San Roman screamed. It sounded like nothing Smalls had ever heard before. He opened his eyes and looked at the man. The whites of the eyes had not just turned black but looked to be blistering as if the thing inside the corpse was being incinerated. Cooper screamed. Smalls had forgotten about her. He had no idea what effect the mantra had on her if any.

More loud pops filled the air, but nothing showered down. Instead a spray of deep red blood spewed from San Roman. The body was hurled against the door by the mantra and crumpled to the floor. The horrible screaming of someone being burned alive ended. Smalls was certain that he saw something like a dark shadow float from the eye sockets of the corpse and disappear like smoke.

"The power of 9mms compels you," Cooper said.

Smalls looked at her. She held out her service pistol. A hint of blue smoke curled from the barrel. The smell of spent gunpowder wafted to him. He realized that the blood had sprayed him from bullet wounds, not from the mantra. He stopped reciting it.

"Why did you do that?"

"He tried to kill you. I'm a cop. It's what I do." She put her gun back into the holster behind her back.

"My mantra was working. It was expelling the spirit."

"That's what you were doing?" she said. "I thought he was doing something to your mind. Doesn't matter, I expelled it." Her face hardened. "I think I saw it leave the body."

"I saw it too. You should have let me finish him with the mantra alone. It's the only way I'm positive it will work without any other kind of intervention. That is the mantra I told Ashe to use to deal with evil spirits. He may try it on the others, and we don't know if it works at expelling them or if killing the host is necessary for expulsion."

Cooper walked to the body and bent over it. She sucked in air through her teeth. "Come and look at this."

He walked behind her. The corpse stared up at them, or

would have if it had eyes. The sockets were empty, charred black to the point that the eyebrows were singed off and the skin around the eye blistered.

"My pistol didn't do that."

"I think you are right. Do you believe me now about the Devil?"

She rubbed her own eyes as if they were burning. Smalls understood the feeling. The sight made his eyes a bit watery as well. He crossed himself and made a quick prayer for the body of whoever's soul had occupied it before San Roman possessed it.

"I don't know about the Devil, but I do know that I've never met a murderer that had his eyes do that. I think I ought to get a warrant to search that warehouse."

"I can go with you when you raid it?"

She looked at him. "I wouldn't have it any other way. That chant is better than a bulletproof vest."

"Only toward evil spirits," Smalls said. "It won't work for actual bullets."

"Let's get out of here."

Smalls nodded. He crossed himself again and said a prayer to purify the room. It was a Buddhist prayer. Although he was a priest, he believed that the power of God and good and the Devil and evil knew no exclusive religion. That room needed good karma to ward off any other problems.

CHAPTER TWENTY-NINE

A she finished the last tweak on the final engram recorder. He slid the small blue device away from him and rubbed his face. Everything twinned as he looked from his fatigued eyes. He couldn't remember working so hard on anything. Even when he created the first engram recording devices, he hadn't spent as much effort or time bent over a magnifying lamp. The muscles in his neck cramped down, not allowing him to fully extend it. A boxer after a prize fight probably didn't feel as rough as he did right then.

He stood and stretched out his back. Czernobog had removed the possessed helpers a few hours ago. He mentioned they had other work to do tonight. Ashe figured it must be sometime pretty late by the way he felt. He hadn't seen the outside in a few days. The Devil had kept all time devices away from him. A quick twist of his neck one way then the other popped the vertebrae and loosened his stiff muscles. The repaired cot that stood against the far wall of his lab enticed him. With everything finished, including programming the chant Smalls had emailed him into the engram recorders, he figured that Czernobog wouldn't care if he slept for a while.

The minimal support the canvas bottom of the cot gave his back didn't matter. The second-hand army cot felt like the plushest bed Ashe had ever slept in. The flimsy, flat pillow under his head cradled it just enough to be soothing. He blinked and rubbed his eyes again, and finally he saw only one image. The only noise he heard was the humming of a few mechanical instruments in his lab. The sound of the other corpses working in the warehouse had ended hours ago. The Devil must have sent them out on some other work as well. He closed his eyes and thought about two people, Cybil and Marianne.

Both of their faces floated in the dark space behind his eyelids. They weren't reconciled with each other in his mind. Worry for Cybil and her safety prodded him into doing the dumbest thing he might ever do. Marianne haunted him both in his conscience and literally. Her likeness walked around the building. He watched Rogers have his way with her. Only because of his promise, strike that, verbal contract with Satan was he sure Rogers hadn't done the same with Cybil.

The door to the lab slammed open. "Wake up."

Ashe opened his eyes and looked toward the door. Rogers hurried across the room. He pulled a long strip of silver duct tape out as he did so. The door to the room remained wide open. Ashe sat up and tossed his feet off the cot. Before Rogers could have known what happened, he was on his feet and hit the other man in the chest with his elbow. Rogers spun and buckled to the floor. Nothing blocked Ashe from the door. He was almost there when orange light flamed up in the doorway. The whole place filled with sulfur odor. The sudden wind and heat from fire knocked him backwards. Czernobog stepped into the room through the curtain of fire. He put his foot on Ashe's chest, pinning him to the floor.

"Hurry up and get this done, you fool," the Devil told Rogers.

The psychologist grabbed Ashe's wrists and put them together. Then he wrapped them with duct tape. Ashe felt the need to yell building up in his chest. Czernobog must have read this in his eyes because he put his finger to his lips.

"I would recommend that you stay very silent, Dr. Shrove. I would hate to have something happen to your dear Cybil." He nodded his head from Rogers to Ashe. "Over his mouth for extra insurance."

Rogers placed the end of the tape at the edge of his mouth and wrapped the tape twice around his head, leaving a two-ply barrier between Ashe's mouth and the outside world. The taste of the tape's glue was bitter on his tongue. Czernobog removed his foot and grabbed Ashe by the wrists. With a mere movement, the Devil pulled him to his feet.

"When you hear the lock on this door rattle, take him out the back door into the main area. When you hear me heading in there, you bring him back in here." Czernobog looked deep into Ashe's eyes. "You do anything stupid, and I will kill Cybil slowly and agonizingly. You will be forced to watch, and I will take great pleasure in doing both."

A puff of acrid, sulfurous smoke enveloped the Devil, and he was gone. The curtain of fire disappeared leaving no trace on the doorjamb as the door slammed and locked on its own. Ashe cut his eyes around. He would have moved away, but Rogers held him. His former partner's grip felt stronger than he had expected. Part of his deal with the Devil must have involved a subclause about strength. They walked closer to a door in the wall that led into the main area of the building where the floats were assembled.

A door somewhere not far from them slammed open. The sound echoed through the metal walls of the building. Voices muffled by distance but obviously shouts followed the boom of the door opening. Ashe strained to hear who it was. One of the voices was definitely female. It bore authoritative undertones.

More loud clattering sounds mingled with yells. Someone slammed desk drawers closed in the main office. Another sound was similar to a chair rolling across the floor ending with an echoing cymbal-like crash. The place was being ransacked.

"The police got their warrant." Rogers' breath felt hot on his ear as he whispered to him.

"They're probably looking for me. I killed a doctor in Mississippi."

Ashe cut his eyes up at his former friend. A childish grin of pride split Rogers' face. He nodded and winked as if to tell Ashe that was just another thing to add to his delinquent record. Ashe wanted to yell but knew it would be wasting his breath.

The door to the lab rattled. Rogers opened the rear door and forced Ashe through it before closing it without making a sound. The wall between the lab and the main chamber was thinner. It looked like little more than tin sheeting held up by two-by-fours, a makeshift lab put up on the fly. Ashe started to believe that the Devil was a little more haphazard than religion would have people believe.

"This is my electronics lab where I have techs mock up and knock together the more technical aspects of my floats." Czernobog's voice came clearly through the wall.

"Where are your techs tonight? I would think troubleshooting would be happening this close to showtime." Ashe recognized the female voice now. It was Detective Cooper.

"All my people have been told to go to the MOT's parade tonight. That society knows how to make a technically impressive series of floats. I want my people to make any last minute adjustments they need to top those guys."

"Where do you build the floats?" Cooper asked.

"In the larger room. Follow me and I will be happy to show them to you."

Rogers put his ear to the wall. After a few seconds he opened the door back into the lab, and dragged Ashe back inside. Making a sound would be so easy, and could be considered a mistake. The Devil couldn't read his mind so blaming him for doing it purposefully wouldn't work. Ashe stopped. Rogers kept a good grip on him and listened at the wall. They stood a long time in silence. The tape around his mouth began to burn and sting as it started to slip, pulling at the whiskers on his face. He mumbled, but Rogers twisted his arm like an Indian burn. Ashe quit.

After another eternal period of standing still taking short breaths to try and keep the tape from slipping more, Rogers let him go.

"They're gone. I guess they didn't find what they were looking for."

Ashe walked to his cot and sat down. He put his elbows on his legs and entwined his fingers. After a span of time Czernobog walked in through the rear door. He smelled overwhelmingly of sulfur. Ashe looked at him, and the Devil's features were more demonlike, sharp and angry.

"Unbind him," he said to Rogers.

The psychologist did what he was told. Ashe rubbed his face when the tape was ripped off unceremoniously. Twin stripes on his wrists were red and bumped from where the tape had torn the hair from his arms.

"Are they on to you?" he asked the Devil.

"Silence!" Czernobog turned to Rogers. "I am very angry. They are looking for you. The Pascagoula Police Department wanted to question you about the murder of a doctor in the Singing River Hospital. You are becoming a liability, Dr. Rogers."

"You told me to get more corpses. I was just doing your bidding."

"I did not mean that you needed to gloat on camera. You have gotten sloppy." The Devil flashed with anger. "I will deal with you later. For now, you have a job to do. Get to it and hope my rage subsides after you do."

"Yes, Master."

Rogers bowed and hurried from the room. Czernobog sat on the cot beside Ashe. His face smoothed out to the swarthy complexion he had the first time they had met. The smell of sulfur still clung to him. He put his hand on Ashe's knee like a father would a son.

"You have finished?"

"Yeah."

"You have done a good job. You have no need to worry about Miss Fairchild's safety. I will uphold my end of the deal completely."

Ashe believed Czernobog, but it didn't help ease his mind any.

Cybil felt her way around in the pitch black. She knew that she was in a basement. When the guards or whatever they were moved her from the closet they kept her in they walked down stairs. They made sure to keep her blindfolded. She wasn't even sure what time it was. Staying in the closet day and night with only the artificial light from a single low wattage bulb screwed up her orientation.

She heard the rumble of noise above her. It wasn't in the house or wherever they kept her. The sound came from the street. The wall felt like old hewn block as she slid her back over it. Cybil felt ahead of her with one hand. After shuffling along for a while, her hand hit a corner. She scooted around it and kept against the wall until her hand no longer ran across a solid wall. Her foot bumped against a wooden step.

"Thank you."

Cybil swung around and placed a shaky foot on the step. Her hand pawed in the darkness until she grabbed a banister rail. Using it as an anchor, she started up the steps. Her steps were quick but short to keep from missing a stair and toppling to the hard floor in the pitch black. The higher she ascended the stairs, the louder the noise from outside became.

Now she heard cheering and felt the bumping of bass coming from speakers. Occasionally the shrill blast from a plastic party horn cut through it all. Her eyes began to perceive a slit of light not far from her. Three more steps and the hand she slid up the banister rail hit the doorjamb. She searched for the doorknob with her free hand. The cold metal of the knob first flirted with the tips of her fingers. Then she wrapped her hand round it and twisted hard. The knob didn't move.

Cybil repositioned herself on the top stair. She took her hand from the rail and balanced as best she could. A quick shifting of her weight down the steps nearly toppled her over, but she flung that momentum into ramming the door with her shoulder.

An involuntary puff of air burst from her, and pings of pain prickled across her shoulder. The door seemed no worse for it. Deep inside her, Cybil knew that this might be her only chance to escape. As best she could tell, Czernobog, the Devil, or whatever he called himself, had ordered all the living corpses out of the house tonight. That's why they locked her in the basement. She flung herself against the door again. More pain and still more of nothing happened to the door. Desperation took over. She slammed into the door with the rhythm of a manic-depressive typing a suicide letter.

The wood on the doorjamb popped. Another ram with her shoulder made the wood crack. A well thought out hard blow with most of her weight splintered wood, and the door pushed open. Cybil fell onto the upper floor. More air forced its way out of her in a large puff.

Sweat ran into her eyes. It stung. As she wiped them with her sleeve, her eyes focused in on the light. They ached from having been so long in the dark. The sound from the street almost rattled the window. She stood up and walked to the window. Outside revelers stood along the street, as a large float passed by. It looked like a dragon and seemed to slither from side to side as smoke billowed from its nose. She hurried through the house looking for a door to the outside. As she ran into the kitchen, the small door with a window in it almost beckoned to her. Cybil ran across the room. She twisted the dead bolt and jerked the safety chain away.

The cold night air gushed in around her when she opened the door. The sound of all the festivities followed as well.

"Thank you," she said again out loud.

Hindered by nothing, Cybil ran down the small back steps into the little yard. A fence cut the yard off from the street, but a gate stood ajar. She rushed it and bounded onto the street. Several of the revelers gave her mean looks when she bumped into them.

"Please help me." She pulled on a man's sleeve. "I've just escaped from that house. They kidnapped me."

The man jerked his arm away and pushed deeper toward the street. Cybil moved down the street and grabbed a man in tuxedo wearing a feathered domino mask.

"You've got to help me. I just escaped from kidnappers. They've kept me for I don't know how long."

"What?" The man pulled up his mask.

"I've been kidnapped. I need help."

"All right, just stand here." The man sounded panicked. He pushed into the crowd toward the street.

Cybil waited. Her heart beat hard, and she kept twisting her head to make sure none of the living corpses were coming up the street. The man in the tuxedo came back with a police officer who had several strands of Mardi Gras beads around his neck.

"This man tells me that you just escaped from some kidnappers?" the cop asked.

"Yes, and I'm afraid they're out here in the crowd. I need your help. Take me to the police station or St. Mary's-by-the-Bay church. I'm friends with Father Smalls. He'll know what to do."

The policeman looked at the tuxedoed man. "I think she's in shock."

"I'm not. They're going to get me," Cybil screamed at him.

A plastic horn squealed out, and a string of beads hit her in the face. She pawed at it knocking it to the ground. The policeman took her by the wrist.

"Please just try and settle down. I'm with you and you'll be safe." He turned to the radio clipped to his epaulet. "This is Simmons. I have a woman who says she's been kidnapped. I'm at Government just past D'Iberville Court. Send a buggy."

"Roger that Simmons. Buggy on the way."

Simmons, the policeman, pushed her back from the crowd and against another fence.

"I've got a golf cart on its way. We'll get you somewhere safe."

She put her arms around his neck. "Thank you."

News Report: Channel 10, Mobile, AL, 2:30 a.m. CST. Sharmaine O'Calley Broadcasting.

"Good morning. We are sorry to interrupt the repeat of Thursday night's *American Idol*, but we have breaking news from downtown Mobile."

Sharmaine O'Calley turns to the second camera as it focuses in closer on her.

"We received a report around two this morning that the Cathedral of the Immaculate Conception Basilica, seat of the Archdiocese of Mobile, was on fire. Not long ago, the

Mobile Fire Department confirmed that the one-hundred-plus-year-old church is engulfed in flames."

Grainy images of flames lapping the sky replace that of O'Calley. Orange fire envelops the large church building. Several laddered fire trucks sit diagonally to the building. Firefighters spray the flames with water from hoses. O'Calley speaks over this scene.

"Maxwell Grady, captain at the downtown firehouse, says that the fire appears to have been set. At this time, the Mobile police will not confirm or deny this. They do report that they are currently reviewing the video from the traffic cameras near the basilica. This video was emailed to us by a reveler heading home from Dauphin Street celebrations after the Mystics of Time parade."

The video of the burning church loops back to the beginning, and O'Calley comes back on screen.

"There is also no word from the Mobile police if this fire might be linked to the kidnapping of Archbishop Harrington, who presides over the Archdiocese of Mobile. The spokesperson for the Mobile police did report they are looking for a suspect in the kidnapping of the archbishop, and will probably question that person about this fire."

She stops and puts her finger to her ear. She listens for a moment.

"We've just been given a report that Fairview Baptist Church on Azalea Road burned to the ground about an hour ago. Late night tipsters are also making unconfirmed reports that West Mobile United Methodist Church and St. Simon's Episcopal School have burned."

The broadcaster looks nervous at this point. Her young face shows the inexperience that landed her on the overnight shift at the television station.

"It appears that we are in the middle of a major news event. Please stay tuned to Channel 10 for the latest breaking news about this rash of church burnings. We are going back to our program still in progress."

A commercial for Zion Presbyterian Church comes on. The minister smiles as a church organ plays "Nearer My God to Thee".

CHAPTER THIRTY

Cybil woke up in a haze. Slits of light came into the room from behind blinded windows. She rolled over to her back, making her head swim. Her eyes felt heavy and hot. Cotton filled her mouth. She lacked enough saliva to swallow.

The sunlight in the room looked older than morning light, more like noon or just after. What time was it? She looked around the room but saw no clock. Nothing in the room looked familiar. She willed her mind to clear so that she could search her memories.

Last night the living corpses left her in a basement, and she escaped and found a policeman along the parade route. He brought her to the police department. She told them her story, and they transported her to University Hospital. Everything got fuzzy after that. Another look around the room confirmed that it looked like a hospital room, but without some of the customary furniture. No chairs sat against the wall. The mirror over the sink looked more like high polished metal than glass. There wasn't a television anywhere, and the bed was more of an uncomfortable mattress on a rectangular block of wood.

She stood up and swooned, catching herself on the wall before she fell back on the bed. Her clothes were the same she had on last night. The floor felt cold on her feet.

"No shoes," she said.

Steadying herself, she staggered to the door and into the hallway. The smell of the hospital washed over her. Chatter from other rooms buzzed around her. A man in dark blue scrubs walked toward her. He carried a clipboard like a tray. A small paper cup was on it.

"Ms. Fairchild?" he asked.

"Yes. That's me."

"I need to give you this." He handed her the cup.

Inside were two small pills. Cybil stared at them but wouldn't take the cup from the nurse.

"What are they?"

"Your medications."

"Why am I getting medications? Where am I?"

"You're in University Hospital. These are what the doctor ordered to help you get your thoughts straightened out."

"What do you mean? I haven't seen a doctor. I don't even remember coming to this unit."

A short, angry-looking woman with wild curly hair stomped past. She mumbled about the queen's tarts and how she'd eaten them all. Realization cleared Cybil's mind quickly.

"I'm on a psych ward?" Cybil said. "How did I end up here?"

"Please just take these," the nurse said.

"I'm not taking anything until you tell me how I ended up here. The last thing I remember was the police bringing me to the ER because I had escaped from kidnappers."

The nurse set the cup back on his clipboard. "In the ER, you told them that you had escaped from zombies, who had to go to the Mystics of Time parade because their master, the Devil, told them to. You became agitated when they tried to orient you to reality so they gave you a shot of Geodon then transferred you to us."

"I'm not crazy. I really did escape from living corpses. They have a house in downtown and a warehouse on Michigan Avenue. Call Father Smalls at St. Mary's-by-the-Bay Church. He'll tell you."

"Ms. Fairchild, I don't want to have to give you a shot, but if you don't take these medicines, I'll have to."

"You can't force me to take medications. I'm here against my will and preference. You've kidnapped me again."

"The doctor made you something called a *no AMA discharge*, which means that tomorrow when the probate office opens he will have you committed, which means we can force medications on you. Please don't make us."

Cybil saw that she had lost this particular battle. She held out her hand. The nurse poured the two pills into her hand. She popped them into her mouth.

"Do you need some water?" he asked.

She swallowed big, using the movement to secure the two pills between her top gum in the back and her jaw. "I don't need it."

"Let me see."

Cybil stuck her tongue out and lifted it. Then she swished it around her mouth, making sure not to dislodge the pills. "We good?"

"Thank you."

"What time is it?"

The nurse looked at his watch. "One fifteen in the afternoon. You missed lunch, but I saved it for you. Would you like it?"

"Yes, please. Can I go back to my room?"

"Of course. I'll have the PCA bring it to you in a minute."

Cybil walked back into her room and then into the bathroom. She closed the door and spat the pills out into the toilet. The swirling water flushed them into the sewers.

Lunch had been surprisingly good. Ashe didn't want to eat, but the smell from the tray that one of the undead minions of Czernobog brought him was too much to resist. The fear of being drugged kept him from eating very often since coming to an agreement with the Devil, although he'd been promised many times that would not be the case. He really didn't trust the Devil beyond their agreed-upon area.

The afternoon drags took hold of him. After finishing his work on the engram recorders, Ashe hadn't much to do except sit in his cell/lab twiddling his thumbs. Czernobog denied him anything to entertain himself. Even a romance novel would have been better than counting the rivets in the ceiling again. His eyelids grew heavy as he started down the third row of rivets.

The door slammed open. Ashe jerked to a sitting position. Czernobog strolled in with a large smile on his face.

"Did I wake you?"

"No, I was just counting the rivets in the ceiling, again."

"Has the number changed since you got here? If so that is a disturbing turn of events."

"It's been the same number the last nine times I counted them."

"You should really get a hobby." Czernobog walked deeper into the lab. "I recommend masturbation. It seems to work wonders for Dr. Rogers."

"I'll keep that in mind. I assume you haven't come here to discuss my recreational interest."

"You are correct. I have come to test the engram recorders. I need to make sure they play the music correctly and then distribute emotions out." He pointed to the box Ashe kept the small devices in. "I'll just help myself."

"No." Ashe jumped to his feet. "Let me get you one."

"I have been around since time began, Dr. Shrove. I can handle getting a device from a box."

"Yes, but you didn't give me a clean room to make these things. Several of the devices malfunctioned during construction because your corpse slaves had too much static electricity in them. If you unload a single charge, it will destroy them all."

"How will the same thing not happen to you?" Czernobog sounded skeptical.

Ashe walked to the worktable and tapped his hand on a metal pad. "Because I've been handling electronics for years. I know how to do it."

"You could not show me?"

"I don't know what kind of electrical makeup you have. I don't know if the Prince of Darkness is AC or DC."

Czernobog laughed. It sounded pleasant and filled with real humor. "Mark Twain was the last of your species to make me really laugh. That man was truly a silver-tongued devil. Please select one. You are correct. I would hate to destroy all of this work with just two days to go. You have shown amazing skill for a human, but I think having to remake those would test your limits. I will not test you that far."

Ashe tapped the metal pad again to make sure he had no static build-up. He didn't need those things frying. The Devil was right; there was no way he could get them completed by Mardi Gras night if he did. He lifted the lid of the box. Ten identical thumb drive–like devices lay in the box. He picked up the one at the end. It was programmed exactly as the Devil had wanted it to be. If it were used, whoever heard the music stored on it would drop dead, and could then be given recorded emotions and be possessed. If the Devil wished to test any others, Ashe intended to make it look like he took a new device from the box, but just give the same one back. It was a plan suited to the Devil himself. He closed the box and handed the device to Czernobog.

"There you are. I hope you know that as soon as you use that thing, you've won."

The Devil appeared puzzled. "How do you mean?"

"You'll have damned my soul."

"Perhaps."

Ashe almost felt the coldness in the Devil's voice, but there was something else hidden in the frigidness. Crystals of doubt seemed to rim the chilly words. He wondered if the Devil was as powerful as everyone thought when it came to Hell and damnation.

"I look forward to seeing if all your hard work has paid off. I hope for Cybil's safety it does."

"Oh, it will."

Czernobog slipped the engram device into the pocket of his suit vest and walked out of the room. As he closed the door, he reached into his coat pocket and removed a small paperback book. It hit the table near Ashe, cover up. Apparently, the Devil had a wit equal to Mark Twain's as well. He was going to let Ashe read *The Exorcist.*

Cybil walked out of her room into the hall of the psych unit. Something had happened. She hadn't heard anything, but the lights blinked out and back on. A single shrill scream echoed from the fire alarm and then went silent. All that caught her interest. With all the weirdness she'd encountered over the last few weeks, she'd come to expect anything.

What she found was a hallway with a few patients walking around in a dazed state. She walked past them to the nurse's station. No one was there.

"Hello," she said loud enough for her words to echo down the hallway.

"Hello." A voice fell flat without any echo.

Cybil turned back toward her room. Archbishop Harrington stood looking at her with dull eyes and an expressionless face.

"What are you doing here, Archbishop Harrington? Did they finally call Father Smalls to come and get me? How is Ashe? Is he is okay?"

"I do not know who you are talking about. I am Gerard Segarelli."

"He's with me." She turned back to look behind her. Rogers stood with a huge grin on his face holding something like a thumb drive in his hand. "Actually, they are all with me. Ashe did a good job on this thing. It works like a charm. Be glad I figured out how to cut off the intercom to your room, or you'd have been one of them too."

All the staff of the unit and the patients surrounded her. All their eyes were dull and flat like Harrington's or rather Segarelli's. Rogers had zombified everyone on the unit except for her. Hope fell away as heavy and flat as Harrington's greeting had.

"Why are you here?" she asked.

"Czernobog has an agreement with your boyfriend. If Ashe found out you'd escaped, he might renege on the agreement. We can't have that. Come with us all quiet like or this could be unpleasant."

Cybil nodded her head to signal her surrender. To resist would get her manhandled by the possessed mental patients.

"Let's go," she said.

"There's a smart girl." Rogers smiled and shoved the small thumb drive–like thing into his pocket.

She followed him off the locked psychiatric unit with Harrington, the nursing staff and patients following.

Ashe paced from his cot to his workstation. Since Czernobog had taken the engram device, he'd worried about the outcome of its use. If he'd accidentally given the Devil the wrong one, Cybil was dead, and he was more damned that he already was.

The lock on the door turned over. He stopped and waited, holding his breath anticipating the worst. The door swung open, and Czernobog stepped in. He smiled his hollow artificial smile.

"It is your lucky day," he said.

"It worked."

"You sound like it would be any other way. That makes me worry."

"I always worry about my product when I make something. Just the perfectionist in me."

Czernobog's smile changed to one of genuineness. "I like a perfectionist. It is a keystone in life. Do not worry. Your device worked flawlessly. So good in fact, I don't have to worry about the rest of them."

Relief dropped through Ashe like a stone down a well. The room even felt cooler. It was good news indeed. The Devil dug into his vest pocket and brought the engram recorder out. He handed it to Ashe.

"I'm glad it worked so well. That is really good news, I guess."

"You guess?"

"If it worked that means people died."

"True but it means that Cybil is safe for another day, which is really the good news." Czernobog waved toward the door.

Harrington pushed Cybil into the room. He held her by both arms. Ashe looked at the archbishop or what had been the archbishop. The man's eyes told him a heretic occupied the place the venerable churchman's soul had once been. Cybil looked both terrified and relieved at the same time.

"You're alive," she said.

"So are you."

Harrington let her go. She ran to him and gave him a hug. Before they could kiss, Czernobog cleared his throat.

"Understand I only put her here because it's easier to guard you both in the same place. I do not require as many workers for such a dull task." He smiled his insincere smile again. "Don't do anything I wouldn't do."

He laughed his dead soulless laugh and walked out.

Harrington followed. The door closed and locked. Cybil looked into Ashe's eyes. He felt all the passion and relief he thought a man could. Tears fought to be released.

"I almost got away," she said. "They found me. Dr. Rogers killed everyone where I was and turned them to those things. *Everyone.*"

"Trust me; Czernobog's plan is far worse." He thought about telling her what he had done, but stopped. As far as he knew, she could be brainwashed or bugged. "It will make what's happened so far a moot point."

"What do you mean?"

He let her go and walked to his workstation. The engram recorder went back into the slot so he would know where it was. "I can't tell you."

CHAPTER THIRTY-ONE

"That's him, isn't it?" Cooper pointed to a blurry image on the television screen.

Smalls squinted. It was hard to make out anything in the grainy black and white still from the video. A line of paused movement obscured part of the picture. Even if he wasn't sure of everyone in the picture, the man in the forefront was Erik Rogers, and he knew the man behind him was Archbishop Harrington.

"I can't be positive, but the other man is Harrington, or was the archbishop."

"You think the archbishop is dead now?" she asked.

"I think he was dead then." Smalls pecked on the screen. "If what I think has been happening is then that's the shell of the man that was once head of the Mobile Archdioceses."

"I still don't buy this whole possession thing."

"How do you explain this?" He pointed to another screen shot of a string of medical staff and patients walking single file down the hall with Cybil at the lead. "Pied piper?"

"There are many explanations better than possession."

"Like?"

"Brainwashing. Threats of harm," Cooper said. "What kind of detective would I be if I jumped straight to demons every time something strange happens?"

"Why can't we recover any more of the images on the screen?" Smalls asked.

"There was a power surge right as that picture was taken." The house supervisor pointed to the distorted picture of Harrington and Rogers. "This one was taken a few minutes later according to the time stamp. According to the tech guys the video system has to reset. It takes about that long."

Smalls stared at the television screens. He looked from the first picture to the later one. Ashe had suspected that Rogers was working with the Russians because they had threatened him. Czernobog seemed to be a Russian with something to hide. Harrington warned of the Devil and now seemed to be in on everything. His head swam with so much information.

"We finally got an ID on the van that kidnapped Harrington," Cooper said. "It belongs to the Mystics of Mayhem parading society. Mikal Czernobog signed the registration."

"So why haven't you moved on this?"

"Just in case you are living in a cave, most of our resources are focused on the church arsons. Over fifteen churches or religiously affiliated buildings were torched including your basilica and the largest Baptist church in the county. Chasing after these kidnappers has been left to me alone." Cooper lowered her voice. "To be honest, they've limited how much longer I can work on this thing."

"How long?"

"Until Ash Wednesday."

"Two days from now." Smalls nodded. "I'm pretty sure everything will be over by then."

"The judge has given me another warrant to check out that warehouse, and one to look through the house that Cybil told the beat cop she escaped from. My usual partner is tied up at St. Simon's School. You game?"

Smalls pulled a small book from the inside pocket of his coat. "As ready as I'm going to be."

"The Bible?"

"A book with incantations to expel evil and vile spirits. It's an old volume considered heretical. It's been in my arsenal for years."

Cooper reached behind her and brought out a pistol. "9mm expels creeps and weirdoes. Been in my holster all day."

The house they strolled up to was unassuming. Nestled behind a plank board fence, the two visible stories of the house sat between a pair of Spanish moss–covered live oaks. The yellow paint peeled from the wooden siding. The hurricane shutters hadn't seen a coat of paint in years. Smalls remembered the place. He'd passed it many mornings on his jogs through downtown. Usually, he came from the front side of the house, where there was not a fence. Today he and Cooper had to approach up the street from the back of the house. The smaller streets around it were no-parking areas, even for police vehicles.

"Cheery place." Cooper stared up at it. "Hard to believe kidnappers would be in there."

"I know you're being sarcastic, but it kind of is. I would expect crack dealers more than anything. I jog through this neighborhood a lot. The fear of getting shot in a drug war or pricked by a used needle is always present."

"You're a priest. Why would you worry about that." She walked the way down the sidewalk that led to the front of the house. "You should be straight with the man upstairs."

"Until now, it was my biggest fear. The world ending at the hands of Satan trumps most everything else."

They stepped into the yard. High weeds flanked the broken concrete sidewalk. The steps to the porch listed to one side, and several of the floorboards stuck up, warped from time and lack of care.

Cooper drew her pistol out. "We're going in fast and hard. I don't want to give anyone time to get out the door."

Smalls nodded. He crossed himself then kissed his fingers. The detective rushed up the steps and kicked the door. He came up after her. The door creaked, popped, and slammed open. She rushed in. Before crossing the threshold, the priest took out the book of incantations and flipped it open. He wanted to try some different ones to see if they worked. Although he feared failure, the Buddhist one did the charm and would be a good fallback point. A quick silent prayer went up as he headed into the dark entryway.

"Mobile police," Cooper yelled. "Come out now with your hands where I can see them."

Smalls followed the direction of her voice. He entered into what would have been a living room at one time. There was no furniture. The wallpaper peeled from the walls, and cob-webs hung from the blown ceiling. The next room looked like a dining area. An old round breakfast table sat in the middle of the room. A large column candle was in the middle. Red wax spread everywhere over the tabletop like a pool of blood. He heard quick footsteps in the room just beyond that one. Smalls headed that way. The kitchen looked as if it had been recently used. A coffee maker sat on the filth-encrusted counter. It still perked. From the corner of his eye he saw movement.

The priest turned as a small black woman lumbered toward him. She held a cleaver in her hand. Her amber eyes had the look of evil and possession in them. The urge to yell out to Cooper for protection filled him up, but he turned to his book. This was not the time to turn tail.

"Bless you." He read from the page he'd turned to. The shock of such a simple phrase children used when people sneezed took him aback but did nothing to the advancing woman. He regrouped and put real meaning into. "Bless you!"

The woman stopped. The cleaver dropped from her hands. The words stunned her. Smalls said them again, but in a Gregorian chant cadence. The amber eyes that stared at him rolled over white. The woman pitched and shook, hitting the floor with enough force to make the boards creak. A few flops like a fish out of water and a dark shadow erupted from her mouth. Smalls kept up his *bless you* chant. The shadow charged him and passed through him at great speed. He felt the heat of a million fires as it enveloped him, but didn't stop. Everything cooled. The body on the floor stayed in place. He stopped his chant.

"That was some pretty singing," Cooper said from behind him.

He turned. She held Rogers by the arm. His hands were secured behind him with handcuffs. Her 9mm poked his ribs at an angle that would send the bullet to his heart.

"I found him hiding in a closet under the stairs."

Smalls nodded toward the dead body. "I found her in the corner ready to chop me up with a meat cleaver."

"They're too slow after a few days," Rogers said. "Rigor

mortis starts to set in, and they all move like Frankenstein."

"So they're dead bodies?" Cooper asked.

"I'm not saying anything without my lawyer."

"Are there any more in here?" Smalls asked.

"I'm not answering."

"I'll remind you that I'm not a cop. I can make it real uncomfortable for you," Smalls said.

Rogers huffed a laugh of derision. "You're a priest, and I'm alive. That little chant won't work with me. It wouldn't have worked with a spirit better entrenched either. Don't think Czernobog isn't aware of that. Fortunately, he's more powerful than those childish chants and stupid witticisms."

Smalls walked to Rogers. He loathed the man at that moment. Although such an emotion should never enter a priest's mind, his former friend brought Satan into all their lives in an overly personal way. The hubris of the Devil bolstered his former friend's confidence.

"The power of Christ compels you." He planted a knee into Roger's groin.

The psychologist bent double, but Cooper wouldn't let him go so that he could crumple to the floor. His face turned red.

"She's all that's here," he said between pained gasps.

"Who is she?" Smalls asked.

"I'm not telling."

"I'll grind it in this time."

"I don't remember her name. I brought her from the Pascagoula hospital a few nights ago."

"The night you killed the doctor. Her name was Debra Henry," Cooper said.

"I'm going to say a prayer for her soul. She didn't deserve the fate she received."

"Do it on the way to the car. I want to get him back to the station so we can get his lawyer to him." She looked at the body on the floor. "I'll call her location in."

Smalls nodded and started his silent prayer for the poor dead woman and one for his own forgiveness for his treatment of Rogers.

CHAPTER THIRTY-TWO

The Devil seemed extra vindictive. Ashe sat on his work stool across the room from Cybil who lay on the cot. The possessed corpse of Marianne kept watch over them from the corner nearest the door. Only Satan himself could have thought up such a diabolical plot. Even though he wasn't one hundred percent sure Cybil wasn't in the Devil's fold, Ashe still wanted to talk to her, but with Marianne's watchful eyes, the thought of even innocent conversation stalled.

The eyes that watched them were nothing like his late fiancée's. These stared like doll's eyes. Nothing of Marianne lived within the shell of her body. The stiffness in her walk told him that the flesh was breaking down already. Still, there was something guilt inducing about her being there. He gave over to the temptation of Cybil too quickly. Maybe that was what mourning did to people sometimes.

He tried to read the novel Czernobog gave him. Although the movie had scared the daylights out of him as a kid, the novel of *The Exorcist* didn't really keep his attention. Many things rattled around in his head though. Holding the book was more to keep Cybil from talking to him than anything else.

"Did he give you that?" Cybil asked, breaking a long silence that Ashe wished would have stayed unbroken.

"Yeah."

"Quite a sense of humor he has."

Ashe set the book down. There was no reason to attempt to pretend he still read it. "That's what I thought when he gave it to me."

"And he leaves us with her."

A twinge of guilt twisted inside of Ashe. Why did Cybil have to acknowledge her? Why did the Marianne thing have to just watch them in silence? A roaring ball of emotion threatened to burst from him, when the door opened. The tall black woman he'd encountered at his first Mardi Gras parade, which now seemed centuries ago, stepped inside carrying several colorful garments over her arm. He remembered that before she walked out of a hospital in Birmingham her name had been Heinz. Now he had no idea what her name was.

"The Master wishes for you to pick out a costume for tomorrow evening." Her voice fell flat and cold to the floor, gray words for bright clothes.

"What if you tell your master I'm happy with the clothes I've got on," Ashe said.

"That is unacceptable," Marianne said. "The Master wishes for you to wear garments like everyone else will tomorrow."

"I'm not planning on riding in your death parade," Ashe said. "I made the deal to build the engram machines, not to toss out beads."

"The Master demands it," Heinz said.

"You will do what the Master says." Marianne shuffled across the room. She took Cybil by the arm. Twisting it, she pulled her to a standing position. "He said that if you did not cooperate I was to deal with her."

Ashe stared into Marianne's dead eyes, then to those of Cybil, which held terror inside of them. Heinz's eyes were as doll-like as Marianne's. The words he had recorded on the engram device came to him. Smalls told him they should expel evil spirits. He licked his lips ready to say them. Before he started, memories surfaced. Several of the possessed corpses were in the room when he recorded the words. Nothing happened to them. If he said the incantation and it worked, then Czernobog would keep his promise to harm Cybil. Also if the chant hadn't worked when he recorded it would it work tomorrow night? Maybe it needed to be said louder than a whisper or more frequently.

Cybil sucked in breath between clenched teeth. Ashe stared at her. Marianne twisted her arm more severely. It looked almost like the twist of a pretzel. He couldn't risk the incantation right now. A blue outfit with silver sequins was on top of the pile Heinz held.

"I'll take the top one," he said.

"Very wise choice, Dr. Shrove." Marianne let go of Cybil. "What color for you?"

Cybil looked at Heinz. Tears pooled in her eyes. "Whatever is next in the stack will be fine."

"Very good." Heinz handed Ashe the blue suit and Cybil an orange one below it. "Try them on. If they do not fit, they must be altered. The Master insists."

"He's being very insistent," Ashe said with as much sarcasm as he could pack in the words. He hoped the long damned heretics would still understand that nuance of language even if contractions mystified them.

"All must be perfect," Marianne said. "The Master insists."

Ashe held his blue parade costume in his hand. He hoped that things wouldn't go perfectly for Czernobog. He hoped that his mechanisms would work. If only Smalls could get him a message or he could get one to the priest, his mind might be better settled. As of now, he could only try on his gaudy parade pajamas.

Security Camera: Mobile County Jail, Mobile, AL, 11:00 p.m. CST

Rogers lies on the lowest bunk on the triple-bunk bed. Two prisoners sleep on the bunks above him. Flames flash up from the floor. Czernobog steps out of them, and they die away. Rogers rolls off the bed and onto his feet. The other two prisoners jump down from their bunks. The Devil touches the bars on the door. They smoke and melt away. He steps into the cell.

The two prisoners stumble away from him. A stream of fire like the blast from a flamethrower erupts from Czernobog's hand. The flash fire burns the two prisoners to a pile of ashes in a few moments. The Devil turns to Rogers. The psychologist backs away until his back is against the bunk. He screams. He claws on the bed trying to get higher up and farther away from the Devil.

Two deputies run to the cell with their weapons drawn. Czernobog turns to them. They press in on him, but he steps up to them. They fire their weapons. Bullets pierce Czernobog in his chest and stomach. They exit from his back. He smiles and extends his arm. Another jet of liquid fire propels from his open palm. The two deputies erupt in flame and smoke. When the flames peter out, only ashes remain.

The Devil turns back to Rogers, who has climbed to the top bed of the bunk. He reaches up and pulls the psychologist down. Rogers appears to bounce on the solid concrete floor. Czernobog picks him up by the hair. With a quick movement of Czernobog's hand, Rogers' body crumples to the floor, blood pouring from the gaping hole in his neck. The Devil holds the decapitated head firm in his hand. He shoots fire against the wall and patterns it in the shape of downward pointing pentagram.

Like an illusionist at a children's party, he disappears in an expanding puff of smoke.

CHAPTER THIRTY-THREE

Smalls woke up from a nightmare. Sweat poured from every pore of his body. He couldn't remember the last time he had such a bad dream. Satan taunted him from a Mardi Gras float, and the possessed corpses of Ashe and Cybil held him at bay while the end of the world raged around him.

He sat up and for a moment lost all sense of where he was. Then he realized that he slept on Detective Cooper's couch. After their adventure in the old house off of Confessor Street and all the church fires, she decided to let him stay with her. It had been a long time since he had stayed in a woman's house without being in bed with her. Much like a drunk sitting in a bar, he was bothered by old urges. He thought that might have given him extra fitful sleep.

"Are you okay?" Cooper walked into her living room. She carried a cup of coffee and wore unflattering pajamas.

"Nightmare."

"I didn't sleep that well either. No nightmares though." She sipped her coffee. "Want a cup of joe?"

"Cup of joe? You are a cop, aren't you?"

"Can't fight who you are."

Cooper's cell phone rang before Smalls could reply. She answered it. Her face fell from a friendly smile to a harsh frown. He didn't care for the look. Something in it transcended normal displeasure to straight disgust. She sputtered a string of profanities as she slammed the phone down on her coffee table.

"That good?" Smalls asked.

"Dr. Rogers is no longer in our jail."

"He busted out?"

"He's dead. According to the chief jailer, the video shows a small dark man appeared in a flourish of fire, killed two deputies and two inmates before ripping Rogers' head off and disappearing into a puff of smoke." She drank her coffee.

Smalls crossed himself and said a silent prayer for his friend. He didn't figure it was going to help since it seemed Rogers sold his soul to Satan, but he figured it might not hurt either.

"What are they going to do about it?" Smalls asked.

"Suppress the evidence. Can you imagine if something like that gets out to the media?"

"What are we going to do about it?"

"Find Mr. Czernobog and kill him." Cooper drank some more of her coffee.

"You know that he's probably Satan, right?"

"That's why I'm taking you along with me."

Smalls knew he had to face this evil but didn't feel very pleased about it. There was little he could actually do in a full assault on the Devil, himself. If Czernobog was connected with the Mystics of Mayhem, then his nightmare might come true. They needed to stop that parade.

"Can you get the police chief to stop the Mystics of Mayhem parade tonight?" Smalls asked.

"I doubt it. Parades bring in big bucks, plus what am I going to say, 'There's a good chance this parade is being put on by the Devil'? They'd laugh me all the way to the psych unit."

"But all the evidence. The reanimated corpses and church burnings."

"None of that can be directly linked to Czernobog or the Mystics of Mayhem."

"So what then?" Smalls knew the answer but asked the question anyway.

"We find him and stop him before the parade gets a chance to start."

Ashe helped one of the possessed corpses wire a speaker to a USB port so that one of the engram storage mechanisms could be played through it. He had no idea where they were, however. During the early morning hours, Czernobog had moved him and Cybil from the warehouse. Blindfolded, he felt like the ride to the new location took forever. They turned onto and off of what felt like a myriad of streets. The large area the floats were set up in was much bigger than the main room at the warehouse.

Assisting in the installation of the speakers helped Ashe figure out the Devil's plan when the parade rolled. The lead float would begin playing unsynced music impregnated with the satanic incantation. Later floats would do the same. Once the music played for a stretch, the engram machines would switch to releasing emotions into corpses lining the street. He planned for the last engram device to contain the deadly chant. That way he had most of the parade to stop Czernobog. The last float would be the one the Devil rode on. Ashe had gotten that impression by the design of the thing. It looked like hellfire had erupted on a flatbed trailer.

"Where are we?" he asked one of the minions.

"At the holding area to wait for our parade."

"Where is that?"

"I do not know. The Master did not tell us. He only told us to get these speakers ready and be in costume by the time the sun sets."

"Did he say if he wanted me to put the engram devices in the drives after we finished with the speakers?"

"He did not say."

"You can't take a guess?"

"My way is to do what the Master says. It is only because of him that I am able to be here. I will not upset the Master."

A burst of heat hit Ashe's back. He turned to see Czernobog step out of flames. He already wore his parade outfit. The suit he wore was red satin with a string of red sequins running down the lapels of the jacket. A few strands of beads hung around his neck. A pair of black and silver horns rested on his head.

"You can insert the engram devices when you have completed rigging the USB ports," he said. "There was no reason for me to tell the others this."

Ashe dug one of the devices from his pocket. All the ones that were rigged to use the incantations were in one pocket. The one that was made to the Devil's specifications was in the other.

He inserted one of the safe devices into the USB port. The small LED screen on the speaker lit up. A string of letters appeared and then the word *play*. A small button underneath the screen lit up.

"Is it working correctly?" Czernobog asked.

"Looks like it." Ashe pulled the wire that connected the system to the power source.

"The world will be ready to end at your convenience."

"Why did you unplug it?" he asked.

"To make sure it doesn't get turned on accidentally. If that thing plays, and I'm around, I'll be dead. What would you do if something happened and you needed troubleshooting? Erik doesn't know how to fix these things. He'd be no good to you."

Czernobog smiled. "You have no idea how right you are."

He looked Ashe over. The beady eyes felt like they scanned his deepest thoughts and soul. Ashe still was not certain that Czernobog couldn't read his mind. Perhaps he was just being toyed with to make his ultimate demise worse.

"That makes good sense. No trickery, mortal, or our deal is void. Your soul is mine and Cybil's body belongs to whoever wants it."

"No tricks."

The Devil nodded and started studying the remainder of the floats. Ashe moved on to the next speaker that needed to be rigged with a USB port. What Czernobog said kept running through his head. Every other time he'd talked about the agreement, Rogers had been part of the threat. This time he clearly said whoever. Something had happened. Ashe had figured out how to stop the onslaught of the possessed corpses, he hoped, but hadn't quite figured out how he would handle Czernobog himself. The smell of sulfur wafted around the place. Ashe kept his head down and rigged the next USB port. Much of his mental effort was put to plotting his next big move.

"They're not going to be here," Smalls said as he, Cooper and a sheriff's deputy pushed through the gate at the warehouse on Michigan Avenue.

"Positive thinking, Padre," the deputy said.

"I'm positive they aren't going to be here."

"Have a little faith, Smalls," Cooper said.

The door to the warehouse opened as soon as she turned the handle. They walked in. The deputy stepped in first with his weapon drawn. Cooper entered second, and Smalls came up third. The office immediately inside the door was empty. Only one fluorescent light flickered and hummed above them. The desks that just a few days before were covered with papers and other miscellaneous flotsam were bare. The air felt cold and stale. The ventilation and heating hadn't been on for a while.

Cooper looked at Smalls. He smiled. After years of investigating and researching strange phenomena, he'd learned that when you expect something it's never there. When they went into the house on Confessor Street, nothing was expected to be found, and they uncovered Rogers and one of the possessed corpses. If Satan was involved like Smalls almost definitely knew was the case, only the unexpected would yield results. This was too much of a diatribe for him to go on about to Cooper and the deputy.

They walked into the lab room, empty. The large area where several floats were being constructed was bare as well. It didn't even look like any work had been done in the vast chamber. Not a scrap of material or speck of sawdust littered the open space.

"I guess we should have listened to Father Smalls," the deputy said. "I guess you really do have a direct line to the Almighty."

"It has nothing to do with my being a priest, but everything to do with being a scientist. Results always come when you don't expect them."

"A lot like police work," the deputy said.

"They've moved to the staging area already." Cooper pulled a radio from her back pocket. "Cooper to dispatch, get me the location of where societies wait for parades to start."

"Civic Center, over." The dispatch didn't miss a beat.

"Do we have any officers, city or county, out there?" Cooper asked into the radio.

"Plenty."

"Raise one of them."

"They won't be there, either," Smalls said.

"Please try some positive vibes." Cooper waited for a voice

from the radio.

"This is Smithfield out at the Civic Center, what do you need, Detective?"

"Is the Mystics of Mayhem set up out there anywhere?" Cooper asked.

"Give me a minute," Smithfield answered back.

Smalls walked to the far corner of the room. He dug into his pocket and brought out a salt shaker. The two police officers watched him as he unscrewed the top of the shaker and started pouring the salt as he walked the perimeter. They would think he was crazy. Maybe he was. Evil had been in that place. It echoed off the walls. Salt purified. The Bible talked about the purifying effects of the stuff. He mumbled some Psalms to help the cleansing. When the first shaker ran out, he removed another and continued.

"Still with me, Cooper?" Smithfield's voice bounced through the cavernous room.

"On pins and needles."

"There is no Mystics of Mayhem here, and no one has heard where they have set up for tonight's parade. A guy with the KORs thinks they'd have to be close by. Over."

"Roger that, Smithfield. Thanks for the info." Cooper put her radio away.

Smalls finished his circuit of the room. He used five shakers of salt on his path. The two police officers looked at him like he'd lost his mind when he came back to them.

"What were you doing?" the deputy asked.

"Salt is believed to help purge evil from places," Smalls said.

"Does it help find needles in haystacks?" Cooper asked. "'Cause we got one now."

"No, but magnets do. Why don't we try to draw them out?" Smalls suggested.

"We could just call the mayor and have this parade cancelled or wait for it to start and get this guy then," the deputy said.

Smalls and Cooper both shook their heads.

"No good waiting. If this guy gets started it's the end of everything," Cooper said.

"Glad you finally believe me."

"What are you two talking about? He can't destroy everything."

Smalls looked deep into the deputy's eyes. "This isn't an ordinary man. It's Satan, and he may very well do just that if we can't stop him before he starts or push whatever he's trying to do over into tomorrow."

"Tomorrow?" Cooper asked.

"Ash Wednesday begins a holy period. It should render him close to powerless."

"I'll try to get the parade stopped," Cooper said. "Father, work on that magnet."

Smalls waited outside the police station for Cooper. Streams of people passed by. Some wore layers of shiny plastic beads; others looked as if they were just getting ready for the festivities. He always enjoyed Mardi Gras. The parades went past his apartment. He could stand at the window and watch the colorful floats and people without getting into the mass of bodies on the sidewalks. Today, however, he wished everything would hurry up.

Cooper walked down the steps to the sidewalk. She shook her head the whole way down. "Chief won't go for shutting the parades down. He says that the mayor would veto it because of the massive amount of money that would be gone."

"Could he just shut the Mystics of Mayhem's parade down tonight?" Smalls asked.

"Thought of that one too, but that particular parading society has asked for no police involvement."

"The city is okay with this?"

Cooper rubbed her first two fingers with her thumb. "Apparently the Mystics of Mayhem dropped a huge amount of money on the city council's desk. I'm sure they could get anything they wanted."

"Mammon, you mean. I suppose Satan has an unlimited supply of wealth."

"He is the Devil." Cooper dug into the bag she had slung across her shoulder and brought out a pack of cigarettes. She bumped one out, pulled it from the pack with her lips, and offered Smalls one. He declined. She lit hers up. "What about that magnet?"

"When did you start smoking?"

"I do under stress. So how about that magnet?"

Smalls rubbed the back of his neck, something he did more when nervous. "You might want to stop by one of those fancy tobacco places near here and get a pipe and a whole lot of loose tobacco. I've known what to use for a magnet since we were at the empty warehouse. Problem is I can't use it."

"Why not?"

"Because it will tip our hand. The only defense and way to stop all this is to use an incantation to ward off evil. You saw what they did the other day at ATU and when you arrested Rogers. We could go to the staging area for the Mystics of Mayhem, which would have to be the parking deck for the cruise line that just pulled out of town. It's the only place big enough to keep floats in that's close to the parade route. I would use a light incantation to make the possessed corpses sick if you will. That might draw Satan out, but if we didn't succeed in stopping the parade, he would know our only working tactic and could plan for it."

"That is pipe-worthy."

"There are other problems. The incantations may work on some but not all of the possessed corpses, and it won't work at all with Satan."

"What will kill him?"

"Nothing can kill him, and I don't know what might cast him back to Hell." Smalls rubbed his neck hard now.

"I know that it's early, but let's get over to Government Plaza. I want to be on the barrier on when the Mystics of Mayhem roll," Cooper said.

Smalls wished that he could feel optimistic about things, but he only knew of one definite way to completely defeat Satan and that was God. He looked at the sky. It began to turn purple as evening crept closer. Something should be different. He figured that the night of the great battle with Satan and humanity would have more electricity in the air. It felt ordinary, like any other Tuesday.

"Peace and safety, then sudden destruction," he whispered as he followed Cooper toward the parade route.

CHAPTER THIRTY-FOUR

A she stood at the back of the second float in line for the parade. Czernobog chained his leg to a sturdy steel pipe welded to the trailer. A garbage bag full of beads rested at his feet. The float looked like a whale on the ocean. He stood at the upsweep of the flukes. One of the possessed copses stood in the blowhole. A few other possessed people flanked both sides of the float. The number of possessed corpses the Devil had assembled shocked Ashe. Apparently, Czernobog had been gathering up his small army since not long after he'd built the original prototype of the engram device.

"Dr. Shrove."

Ashe looked down at Czernobog. "Yes?"

"Don't forget to throw the beads, and have a good time."

"What's the point?"

"Not everyone in the city is present," Czernobog said. "I don't want mass hysteria when the folks watching TV sees what happens."

"What about Cybil?"

"She'll be safe with me on the last float, or safe as long as your end of the deal holds up." He smiled his insincere smile. "Don't forget to put your earplugs in. I'd hate for you to get possessed before the end of the parade."

The Devil disappeared in a puff of acrid smoke. Ashe thought that he was getting a little more histrionic as the time for the parade neared. He took his advice, however, and plugged his ears. Czernobog had given him some earplugs made from a strange waxy substance. Although he had crammed them well into his ears, he could still hear everything as if they weren't plugged. Something seemed wrong about it. A nagging idea that the Devil might have tricked him tugged at Ashe's mind, but he kept them in place. Perhaps the plugs would work like some kind of sunglasses, just block the bad stuff.

A flourish of horns filled the air. The float lurched forward. Ashe caught himself before he could tumble over into the depths of the float. The corpses who shared the float seemed to have little concern about the movement. Somewhere in front of him, the sound of a marching band flourished. The tune was a high school halftime show version of "Sympathy for the Devil". Ashe tried to see to the front of the parade, but the mass of the whale float kept him from seeing anything. No sooner had the float come out of the parking garage, than people began to scream for beads. The corpses on his float began tossing out handfuls of the plastic trinkets. Ashe bent low as if he were going to dig out some throws, but instead he tried to free his leg.

The metal wouldn't give. He needed something to pry at the pole with. There was nothing. He stood back up with a handful of beads and tossed them out. When the time came for the engram devices to begin, the confusion might give him time to try something. Ashe looked back down the line of parade floats. At the very end he could see the one Czernobog and Cybil rode on. It was also the only one with the actual working engram machine. The last float was taller than the others. A large column of painted fire went into the sky. At the top, Czernobog stood in his devil costume. A large gong that looked like a silver moon was behind him. As soon as that float cleared the garage, the Devil reached below him. He brought up something that looked like a human head. Holding it by the hair, he slammed the head against the gong. The deep sound resonated out like the loudest thunder. It drowned out all the other sound.

Ashe looked forward. The float turned onto another street. One of the buildings that loomed over the street was the courthouse. The people lined along this stretch of road looked four deep on both sides, if not more. The cry for beads was deafening. The music from the gong continued to echo around.

A flash of light erupted all around. The sky ripped open with a bolt of orange lightning and all the bulbs in the street lamps exploded. Sparks showered down on the revelers. The time had come. Ashe ducked back down to work on freeing himself from the chain. He looked toward one of the speakers that contained a USB port and engram device. One of the possessed corpses switched it on. The sound of his voice boomed from the speakers. He chanted the mantra that Smalls had emailed him.

More lightning streaked the sky. The wind kicked up, blowing the smell of sulfur around the street. Ashe pulled on the chains, trying to get them up and over the loop in the pipe he had been secured to. He kept his eyes on the corpse closest to him. It covered its ears with its hands. The float began to swerve back and forth down the street. People on the sidewalks screamed.

Ashe popped up long enough to see his float hit one of the crowd barriers. Revelers scattered from the sidewalks trying to get away from the out-of-control float. His words kept repeating over and over. He looked at another corpse. It lay on the floor flopping like a fish. Then it stopped, and a dark shadowy thing escaped from the eyeholes of the mask.

The float jerked hard the other way. The force tossed Ashe to the floor. He slid along until he hit the side of the float. More people screamed. Metal popped, and the float bounced hard. He felt the dizzying sensation of being thrown head over heels. The body in the blowhole fell out as the float flipped to its side.

Ashe fell over the side of the float. His shoulder hit cement and felt as if it had popped out of place. The pain radiated throughout his whole body, but he noticed that the pipe that the chain was attached to had broken. Gritting his teeth against the pain, he tossed the chain off the stub of pipe and tried to free himself from the wreck of the whale float.

As he gained his footing on the steps that led into the courthouse, he pulled the hooded mask that was part of his costume from his face. Glittery beads scattered across the street like grains of sand. Costumed bodies lay at assorted angles on crashed floats that lined the street. His voice echoed as the ruined floats still played his recording over their PA systems.

Hundreds of people ran up and down the sidewalks. Many were trapped by the floats. Screams echoed into the flashing sky. Ashe, holding his arm limp, moved toward the back of the parade. He had no idea what he would do to stop the Devil, but he had to try. The fire column float hadn't made it onto Government Street before the engram machine expelled the heretics from the corpses.

A jackknifed float made to look like a koi pond took up most of the intersection at Government and Royal Streets. It didn't deter Ashe. He rounded the corner. The fire column float sat in the middle of the street. Czernobog was nowhere to be found and neither was Cybil.

"Czernobog!" Ashe yelled, digging the earplugs from his ears.

"Ashley Shrove!" the Devil yelled back from somewhere on the float. "You did not uphold your end of the bargain."

Czernobog appeared on the float. He held Cybil by the arm. In his other hand, he held the head he smashed the gong with. It was Rogers'.

"Let her go," Ashe yelled.

"No. You know the consequences for breaking our agreement."

A group of teenagers ran between Ashe and the float. They screamed. Czernobog dropped Rogers' head. He held his hand out toward the kids. They burst into flames. Screams grew louder. Ashe became aware that a mass of humanity scrambled around him. Parade goers ran for any kind of safety. Some huddled in the meager stoops of closed lawyers' offices.

"Do you think it is over just because you stopped those corpses?" Czernobog said. "It's not midnight yet. I still have time to bring this world to an end. A stupid chant you learned from that meddlesome priest cannot stop me."

The ground began to shake. A crack opened up in the street between Ashe and the float. Water jetted up from a broken water main. It rained down on the pavement making it slick and reflective like glass. The image of the burning teens flickered in the forming puddles.

"Let the woman go."

Ashe turned to see Detective Cooper standing just behind him with her service pistol drawn. Smalls stood beside her. He fell back to their side.

Czernobog let go of Cybil's arm and held his hands up as if he were surrendering. Then he laughed. The sky thundered, and lightning struck the ground around him.

"You stupid bitch," he said with a voice that seemed to come from the sky. "I am Lucifer, the bright star. Satan, the prince of the damned. What is your gun going to do to me?"

She didn't answer, but fired. Several bullets flew into the Devil. The impact flung him over the side of the float.

"More than what you thought it would," she said.

Ashe ran to the crack in the street and hurtled it. The impact on landing sent a new flare of pain through his shoulder.

"Cybil!"

Her head appeared over the edge of the float. He held his good arm up to her. Cybil pushed herself onto the edge of the float and slid down. They didn't need words to express what they felt. Ashe motioned with his head for her jump across to Smalls. She did.

Ashe ducked under the float to look for the Devil. As he suspected, the demon was gone. Three bullets hit the ground in front of him. Ashe looked up. Czernobog stood on the edge of the float beside the column of painted fire.

"Did you really think bullets would stop me?"

"No, that's why I came around. This is between you and me."

The Devil chuckled and hopped down. "Me and you? This is far more than just us. The world is in my grasp. I can taste it. For the first time since I tricked Adam and Eve, I am on the verge of victory."

His features changed. His nose crinkled and deep lines sank into his face. His eyes flashed red, and his tongue forked. Ashe stood his ground and tried his hardest not to show any of fear.

"Tremble before me, human."

"No."

The Devil roared. He held out both hands to the sky. Fire erupted from them. He spread it around like a farmer sowing seeds. The buildings, trees and grass caught alight. The float began to drip with real flames.

"There is nothing that you can do. It is my time. I will rule this planet. I will own you."

"Yea, though I walk through the valley of the shadow of death I will fear no evil." Ashe had no idea why he said it. That Psalm was just the first thing that came to his mind.

"Always with the Psalms. You mortals will never learn. That works on spirits and demons but not on me. I am Beelzebub, the Lord of the Flies. I am more powerful than that."

"Are you more powerful than God?" Smalls said. He touched Ashe's arm as he took his place beside him.

The priest's sleeve was singed, and the skin underneath looked blistered from where he had come through the fire. Those flames reflected in his eyes.

"You are not God," the Devil said.

"True but God created time." Smalls pointed to his watch. "And you are out of it."

"What do you mean? I am immortal. Time means nothing to me."

"What time is it?" Ashe asked, looking at his watch. The face was cracked and the hands no longer moved.

Lightning raced across the sky. This time it was golden, not orange. Rain began to sprinkle from above. This became steady, dousing the hellfire. The water felt warm like a summer rain.

"It's midnight, Ash Wednesday," Smalls said.

"No!" The Devil raged.

He tossed his hands out. Fire flew from his fingers but sputtered to wisps of smoke in the rain. He grimaced, and the rain poured from his wrinkles like water from the mouth of a gargoyle. Yellow, sulfur-smelling smoke surrounded the Devil. When it cleared, a stone image of Czernobog remained. The rain ceased as quickly as it had started.

"What happened?" Ashe asked, truly confused.

"You kept him occupied until Lent began," Smalls said.

"And?"

"He had to get everything done before the strike of midnight. It is believed there are days when humanity is the most susceptible to the Devil and his satanic powers. Mardi Gras is one. By keeping him from rallying, you saved us all."

Ashe walked to the statue. The look in the eyes seemed as lifelike as if Czernobog stood before him at that moment. He pushed hard on the rock. The figure toppled over and broke on the pavement.

He ran his fingers through the black dust and smeared it on his forehead in the shape of a cross. Ash Wednesday had come. He had a lot of things to give up, but Ashe knew his soul wasn't one of them.

About the Author

Vic Kerry lives in Alabama with his wife, four dogs, and two cats. He has an MFA in writing popular fiction from Seton Hill University and is haunted by the ghost of his dearly departed Lovecraft-loving cat, Possum H. Puss Lovecraff. You can like him or friend him on Facebook or stalk him through Twitter and Instagram.

Curious about other Crossroad Press books?
Stop by our site:
http://store.crossroadpress.com
We offer quality writing
in digital, audio, and print formats.

Enter the code FIRSTBOOK
to get 20% off your first order from our store!
Stop by today!